OTHER BOOKS BY JEFF VANDERMEER

FICTION
Dradin, in Love
The Book of Lost Places
Veniss Underground
City of Saints & Madmen
Secret Life
Shriek: An Afterword
The Situation
Secret Lives
Predator: South China Sea
Finch

NONFICTION
Why Should I Cut Your Throat?
Booklife: Strategies & Survival Tips for the 21st-Century Writer
Monstrous Creatures

ANTHOLOGIES (EDITED OR CO-EDITED)
Leviathan 1
Leviathan 2
Leviathan 3
Album Zutique
The Thackery T. Lambshead Pocket Guide to Eccentric and Discredited Diseases
Best American Fantasy 1
Best American Fantasy 2
The New Weird
Steampunk
Fast Ships, Black Sails
Last Drink Bird Head
The Leonardo Variations

"Vandermeer's stories hit one's hindbrain slantwise – they offer no easy answers and no comfort. Rather they are hard, brilliant gems meant to cut and shine – these are some of the most beautiful, upsetting, and accomplished tales I have ever read."

— Catherynne M. Valente, author of *The Orphan's Tales*

"*The Third Bear* contains some of my favorite stories of recent years. There's the meticulous workplace surrealism of 'The Situation,' the remorseless multi-world cataclysms of 'The Goat Variations,' the beautiful eldritch heartsickness of 'The Surgeon's Tale.' Jeff VanderMeer is one of the very best."

— Kevin Brockmeier, author of *The Brief History of the Dead*

"Jeff VanderMeer knows what story can do to human consciousness, as is delightfully evident in his latest collection, *The Third Bear*. These stories are smart, gorgeous, allusive, and tricky. VanderMeer is a fantasist extraordinaire."

— Jack O'Connell, author of *The Resurrectionist*

"Annexing the weird half-lit spaces between genres, these stories lean sometimes into fantasy and sf, sometimes into metafiction, but are always deft and pleasurable reads. VanderMeer is one of the few writers out there able to coax something startling and necessary from anything…a very strong collection."

— Brian Evenson, author of *Last Days*

"Jeff VanderMeer's work is subversive and disquieting, possessed of an almost kinetic force in its impact upon the mind. Body horror gone viral, fairy tales wrapped in their own entrails, and metafictional murder; these and other images herein are sure to leave their mark and fester in the subconscious. Already a well-regarded fantasist, *The Third Bear* reveals VanderMeer at his most fearsome."

— Laird Barron, author of *The Imago Sequence and Other Stories*

The
Third Bear

JEFF VANDERMEER

The Third Bear
Jeff VanderMeer

Copyright © 2010 by Jeff VanderMeer

Interior and cover design by Jacob McMurray

Tachyon Publications
1459 18th Street #139
San Francisco, CA 94107
(415) 285-5615
www.tachyonpublications.com
tachyon@tachyonpublications.com

Series Editor: Jacob Weisman
Editor: Jill Roberts
ISBN 13: 978-1-892391-98-8
ISBN 10: 1-892391-98-8

Printed in the United States of America by Worzalla
First Edition: 2010
9 8 7 6 5 4 3 2 1

Dedicated to my wife, Ann

TABLE OF CONTENTS

The Third Bear

THE THIRD BEAR

❧

It made its home in the deep forest near the village of Grommin, and all anyone ever saw of it, before the end, would be hard eyes and the dark barrel of its muzzle. The smell of piss and blood and shit and bubbles of saliva and half-eaten food. The villagers called it the Third Bear because they had killed two bears already that year. But, near the end, no one really thought of it as a bear, even though the name had stuck, changed by repetition and fear and slurring through blood-filled mouths to *Theeber*. Sometimes it even sounded like "seether" or "seabird."

The Third Bear came to the forest in mid-summer, and soon most anyone who used the forest trail, day or night, disappeared, carried off to the creature's lair. By the time even large convoys had traveled through, they would discover two or three of their number missing. A straggling horseman, his mount cantering along, just bloodstains and bits of skin sticking to the saddle. A cobbler gone but for a shredded hat. A few of the richest villagers hired mercenaries as guards, but when even the strongest men died, silent and alone, the convoys dried up.

The village elder, a man named Horley, held a meeting to decide what to do. It was the end of summer by then and the leaves had begun to disappear from the trees. The meeting house had a chill to it, a stench of thick earth with a trace of blood and sweat curling through it. All five hundred villagers came to the meeting, from the few remaining merchants to the poorest beggar. Grommin had always been hard scrabble and tough winters, but it was also two hundred years old. It had survived the wars of barons and of kings, been razed twice, only to return.

"I can't bring my goods to market," one farmer said, rising in shadow from beneath the thatch. "I can't be sure I want to send my daughter to the pen to milk the goats."

Horley laughed, said, "It's worse than that. We can't bring in food from the other side. Not for sure. Not without losing men." He had a sudden vision from months ahead, of winter, of ice gravelly with frozen blood. It made him shudder.

"What about those of us who live outside the village?" another farmer asked. "We need the pasture for grazing, but we have no protection."

Horley understood the problem; he had been one of those farmers, once. The village had a wall of thick logs surrounding it, to a height of ten feet. No real defense against an army, but more than enough to keep the wolves out. Beyond that perimeter lived the farmers and the hunters and the outcasts who could not work among others.

"You may have to pretend it is a time of war and live in the village and go out with a guard," Horley said. "We have plenty of able-bodied men, still."

"Is it the witch woman doing this?" Clem the blacksmith asked.

"No," Horley said. "I don't think it's the witch woman."

What Clem and some of the others thought of as a "witch woman," Horley thought of as a crazy person who knew some herbal remedies and lived in the woods because the villagers had driven her there, blaming her for an outbreak of sickness the year before.

"Why did it come?" a woman asked. "Why us?"

No one could answer, least of all Horley. As Horley stared at all of those hopeful, scared, troubled faces, he realized that not all of them yet knew they were stuck in a nightmare.

Clem was the village's strongest man, and after the meeting he volunteered to fight the beast. He had arms like most people's thighs. His skin was tough from years of being exposed to flame. With his full black beard he almost looked like a bear himself.

"I'll go, and I'll go willingly," he told Horley. "I've not met the beast I couldn't best. I'll squeeze the 'a' out of him." And he laughed, for he had a passable sense of humor, although most chose to ignore it.

Horley looked into Clem's eyes and could not see even a speck of fear there. This worried Horley.

"Be careful, Clem," Horley said. And, in a whisper, as he hugged the man: "Instruct your son in anything he might need to know, before you leave. Make sure your wife has what she needs, too."

•

Fitted in chain mail, leathers, and a metal helmet, carrying an old sword some knight had once left in Grommin by mistake, Clem set forth in search of the Third Bear. The entire village came out to see him go. Clem was laughing and raising his sword and this lifted the spirits of those who saw him. Soon, everyone was celebrating as if the Third Bear had already been killed or defeated.

"Fools," Horley's wife Rebecca said as they watched the celebration with their two young sons.

Rebecca was younger than Horley by ten years and had come from a village far beyond the forest. Horley's first wife had died from a sickness that left red marks all over her body.

"Perhaps, but it's the happiest anyone's been for a month," Horley said.

"All I can think of is that he's taking one of our best horses out into danger," Rebecca said.

"Would you rather he took a nag?" Horley said, but absent-mindedly. His thoughts were elsewhere.

The vision of winter would not leave him. Each time, it came back to Horley with greater strength, until he had trouble seeing the summer all around him.

•

Clem left the path almost immediately, wandered through the underbrush to the heart of the forest, where the trees grew so black and thick that the only glimmer of light came from the reflection of water on leaves. The smell in that place carried a hint of offal.

Clem had spent so much time beating things into shape that he had not developed a sense of fear, for he had never been beaten. But the smell in his nostrils did make him uneasy.

He wandered for some time in the deep growth, where the soft loam of moss muffled the sound of his passage. It became difficult to judge direction and distance. The unease became a knot in his chest as he clutched his sword ever tighter. He had killed many bears in his time, this was true, but he had never had to hunt a man-eater.

3

Eventually, in his circling, meandering trek, Clem came upon a hill with a cave inside. From within the cave, a green flame flickered. It beckoned like a lithe but crooked finger.

A lesser man might have turned back, but not Clem. He didn't have the sense to turn back.

Inside the cave, he found the Third Bear. Behind the Third Bear, arranged around the walls of the cave, it had displayed the heads of its victims. The heads had been painstakingly painted and mounted on stands. They were all in various stages of rot.

Many bodies lay stacked neatly in the back of the cave. All of them had been defiled in some way. Some of them had been mutilated. The wavery green light came from a candle the Third Bear had placed behind the bodies, to display its handiwork. The smell of blood was so thick that Clem had to put a hand over his mouth.

As Clem took it all in, the methodical nature of it, the fact that the Third Bear had not eaten any of its victims, he found something inside of him tearing and then breaking.

"I...." he said, and looked into the terrible eyes of the Third Bear. "I...."

Almost sadly, with a kind of ritual grace, the Third Bear pried Clem's sword from his fist, placed the weapon on a ledge, and then came back to stare at Clem once more.

Clem stood there, frozen, as the Third Bear disemboweled him.

●

The next day, Clem was found at the edge of the village, blood-soaked and shit-spattered, legs gnawed away, but alive enough for a while to, in shuddering lurches, tell those who found him what he had seen, just not coherent enough to tell them *where*.

Later, Horley would wish that he hadn't told them anything.

There was nothing left but fear in Clem's eyes by the time Horley questioned him. Horley didn't remember any of Clem's answers, had to be retold them later. He was trying to reconcile himself to looking *down* to stare into Clem's eyes.

"I'm cold, Horley," Clem said. "I can't feel anything. Is winter coming?"

"Should we bring his wife and son?" the farmer who had found Clem asked Horley at one point.

Horley just stared at him, aghast.

•

They buried Clem in the old graveyard, but the next week the Third Bear dug him up and stole his head. Apparently, the Third Bear had no use for heroes, except, possibly, as a pattern of heads.

Horley tried to keep the grave robbery and what Clem had said a secret, but it leaked out anyway. By the time most villagers of Grommin learned about it, the details had become more monstrous than anything in real life. Some said Clem had been kept for a week in the bear's lair, while it ate away at him. Others said Clem had had his spine ripped out of his body while he was still breathing. A few even said Clem had been buried alive by mistake and the Third Bear had heard him writhing in the dirt and come for him.

But one thing Horley knew that trumped every tall tale spreading through Grommin: the Third Bear hadn't had to keep Clem alive. *Theeber* hadn't had to place Clem, still breathing, at the edge of the village.

So *Seether* wasn't just a bear.

•

In the next week, four more people were killed, one on the outskirts of the village. Several villagers had risked leaving, and some of them had even made it through. But fear kept most of them in Grommin, locked into a kind of desperate fatalism or optimism that made their eyes hollow as they stared into some unknowable distance. Horley did his best to keep morale up, but even he experienced a sense of sinking.

"Is there more I can do?" he asked his wife in bed at night.

"Nothing," she said. "You are doing everything you can do."

"Should we just leave?"

"Where would we go? What would we do?"

Few who left ever returned with stories of success, it was true. War and plague and a thousand more dangers lay out there beyond the forest. They'd as likely become slaves or servants or simply die, one by one, out in the wider world.

Eventually, though, Horley sent a messenger to that wider world, to a far-distant baron to whom they paid fealty and a yearly amount of goods.

The messenger never came back. Nor did the baron send any men. Horley spent many nights awake, wondering if the messenger had gotten through and the baron just didn't care, or if Seether had killed the messenger.

"Maybe winter will bring good news," Rebecca said.

•

Over time, Grommin sent four or five of its strongest and most clever men and women to fight the Third Bear. Horley objected to this waste, but the villagers insisted that something must be done before winter, and those who went were unable to grasp the terrible velocity of the situation. For Horley, it seemed merely a form of taking one's own life, but his objections were over-ruled by the majority.

They never learned what happened to these people, but Horley saw them in his nightmares.

One, before the end, said to the Third Bear, "If you could see the children in the village, you would stop."

Another said, before fear clotted her windpipe, "We will give you all the food you need."

A third, even as he watched his intestines slide out of his body, said, "Surely there is something we can do to appease you?"

In Horley's dreams, the Third Bear said nothing in reply. Its conversation was through its work, and Seether said what it wanted to say very eloquently in that regard.

•

By now, fall had descended on Grommin. The wind had become unpredict-able and the leaves of trees had begun to yellow. A far-off burning smell laced the air. The farmers had begun to prepare for winter, laying in hay and slaughtering and smoking hogs. Horley became more involved in these preparations than usual, driven by his vision of the coming winter. People noted the haste, the urgency, so unnatural in Horley, and to his dismay it sometimes made them panic rather than work harder.

With his wife's help, Horley convinced the farmers to contribute to a communal smokehouse in the village. Ham, sausage, dried vegetables, onions, potatoes – they stored it all in Grommin now. Most of the outlying farmers realized that their future depended on the survival of the village.

Sometimes, when they opened the gates to let in another farmer and his mule-drawn cart of supplies, Horley would walk out a ways and stare into the forest. It seemed more unknowable than ever, gaunt and dark, diminished by the change of seasons.

Somewhere out there the Third Bear waited for them.

●

One day, the crisp cold of coming winter becoming more than a promise, Horley and several of the men from Grommin went looking for a farmer who had not come to the village for a month. The farmer's name was John and he had a wife, five children, and seven men who worked for him. John's holdings were the largest outside the village, but he had been suffering because he could not bring his extra goods to market.

The farm was a half-hour's walk from Grommin. The whole way, Horley could feel a hurt in his chest, a kind of stab of premonition. Those with him held pitchforks and hammers and old spears, much of it as rust-colored as the leaves now strewn across the path.

They could smell the disaster before they saw it. It coated the air like oil.

On the outskirts of John's farm, they found three mule-pulled carts laden with food and supplies. Horley had never seen so much blood. It had pooled and thickened to cover a spreading area several feet in every direction. The mules had had their throats torn out and then they had been disemboweled. Their organs had been torn out and thrown onto the ground, as if Seether had been searching for something. Their eyes had been plucked from their sockets almost as an afterthought.

John – they thought it was John – sat in the front of the lead cart. The head was missing, as was much of the meat from the body cavity. The hands still held the reins. The same was true for the other two carts, their wheels greased with blood. Three dead men holding reins to dead mules.

7

Two dead men in the back of the carts. All five missing their heads. All five eviscerated.

One of Horley's protectors vomited into the grass. Another began to weep. "Jesus save us," a third man said, and kept saying it for many hours.

Horley was curiously unmoved, his hand and heart steady. He noted the brutal humor that had moved the Third Bear to carefully replace the reins in the men's hands. He noted the wild, savage abandon that had preceded that action. He noted, grimly, that most of the supplies in the carts had been ruined by the wealth of blood that covered them. But, for the most part, the idea of winter had so captured him that whatever came to him moment-by-moment could not compare to the crystalline nightmare of that interior vision.

Horley wondered if his was a form of madness as well.

"This is not the worst," he said to his men. "Not by far."

At the farm, they found the rest of the men and what was left of John's wife and children, but that is not what Horley had meant.

•

At this point, Horley felt he should go himself to find the Third Bear. It wasn't bravery that made him put on the leather jerkin and the metal shin guards. It wasn't from any sense of hope that he picked up the spear and put Clem's helmet on his head.

His wife found him there, ready to walk out the door of their home.

"You wouldn't come back," she told him.

"Better," he said. "Still."

"You're more important to us alive. Stronger men than you have tried to kill it."

"I must do something," Horley said. "Winter will be here soon and things will get worse."

"Then do something," Rebecca said, taking the spear from his hand. "But do something *else*."

•

The villagers of Grommin met the next day. There was less talking this time. Horley tried to gauge their mood. Many were angry, but some now seemed resigned, almost as if the Third Bear were a plague or some other force that could not be controlled or stopped by the hand of Man. In the days that followed, there would be a frenzy of action: traps set, torches lit, poisoned meat left in the forest, but none of it came to anything.

One old woman kept muttering about fate and the will of God.

"John was a good man," Horley told them. "He did not deserve his death. But I was there – I saw his wounds. He died from an animal attack. It may be a clever animal. It may be very clever. But it is still an animal. We should not fear it the way we fear it."

"You should consult with the witch in the woods," Clem's son said.

Clem's son was a huge man of eighteen years, and his word held weight, given the bravery of his father. Several people began to nod in agreement.

"Yes," said one. "Go to the witch. She might know what to do."

The witch in the woods is just a poor, addled woman, Horley thought, but could not say it.

"Just two months ago," Horley reminded them, "you thought she might have made this happen."

"And if so, what of it? If she caused it, she can undo it. If not, perhaps we can pay her to help us."

This from one of the farmers displaced from outside the walls. Word of John's fate had spread quickly, and less than a handful of the bravest or most foolhardy had kept to their farms.

Rancor spread amongst the gathered villagers. Some wanted to take a party of men out to the witch, wherever she might live, and kill her. Others thought this folly – what if the Third Bear found them first?

Finally, Horley raised his hands to silence them.

"Enough! If you want me to go to the witch in the woods, I will go to her."

The relief on their faces, as he looked out at them – the relief that he would take the risk – it was like a balm that cleansed their worries, if only for the moment. Some fools were even smiling.

●

Later, Horley lay in bed with his wife. He held her tight, taking comfort in the warmth of her body.

"Rebecca? I'm scared."

"I know. I know you are. Do you think I'm not scared too? But neither of us can show it or they will panic, and once they panic, Grommin is lost."

"What can I do?"

"Go see the witch woman, my love. If you go to her, it will make them calmer. And you can tell them whatever you like about what she says."

"If the Third Bear doesn't kill me before I can find her."

If she isn't already dead.

•

In the deep woods, in a silence so profound that the ringing in his ears had become the roar of a river, Horley looked for the witch woman. He knew that she had been exiled to the southern part of the forest, and so he had started there and worked his way toward the center. What he was looking for, he did not know. A cottage? A tent? What he would do when he found her, Horley didn't know either. His spear, his incomplete armor – these things would not protect him if she truly was a witch.

He tried to keep the vision of the terrible winter in his head as he walked, because concentrating on that more distant fear removed the current fear.

"If not for me, the Third Bear might not be here," Horley had said to Rebecca before he left. It was Horley who had stopped them from burning the witch, had insisted only on exile.

"That's nonsense," Rebecca had replied. "Remember that she's just an old woman, living in the woods. Remember that she can do you no real harm."

It had been as if she'd read his thoughts. But now, breathing in the thick air of the forest, Horley felt less sure about the witch woman. It was true there had been sickness in the village until they had cast her out.

Horley tried to focus on the spring of loam beneath his boots, the clean, dark smell of bark and earth and air. After a time, he crossed a dirt-choked stream. As if this served as a dividing line, the forest became yet darker. The sounds of wrens and finches died away. Above, he could see the distant dark shapes of hawks in the treetops, and patches of light shining down that almost looked more like bog or marsh water, so disoriented had he become.

It was in this deep forest that he found a door.

Horley had stopped to catch his breath after cresting a slight incline. Hands on his thighs, he looked up and there it stood: a door. In the middle of the forest. It was made of old oak and overgrown with moss and mushrooms, and yet it seemed to flicker like glass. A kind of light or brightness hurtled through the ground, through the dead leaves and worms and beetles, around the door. It was a subtle thing, and Horley half-thought he was imagining it at first.

He straightened up, grip tightening on his spear.

The door stood by itself. Nothing human-made surrounded it, not even the slightest ruin of a wall.

Horley walked closer. The knob was made of brass or some other yellowing metal. He walked around the door. It stood firmly wedged into the ground. The back of the door was the same as the front.

Horley knew that if this was the entrance to the old woman's home, then she was indeed a witch. His hand remained steady, but his heart quickened and he thought furiously of winter, of icicles and bitter cold and snow falling slowly forever.

For several minutes, he circled the door, deciding what to do. For a minute more, he stood in front of the door, pondering.

A door always needs opening, he thought, finally.

He grasped the knob, and pushed – and the door opened.

●

Some events have their own sense of time, and a separate logic. Horley knew this just from the change of seasons every year. He knew this from the growing of the crops and the birthing of children. He knew it from the forest itself, and the cycles it went through that often seemed incomprehensible and yet had their own pattern, if you could only see it. From the first thawed trickle of stream water in the spring to the last hopping frog in the fall, the world held a thousand mysteries. No man could hope to know the truth of them all.

When the door opened and he stood in a room very much like the room one might find in a woodman's cottage, with a fireplace and a rug and a shelf and pots and pans on the wood walls, and a rocking chair – when this happened, Horley decided in the time it took him to blink twice that he had no need for the *why* of it or the *how* of it, even. And this was, he realized later, the only reason he kept his wits about him.

The witch woman sat in the rocking chair. She looked older than Horley remembered, even though no more than a year had passed since he had last seen her. Seeming made of ash and soot, her black dress lay flat against her sagging skin. She was blind, eye sockets bare, but her wrinkled face strained to look at him any way.

There was a buzzing sound.

"I remember you," she said. Her voice was croak and whisper both.

Her arms were mottled with age spots, her hands so thin and cruel-looking that they could have been talons. She gripped the rocking chair as if holding onto the world.

There was a buzzing sound. It came, Horley finally realized, from a halo of black hornets that circled the old woman's head, their wings beating so fast they could hardly be seen.

"Are you Hasghat, who used to live in Grommin?" Horley asked.

"I remember you," the witch woman said again.

"I am the elder of the village of Grommin."

The woman spat to the side. "Those that threw poor Hasghat out."

"They would have done much worse if I'd let them."

"They'd have burned me if they could. And all I knew then were a few charms, a few herbs. Just because I wasn't one of them. Just because I'd seen a bit of the world."

Hasghat was staring right at him and Horley knew that, eyes or no eyes, she could see him.

"It was wrong," Horley said.

"It was wrong," she said. "I had nothing to do with the sickness. Sickness comes from animals, from people's clothes. It clings to them and spreads through them."

"And yet you are a witch?"

Hasghat laughed, although it ended with coughing. "Because I have a hidden room? Because my door stands by itself?"

Horley grew impatient.

"Would you help us if you could? Would you help us if we let you return to the village?"

Hasghat straightened up in the chair and the halo of hornets disintegrated, then reformed. The wood in the fireplace popped and crackled. Horley felt a chill in the air.

"Help you? Return to the village?" She spoke as if chewing, her tongue a thick gray grub.

"A creature is attacking and killing us."

Hasghat laughed. When she laughed, Horley could see a strange double image in her face, a younger woman beneath the older.

"Is that so? What kind of creature?"

"We call it the Third Bear. I do not believe it is really a bear."

Hasghat doubled over in mirth. "Not really a bear? A bear that is not a bear?"

"We cannot seem to kill it. We thought that you might know how to defeat it."

"It stays to the forest," the witch woman said. "It stays to the forest and it is a bear but not a bear. It kills your people when they use the forest paths. It kills your people in the farms. It even sneaks into your graveyards and takes the heads of your dead. You are full of fear and panic. You cannot kill it, but it keeps murdering you in the most terrible of ways."

And that was winter, coming from her dry, stained lips.

"Do you know of it then?" Horley asked, his heart fast now from hope not fear.

"Ah yes, I know it," Hasghat said, nodding. "I know the Third Bear, *Theeber, Seether*. After all I brought it here."

The spear moved in Horley's hand and it would have driven itself deep into the woman's chest if Horley had let it.

"For revenge?" Horley asked.

Hasghat nodded. "Unfair. It was unfair. You should not have done it."

You're right, Horley thought. *I should have let them burn you.*

"You're right," Horley said. "We should not have done it. But we have learned our lesson."

"I was once a woman of knowledge and learning," Hasghat said. "Once I had a real cottage in a village. Now I am old and the forest is cold and uncomfortable. All of this is illusion." She gestured at the fireplace, at the walls of the cottage. "There is no cottage. No fireplace. No rocking chair. Right now, we are both dreaming among the worms and the beetles and the dirt. My back is sore and patterned by leaves. This is no place for someone as old as me."

"I'm sorry," Horley said. "You can come back to the village. You can live among us. We'll pay for your food. We'll give you a house to live in."

13

Hasghat frowned. "And some logs, I'll warrant. Some logs and some rope and some fire to go with it, too!"

Horley took off his helmet, stared into Hasghat's eye sockets. "I'll promise you whatever you want. No harm will come to you. If you'll help us. A man has to realize when he's beaten, when he's done wrong. You can have whatever you want. On my honor."

Hasghat brushed at the hornets ringing her head. "Nothing is that easy."

"Isn't it?"

"I brought it from a place far distant. In my anger. I sat in the middle of the forest despairing and I called for it from across the miles, across the years. I never expected it would come to me."

"So you can send it back?"

Hasghat frowned, spat again, and shook her head. "No. I hardly remember how I called it. And some day it may even be my head it takes. Sometimes it is easier to summon something than to send it away."

"You cannot help us at all?"

"If I could, I might, but calling it weakened me. It is all I can do to survive. I dig for toads and eat them raw. I wander the woods searching for mushrooms. I talk to the deer and I talk to the squirrels. Sometimes the birds tell me things about where they've been. Someday I will die out here. All by myself. Completely mad."

Horley's frustration heightened. He could feel the calm he had managed to keep leaving him. The spear twitched and jerked in his hands. What if he killed her? Might that send the Third Bear back where it had come from?

"What can you tell me about the Third Bear? Can you tell me anything that might help me?"

Hasghat shrugged. "It acts as to its nature. And it is far from home, so it clings to ritual even more. Where it is from, it is no more or less bloodthirsty than any other creature. There they call it 'Mord.' But this far from home, it appears more horrible than it is. It is merely making a pattern. When the pattern is finished, it will leave and go someplace else. Maybe the pattern will even help send it home."

"A pattern of heads."

"Yes. A pattern with heads."

"Do you know when it will be finished?"

"No."

"Do you know where it lives?"

"Yes. It lives *here*."

In his mind, he saw a hill. He saw a cave. He saw the Third Bear.

"Do you know anything else?"

"No."

Hasghat grinned up at him.

He drove the spear through her dry chest.

There was a sound like twigs breaking.

●

Horley woke covered in leaves, in the dirt, his body curled up next to the old woman. He jumped to his feet, picking up his spear. The old woman, dressed in a black dress and dirty shawl, was dreaming and mumbling in her sleep. Dead hornets had become entangled in her stringy hair. She clutched a dead toad in her left hand. A smell came from her, of rot, of shit.

There was no sign of the door. The forest was silent and dark.

Horley almost drove the spear into her chest again, but she was tiny, like a bird, and defenseless, and staring down at her he could not do it.

He looked around at the trees, at the fading light. It was time to accept that there was no reason to it, no *why*. It was time to get out, one way or another.

"A pattern of heads," he muttered to himself all the way home. "A pattern of heads."

●

Horley did not remember much about the meeting with the villagers upon his return. They wanted to hear about a powerful witch who could help or curse them, some force greater than themselves. Some glint of hope through the trees, a light in the dark. He could not give it to them. He gave them the truth instead, as much as he dared, but when they asked questions he could not stand the truth, either, and hinted that the witch had told him how to defeat the Third Bear.

Did it do much good? He didn't know. He could still see winter before them. He could still see blood. And they'd brought it on themselves. That was the part he didn't tell them. That a poor old woman with the ground for a bed and dead leaves for a blanket thought she had, through her anger, brought the Third Bear down upon them. Theeber. *Seether.*

"You must leave," he told Rebecca after the meeting. "Take a wagon. Take a mule. Load it with supplies. Don't let yourself be seen. Take our two sons. Bring that young man who helps chop firewood for us. If you can trust him."

Rebecca stiffened beside him. She was quiet for a very long time.

"Where will you be?" she asked.

Horley was forty-seven years old. He had lived in Grommin his entire life. "I have one thing left to do, and then I will join you."

"I know you will, my love." Rebecca said, holding onto him tightly, running her hands across his body as if as blind as the old witch woman, remembering, remembering.

They both knew there was only one way Horley could be sure Rebecca and his sons made it out of the forest safely.

•

Horley started from the south, just up-wind from where Rebecca had set out along an old cart trail, and curled in toward the Third Bear's home. After a long trek, Horley came to a hill that might have been a cairn made by his ancestors. A stream flowed down it and puddled at his feet. The stream was red and carried with it gristle and bits of marrow. It smelled like black pudding frying. The blood mixed with the deep green of the moss and turned it purple. Horley watched the blood ripple at the edges of his boots for a moment, and then he slowly walked up the hill.

He'd been carelessly loud for a long time as he walked through the leaves. About this time, Rebecca would be more than halfway through the woods, he knew.

•

In the cave, surrounded by all that Clem had seen and more, Horley disturbed Theeber at his work. Horley's spear had long since slipped through numb fingers. He'd pulled off his helmet because it itched and because he was sweating so much. He'd had to rip his tunic and hold the cloth against his mouth.

Horley had not meant to have a conversation; he'd meant to try to kill the beast. But now that he was there, now that he *saw*, all he had left were words.

Horley's boot crunched against half-soggy bone. Theeber didn't flinch. Theeber already knew. Theeber kept licking the fluid out of the skull in his hairy hand.

Theeber did look a little like a bear. Horley could see that. But no bear was that tall or that wide or looked as much like a man as a beast.

The ring of heads lined every flat space in the cave, painted blue and green and yellow and red and white and black. Even in the extremity of his situation, Horley could not deny that there was something beautiful about the pattern.

"This painting," Horley began in a thin, stretched voice. "These heads. How many do you need?"

Theeber turned its bloodshot, carious gaze on Horley, body swiveling as if made of air, not muscle and bone.

"How do you know not to be afraid?" Horley asked. Shaking. Piss running down his leg. "Is it true you come from a long way away? Are you homesick?"

Somehow, not knowing the answers to so many questions made Horley's heart sore for the many other things he would never know, never understand.

Theeber approached. It stank of mud and offal and rain. It made a continual sound like the rumble of thunder mixed with a cat's purr. It had paws but it had thumbs.

Horley stared up into its eyes. The two of them stood there, silent, for a long moment. Horley trying with everything he had to read some comprehension, some understanding into that face. Those eyes, oddly gentle. The muzzle wet with carrion.

"We need you to leave. We need you to go somewhere else. Please."

Horley could see Hasghat's door in the forest in front of him. It was opening in a swirl of dead leaves. A light was coming from inside of it. A light from very, very far away.

Theeber held Horley against his chest. Horley could hear the beating of its mighty heart, loud as the world. Rebecca and his sons would be almost past the forest by now.

Seether tore Horley's head from his body. Let the rest crumple to the dirt floor.

Horley's body lay there for a good long while.

•

Winter came – as brutal as it had ever been – and the Third Bear continued in its work. With Horley gone, the villagers became ever more listless. Some few disappeared into the forest and were never heard from again. Others feared the forest so much that they ate berries and branches at the outskirts of their homes and never hunted wild game. Their supplies gave out. Their skin became ever more pale and they stopped washing themselves. They believed the words of madmen and adopted strange customs. They stopped wearing clothes. They would have relations in the street. At some point, they lost sight of reason entirely and sacrificed virgins to the Third Bear, who took them as willingly as anyone else. They took to mutilating their bodies, thinking that this is what the Third Bear wanted them to do. Some few in whom reason persisted had to be held down and mutilated by others. A few cannibalized those who froze to death, and others who had not died almost wished they had. No relief came. The baron never brought his men.

Spring came, finally, and the streams unthawed. The birds returned, the trees regained their leaves, and the frogs began to sing their mating songs. In the deep forest, an old wooden door lay half-buried in moss and dirt, leading nowhere, all light fading from it. On an overgrown hill, there lay an empty cave with nothing but a few old bones scattered across the dirt floor.

The Third Bear had finished its pattern and moved on, but for the remaining villagers he would always be there.

The Quickening

In the old, tattered photo Sensio has been dressed in a peach-colored prisoner's uniform made out of discarded tarp and then tied to a post that Aunt Etta made me hammer into the ground. Sensio's long white ears are slanted back behind his head. His front legs, trapped by the crude arm holes, hang stiff at a forward angle. The absurdly large hind feet with the shadows for claws are, perhaps, the most monstrous part of Sensio – the way they seem to suddenly shoot from the peach-colored trousers, in a parody of arrested speed. The look on Sensio's face – the large, almond-shaped eye, the soft pucker of pink nose – seems caught between rage and a strange acceptance.

Sensio was, of course, a rabbit, and in the photo, Aunt Etta's stance confirms this bestial fact – she holds the end of the rope that binds Sensio to the post, and she holds it, between thumb and forefinger, with a form of distaste, even disdain? Such a strange pose, delicate against the roughness of Sensio; even a gentle tug and his humiliation would be undone.

Or maybe not. I don't know. I know only that Aunt Etta's expression is ultimately unreadable, muddied by the severe red of her lipstick, by the bookending of her body by a crepe-paper bag of a hat and the shimmering turquoise dress hitched up past her waist, over her stomach, and descending so far down that she appears to float above the matted grass. (Between the two, a flowsy white blouse that seems stolen from a more sensible person.) I'm not in the photo, but she'd dressed me in something similar, so that I looked like a flower girl at a wedding. The shoes Aunt Etta had dug up out of the closet pinched my feet.

Sensio had said nothing as he was bound, nose twitching at the sharp citrus of the orange blossoms behind them. He'd said nothing as we'd formed our peculiar circus procession from the bungalow where we lived to the waiting photographer. No reporters had come, despite Aunt Etta's phone calls, but she'd hired the photographer anyway – and he stood there in white shirt, suspenders, gray trousers, black wingtip shoes. He looked hot even though it was only spring, and was so white I thought he must be a Yankee. His equipment looked like a metal stork. A cigarette dangled from his lips.

"That's him," Aunt Etta said, as if Sensio were her rabbit and not mine. Shameful, but that's what I felt that long-ago day: Sensio is mine, not hers. I was twelve in 1955, and big for my age, with broad shoulders that made me look hunched over. I did chores around the orange groves. I helped to get water from the well. I'd driven the tractor. In the season, I'd even harvested the oranges, just for fun, alongside the sweating, watchful migrant workers, who had no choice. But I was still a kid, and as Aunt Etta put Sensio down and bound him to the post I'd pounded in the day before, all I could think was that Aunt Etta had no right to do anything with him.

"Do you have to tie him up like that?" the photographer asked Aunt Etta, but not in a caring way. He reached down to ruffle my hair and wink at me. I flinched away from him, wrinkling up my nose. People were always touching my head because of my curly red hair, and I hated it.

Aunt Etta just looked at him like he was stupid. She was stiff that morning – a broken hip that had never completely healed – and further trapped in her ridiculous dress. She grunted with effort and no little pain as she leaned precariously to loop the rope over and over again across Sensio's chest. "Shit," she said. I heard her, distinct if soft. She looked over as she straightened, said, "Rachel, finish it for me."

So it was I who tied the last knots, who knelt there beside Sensio, smelling the thick yet sweet musk of his fur.

"It's okay," I said to him, thinking, *Aunt Etta's just gone a little cracked. She'll be better soon.* I tried to will the message into that deep, liquid eye, through to the brain beyond.

Aunt Etta tapped my shoulder with her thick fingers. "Come away."

"Are we ready, then?" the photographer asked. Aunt Etta wasn't paying him by the hour. He was already looking at his watch.

In the photo, Aunt Etta has the end of Sensio's rope in her right hand, arm extended down, while her left arm is held at a right angle, palm up, thumb against the index finger. At first, people think she's holding a cigar in her hand, because the photograph is so old. Then they realize that's just a crease in the image and they think she holds something delicate – something she's afraid to close her hand around for fear of damaging it.

But I know there was nothing in Aunt Etta's hand that day.

•

We lived in a land of gentle hills, farms, lakes, and small towns. We lived on an orange grove in the middle of the state of Florida, near a place that's now a favorite truck stop on the freeway, Okahumpka. The attraction called Dog Land lay to the west and Orlando to the east – a sleepy town that didn't know that Walt Disney's touch would one day awaken it. My parents had died in an automobile accident when I was four. I had a confused memory or two of life with them that involved the snow in Minnesota and bulky, uncomfortable coats, but nothing more. At age five, after living for a few months with a cousin who didn't really want me, I was sent to live with Aunt Etta, who, it soon became clear, wanted me mostly for the modest life insurance my parents had left for me. Etta Mary Pitkaginkel was her full name, but no one dared call her that because no one could say it without laughing.

She worked for A. C. Pittman, who owned over ten thousand acres of orange groves all over the state. She'd started off cleaning and taking care of his big house, which he never lived in because he had taken a mistress in Cleveland. Pittman's wife lived in California, at their other house. Aunt Etta also helped with the orchards next to the house during the picking season, assisting the foreman. Sometimes it seemed like she was the foreman. In the off season, with almost no one around, Aunt Etta took up the position of being in charge almost by default.

I'd like to think that the Aunt Etta I met as a child was very different from the Aunt Etta from before, that the rare hints of good humor and of kindness had once been a fireworks display. She, like me, had come from up north, from near Minneapolis, and she had also been fleeing disaster: a bad marriage, and dead-end jobs afterwards that never matched up with the comfortable, even rich, life she'd had before. She never talked about her brother, my father, but she'd so loathed those crappy jobs that she still muttered about them, couldn't let go of past slights and injustices. Other muttering came from resentment over Pittman keeping an exhaustive catalog of the house's many treasures – and having someone come and check that they

were still there every six months, "as if I'm not to be trusted." Revenge for
Aunt Etta came in the form of pretending she was related to Pittman, and
using that to control the foreman, in a variety of ways.

She had what looked to me like a boxer's hands, all knuckles and cal-
luses, and she used them like a boxer sometimes, too. The pickers, behind
her back, called her "Auntie Dempsey" after Jack Dempsey. A tall woman
with some meat on her, she used to boss the Mexican immigrants around
– she stood over them like a stern, plump statue of liberty. They all feared
her, endured her.

For my part, as soon as I had sense enough to understand Aunt Etta, I
tried to keep out of her way. The rest of the time, I obeyed her the best I
could, and looked forward to each and every day of school at Littlewood El-
ementary and, later, Westwood Middle School. I didn't make many friends,
never felt comfortable, but at least other kids were around. No kids on the
Pittman land, except for the children of the Mexican laborers, and they
wouldn't play with me by the bungalow because of Aunt Etta. I had to sneak
off into the groves. Even then, they were wary as the deer that sometimes
appeared at dusk, while I, husky and my face ruddy with acne, felt like some
clumsy monster barging in on their peace and quiet. Sure, there were kids at
the Episcopalian church we sometimes went to on Sundays, but with Aunt
Etta it was always go in, worship, and, as she put it, "get the hell out." I always wanted to "get the hell out," too, so in a way perfunctory church-going
formed a bond between us.

I guess maybe that's why I said yes to Sensio in the first place – to have
someone to play with, even if a rabbit was just a couple steps up from a
doll. It was a summer day, I remember. I was just hanging around the pond
behind the bungalow, in my bathing suit, watching the water ooze into the
soil and wondering how the smell of oranges could have gone from smelling good to being an awful stench, and then a nothing, a scent that had no
texture, no impact. I was in that good, silent place where the sun's warm on
your skin and the breeze moves lazily over the hairs on your forearms.

The man was a presence leaning over me, and then a shadow through
the sunlight from which appeared a darkened face, alongside a voice like
the soft rasp of weather-beaten leather that said, "Would you like a rabbit?"
Then through my squint the figure resolved into a withered old man with
only one eye and one arm. Where the eye should have been there was just an

obsidian-black hole. Where the arm should have been, there was just a blue sleeve flapping in the breeze. He had a strange whispering rasp to his accent that drifts away from me whenever I try to identify it. A vague thought in my head that maybe he'd served in the War, although I didn't know much about "the War" beyond what I'd heard some men at the church say.

He carried a cage full of rabbits with the other hand. His remaining arm was what an adult would have called hypertrophied, the muscle in his bicep, triceps, and forearm thick, shoulders almost splitting his shirt seam.

"I'm not supposed to talk to strangers," I said. For some reason, he was a curiosity to me. I didn't feel threatened even as I said the words.

"Then don't talk," he said, and set down the cage. He reached down and undid a latch, and suddenly there was something soft and white and heavy on my lap. The man said, "His name is Sensio," and then he was lurching away with the cage, saying over his shoulder, "Tell Aunt Etta I said hello."

I stared after the man long enough for him to become a flicker of light and dark moving through the orange groves. Then I turned to the rabbit.

Sensio was nuzzling up against my shoulder as he searched for a carrot or a lettuce leaf. To a bored kid in an orange grove in Florida, he looked like any old rabbit. He looked like my best friend.

I never told Aunt Etta the truth about where I got him. Something about the way the man said, "Tell Aunt Etta I said hello," had bothered me. It wasn't that I wanted to protect Aunt Etta; in my kid's logic, she was as much of a problem as she was the person feeding me, putting a roof over my head. It was more that I didn't know how the man knew Aunt Etta. What if she hated him? Did that mean she wouldn't let me keep Sensio?

•

Aunt Etta kept giving the photographer suggestions that he didn't take to, like "Move the tripod to your left, young man, so you can get the trees behind me." She had an odd sort of pride about those trees, I realized later. A kind of pride not in keeping with her actual role as servant, as if she thought she owned the orchard.

"Ma'am," the photographer would say, "the light won't be right if I do that." Or, "That will take another half hour."

Whatever patience the man possessed had been used adjusting to the oddness of the assignment. He was a young man, yes, but he had shadows under his eyes, and wrinkles at the corners. I remember thinking that his face shone oddly in the same way as Sensio's as he suffered his humiliation bound to the post.

As Aunt Etta tried to settle down for the photograph, even as she kept primping and fussing, I almost said something to her, but it was Sensio who broke in first.

"Take the picture," he said in his voice, which always had a gruffness to it. "Take the picture and be done with it."

The photographer stepped back, knees bent. The cigarette fell to the grass as his mouth opened so wide his jaw must have hurt. He looked like he'd just realized he was standing in quicksand or something.

Aunt Etta cackled, jumped up and down, which looked less dramatic than it sounds because of the length of her dress. Every utterance from Sensio's mouth must have sounded like a celestial chorus of dollar bills to her.

●

Sensio first spoke one night in my room, about a week after he came into my life. I had the windows pulled open because of the heat, hoping for a cross-breeze or anything to stop the sweat. I was on top of the sheets, naked except for my underwear. I was in a typical wretched, self-pitying mood. I had no friends. I was bored. I would never have a life in this place. The moon through the window was like a huge round cross-section of bone. The strange cries of nighthawks seemed to come from that whiteness, not the darkness into which their silhouettes disappeared.

Sensio was in the cage in the corner near the closet, next to my old dolls and other toys. I'd told Aunt Etta I'd found him cowering under an orange tree, even attached a crude splint to his paw to support my lie that he'd been injured, needed my help. "He must have been someone's pet," I said.

I don't know if she believed me, but she'd let me keep him, making it clear that if he became a nuisance, "into the pot he'll go." Although she'd never killed an animal in her life except mice, Aunt Etta loved rabbit stew. She said it reminded her of "her youth" growing up in Minnesota. I thought there must be better memories than that, even if my own childhood hadn't yet amounted to much. Still, four or five times a year, she paid the Mexicans to get her rabbits. They tended to be stringy things, marsh rabbits taken from the shores of nearby lakes.

That night, as I lay there, so uncomfortable, staring out the window, listening to the sound of mosquitoes kissing the window screen, I heard a voice.

"Let me out of my cage," it said, gruffly. "Let me out."

I sat bolt upright in my bed, grabbed a plastic doll for protection. I listened carefully but heard nothing except my own breathing.

After a minute, I lay back down, chest tight and heart devouring my blood.

But a little later, the voice spoke again: "Please let me out of this cage, Rachel."

This time when I sat up brandishing my doll, I dared look over at the cage. Sensio was staring at me, his white fur darkly glowing against the cross-cut shadows.

"Was that you?" I whispered, almost hoping it had been, and not someone who had broken into our home. An absurd little part of me was almost more afraid of waking up Aunt Etta than of a talking rabbit.

"Yes, it's me. Sensio."

I couldn't see Sensio's mouth, but the sound definitely came from his cage. That's when I thought I must be asleep, and that the heat was giving me strange dreams. I would wake soon.

In the meantime, it was the most natural thing in the world to climb down off my bed made for an adult and kneel down in front of the cage and say to Sensio, "If I let you out, will you go back in when I tell you?"

Those eyes, so full and dark against the ghost-white of his face, *saw* me.

"Yes, Rachel," Sensio said.

Had I, in my loneliness, *created* a voice for Sensio? Something like this thought passed through me.

Watching myself do it, I opened the cage, and even then it was as if I had opened more than just a cage. I flinched from the slight electrical discharge as the latch shocked me.

But nothing odd happened afterwards, not really.

Sensio hopped forward, snuffled against my knee, asked in a low, deep voice, "Do you have any lettuce? Any carrots?"

Just like any rabbit.

•

The photographer laughed weakly when he'd recovered his composure. He turned to me and pointed and said, standing straight again, a new cigarette held in one shaking hand, unlit: "Nice trick, kid. You should take that act out on the road." While Sensio stared up at him from his position as prisoner at the post.

Aunt Etta became livid, all the cheer dropping from her face and a pink blush steadily moving up her face from her neck.

"It was the rabbit, you idiot!" she shouted at him, her lipstick a ragged blood-snarl in the heat. "You heard it! You heard it *speak!* You heard it and you think she could do that? *That stupid little kid?*"

The photographer stared at Aunt Etta much as he'd stared at Sensio. I was staring, too, but Aunt Etta hadn't really said anything I hadn't heard before.

He worked much faster after that, and Sensio said nothing. Nothing at all. But from the look he gave me, I thought there was must be much more he wanted to say.

•

At first, we talked mostly at night, when I thought Aunt Etta couldn't hear us. I'd forgotten the strange ways in which that old bungalow could carry sound, or I'd just decided to risk it. I can't remember.

These weren't conversations like the ones between two people. For one thing, I sometimes still believed I'd made it all up and was talking to myself. For another, Sensio sometimes made sense and other times talked in riddles, or with some kind of veil between what I wanted him to mean and what he actually meant. I mimicked Aunt Etta's mutterings for a while around the cottage, but my favorite phrase was "Just the tip of the iceberg," to remind me of larger mysteries. My forehead became taut with the strain of thinking all the time, trying to interpret Sensio.

"How come you can talk?" I asked him this question the second night; I hadn't had the nerve to interrogate what seemed like a miracle the night before, had been afraid it might turn out to be a dream, or a nightmare.

"I have always been able to talk," Sensio said, with the stiffness of a Russian count from a fairy tale. "It is just that no one could understand me."

"What do you mean?" That was a favorite question of mine at the time, along with "Why?"

"I do not mean anything," Sensio said, and nibbled on a carrot.

"How old are you?"

"I do not know. Very old."

For a rabbit? For a person? Sensio did not know.

Then I asked a question that I kept coming back to in my feverishly alert child's mind – about the man who'd brought Sensio to me.

"That man. The one who gave you to me. Who was he?"

"A friend from another country."

"What's the country?"

"A place far from here."

I paused, frowning. I tried a different approach.

"Where did you come from?"

"Somewhere else."

"Where?"

"A place far from here."

"Have you ever been to school?"

"What is school?"

"A place where you learn things."

Sensio had nothing to say to that, but he seemed to give me a disapproving look. I tried again.

"How long have you been able to talk?"

"As long as I have been able to talk."

I really didn't like that answer. Impatient, almost imperious, I asked, "Are you the only rabbit that can talk?"

"I am not a rabbit."

And there it was: *I am not a rabbit.* Even now, so long after, it makes me shiver. But at the time, it made me giggle. It seemed like a funny answer. Of course Sensio was a rabbit. He looked like a rabbit, ate like a rabbit, and definitely crapped like a rabbit.

"So what are you then?" I asked. "A ham sandwich? A can of beans? A witch?" I was delighted with myself for these guesses.

"I am not a rabbit," he said again.

This time I didn't giggle. It was said with such a sense of aloneness, that it's impossible to convey. It made me stop asking questions, because I felt I understood him. He was just like me.

That was the day before Aunt Etta found out.

•

After the photographer had taken his pictures and left along with all of his strange equipment, giving us a brusque promise of samples in a week, we stood there for a little while. It was dusty. It was uncomfortably hot. My throat felt parched and the green of the orange groves quivered in an air thick and humid.

Aunt Etta licked her lips, asked Sensio, "Don't you have anything to say?"

Sensio said nothing.

"Not one damn thing?" Aunt Etta asked again.

Sensio still said nothing. I felt the moment turn, like we were all balanced on the same thin plank high in the air, and at least one of us was going to fall off.

"Not one damn thing," Aunt Etta muttered. "You've got nothing to say to me after all of that. I feed you, I give you shelter, and you won't give me one word when I need it."

"There is nothing to be said," Sensio growled after a moment.

Turning his head to the side in a very unrabbit-like way, Sensio stared up at Aunt Etta. Aunt Etta stared back, just as implacable.

Right then, the rope in Aunt Etta's hand looked less like a leash and more like a fuse.

•

"Remember, it's just an animal," Aunt Etta said to me, during that first meal after she discovered me talking to Sensio. This was back when she thought she might flatter Sensio into cooperating with her plans. I know she was wearing something else, but in memory she is wearing the same outfit as she did to the photo shoot.

We sat, the three of us, at the dining room table in A. C. Pittman's house, which almost qualified as a mansion. Eating there was something Aunt Etta did rarely, and only when she wanted to impress. Sometimes the foreman – a tall, rangy Mexican originally from Tijuana – would visit, and the two of them would walk up to Pittman's house laughing, with some bottles of beer, and be gone for hours. That was the happiest I ever saw her, and the house had something to do with it.

Chandeliers from Paris, Waterford crystal, decanters of brandy, rosewood chairs and tables, carpet from the Orient, and even an awful lion's pelt rug in the study. Pittman made money from more than just orange groves, and he spent it on only the most obvious things.

The dining room table could seat twenty along its length, and its surface was a rich, shining mirror from which none of us could hide. Aunt Etta sat at the head of the table, me to the left, sullen and on edge. Sensio sat on the other side – balanced atop five cushions to begin with, Aunt Etta having, absurdly I realize now, pulled up Pittman's ornate French chair from the study to impress the rabbit.

After a time, Sensio hopped onto the table, onto his plate.

"Rachel, move that for him," Aunt Etta snapped at me. Since she'd found out Sensio could talk, her whole world had been Sensio, except when she needed something done.

"Isn't this nice?" she said to Sensio.

That afternoon, when she'd burst into my room in the bungalow and admitted she'd been listening at the door on and off for a while – when she saw I had neither imaginary friend nor actual friend – she'd at first let out a kind of horrible shriek, followed by the hiss of an intake of breath. Her face had seemed for a moment to crumple. Ever since there had been in her eyes a light that was too bright. Her actions, her movements, were also too "bright," as if under such tight control that she might at any moment explode.

Isn't it nice?

Perhaps, in that moment, I did find it nice, almost as if I were younger and having a teddy bears' tea party in the orchard by myself. Those bears had talked to me, too, but I'd always known what they were going to say.

But Sensio said nothing in reply. The tock-tock of the inlaid mother-of-pearl grandfather clock in the hall became oppressive. Even the savory but thick smell of dinner cooking in the kitchen added weight to the air.

"Your friend is a little shy," Aunt Etta said to me.

I shrugged, not sure what to make of the situation. Aunt Etta's discovery that Sensio could talk had been a different kind of shock for me. It meant that Sensio's ability was definitely real. There was relief in knowing I wasn't imagining things, and another kind of relief in hoping that the rabbit might create a kind of truce between Aunt Etta and me.

"What's for dinner?" I asked, but she had already turned her back on me.

"Why are you here?" she asked Sensio.

I sat up straight in my chair. It was a question that would have seemed like nonsense if I'd asked it. Coming from Aunt Etta, it seemed like the only question.

Slowly, Sensio stirred and turned toward Aunt Etta.

"Does it matter?" he replied. "It only matters what you think I'm here for."

Suddenly, a coldness crept into me. Suddenly, I was not Sensio's friend. Instead, it felt as if he were an adult just like Aunt Etta.

Aunt Etta leaned forward, said, almost primly, "I think you are here to make all of us very rich," as if she'd invited an oil derrick or a shipment of gold bullion to dinner. Then she went to get our meal.

That was just the first of three fancy dinners, each more tense than the last. In memory, they are all mixed together, but they each had their own characteristics: in the first, vegetarian lasagna, as Aunt Etta tries to flatter what cannot be flattered; in the second, steamed vegetables, rice, and (for us) chicken, as Aunt Etta tries to plead with that which cannot negotiate; in the third, Aunt Etta outdoes herself in more than one sense.

Later, I would think about what she did and wonder if she just had limited ways of coping with the impossible without going insane. Yet, her solution – that Sensio would make us rich – made her even crazier.

•

The day after Aunt Etta discovered Sensio could talk, she shoved a cot into her room for me to sleep on and also brought Sensio's cage in there. She made sure he only got the best carrots, lettuce, and other produce.

I was mad about this, and not just because my feet dangled off the end of the cot and my back became stiff from the mattress, or that she didn't care. I was mad because now there was almost no time for me to talk to Sensio without Aunt Etta around. Sensio didn't talk as much during the day.

Then Aunt Etta started to call newspapers. First, national newspapers, from telephone numbers she found rummaging through Pittman's business office, and then the Florida papers, because the national papers thought she was a kook.

"I'll show them kook," she'd say, dialing yet another number.

I admit I became caught up in the idea of Sensio becoming famous, and the thought of it almost made up for Aunt Etta making us sleep in the same room with her. I don't know what Aunt Etta envisioned, but in my daydreams Sensio did make us rich, and we went on the road with him as part of a traveling carnival a little like the one painted in a picture in Pittman's house: all garish reds and greens, and smiling carnies standing to one side of cages with dancing bears in them and jugglers practicing their trade on the other. All sorts of exotic ideas came out of my head. As Sensio's trainer I would be much interviewed and admired. I'd have someone to help me with my makeup and buy me clothes. The other kids in the carnival would seek me out. When we weren't working, we'd take holidays, going to fancy restaurants and staying in swank hotels. I had a fixation with chocolate ice cream back then, so I dreamed of eating mountains of it.

But more important, it began to dawn on me that if Aunt Etta was successful, her attention wouldn't always be on me and all the things I was doing wrong. That I would have some relief, and maybe even some control, even though I knew that, thankfully, she didn't yet realize this fact. I could also, during those handful of days, pretend that, for once, Aunt Etta and I wanted the same things – for Sensio and for ourselves.

A couple of reporters finally came down, one from the *Orlando Sentinel* and one from the *St. Petersburg Times*, but Sensio wouldn't talk to them. Aunt Etta had made him clothes by then, so he'd look more human, but I thought he looked more foolish that way, like he was playing dress up, and it didn't help with the reporters, who only cared if he talked or not. The second reporter left angrier at the waste of time than the first, maybe because he'd had to drive a longer distance or maybe because he'd already been having a bad day.

When no one else would come out Aunt Etta made a fool of herself trying to get Sensio to talk to people over the phone, which he wouldn't do. The sight of Aunt Etta, on her hands and knees, holding the phone down to Sensio's mouth and pleading with him to talk should have made me feel bad for her.

When I hesitantly tried to tell Aunt Etta that no one thought of a rabbit talking over the phone as proof of anything, she snapped, "He still sounds like a rabbit."

Except, I realized he didn't sound like a rabbit. He didn't make a chuttering purr or the kind of warbling squeak I'd heard from other rabbits. All he did was talk in a voice like a man, and he snored sometimes at night, a sound that made me smile because sometimes he formed a chorus with Aunt Etta. Once, waking up suddenly, he made a sound like a high-pitched sonic boom.

"Maybe he's more comfortable staying in my room," I said, but Aunt Etta wasn't having any of that, either.

●

After the photo session, the moments extended out into a kind of standoff while I watched, Sensio staring at Aunt Etta and Aunt Etta staring at Sensio. They were like battle-scarred emissaries from two different countries that would never speak the same language and never admit to the need for an interpreter.

Almost as if to make him stop, she yanked on the rope and Sensio fell over like a child's toy. Silent. Still looking up at her. I was so surprised I just stood there.

Aunt Etta nudged Sensio with her foot as he tried to right himself. Then she kicked him in the side.

I beat on her then, my fists on that impenetrable, ridiculous skirt that seemed made of something more like aluminum siding than fabric.

I imagine I was screaming at her, although I can't remember making a sound.

●

A week or two before Aunt Etta contacted the photographer, she called the Ringling Brothers Circus, which kept a permanent headquarters in Tampa. The woman who came out surprised us both. I'd expected a bearded lady and Aunt Etta had expected a trapeze artist. What we got was a slim, gray-haired woman dressed smartly in slacks and a blouse. Her shoes were flat and black and simple. She had hazel eyes tinged with green. She could have been from Sears, except for her mysterious smile that made everything ordinary and normal about her seem just a disguise. I liked her. She seemed the opposite of Aunt Etta in almost every detail.

We went to the screened-in Florida Room of Pittman's house, a ceiling fan lazily revolving above our heads. The circus woman, whose name I can't remember, sat on the couch and looked out at the orange orchards in the distance while I brought Sensio in and put him on the wicker chair to her left. Aunt Etta had gotten a fancy tea service with a hummingbird pattern out of the basement, and handed the circus woman a cup of orange blossom tea.

From his comfortable wicker chair, even with me petting him, Sensio steadfastly refused to speak. Long minutes passed by in uncomfortable silence, broken only by the staccato, almost garish attempts by Aunt Etta at small talk. I remember feeling a perverse pleasure at being a kid, at not being expected to put forth the effort. All I'd had to do to prepare was put on a sun dress and let Aunt Etta tie a pink bow in my hair. All I had to do now was smile and pet the rabbit, and dangle my legs off the edge of the chair.

The circus woman was patient, and she waited for longer than most people. She even waited while Aunt Etta squatted and sidled up to Sensio on the side of the chair opposite me, and then poked him in his side as he nibbled on a carrot.

"C'mon, Sensio," she said in a wheedling voice. "Come on. Talk for the nice lady."

I didn't like those pokes. Those pokes were deceptive. When the foreman was around and I did something Aunt Etta disapproved of, she'd poke me in the side like it was a joke, but it always hurt. Sometimes it left a bruise.

Near the end of this thankless and uncomfortable sitting, with Aunt Etta's pokes becoming more like jabs, a strange thing happened. Sensio lifted his head and a look of recognition, almost sympathy, passed between the rabbit and the circus woman, her mysterious smile growing momentarily larger and fuller before fading. It was so quick and so ambiguous, I couldn't tell if I'd imagined it, let alone begin to understand its meaning.

A few minutes later, as if on a pre-arranged signal between her and the rabbit, she rose, giving a nonchalant pat to Sensio that, in my imagination, now is elongated and slowed down so that some kind of communication or comment is occurring there. Then, with a smile of sympathy toward me that I warded off by looking away, she ignored Aunt Etta's pleas to give Sensio another chance with some polite collection of words like "a lovely rabbit, but I don't think it's the kind of act we're looking for."

She handed Aunt Etta a business card and, on the way out, managed to – while giving me the solemn, leaning-over handshake of adult to child – slip a tiny deck of tarot cards into a pocket of my dress. If there was something serious in her gaze, I couldn't understand what it might be any more than I could understand Sensio.

After the circus woman had left, Aunt Etta folded her arms, stared down at Sensio, and said, "No dinner for you." And then, looking over at me, "For either of you."

No dinner because of someone else's failure wasn't unknown in our strange, sealed-off household, but this seemed so unfair I began to cry. Or maybe I was upset because the circus woman had left.

"I'm sorry," I said to Sensio through my tears. "I'm sorry." After all, I had led him into this trap.

"It would all be the same anyway," he said very seriously.

"No, it wouldn't be," I said. I don't know what I meant by that, though. Did I mean if he'd talked to the circus lady or something else?

"I am not what she wants me to be," Sensio said.

"What are you then?" I asked him, bringing his warm fur up to my face as I hugged him close. "What are you?"

"Does it matter?"

•

After Aunt Etta kicked Sensio, she dragged him through the dirt back toward our bungalow, holding the rope tightly in her boxer's fist. There was no one to see her do it. The workers had the afternoon off and the foreman was out at a local bar.

I was screaming, kicking at her, but she didn't even notice. Sensio remained silent. Not a squeal, not a squeak, although it must have hurt him terribly.

"Stop," I kept shouting. "Stop!"

But she wouldn't stop. She was caught up in the moment. She couldn't stop. Something hidden at the core of her had come out. She would have dragged him through the rows of orange bushes, choking, until his fur came off and he was raw and spasming. She would have turned him into rabbit stew without any protest from Sensio, as if this was what he had been set on earth to become. There wasn't even anything personal about it, and that made it worse, like she'd planned it all along. Like she'd wanted it to happen that way. Was it because she couldn't stand being turned into a fool? Was it from sheer frustration?

All I know is that I ran back to the post. With a grunt, bending my knees, I put my bulky frame to use and pulled the post out of the ground in an explosion of dirt, splinters ripping into my hands. When I caught up to Aunt Etta – she was still dragging Sensio by the rope around his neck, his paws flopping in the dirt – I shouted "Stop!" again in my loudest voice. But still she refused to hear me, so I had to make her hear.

I hit Aunt Etta across the shoulders with the post. She turned to me with a distant look on her face. I couldn't tell you what that expression meant. It didn't stop me from smashing her in the knees, through that ridiculous armored skirt. It absorbed some of the force of the blow, but she still let out a loose, oddly high-pitched cry of pain. She lurched to the side, but regained her balance.

"Stop it, Rachel," she said. "Just stop it. It's just a rabbit." She was breathing heavily, and her words sounded like they'd been said in a foreign language.

I hit her in the knees again, with all my strength. She cried out again, this time more piercing. She fell almost like a statue, straight down, as if she had no joints, the skirt settling around her like a parachute. She was slapping out at me as she fell like I was some sort of insect rather than a big, clumsy twelve-year-old with a wooden post in her hands. Even then she refused to let go of Sensio, her hand clenched white against the rope. Maybe it was just a reflex, but I saw it as more refusal, more proof that Sensio was in danger.

I hit her in the head. Once, twice. She gasped like all her breath was rushing out of her, tried to get up, and my anger turned to fear. If she got up, she would do to me what she was doing to Sensio. And I could not let that happen. I hit her one last time.

Aunt Etta groaned and slumped and lay still while I freed Sensio from the rope. His fur had been ripped off in places, revealing pink, bloody skin. There was sand and grass and dirt all over him.

"Are you okay?" I asked him, frantic as I cradled him in my arms.

But he said nothing.

JEFF VANDERMEER

•

You can see the photograph now, as a postcard, in antique stores and gift shops in Florida. Sometimes it comes with a funny title, like "She dealt swiftly with evildoers." It has been doctored to include shadows for both Sensio and Aunt Etta. Her clothes have been colored, as has his straitjacket uniform. Because of these changes, which make the photo look even less real, there is no chance that anyone would ever believe Aunt Etta really tied a talking rabbit to a post and, dressed in her Sunday best, had someone take a photograph of her with the rabbit. No one will ever know that I was there, too, or what happened after.

I came to my senses a few minutes after I'd hit Aunt Etta for the last time. She was making little broken sounds in the dirt and had a big, bleeding dent in her forehead. Her eyes were open but glassy, as if she had already turned inward. Every couple of minutes her body would convulse. I knew that I had hurt her badly.

I'd dropped the post and was babbling to Sensio as I held him against my chest. We'd escape together. We'd hide out in the orange groves, or we'd make our way to Key West and hide out there, like I'd seen in a movie once. Or maybe we'd even travel to Tampa and find the circus woman and she'd help us out. "She liked you, Sensio," I remember telling him. "She'd definitely help us." As if I were an adult, or had any money, or any sense.

After a while I realized Sensio wasn't answering, which to me, in that state, meant he didn't agree. Slowly, a cold, clear mood came over me, and I knew what we had to do, what we could do to survive this together.

I scuffed up the trail from the photo shoot to where Aunt Etta's body lay to make it harder to tell what had happened. I used leaves and a branch to obscure any of my footprints. I took the post with me, and later burned it. Then I went back to the bungalow, treated Sensio's wounds, and put him in his cage, telling him, "No matter what questions they ask, don't say anything." I thought I saw him nod.

Then I had the operator call the foreman at the bar and told him I'd found Aunt Etta, "beaten up by someone." The foreman called an ambulance and the police, and came barreling back in his ancient truck. I was bawling by Aunt Etta's side just like a kid of twelve would bawl if she found her aunt

36

brutally attacked and left for dead. I did it because I had to, yes, but also because by then the madness had left me and I was truly sorry.

As the ambulance took Aunt Etta away to three months in a coma followed by brain death, the policeman on the scene asked me, "Have you see anyone you don't know around here lately?"

Through my sobs and hiccupping and snot, I told him that an old man with a face like weather-beaten leather and missing an eye had come looking for Aunt Etta, but I'd only seen him the once. I figured telling them the man was missing an arm, too, would be laying it on too thick.

"Could you identify him if you saw him again?" the policeman asked. He was in his late forties, losing his hair, and had a kindly voice that made me feel bad.

Yes, I nodded, although I knew they'd never find him.

After they'd finished questioning me, I stayed with the foreman's family for a few weeks before being picked up and sent back north to live with the cousin who hadn't wanted me before. I guess the sympathy money A. C. Pittman threw at him made me more appealing. I even got to take Sensio with me, in a little cage in the backseat next to me. No one was willing to tell the girl who had suffered such a trauma that she couldn't keep her only friend in the world.

I talked to Sensio the whole way up, but in the way a child might to an imaginary friend so the cousin, who smelled of too much cologne and was throwing me strange glances from the driver's seat, wouldn't get too concerned. Sensio didn't answer me. That was okay, I reasoned. He'd suffered a trauma, too. It would take time for both of us to recover.

The same newspapers that had ignored Aunt Etta when she'd tried to sell them on a talking rabbit, now splashed the details of her injuries all over their pages, referring in lurid tones to the mysterious man I'd described for the police. They even interviewed the photographer, whose account of that day didn't include the fact that he'd witnessed Sensio talk. But the man did leave the strong impression that Aunt Etta had been both a fool and a witch. Then it all died down, and Aunt Etta passed on without them having caught her murderer, and I imagine life went on in the orange groves much as it had before for the migrant workers and the foreman and whomever Pittman got to look after his house full of expensive junk.

●

It's been many, many years since that day captured by the photograph, and in most ways there's been nothing special about my life. I grew up, went to college, mostly on money it turned out Aunt Etta had kept for me in a trust fund. I left my cousin's house as soon as I could, became an accountant, and did well enough to come back to the small town in Minnesota where I'd been born and have a respectable career, live a respectable life. I found religion and lost it again. I dabbled at children's stories but never found the right voice. I fell in love on a cruise and married my husband John two years later. He's an attorney, and we have two kids, Bobby and Sandy, who've left home already for families and lives of their own. I used to go to a lot of PTA meetings and high school football games. Now I've retired from accounting, serve on the city council here, and do a bit of gardening. My marriage has had the highs and lows you'd expect, but there are some things you can't tell anyone, and the possibility becomes more remote every year. In short, there's nothing unusual about me. I could be anyone, anyone you know, and think after meeting her, "She's a nice older lady, but a little boring." I am more a ghost in my life now than as a presence beyond the edge of that postcard.

But even while I listen to some citizen talk about storm drains at a city council meeting, or weed the garden, I am still having conversations with Sensio in my head. So many conversations that I don't know what to do with them sometimes, don't know how to distinguish between what's been said and what's always been left unsaid, so that there are moments when something rises inside of me, unable to get out but unable to rest. Useless questions. Useless thoughts.

•

That third dinner, the night before the photo shoot, Aunt Etta made a fuss, wanted it to be formal and "just right." She'd suffered what I thought of as a change of mood that I found suspicious; she seemed almost giddy, almost happy. We waited at the foot of the stairs while Aunt Etta brought down a silver serving set. She claimed Pittman had bought it in Paris and kept it hidden in a cupboard on the second floor.

Aunt Etta had put on one of her best dresses: a silvery, shimmering thing that caught the light at odd angles so that one moment it was drab, lifeless, and the next it seemed full of tiny shooting stars. She'd taken special care with her makeup so it wasn't so thick or approximate, and she'd wrapped her hair up into a bun. A silver bracelet matched a silver necklace, both of which, up close, consisted of tiny dragon heads. I could smell her sickly sweet perfume from the bottom of the stairs as she came lurching down the steps in her black high heels. Sensio could smell it too; his nose twitched like crazy. But, I have to say, I liked her then. There was a sense, for a moment, of an Aunt Etta I barely knew.

With exaggerated care she swept by us with her serving set, giving us a smile of benevolent regard, and saying, "Sensio, I just know you will love this dinner. You will love it."

Sensio said nothing.

She disappeared into the kitchen that abutted the dining room. Interesting smells and sounds had been coming from the kitchen for hours.

The table had already been set. The cutlery gleamed in the fractured light from overhead lamps. I arranged Sensio atop his pillows again, to the left of Aunt Etta's place at the head of the table. I sat next to Sensio, in case he needed help.

"It smells good," I said to Sensio.

Sensio made a sound between a grunt and a sneeze.

Aunt Etta brought out the first dishes, which were to be served, buffet-style, in silver bowls. Squash and broccoli and green bean casserole, and potatoes au gratin with cheese crisped in frozen waves on top.

We ate silently because it was delicious and we were starving, Aunt Etta smiling at us from time to time from her newfound "shining city on the hill" as the church preacher might've put it.

Sensio didn't eat much, but this didn't seem to bother Aunt Etta. Mostly, Sensio had a sense of watchful waiting about him. But I ignored that, just as I put aside any misgivings about Aunt Etta's cheer.

Finally, Aunt Etta disappeared once more into the kitchen and came out wearing oven mittens and carrying a huge silver bowl, twice as large as the others, with an ornately etched lid.

She placed it on the table in front of us, and produced a ladle. A stillness had come over her, a kind of grand anticipation.

"This is something extra special for you, Sensio," she said. "I hope you like it."

39

With a flourish, Aunt Etta uncovered the bowl. Steam rose, and with it a smell familiar to me. Rabbit stew.

You might think I would've been horrified. But, oddly, I wasn't. Some cruel little part of me perked up in sudden fascination. What would Sensio do? Perhaps I was mad Sensio didn't talk to me as much anymore, even though that impulse would've been perverse, irrational. It was Aunt Etta who had ruined our conversations, after all.

Aunt Etta placed a generous portion in Sensio's bowl.

Sensio sniffed it hungrily, jumped onto the table, put his forelegs on the lip of his bowl. With extraordinary grace and agility, he used his teeth to pick out a carrot next to a meat-rich bone in the thick gravy.

"It's rabbit stew," Aunt Etta said, as if revealing the twist in a thriller on the radio. Her voice was slick with a kind of self-satisfaction, a sort of smugness.

Sensio sniffed again, looked over at Aunt Etta, said, "I am not a rabbit," lifted a bone out of the bowl, and crunched down on it with teeth never intended for the task. The sound of the bone cracking and then splintering was loud and grotesque. A sloppy, brutal sound that made mockery of the silver dining service, the opulent dining room, and, especially, of Aunt Etta.

The air had disappeared from my lungs without me noticing it, and I took a huge gulp. Neither Aunt Etta nor Sensio took any notice of me. Aunt Etta slowly sat back in her chair, struggling with emotions that only occasionally broke the surface of her face in the form of a tic, a tightening of the jaw, a strange look that hinted at both hatred and defeat. All those dollar signs were receding from eyes grown small and cold. Except, thinking back, I don't think it was really about making money off of him anymore.

But the crunching continued as Sensio, with great delight and deliberation, ate his stew, sucking out marrow as well as he was able, the pink of his nose, the white fur of his muzzle, soon muddy with the gravy.

It wasn't quite over, but it might as well have been. Aunt Etta attempted a kind of recovery, to overcome the moment with halting conversation, to somehow undercut the enormity of not just one, but *two* things that defied explanation. As I glutted myself to shut them out, and became drowsy, I seem to recall Sensio saying matter-of-factly, "…there is no time" or "…there isn't time yet," while Aunt Etta whispered over and over, as if to confide in Sensio, "Don't make me look like a fool. Don't make me look like a fool."

Their conversation seemed to narrow and narrow, like light withdrawing until it was only a single bright point reflected in the darkness of the dining room table.

•

I know I should think of Aunt Etta every day. I know I should be kinder to her memory. I know I should be sorrier about what happened. But even when I came across the photo again yesterday, while cleaning up the attic, all I could see was Sensio, and all I had inside of me was frustration, and a kind of anger that won't go away. That I didn't ask the questions before, or the right way, and that this would've made all the difference. Whenever I catch a glimpse of rabbits on TV, or at the mall pet shop, I hope to see one more time that great, that animating impulse in a large, almond-shaped eye, but I never do.

Although I had Sensio for another four years after I was sent back north, he never spoke to me again. Not a single word. Not even to tell me, one more time, that he was not a rabbit. I woke one morning and he was dead: just an old white rabbit with patchy fur, lying on his side, and looking out toward something I could not see.

Finding Sonoria

*

John Crake and Jim Bolger sat in Crake's living room. A small blue-green postage stamp lay on the old, low coffee table in front of them.

Bolger was a private detective once known all over Minnesota for his skill at finding people. He had the face of a pug and the build of a construction worker, or a weightlifter gone to seed. The jacket he wore made him seem even bigger, almost rectangular.

Crake had retired as a surveyor for the county three years ago. He'd been used to getting up at dawn and walking and driving around for hours. He had gained a little weight since his retirement, but not much, and he still wore bright plaid shirts, the kind of clothing that might distinguish him from a deer.

To Crake, the slopped-on cologne smell rising from Bolger was a surprise. To Bolger, Crake looked too tall even sitting down, but also like easy money.

"You want me to find a fucking country?" Bolger said. He picked up the stamp. In his palm, it looked like a strange Band-Aid. "Ever heard of the Internet, or the library?"

Crake had to resist the urge to tell Bolger to put it down, and Bolger, noticing that hesitation, moved the stamp to his other hand, then back again.

"I've checked the Internet, but there's no 'Sonoria,' just Sonora. Now I want you to try. Is that a problem?" Crake said. Ever since a throat cancer scare, Crake's voice had been low, and sometimes, whether he wanted it to or not, it sounded menacing. His wife Grace had loved the new voice, but she'd died of breast cancer the next year. He'd had no kids with Grace, had restarted his stamp collection after she was gone.

"If it's there, I want you to find it," Crake said. Crake's mind worked one way. He wanted a mind that worked another way.

43

Bolger just looked at him. But the fact was, Bolger's business had been in the crapper ever since he'd been hired by a state senator to spy on the man's wife. Bolger had entered into the case with gusto and delivered the news of the wife's multiple affairs with a cheerfulness that, looking back, Bolger figured he should have dialed down a bit. It wasn't so much "kill the messenger" as "kill the messenger's business."

In the old days, Bolger wouldn't have been in Crake's house, drinking tap water out of a dirty glass. In the old days, Crake would've come to the Imperial Hotel and paid for good whiskey and they would've sat in leather chairs, Bolger messing with his gold cufflinks or his expensive watch while Crake got smaller and smaller in Bolger's presence.

Crake had offered Bolger sardines, too, because Grace had liked them, so Crake still stocked up on them. Crake, staring across at Bolger, thought, *This is the kind of person who would blast a warning shot if I crossed his lawn.*

"Look," Crake said, "it'll be worth your while. And if the place doesn't exist, that's not your fault."

Bolger snorted. "You got that right." It was the kind of snort Crake would've expected from a sausage, if a sausage could snort.

"So what do you say, Mr. Bolger?"

"Sonoria. A country not on the map. You want it found. Okay, I'll find it for you, Mr. Surveyor. Four hundred a day plus expenses – and that's cheap."

Even as he said it, Bolger knew he was willing to go as low as two hundred a day, but what kind of client had faith in someone who *started out* as a discount detective?

"I can't afford that," Crake said, lying. He had a good pension, and a couple hundred thousand he'd stolen from people while surveying, buried out in the yard.

"Well, fuck, Crake, why did I come all the way over here, then?"

"I can't afford it. I'm sorry." Crake wasn't stingy, but he didn't want to pay too much for something this risky.

"How about two hundred a day?" As soon as he said it, Bolger was cursing himself. Too large a drop; it looked bad.

"I can't afford that, either." Crake thought: *I can't afford to spend that much just because I've been having dreams about the place.*

Bolger looked down at the table, back up at Crake. "You're a cheap motherfucker."

"And your business is in the toilet."

There. Crake had said it, and now Bolger thought he knew why Crake had called him.

Bolger half-rose, sat back down, feeling awkwardly like some kind of caged animal.

"You bastard. Well, what the hell can you afford?" Bolger said.

"Fifty a day."

"Fifty? Fifty." Bolger felt for a second like his heart, which sometimes seemed lodged in his large gut, was going to stop beating.

"There shouldn't be much in the way of expenses."

"Fifty, huh."

That should cover his daily rent at least, a little gas. He still had some savings and a couple of residual clients.

Crake rose suddenly and put out his hand, forcing Bolger to rise awkwardly and do the same.

"I know you can do it," Crake said as they shook hands, as if Bolger'd already agreed.

Bolger sighed. "And I know it's fucking insane, Crake. But I guess that's your problem, right?"

Crake's grip was stronger than the man looked, and Bolger's hand ached as he walked through the snow back out to his car.

•

As a child, Crake had collected stamps for their exotic qualities, and the colors. His mother approved, but his father, a tough bastard who claimed he'd been a Golden Gloves champ and had once made his living selling women's deodorant door-to-door, thought it was a hobby for "sissies." By the time his father was prematurely forcing him to learn how to drive with a clutch and signing him up for baseball, Crake had put aside the stamps.

Once, though, before he gave it up, his mother had given him a dozen stamps from "Nippon." Delicate traceries of cherry blossoms and storks and other images had conveyed a kind of distant otherness that made him shiver. At the time, he hadn't realized "Nippon" meant "Japan," and so the country itself had been a mystery, a place not found on the globe, waiting to be discovered. Even as late as eighteen or nineteen he'd remember those stamps and think that someday he would have a job that allowed him to travel a lot. Instead, he'd fallen into the path of least resistance: easy surveying job, wife, and inheriting his parents' home when they died.

Now, though, Crake had found another undiscovered country: Sonoria. Only, he couldn't find it on the map. The stamp had come with a Lewis & Clark commemorative set: small, triangular, trapped in a corner, the illustrated side facing away. The back of the stamp had yellow discoloration, indicating some age, the glue having melted.

Memories of the Nippon stamps, long lost, came to him as he sat at the worn table in the dining room, under a single light bulb. The bass of someone's idling car outside throbbed on and on despite the late hour. The neighborhood had changed; now he knew only Mrs. Stevenson and her daughter Rachel, who lived on the corner.

When he had found it, Crake had taken a pair of tweezers and extracted the odd stamp from the envelope. He turned it over and set it down on the table, on top of the envelope. It was an etching, very carefully rendered, of a mountain range, with a river winding through the foreground. Whoever had created the stamp had managed to mix muted colors – greens, blues, purples, and browns – into a clever tapestry of texture. For a moment, the river seemed to move, and Crake drew in his breath, sat back, magnifying glass clutched tightly in his hand. Across the three corners of the stamp, he read the words "Republic of Sonoria."

Crake raised an eyebrow. Sonoria? He'd never heard of it. It sounded faintly Eastern European – Romania? – and it was true he still had trouble identifying the former Soviet republics, but it still sounded false to him. He stared at the picture on the stamp again, shivered a little as if a breeze blew across the grassy plains surrounding the river. Something about the image stirred some deeply buried recognition.

Carefully, as if the precision were important, he picked up the stamp using the tweezers and placed it back in the envelope, in the same position, with the front facing inward. Then he walked over to the map of the world framed in his bedroom, and he looked for Sonoria. First, he tried Eastern Europe, then Central Asia, then random places, then systematically from left to right. No Sonoria in Asia, Europe, South America. No island named Sonoria. No isthmus. No province. No state. No city. Nothing. Unless it was so small it wouldn't show up on a map? Or it was one of those countries that had disappeared into the maw of another country?

Then he stood back, gazing at the map. It was probably a fake stamp someone had stuck in there as a joke. That's what Grace would've said. Just a joke. Why should he waste his time with it?

But that night, as Crake tried to get to sleep, he recalled the weathered quality of the stamp, the yellowish stain on the back, the high quality of the image on the front, and something about it worried at him, made him restless. He felt hot and out of sorts. When he did finally get to sleep, he dreamed he stood in front of a huge rendering of the stamp that blotted out the sky. The image in the stamp was composed of huge dots, but the dots began to bleed together, and then swirled into a photograph that became a living, moving scene. On the plains, strange animals were moving. Over the wide and roiling river, kingfishers dove and reappeared, bills thick with fish. The mountains in the distance were wreathed with cloud. A smell came to him, of mint and chocolate and fresh air far from the exhaust and haze of cities. Then the stars came up in a sky of purest black and blotted it all out, and he woke gasping for breath, afraid, so afraid, that he might forget this glimpse, this door into the Republic of Sonoria.

•

Bolger had heard none of this from Crake, of course, but had managed in his rough but uncanny way to intuit a narrow vein of madness in Crake's words during their initial meeting. It hadn't hurt that he'd bugged Crake's phone, though, and learned that Crake continued to call the post office about "Sonoria" and to make other calls that suggested Bolger could've charged much more than fifty dollars an hour.

47

He had also talked to a few of Crake's friends from the surveyor's department as well as the neighbors. Bolger had ruled out the stamp as a prank as a result. Everybody said Crake was a straight arrow – so straight it was ridiculous.

Truth was, Bolger still thought the joke might be on him. Sonoria. Was Crake in cahoots with the state senator, trying to make him look stupid? The whole story sounded like one of Bolger's mother's stories. He always knew the stories were bullshit, but at night, lying in bed with the sounds of his father knocking things over in the garage, he'd liked them anyway.

Bolger had a color photo of the stamp that he kept on the bed stand in his room at the Murat by-the-hour motel. It was the last thing he saw when he went to bed at night, and the first thing he saw when he woke up. When he had a hooker come by, they almost always noticed the damn stamp, maybe because it was the only thing in the place with any color to it.

At first, Bolger's own dreams focused on the councilman, and how this Sonoria assignment was all a big hoax to harass him. He saw a headline in his dreams: Discount Detective Looks For Imaginary Country.

But then the dreams began to change. The Republic of Sonoria. Where might that be? He didn't know, but he did know that in his dreams he had drawn his hand across the surface of a mighty river and felt the thick wet weight of it slap against his palm. He knew that his pants leg had been stained with the yellow-green of the grasses of the plains. His face had felt the breath of the place upon it. Jeez Louise, he'd smelled the fucking dirt, for chrissakes! No dream had ever been so real, so true, and sometimes even when he woke to the warm body of a woman in his bed, he wished he was still in dream. Sometimes, too, when he woke, Bolger remembered Crake's firm handshake and wondered if it had been a kind of trigger.

Bolger told none of this to Crake. All Crake got were the standard progress reports Bolger gave him over the phone. For reasons Bolger couldn't put into words, he didn't want to visit Crake's house again if he could help it. Maybe because it reminded him too much of his old man's place, and getting the shit kicked out of him every other week.

Bolger would open the bed stand drawer and take out the gun given to him by his father, and an old color photo of his mother standing on a bridge in Prague.

Then he would call Crake.

"Yeah, Crake? I went to the post office. I asked the stupid questions you didn't have the balls to ask. They've never heard of Sonoria. It's not in their computers. You can't send a package there. I mean, you could try – you could address something to Bumfuck, Sonoria, and see if it came back – but it's not in the computers. And, listen, they don't have anything close to it, either. No 'Slonoria,' 'Shonoria,' 'Snoria,' or whatever. Sonora's a fucking desert, not a country, just a county, with no 'i.' So much for misspellings. Over and out."

•

Crake didn't know why Bolger said "over and out," and Bolger never told him it was left over from a brief stint driving a truck for his dad. Mostly they'd hauled timber out of Canada, and it had been the most boring work Bolger had ever done. Getting out of it had also meant getting the fuck away from his dad, so he'd split. But he still liked that phrase, "over and out." It had a way of shutting up whoever was on the other end.

Crake appreciated "over and out," because he'd been about to make a big mistake. If Bolger hadn't cut him off, Crake would've blurted out, "But I know it's real! I've been there. I've walked along the riverbank. I've run through the plains. I've walked toward the mountains."

Crake, in his house by himself, no longer got any satisfaction from his stamps. Instead, he thought about Sonoria a lot, and Bolger. He wondered what Bolger's life must be like, solving mysteries for a living. As a surveyor, he'd spent a lot of time outside, measuring – a lot of time in the spring and summer hammering little stakes with red flags into the ground so people could sell properties or rezone them. This seemed so far from Bolger's experience of life. And yet now their worlds were the same world, all because of a stamp.

Bolger, meanwhile, kept looking, needing that fifty dollars a day, dutifully mailed to him by Crake in six-day increments. Bolger didn't know why Crake insisted on six-day increments, and it pissed him off because it seemed arbitrary and yet *organized*. Crake did it because he had a thing about threes, and because it fit the increments in which he'd buried the stolen money, but Bolger never figured that out.

The Internet and the library came next on Bolger's list, simultaneously because he no longer had a computer. In a particle-board stall at the library, he found out that "Sonora" was also a music company, a snake, and a kind of thunderstorm in California. "Sonoria" was nothing. Wondering, in a purely theoretical way, if a piece of information had fallen through the cracks, he spent hours huddled over remaining archives of decaying microfiche, focusing on obscure newspapers and old travel magazines. Maybe it *had* been a place, a long time ago. Over time, Bolger's vivid dreams of the place had begun to infiltrate his days. He had them idling in the car at a stop light, in line at the mini-mart to buy some beer. But the closer he got, the farther away he got, too, in some strange way. And he knew it.

One night, drunk, Bolger called Crake up.

"It's getting away from us, my friend," Bolger said, taking a swig of vodka. Everyone was his friend when he was drunk, in that cozy, soft light way particular to some television interview shows.

Crake's voice was so low that Bolger couldn't understand him over the crappy connection.

"What, Crake? What did you say, my friend?"

"I said I'm paying you to do a job, not be my friend. Do you have anything new to report?"

"Well, all right, then, my friend. Tough love. I get it." Bolger hung up.

It was just him in the Murat Motel.

It was just Crake in his little rotting house.

And Sonoria – out there, somewhere.

●

Crake couldn't stand waiting around for Bolger to call. It got to him mostly because he was smart enough to know it meant he didn't have enough to do. So he took to plotting out and measuring and marking the limits of his backyard, which, being on the last row in the neighborhood, opened up onto a new-growth forest of pines, all planted in straight lines. He dug up parts of the backyard, took the packets he found and put them somewhere else in the yard. Even Grace hadn't known about the money; or, rather, he'd never told her. Crake had always figured Grace knew his secrets whether he told her or not.

When he got tired of digging, Crake pored over old surveying maps, looked up the owners of the house from before his parents' time. This got stale fast, and because he was bored and because he couldn't help himself, he started writing about Sonoria. He did this chiefly because no matter how often he took the stamp out now, fixing it in his imagination, the stamp gradually lost its intensity for him. After a time, so did the dreams. The dreams became as faded as the stamp. The stamp became as faded as the dreams. Finally, Crake's vision of Sonoria faded to a single pixel.

So he wrote. He got out an old oversized blank book full of graph paper and he began with a small map. It didn't have much detail, because he had no idea what the real names for things like the river might be, but it was a start. Then he described the river, the plains, and before he knew it he had the beginnings of a fake history for the place. Fake because when Bolger finally found Sonoria almost everything detailed in his book would turn out to be untrue. *An oligarchy for a government, exports mostly agricultural, but also gold reserves. In the mountains, there lived a species of mountain goat with curved horns much prized for its meat.* Aware also, with irritation, that his imagination might not be up to the task.

Sometimes he babysat for Mrs. Sanderson, and the Sanderson kid Rachel, a quiet, brown-haired, big-eyed ten-year-old, would sit on a stool next to him while he wrote. Crake had no kids of his own, and how to engage Rachel was sometimes a puzzle to him.

"What are you writing?" Rachel would ask him after he'd gotten her some canned sardines and some water, which was all he really had in the house most of the time.

"A novel."

"What about?"

"About an imaginary country."

"What's it called?"

"The country?"

"No, the book."

"*A History of Sonoria.*"

"Sounds boring."

Crake laughed. "It sure does."

"And I don't like sardines."

"Nobody does," Crake told her.

•

Bolger knew about *A History of Sonoria* because the Sanderson kid told him about it for a dollar and a jawbreaker.

After the interrogation, he was walking to the car when he turned back to her.

"Hey, kid. Do you think Crake is crazy?"

The kid thought for a second, said, "Nope. Just hasn't got anything else to do."

True enough, Bolger thought. *Wonder what a surveyor's salary is these days?*

That's when he realized he'd begun to split his time between finding Sonoria and investigating Crake, as if investigating Crake might lead him to Sonoria.

When he got back to the motel, he called up Crake.

"Hey, Crake. I've got an update. I need more money per day for this wild goose chase."

"I don't have more money."

"Yeah, yeah, I know. It's like a mantra with you. Listen, I checked with a few relics from the Old Country. I found out they can't remember for shit, and especially nothing sounding like Sonoria. I've been to three old folks' homes and found out nothing except I hate the smell. I've checked the libraries. I've rechecked the Internet. I've checked with foreign embassies. I've read through some goddamn boring history books. Nothing."

"Nothing?"

"Not a damn thing. You got any suggestions?"

"You're the detective."

"Yeah, and I'm working on it," Bolger said, scowling. "I still got some more old people to visit. And other stuff I can do. But, really, why don't you just give me a map or something, Crake. Make it easier."

"Let me send you some photocopies."

"What?" Bolger asked.

But Crake had hung up.

Crake knew it was crazy as he said it. He knew it was like starting out on the surface, seeing a hole in the Earth, and after climbing down into it and seeing the light above begin to fade, to just keep traveling down rather than climbing back up.

•

Bolger took the envelope Crake sent him down to Curly Sue's, the corner dive, took a stool next to the jukebox because it shed enough light to read by, and asked the bartender for a shot of Irish Highlands whiskey.

He sat there for a while, nursing the whiskey, the envelope on the counter in front of him. Crake's handwriting on the front was as spidery and lucid as Crake.

Part of Bolger wanted to rip the envelope open. Part of him just didn't, not ever. By now, Bolger felt like he had one foot in the Murat and one foot in Sonoria. He could handle that. There was a kind of balance, a kind of balancing act, to it that he could maintain. That he didn't mind maintaining.

But, finally, Bolger ordered another shot and tore open the envelope, began to skim the pages. After a while, Bolger began to get a sense of it. Crake's observations tended to be precise but dry, things like "22 feet from the river, approximately 50 yards from the base of the first rise of hills preceding the mountains, you will find a village of about 70 people, mostly fishermen." Or, "There was a battle three years later. The lancers of the plains won, leaving 20 foot soldiers dead or dying." *A History of Sonoria* read like something bloody rendered bloodless. It read like the biography of a country written by a surveyor.

Bolger kept muttering "That's bullshit. That's bullshit" under his breath, once so loud the bartender came over to ask if he wanted another shot.

It all sounded so right, and yet Crake had gotten it all wrong. The images in Bolger's head, the raw, vibrant hues, the *movement* – none of it was as tepid, as careful as Crake made it out to be. Everything Crake had come up with was crap, and now it was in Bolger's head.

But when Bolger turned to the final page, in full color, he gasped, almost choked on his whiskey. Crake's map of Sonoria was a thing of beauty. Crake had used a medley of blues, greens, and sepia browns, with burgundy for the dots of cities. Rachel had helped him pick the colors because Crake was color blind. She'd helped him shade it in, too. It showed topographical changes, roads, rivers, mountains. All names had been written with brackets around them, which Bolger thought meant Crake was guessing.

But, of course, he was guessing about the whole thing. There was no Sonoria. Bolger knew that.

Ahmed, the manager of the Murat, slid into the stool next to Bolger at some point. He was a young, ambitious man who always looked more put together than anything in the Murat.

"Hey, Bolger – " Ahmed started to say, but Bolger cut him off, still staring at the map.

"Ahmed, you ever heard of a place called Sonoria?"

"No," Ahmed said. "You ever heard of a place that kicks you out when you owe more than two months' rent?"

●

Crake kept working on the book. As long as he worked on the book, he didn't notice the tiny house around him. He forgot that he was alone. Day after day, Crake filled more pages in the book, and when he was done, he pulled out another and began to write and draw in that one. He'd developed a sympathy not just for the farmers and tradespeople on Sonoria, but also its rulers, who had to navigate a treacherous diplomatic landscape to survive in the midst of much greater powers.

Rachel continued to help him. When Mrs. Sanderson dropped her off, Crake would sit her up next to him at the kitchen table with a glass of water, some sardines, and cookies he'd finally remembered to buy.

Then Crake would read Rachel his work from the previous day and night and Rachel would give Crake her opinions.

Rachel had a serious, conscientious streak, and never let him off lightly for a mistake.

"You said that bit already. Days ago."

"I like the story about the sisters who have to climb the mountain to save their father."

"I didn't understand that bit at all. You have to explain it."

Crake noticed that during these sessions time no longer had a static quality, and that when he wasn't writing, he didn't think about Sonoria much at all. Instead, he thought about things like what he wanted for dinner or what was on TV or a book he wanted to read. Or, about Bolger and the investigation. Crake wanted to call off the investigation, but the way Bolger ignored what other people said made it hard to stop Bolger.

●

Crake's payments stopped coming. At first, Bolger didn't care. He sat in bed staring at the map of Sonoria. Around him on the sheets he'd spread the pages of the history, which he'd heavily marked up. Every once in a while he'd think of some new lead, and he'd take out the phone book and call someone or get into his battered car and take a trip. Soon he stopped doing even that. Some days Bolger didn't even make it down to Curly Sue's. Some days he'd just watch bad TV with Sonoria bleeding through and drink until he slept. Those dreams were odd ones, his face all distorted and Sonoria full of demons that flew and swam and crawled. He'd wake up from them with a jolt, like he'd fallen into his bed from a great height, his breathing shallow, hard, and fast.

One day the jolt was a banging on the door.

Ahmed. Again. Even with Crake's money, money never went far enough. Not with Bolger's debt.

"Get the fuck away from my door!" Bolger shouted. "You don't want to fuck with me!"

Ahmed's voice, tinny through the door: "Get out. Get out by tonight or I'll call the cops. Or pay me. Your choice."

Bolger took the bottle of cheap whiskey on the night stand and threw it against the door. It only bounced, but at least it made a loud sound. His dad used to do that in the middle of the night with a glass bottle, if the dogs started barking outside the bedroom door.

"I'll leave when I want to leave," Bolger said, largely to himself.

Bolger had never done anything but drink and play detective. He looked around the motel room, at the faded, discolored lamp shades, at the chairs with the uneven legs, at the old, dusty TV, and wondered why he bothered.

•

The next day, a Saturday, Bolger showed up on Crake's doorstep. It was around noon and the sun glistened on the crackling snow. Bolger had a five o'clock shadow, bloodshot eyes, and a stain on his white shirt. His jacket showed a slight bulge from Crake's envelope about Sonoria. The gun was shoved into his jeans, in the back, and the photo of his mother was in his front shirt pocket. All of his belongings were out in his 1990 Corolla hatchback.

Bolger had only rung the doorbell after a pattern of indecision that had him pacing up and down Crake's walkway, until a few kids passing by on bikes made him self-conscious.

Crake looked at Bolger and almost closed the door.

Almost.

"Here're some notes on your book," Bolger said, taking out the wad of dirty, marked up pages, shoving them into Crake's chest, and pushing past him into the house.

•

So here they were now, in Crake's living room, again, two months later. Crake had put the pages away, not even insulted but more puzzled. He'd thought of Sonoria in his book as a kind of truth, transcribed from reality. How did you change that?

Bolger got right down to it: "Crake, I think I've found Sonoria."

The stare Bolger gave Crake tried to tell Crake that fifty a day wasn't enough to fund this kind of inventive bullshit. Crake's stare back tried to indicate polite interest, but nothing could hide his shock.

"You've found it?"

"Fuck yes I have."

The unspoken information lay between them – half-curse, half-blessing.

"In a stuffy old literary magazine. I was just about to throw it across the reading room because this essay on how tough the Serbs have it was putting me to sleep. And then I found it – in a footnote. It said something like 'Sonoria, a hidden valley in the mountains between Bulgaria and the Czech Republic.'"

Bolger pulled out a map of Europe he'd ripped from a library book.

"Right here," he said, slapping a fat finger down. "Right there."

Bolger almost believed it, in that moment. But the visions in his head said it wasn't true. Sonoria didn't exist in this world, and maybe the sadness over that led to the anger.

Crake looked over at Bolger and then down at the blank spot on the map. The mountains, the valley, the river. A chill, a shiver, that started in his brain and traveled down to his feet.

"Could it really exist?" Crake said, looking at all those jagged boundary lines. He hadn't considered it for weeks. Sonoria kept receding in one way and coming into focus in another.

Bolger tried to read Crake's face, couldn't tell what he saw there.

"So now you pay me what you owe me for the past weeks and we go there."

Crake frowned, and Bolger thought: *Shit, but now I've said it.*

"Go there?" For a second, Crake really didn't know what Bolger meant.

"Are you retarded, Crake? Didn't you hear me? We need to go find this place."

Did he? Crake looked around at the faded clutter, dim lighting, the dust, and stamp on the coffee table. Thought about his book and the sessions with Rachel.

Bolger followed his gaze, said, "It's kind of a shithole if you ask me." He was acutely aware of the cold metal of his revolver shoved into his pants. The muzzle kept cutting into his waist.

Crake said, "It was my parents' place. It's not a shithole."

Bolger laughed. "Okay, so it's not a shithole. It's a fucking mansion. Still no reason why you can't pay what you owe me and let me book us a flight to Prague, to start." Bolger's mother had been born in Prague, managed to visit once or twice. It wasn't Sonoria, but it was a lot closer than Minnesota.

Crake felt a flare of anger. Sonoria was his vision. Bolger was just a born-again.

"You've done your job. I'll pay you what I owe you. And then we're done."

Bolger sat up straight across from Crake, stared at him. "No," he said, "no. It's not just about the money anymore." Bolger saw the place every time he shut his eyes, but that couldn't pay the rent or get him more work.

"So go," Crake said. "You can do that yourself."

Bolger rose. "Is that your final word, asshole?"

Crake stared up at Bolger, acutely aware of all the unspent, buried money he still had, waiting for him.

"I'm supposed to babysit the Sanderson kid in a little while. I think you should take your money and leave."

Crake took out a wad of bills and put them on the table.

Bolger looked at the money, looked at Crake, pulled out the revolver and pointed it at Crake.

Crake blinked, sighed, and kept staring just past Bolger's left ear. He really wanted one of those cigarettes he'd given up, and he was thinking about the most impulsive things he'd ever done besides hiring Bolger. The first was pro-posing to Grace after only a month of dating. The second was slowly stealing two hundred thousand over thirty-five years from house after house. Crake hadn't stolen the money because he needed it. He'd stolen it because he was bored. Not much of a risk in the sense of looking down the barrel of a gun, but still a substantial risk.

"Fuck the money," Bolger said, both hands on the gun. "Fuck the money and fuck you. You're going with me to Prague."

Crake considered the bearlike Bolger and his gun for a lot longer than Bolger would have liked, then said, "I'm not going to Prague, Bolger. There is no Sonoria. I made a big mistake. Just take your money and get out of here." The Sanderson kid would be there in minutes.

Bolger laughed, although it came out more like a coughing whimper. He didn't really know what he was doing anymore, he realized that. He'd come here with a stupid bluff, one that he'd thought Crake might recognize as a way for them both to get the hell out of their situation. And now he was holding a gun on him.

"You're damn right about the money. I've seen your checking account bal-ance. I know you haven't been paying me from that. So it's got to be in the house somewhere. You just sit right there."

Still training the gun on Crake, Bolger searched the living room and the kitchen, ordered Crake into the bedroom, searched there, again nothing, and they came back to the living room, where Bolger pushed Crake back into his chair. Pain flared in Crake's hip, but he said nothing.

"Who doesn't have some money salted away, asshole?" Bolger said. But even though he held the gun, he didn't feel like he was in control. He picked up the Sonoria notebook Crake had set on the table, pointed the gun at it like he was going to shoot it.

"And now what?" Crake asked. "And now what?" Inside, Crake was shak-ing, but he'd never show Bolger that. "Go ahead and do it if you're going to do it, or get out." Crake felt an emotion he hadn't felt in a long time – a rage mixed with the sadness. He wanted Bolger gone or he wanted to kill Bolger.

Bolger knew when someone was about to fold. Crake wasn't going to fold. Crake wasn't going to give up anything, because he just didn't care. And the Sanderson girl would be there soon.

Suddenly, he felt ridiculous. Suddenly, caught in the weight of Crake's gaze, he saw himself as Crake saw him. Bolger's shoulders slumped. He put down Crake's book. He stuck the gun back into his pants.

"Well, I'm going. I'm going to Prague. I'm going to find Sonoria. And I'm taking the damn stamp." It was dry, almost brittle, in his hand.

"Go ahead," Crake said quietly. It hurt, a little bit, but he just wanted Bolger gone. He could already see the detective in Sonoria, written into Crake's book as the loud foreigner walking along the river, not able to be understood by anyone but talking anyway. It solved some problems he'd been having with the narrative. Crake wondered if Rachel would like the idea.

"Write when you get there," Crake said, relenting a bit. "Send a postcard." Almost said, "with a stamp on it."

Bolger was already at the door, not looking back. He'd taken his marked-up pages from Crake's book, stuffed them in his jacket pocket. Somewhere out there, somewhere *in here*, Sonoria was waiting for him. It had to be better than this.

Then Bolger was gone, driving slowly off in his car, and Sonoria with him, and Crake rose to see Rachel walking up to the door.

LOST

✳

"Are you lost?" it says to me in its gravelly moan of a voice and for a long moment I can't answer. I'm thinking of how I got here and what that might mean and how to frame an answer and wondering why the answer that came to mind immediately seems caught in my throat like a physical form of fear, and that thought leads to this: remembering the line of color that brought me here: the spray of emerald-velvet-burgundy-chocolate mushrooms suddenly appearing on the old stone wall where yesterday there had been nothing, and me on my way to the university to teach yet another dead-end night class, dusk coming on, but somehow the spray, splay of mushrooms spared that lack of light; something about the way the runnels and patches of exposed white understone contrasted with the gray that brought me out of my thoughts of debt and a problem student named Jenna, who had become my problem, really, and I just

stopped.

right there.

and stared at the tracery of mushrooms, the way they formed such a uniform swoop across that pitted stone, and something about them, something about that glimmer, reminded me of my dead wife and of Jenna – the green was the same as my wife's eyes and that of Jenna's earrings, and I remembered the first time I noticed Jenna's earrings, and how it brought a deep, soundless sob rising out of my chest, my lungs, and I stood there, in front of the whole class, bent over, as if struck by something large and invisible, and how ever since I cannot tell if my fascination with her has to do with that color and my need for companionship or some essential trait in her, and how ironic, how sad, that she misunderstood my reaction and began wearing the earrings every day, until that physical pain inhabiting my body became a dullness, like

61

the ache in an overused muscle, which I hated even as I found myself falling for Jenna…

and all of the time.

the whole time.

The light was fading except across the wall, and people in overcoats were walking past in the clear chill, under the streetlamps, and I could smell something other than the dankness of the wall as I traced its roughness with my fingers. It must have been a woman's passing perfume, but for a moment I smelled my wife and the emerald color of the mushrooms, the memory of her beneath me, the solid, comforting feel of her – all of this was the same thing, and when I started walking again, I didn't go straight. I didn't head for the ivy-strewn facades of the campus buildings. Instead, I turned

I turned and turned and turned.

turned as if turning meant wrenching my life from a stable orbit.

To the right I turned to follow the scatterings of mushrooms, and I don't know why, if I was just curious or if I'd already been captured in some way, because it wasn't like me. My dad had always said, before he passed from cancer in a very orderly way, that "you have to make a plan and keep to it." He said it to me, my mother, and my estranged sister, and he meant it. Routine was a religion for him, and we made it ours. Set meals. Set appointments. Set activities. I remember, when I turned eighteen, planning my rebellion, figuring out what I was going to do first and second and last, so I could savor my rebellion even as I…planned it. Less satisfying in the execution, the sex quick and lonely and not with someone I loved, the beer and pot putting me to sleep too quickly, waking to a cat licking my face, out cold on someone's sour-smelling lawn.

But I turned the corner, followed the mushroom trail, which moved up and down the wall like a wave, now mirrored on the wall that had sprung up opposite it – and ahead the ache of a dull red sunset, which bathed the mushrooms in a crimson glow, and,

suddenly, it wasn't that night

that place,

but a two-lane road the year before, the lights of our car projecting through the murk as we drove down a corridor of night. She was driving, and had the pursed lip look of concentration that I loved about her, and which I never told her I loved because I was afraid that if I told her, the expression would become different in some essential way, and I never wanted that to happen – never wanted her to be a different person, either, when we made love, staring at her face and seeing that same look of concentration, of being fully engaged.

wanted no self-consciousness from her.

wanted her lilting laugh to remain spontaneous.

wanted her.

to always preface her questions to me with "Let me ask you a question."

But a look of concentration doesn't mean concentration, and when I said later, in response to the ever-present question, until I had exhausted the gauntlet of friends, family, strangers who didn't know, the ordinary words "car crash," I couldn't help but associate that look with her death, and thus her death with our sex and our conversations and our holidays, and all I really wanted was a way to break that linkage, in almost the same way I wanted the trail of mushrooms to come to an end, because, honestly, where could they possibly lead that would be good for me? Ordinary thoughts, the thoughts we all have: that I was already late for work; that Jenna would miss me or she wouldn't; that this would be my fifth absence this semester and how many did there have to be before they let me go?

My legs didn't seem to have questions, though – they carried me forward. I followed the mushrooms because of the sparkle in Jenna's earrings, the gorgeous color of my wife's eyes. I followed the mushrooms because I can't say my wife's name. If I say her name, if I write her name, I will lose it – the name and my self-control. When I hear her name said, that is enough to conjure up the trail of evidence, the linkage. Unbearable.

The red of the sunset had become as green as...

A few people dressed in the outlandish garb I'd become accustomed to on campus pushed past me, and ahead, partially obscured by the lack of light, the spires of an old church or series of churches. Crenelations. A darkness that came from age, inhabiting the corners of the spires. A few circling birds or bats. It reminded me of the vacation my wife and I took to Eastern Europe one year, which made all that was ancient about my place of employment look petty and cheap and just-yesterday. She fell asleep in the train from Berlin to Prague. I saw her face, framed by the reflection of the landscape rushing past the window, without lines or care, saw how her arms lay at her sides. She felt secure. She felt safe, I could tell.

Spires, though. I couldn't remember spires anywhere off-campus. I couldn't remember churches. Had I somehow ended up back on campus? It's true I had certain routines, certain blind spots, that meant I hadn't explored the city as I might have, and my wife to distract me, and then my grief.

Two youths ran by holding flags with symbols on them that I'd never seen before. I saw a man wearing a goat costume. I saw a woman with no legs "walking" on stilts. Fraternities and fraternity jokes came to mind, although there was something too solemn and formal about them. I had lost the thread

of the mushrooms.

no longer followed them.

just walked forward.

randomly.

Bathed in the green light of my wife's death, I turned as if to head back, except where I had come from no longer existed. It was as disappeared as the swathes of darkness my wife and I left behind us in our little car, headed home from a colleague's party, on the two-lane road at three in the morning.

People crowded out onto the streets and I came under the weird light of gargoyled lampposts and buildings crowded and hunched in shadow to all sides, cut through by the narrowest of alleys. A festival of some kind, and I was in it or out of it or outside of it but caught up in it and the people kept pouring out of nowhere in their strange clothes and their strange accents and the strange look in their eyes and so I laughed with them and clapped my hands when they clapped their hands, and when the parade came by with animals foreign and fey, when the jugglers and the fire-eaters and the retired soldiers from distant wars, wearing uniforms I'd never seen before, when all of this converged, I tried not to think about it, tried not even to smell the stench of beer in the drains, the stench of vomit, of piss, tried to misread the mischief and malice in the eyes of those whose gaze I met. I realized this might be

a break in the linkage.

a severing of routine.

a way out.

Had I missed how random my world had become since my wife had died? Had my grief obliterated the real world for me?

•

And so all of these thoughts overwhelmed me when I woke from my hiding place in an alley the next morning, having slept on garbage and filth, to find *it* – wearing a large gray hat, small as a child but with the wizened features of something already dead – staring down at me. It had long claws that dragged down below the sleeves of its robes. I could not look it in the face. It swayed back and forth as if in trance, and it said to me, as I looked up at it with a disbelieving smile on my face, "Are you lost?"

And.

I thought about how I had gotten to this point.

I thought about Jenna and I thought about my wife and I realized I didn't love Jenna, that I didn't even really like Jenna, and with that thought came a kind of release and I was back on the two-lane road in the darkness and this time I welcomed it, brought it to me, soaked up those last few miles before she lost control of the car and swerved into the path of oncoming headlights connected to god-knows-what kind of vehicle, the same look of concentration on her face mixed with anger, because I was looking at her not at the road, arguing with her about some stupid point of routine that didn't make any sense to anyone but my father, and I wonder if she saw, in those last moments, some kind of entry to this place, and if she saw something that made her swerve, and it wasn't my fault at all, I wasn't the distraction that killed her.

"Are you lost?" it says to me and I'm more frightened than I've ever been before, even when my wife died in front of me, and I say, "No. I'm not lost. I belong here."

And I do.

The Situation

✳

How It Began: Degradation of Existing Processes

My Manager was extremely thin, made of plastic, with paper covering the plastic. They had always hoped, I thought, that one day her heart would start, but her heart remained a dry leaf that drifted in her ribcage, animated to lift and fall only by her breathing. Sometimes, when my Manager was angry, she would become so hot that the paper covering her would ignite, and the plastic beneath would begin to melt. I didn't know what to say in such situations. It seemed best to say nothing and avert my gaze. Over time, the runneled plastic of her arms became a tableau of insane images, leviathans and tall ships rising out of the whorling, and stranger things still. I would stare at her arms so I did not have to stare at her face. I never knew her name. We were never allowed to know our Manager's name. (Some called her their "Damager," though.)

The trouble at work began after I came back from a two-week vacation at my apartment in the city, for this is when my Manager changed our processes. For as long as I could remember, the requests for the beetles we made came to Leer, my supervisor. I had made beetles for almost nine years in this way, my office carpet littered with their iridescent carapaces, the table in the corner always alive with new designs and gestation. However, when Scarskirt was hired to replace Mord, who had moved to Human Resources, we no longer followed this process.

Worried, I pointed this out to Scarskirt during the brief interlude when I taught her how to make her own beetles. She just laughed and said, "Maybe a change is good. We all do such good work, it shouldn't matter, right?"

I should note that "Leer," "Scarskirt," and "Mord" are not their real names. And all three were flesh-and-blood like me when I first knew them. Leer looked a little like a crane, and I had counted her as a friend, just as Mord had been a friend before his move. Scarskirt, though, stared at reflective surfaces all day and flattered so many people that I was wary of her.

After I came back, I found that Leer and Scarskirt shared an office and did everything together. Now, when the requests came in, all three of us were notified and we might all three begin work on the same project.

I remember coming into one meeting with the Manager, holding the beetle I had just created in my office. It was emerald, long as a hand, but narrow, flexible. It had slender antennae that curled into azure blue sensors on the ends, its shining carapace subdivided in twelve exact places. The beetle would have fit perfectly in a school child's ear and clicked and hummed its knowledge into them.

But Scarskirt and Leer had created a similar beetle.

My Manager immediately thought it was my fault, and erupted into flame.

Leer stared at Scarskirt, who was staring at the metallic table top. "I thought we talked to you about this," Leer said to me, still looking at Scarskirt.

"No, you didn't," I said, but the moment belonged to them.

My Manager forced me to put my beetle in my own ear, a clear waste, and an act that gave me nightmares: of a burning city through which giant carnivorous lizards prowled, eating survivors off of balconies. In one particularly vivid moment, I stood on a ledge as the jaws closed in, heat-swept, and tinged with the smell of rotting flesh. Beetles intended for the tough, tight minds of children should not be used by adults. We still remember a kinder, gentler world.

After this initial communication problem, the situation worsened.

•

My Manager's Existing Issues

Twice a year, my Manager would summon me to her office on the fiftieth floor. A member of Human Resources would meet me at my office and attach a large slug to my spine through a specially-designed slit in the back of our office uniforms. This would allow me to walk to the elevators and then up and out to the Manager's office with no memory of the experience.

When it was time to return, the HR representative would reattach the slug. It always felt sticky and smooth at the same time. And wet, like an oyster.

What was Management trying to hide between floors three and fifty? I don't know, but as with the beetle intended for children, I would have nightmares after these meetings. In the nightmares, I was falling forever down a shaft lined with thousands of decomposing bodies. Plastic bodies. Human bodies. Bodies of leopards and of rats, of baboons and of lizards. I could smell the rot of them, sense their spongy softness. And yet my horror would be mixed with delight: so many animals in one place. A sparrow sometimes settled on the tiny patch of yellowing grass outside of my apartment, but I never saw more than that in real life.

●

Every meeting with my Manager was the same. In her office, the walls decorated with pleasant if banal scenes of woods and splashing brooks and green fields out of some fantasy land, she would be sitting behind her desk, smiling. Her hair would be fresh-cut, falling in straight blonde waves. The bland paper of her skin would be newly replaced by the kind of colored crepe paper common to the festivals of bygone eras. I would always catch the elusive scent of some decorative perfume. For some reason, this smell frightened me.

"Hello, Savante," she would say, although this was not my name.

"Hello, Manager," I would reply.

Up close, her eyes were like the glistening grit you find at the edges of drying asphalt. In the quiet, I could hear the leaf in her chest – just the slightest whispering shift of dead plant matter against plastic as it touched the sides of her ribcage. I wondered if each time another piece disintegrated into the dust at the bottom of her chest cavity.

"Do you love me?" she always asked.

I could remember a time and a world where such a question could never have been asked.

Did I love her?

Between meetings this became the question that filled my life. Ever since she had become my Manager, my raises had become smaller and smaller. The last raise had been a huge leech shaped like a helmet. It was meant to suck all the bad thoughts out of your head. It smelled like

69

bacon, which seemed promising. I had invited Mord and Leer over to my apartment and we'd fried it up in a skillet. I'd gotten a week's worth of sandwiches out of it.

And so as I sat in her office, I'd think: *Is it because of how I answer this one question?* And: *Does she think she is giving me good raises?* And, finally: *If I tell her I love her, will it go better or worse for me?*

"Do you love me?"

I always replied, "No, I do not love you."

Her response varied. Sometimes my reply pleased her. She would hum and sing and even burble in a contented way. Other times, my reply exhausted her. She would sit staring blankly into space until I left. A few times, flames would appear at her tiny wrists and she would reach out and try to burn the sides of my face. I could not predict her reaction, so at first I always raced to reattach the slug to my spine immediately after my answer, wanting the sure clean rush of extinguished memory. This seemed the best way to avoid punishment. But after a while, the process grew too familiar and I found I no longer really cared about her reaction.

I mention this because in the six months since Scarskirt had been hired, my Manager had accelerated the rate of these meetings. She called me into her office once each month.

"Do you love me?"

"No, I do not."

"Do you love me?"

"No. I do not."

"Do you love me?"

"No – I do not."

"Do you love me?"

"No. I. Do. Not."

"Do you love me?"

"No."

I always wondered what would happen if I replied, "Yes, I love you. With all my heart."

Could it be worse? Yes, obviously I thought it could be.

●

Memories of Mord

Although harrowing at the time, my two-week vacation in my apartment now seems like a calm respite from all my worries – this even though half a dozen times marauders tried to get through my defenses and the electricity flickered on and off, off and on.

I've thought of my vacation as the turning point, and perhaps it was, for during the time I was gone Scarskirt and Leer bonded ever more closely. But the more I review the events of the last few months in my head, the more I think the beginning of the end came well before that – when Mord departed from our team.

Heavy and strong, Mord had a light wit and an engaging manner before he moved to Human Resources. Outside of the company, he often appeared nervous, but while within its walls his assertiveness bound us together.

I remember that the week before he left us, Mord and I stood in an old stairwell of the company building, one with skylights built into the wall, although they were grimed over with filth and pollution. Outside, in the city, it was almost impossible to find a bird, but the building was so large and had such resources that a bird might survive for years. If it found the right floor.

Mord liked real animals, hinted that he had had contact with them in his former job. One year he even had a bird count of seventy-five sparrows, more than anyone in the company. He told me he loved the "simple functionality" of sparrows, their durability, their instinct to survive. Me, I just liked hanging out with Mord while the bird watched. Or inviting him and Leer to my apartment to stare at the yellowing grass of my front lawn in hopes a bird would appear there.

So it came as a shock to me that day when he said, "I'm moving to Human Resources," as the landing beneath us undulated like a tongue.

"What?" I said. "You can't do that."

"Don't worry. It won't matter." He stared through his roving binoculars up the twisting stairwell for a hint of flutter, of flight. "Everything will be the same."

"Will it?" I asked him in a moment of candor. "Will we still be friends?"

Mord smiled, the binoculars still clamped over his eyes in a possessive grip. "Of course. We'll be friends like we're friends now."

"And Leer, too?"

Mord laughed. "Don't worry. That will never change."

In a weird way, I think Mord meant it. And this at least is true: in my mind it never changed, and that was part of the problem.

We never found a sparrow, or any other bird, that day, so when we got back to the office Mord and Leer made a bird. It was a strange elongated bird with a tail that looked like a wisp of smoke.

They set it free in the stairwells and for months we would catch teasing glimpses of it. For some reason, it made me happy every time I saw it. But, eventually, I found it on a step. Someone had crushed its skull.

•

Confusion Due to Continued Degradation of Processes

Before the hiring of Scarskirt, when Leer was still my friend, we used to, as I mentioned, assign projects through a hierarchy. When this practice ended, we found ourselves locked in endless meetings in the cavernous meeting rooms on the forty-fifth floor. The rooms were more like the mess halls for refugees that I remembered from my teens. The windows provided an excellent view of the dying city, for those who wanted a reminder, but this was offset by the fact that we had to wear the slugs on our spines almost continually, and a herd of Human Resources people had to be ready to escort us at a moment's notice.

Mord walked among them, but only to supervise, and at first he was quite friendly.

•

The reason for the meetings was a new "fish" project. Our main client had asked for more products aimed at helping students. The latest project required the design of a grouper-like fish five times larger than the average nine-year-old child. By our various and immersive processes, we were to make being swallowed by this fish an educational experience. The student would be swallowed and subjected to sensory deprivation deep in the fish's guts. Then the student would be introduced to a number of neural stimuli, some to do with proper social adjustment, but most further enhancing their math/science skills.

We worked from the flesh-and-blood scale model I had made in my office, which was linked to a chart on the meeting room wall that showed the fish-as-blueprint, almost like the schematic of a ship's hull.

The team had to solve numerous technical issues. For example, would the fish be terrestrial or aquatic? We could create it to move on land using hyper-muscular fins while it sucked air like a mudpuppy. If we went with this approach, the fish could be summoned to the classroom so the student could be engulfed during class sessions. Otherwise, each school would need a communal tank into which the student would dive. I liked this solution because the children could change into swimming gear and thus not ruin their school clothes. It also provided more privacy.

In addition to the need for including defensive bioweaponry, we had to consider many other important issues. What shape and size should the fish's jaws be to cushion the child and minimize trauma? Should the fish talk in a reassuring manner to calm the child's fears of being eaten alive? Should it remain silent and allow the burden of providing reassurance to fall on the teacher?

•

The meetings to answer these questions while developing the basic concept now involved the entire creative team. Everyone was ordered to contribute, and to this end the Manager issued us all brainstorming cockroaches. These were the tiny burrowing variety, suitable for inhaling through the nose, with only a whiff of sulfurous decay. A slight, scrabbling discomfort and then they released their calming pheromones and you could see more clearly than ever before and ideas came out of your mouth almost faster than you could speak them.

This method worked fine in moderation, but not when *everyone* was issued the brainstorming cockroaches. The meetings became a babble of tongues, hours and days filled with circular thinking and unproductive repetition.

"I-think-we-should-have-it-walk-on-its-fins-and-talk-with-a-gravelly-old-grandfather-voice-like-my-grandfather-had-when-we-visited-him-in-the-home," Leer would say and I would say, "My-father-was-a-terse-man-but-a-depth-

of-feeling-often-welled-up-in-him-beneath-that-made-me-think-of-him-
as-generous-and-so-this-fish-should-be-all-efficiency-of-motion-but-deep-
deep-deep" and Scarskirt would say "I-think-it-should-have-my-face-and-
my-voice-whether-it-walks-on-land-or-just-swims-because-people-will-like-
that-and-it-will-reassure-them."

This high-volume stream of babble continued without end and without
resolution while we remained euphoric within the cramped quarters of our
own skulls.

•

A Relevant Note on Office Culture

I didn't know Scarskirt's background; nor did I know Mord's or Leer's background. We had all come to the company fleeing something in the city.
People had to be hard to survive, and of necessity you looked past this to
what the person was *in the current moment*. When I found my apartment, I
brought with me only what I could carry from the disaster that lay behind
me, and I furnished my apartment only with what I discovered already in
it and immediately outside the front door. I started with the clothes on my
back, an old dead stuffed dog from my childhood, some books my father
had given me, half-rations in packets, three memory eels, and a few worthless coins that kept changing colors as their batteries ran down. I had to do
many things I was not proud of to hang on to even those few possessions
before the company accepted me under its protective aegis.

My point is, records these days are terse, vague, or imaginary. Scarskirt
could have been anyone – and was. For the one truth of working for the
company had become this: whatever you had been before, you could be
someone else now.

My mistake, if I can call it that, was trust – to think a smile was a smile
and not a show of teeth. I thought that the point of being part of a team was
to be trusting and trustworthy.

I was wrong.

•

Conflict Due to Continued Degradation of Processes

As the months progressed, it became clear that no one had the ability to make a decision on the fish project. My Manager did not attend enough meetings to be useful. We had meeting minutes, of course. They were taken by a veined slab of purpling meat whimsically shaped like an ear. This minutes-taker lay in a far corner of the room, on a raised dais, and printed out its observations on the usual paper that reflected mood, tone, and intent. Alas, in this particular case, the minutes came out thick, viscous, and smelling sickly sweet. Very little could be intuited from them.

The design of the fish on the meeting wall, indigenously linked to the results of the meeting minutes, changed for the worse. Sometimes we would enter to find that it was missing a fin. Sometimes it had transmogrified to have the attributes of a bear, a dragon, or a whale. Once, it had become a girl in a sunflower dress huddled in a dark corner of the room. She had the eyes of a fish, but she was not a fish, and something in her posture reminded me of familiar paper and plastic.

The day we entered the meeting room and the fish had the head of my Manager, I knew I had to change the paradigm.

I drove a knife into the quivering slab of recording material, which relaxed into senility with a sigh, and thus froze the fish design in place on the wall. It might have had the Manager's face, but the rest of it was much closer to completion than we'd been in months.

"From now on, I will lead these meetings," I said to Leer, Scarskirt, and the others. "Some of us will use the brainstorming cockroaches and some will not. We will design the fish, by hand, on the meeting table, using plastics and self-regenerating bits of fish flesh. There will be no more endless meetings or Manager-headed end results."

"Is that wise?" Leer and Scarskirt both asked, words intertwined. Scarskirt said it with a hint of disdain in her voice. Leer said it in a clipped tone. She had a worried look on her face. Scarskirt seemed more amused than concerned. She picked dirt and beetle feelers out from beneath her painted fingernails with a knife that seemed too robust for the delicacy of the task.

"Is that wise?" Leer said again while Scarskirt fell silent. "I mean, ultimately it is the Manager's project."

Leer was always changing her body, but could never set her mind on what

75

she should change it to, as if restless. I could almost imagine her tossing and turning in bed, transforming with each abrupt movement. When she asked the question, Leer had the dynamic skin coloration of a parrotfish and the mouth of one as well.

"It may not be wise," I said, "but I don't think any of us can survive months of meetings like this. My back is sore from the slugs and I'm weary of the journey."

"You may or may not be right," Leer said, "but regardless the Manager will not approve."

"That is my responsibility," I said, confident in my many years of experience.

Scarskirt offered no further comment either way, but just sat there staring at me as she picked at her nails. The blade, I noticed, was double-edged and had a point. No matter how it touched you, it would cut you.

●

For a while, everything went well. We built the fish by hand and it took shape with a coherent design. I noticed a certain reluctance on the part of Scarskirt and Leer, but in general everyone seemed happy with my efforts.

Then my Manager finally decided to attend a meeting. Ten minutes into the meeting, she burst into flames and stood up.

We all shied away from her as she said, "The fish was to have my face. That is the last design to materialize in my office and none of what you have done since has been sent to me for my approval, or is acceptable to me in any way."

This business about approval was blatantly untrue. I had sent her several messages about the changes. I had used her favorite message method: tiny crunchy bats that spurted the long-lost flavors of marzipan, chocolate mousse, and apple pie into your mouth even as you cracked down on the bones to receive the information.

But when my Manager visited my office later, she professed ignorance. She said she had not gotten any of my messages.

Later, I would discover that Mord, gone half-feral, had intercepted the bats as they flew through some long-darkened hall and eaten them all, licking his muzzle with great pleasure afterwards, no doubt. I do not know if he shared them with Scarskirt or not. I do not know how far their relationship had progressed by that point.

"Unacceptable," my Manager said. "I am the lead on this project, and the fish shall have my face."

All of the paper had already burned off of her, and by the light of the thousand phosphorescent fireflies I had created and painstakingly inserted into the walls of my office over the years, her plastic seemed impossibly bright and lacquered, more like armor than it ever had before.

After this encounter, I took to calling the project the Fish-Rots-From-The-Head Project.

•

Increasing Social Isolation

Even before the problems with my Manager, I had indeed grown apart from Leer and Mord, to say nothing of Scarskirt. Several new employees had been hired, some flesh-and-blood, some not. Human Resources made Leer's office larger by demolishing the adjoining offices, some with people still inside them. The new employees took up positions all around Leer and Scarskirt like some kind of defensive perimeter. Scarskirt ran linking worms between all of them, and thus became intimate friends with them overnight. These worms hooked into their ankles and allowed them to communicate soundlessly amongst themselves. No one had thought to invite me, so at night I sent non-combat interceptor beetles to try to tap into the worm links, but they were too tough and all of my beetles came back with broken mandibles.

From that moment forward, I was shut out.

Complicating matters, Mord, I soon discovered, had also become part of their network. Despite all of his promises, Mord had changed once he moved to Human Resources. He was now partially composed of some large furred animal, almost like a bear. He began to emit a musk that someone told me was supposed to have a calming effect on employees. He retained his hands, but they morphed to become more like those of a raccoon. His eyes had been enlarged and refitted so he could see at night. In the dark hallways of some floors it was rumored that he whirled around and snarled and bit the air, as if a clumsy ballet dancer trapped in a straitjacket.

For a month or so, Mord had taken to following me around, and this gave me hope that all would be normal. He wouldn't talk to me, but he would stand in the doorway of my office. Waiting.

Soon, though, I discovered it wasn't really Mord. It was just a shadow Mord had made of himself, and at my Manager's direction each employee had been assigned shadows. After a time, I ignored Mord's shadow and it went away.

As for the real Mord, he rarely came to our floor anymore, and if he did it was to visit Leer's office. I only saw him if he had official business.

When I suggested he come over to my apartment sometime, he ignored me. When I suggested we go looking for sparrows, he ignored me.

For all intents and purposes, Mord had forsaken me. He had become Other.

•

You must understand how much anguish all of this made me feel. All any of us had were the relationships at the company. All the information we had came from each other. What waited for us each night in the city did not bear describing.

These employees had been to my apartment. I had shared my raise with them. I had been over to Leer's house and Mord's house during the holidays, despite the danger in the streets. We had gone hiking in neighboring buildings as an excuse for long lunches. Mord had shared the sad situation of a wife half-plastic, half-flesh. Leer had told of her unhappiness at home, with a husband who preferred shoving memory eels into his rectum to spending time with her. I had shared my loneliness, of how difficult it was to find love if one had not brought it with them while fleeing the disintegration of the world. I had shown them my few remaining photographs of my parents on vacation in some exotic place by the sea, marble columns behind them. Their faded crumbling smiles from which I had to interpret so much. We had talked about how we missed the rigidity of the old times, how much the fluid quality of what happened now, at home and at the office, frightened us no matter how we tried to deny it. How no one born now would understand how different it had been, once.

For this reason, because we had been so close for so long, I blame Scarskirt for my growing isolation. She was gorgeous and lively and everyone loved her, but I now believe she hid a secret wound from us, that she was scarred from before we knew her. That she never cared about anyone, and that she coveted my job from the moment she was hired, despite my friendliness. Despite my openness. Despite the fact I had shared all of my training beetles with her. I did not alter a single one before giving them to her. Three or four new employees died each year from beetles poisoned by their trainers. But I had accepted her into the group, without malice in my heart.

Nonetheless, my trust now meant my isolation. The only solace came from my office, where I still controlled my beetles and the talking crocodile head that I made tell me jokes when I was feeling depressed.

I could still communicate with others in a limited way using the small pool of water on my desk. At the bottom of the pool lay a flounder, modified so that messages played out across the preternatural white of its back, the sweet brine smell a comfort. I would work in my office for hours without any outside contact, content to talk to my diminishing circle of friends spread out across the company. It was, in a sense, like being in my apartment, only safer.

Thus hemmed in, I worked on my small part of the fish project. My Manager had ordered that I could continue fleshing out the dorsal fin, and I had resolved that by meticulous, patient work I would make the dorsal fin so fine a product that no one seeing it as it walked down a school's hallway would remember anything but the perfect geometry of my contribution.

•

A New Manager in an Old Paradigm

Every once in a while I would hear an odd belch or rumble, far distant, coming from above, and remember the behemoth grub that reclined above us, and in the remembering realize again that my Manager did not rule the company. Above her office on the fiftieth floor rose another ten floors. The last five floors consisted of a vast and rippling beetle-grub continually devouring its own self-regenerating flesh. Within this grub resided the company's owners, who had been attached to the succulent meat and milk of the grub. It was the company's finest creation. Nothing could get at them inside the grub. It was not connected by worms. No leeches or slugs were allowed inside.

Once, the remnants of a government had attacked the grub, but their weapons bounced off of the grub's glossy, impenetrable skin. The infiltrations of flesh-and-bloods they sailed down upon the grub were legion, but they slid away or were repelled by the poison coating the grub's skin. Large parasites that kept the grub's skin clean ate the rest of them.

Now, in the owners' infinite, grub-defended wisdom, they decided to send a second Manager down to our floor. His name was a secret, of course, but Leer nicknamed him "Slumber," because he was large and lumbrous like the Mord, only not as unpredictable.

This development did not please my Manager. Slumber began to attend more and more of our meetings, while my Manager was given other tasks. She was still our personnel manager, but rumor claimed we would eventually move to Slumber's team.

All through this period, my Manager continued to call me into her office and ask me if I loved her. I kept telling her no. She looked agitated, unwell – even more so when Slumber finally decided to put an end to the fish project. The fish with my Manager's face was discarded, the prototype set loose to live or die roaming distant halls. I had an image of it in my mind's eye, scavenging scraps and croaking to itself, devoid of any educational purpose other than survival, held together by its magnificent dorsal fin.

I felt sorry for it. I could sympathize, for soon Slumber hooked up to the worm tendrils of Leer's network and began to ignore me and my suggestions. Two more employees had been moved into what was now effectively Scarskirt's office. I was the only member of the creative team not in that office. Scarskirt frequently visited Slumber on the fiftieth floor and would come back with her slug pulsing and a sickly smile on her vacant face.

For this reason, the next time Slumber came down to our floor, I intercepted him and asked him to visit me in my office. After an hour of speaking to Leer, Scarskirt, and the rest, he finally stood, reluctant, in my doorway. He was as wide as two normal people and had but a single hair that he grew in a circular fashion across the middle of his head and chin, and down his chest. He smelled like melted beans and cheese.

"What do you need?" he asked. "I have meetings to go to."

"I am having trouble with communication," I told him. "The others are discussing projects and brainstorming and going to lunch without me. I need to be attached at the ankle like the rest of them. How can I be proactive if I am ignored?"

Slumber frowned. "You're not being ignored. Nothing of importance is being discussed. You still go to the status meetings, and we discuss everything there."

Yes, the status meetings. During these meetings I now learned what Leer and Scarskirt and the others had decided during the prior week. I learned what lack of role I was to have during the next week. I would stare at Leer, willing her to return my gaze, to understand from the pained look on my face just how much this was hurting me. But she never did. Scarskirt would stare, though. A kind of measuring look. An appraisal. I did not like the hardness of that glance, given while she told a joke. A stolen glimpse to test my resolve.

I tried to argue with Slumber, but he cut me off. "We can always give you another leech if you like, to cure your discomfort," he said. "But don't worry, we all value you."

He left, and five minutes later was laughing and joking with Leer and Scarskirt.

•

Now I had to send out my beetles as spies, just so I would know the basics of what was happening, just so I could do my job. But beetles are not meant as spies; they are made to disseminate information, not capture it. Despite all my efforts to change them, most did a poor job. Several never came back and I had to destroy others that had been tampered with by Scarskirt so they would not infect the rest.

I could not complain to the Mord by then. I had discovered he was not my friend. While seeking solace in isolation, I came upon the Mord and Scarskirt in a forgotten part of the third floor, among the musty ruins of some sort of outdated cathedral. They stood upon a crumbling platform decorated with gold leaf, leaning toward each other, connected at the forehead by the disembodied siphon of a long-necked clam. I watched them for half an hour, noting the bliss on their faces. I could see that they were far, far away. The Mord was now much more animal than flesh-and-blood. I could smell his musk even from my hiding place.

I had begun to call him "the Mord," as had many others.

•

Unacceptable Disregard for Good Practice

One day, a design was presented at a status meeting and it had the face of my remote friends, "Winterlong," looking slack and haggard. The cat-thing with pigeon legs meowed and Winterlong's face contorted into a meow.

I was shocked. I had just talked to him that morning.

After the meeting, I took Leer aside. Leer was wearing a ridiculous pink jacket made of living shark scales that Scarskirt had given her. She had been parading around in it all week, delighted with her office mate's castoffs.

"That was Winterlong," I said. "Butchered."

Scarskirt came up behind us without warning. She spoke before Leer could reply.

"Don't be ridiculous or paranoid," Scarskirt said. She laughed, but it was not her pretty laugh. It was more like a horsehead laugh. Her eyes were wide and bright and the blade of her smile cut me.

"You're imagining things," Leer said, staring at Scarskirt. "That wasn't Winterlong. Not really." But her eyes were moist and her voice was thin and sad.

Winterlong's personal effects showed up on Scarskirt's desk soon after.

"He had no relatives," Scarskirt explained at the next status meeting, batting her eyes at Slumber, who made a sound like the world's laziest orgasm.

•

The First of My Proactive Efforts

Once, when things were still good, Leer and I had shared beetles. We had even created a few just for fun. At lunch, we would sneak out behind the company building with a blanket and sit on the little hill there, looking out onto a ravaged landfill heavy with the skeletons of vultures and then, beyond that, the city in all its strange mix of menace and vulnerability. The grass was yellowing rather than dead. A wiry tree stood on the hill at that time. We would eat crackers and old cans of shredded meat, the smell in that context almost unbearably tantalizing.

After lunch, we would unlock the cases containing our beetles. The shining green-and-crimson carapaces would open like the lids of eccentric jewelry boxes to reveal their golden wings, and we would release them into the world.

Those beetles contained every joyous thing we had ever known, and we loved to watch them fly out into the distance.

"My father's dry laugh!" I would shout.

"My mother's mock frown!" Leer would reply.

"The color of the faded cover of my nursery rhyme book!"

"The taste of real potato soup!"

"The feel of thousand-thread-count clean sheets!"

"The ache of muscles after playing stick ball!"

Our voices would get softer and softer until I was whispering things like "The smell of my father's aftershave when he reached down to hug me."

Then we would stand there, trailing off into silence, and get so much satisfaction out of wondering who would find them and what impact they would have on their discoverers. Sometimes we would even have tears in our eyes.

I can remember Leer saying once, "This hill makes me happy."

•

So it was that when I decided to become proactive in the midst of my worsening situation, I persuaded Leer to join me on the hill, "for old time's sake."

The grass was mostly gone by then and the tree, too. Earthworms writhed and died in the naked dirt. The day was cold and gray, and the city did not bear looking at. The muffled sound of explosions, the smells of smoke and intense rot, told the story well enough. We stood there and turned our backs on the city, looking up at the company building and searching for glimpses of the behemoth grub, lost in the low-lying clouds.

"What has happened, Leer?" I asked her. "I haven't changed. I'm still the same as I ever was."

Leer refused to look at me. She stood with arms folded and stared into the blank windows in front of her. On this day, she had revisited her true form. There was no artifice to her.

"You're imagining things," Leer said.

"Like I imagined Winterlong's face," I said.

"Yes," she said, but so quietly I almost couldn't hear her.

"Leer, I know things have changed. It's not my imagination. We all used to be so close."

"Do you know," Leer said, "how much I hate this place? I hate my job. I hate being here. And I hate the world out there."

I shuddered at that. To think of the past, the distant past, before all of this – she was right. Who could bear it? Sometimes I wondered if we had been sending out those beetles not to help others but to help get rid of the horrible weight of happy memories.

"I know you hate it," I said. "I've known that for a while. I'm not stupid. But what does that have to do with me?"

Leer said, "Why do you fight it? Why do you care about any of it?"

"In the old days, we were all friends," I said.

"It can't be that way anymore. It's just work."

"But why?"

Leer just shrugged.

I think I started to cry then.

Leer took pity on me and said, "It'll be better. It'll be better, I'm sure of it. When we're under Slumber. Then it will all be fine."

By then, we had both noticed the Mord coming up the hill. He was larger than I remembered and his thick fur had a golden brown luster to it. His eyes and fangs stood out more.

The Mord wasn't walking up the hill. The Mord was levitating up the hill, effortless.

I expelled my breath all in a rush.

Leer blanched and a look of terror came over her face.

"I couldn't bear to be disconnected from the worms," she whispered to me. "And Mord can read lips."

The Mord settled down in front of us. Even sitting on the incline, he was taller than us, and his shadow unfurled itself across us and across the entire top of the hill. I had the curious sensation of seeing his human face superimposed over his animal features, for just a second.

Then I caught a hint of movement behind him, at the bottom of the hill. Scarskirt stood there, her arms folded, her legs apart, sentinel-silent.

Leer looked me in the eyes and said, "We don't want you here. We aren't the same. You've changed. You don't do good work anymore."

The Mord let out a roar that pushed its blood-shot, crazed eyes half out of their sockets and pressed my hair flat against the sides of my head. In the Mord's breath I could smell a thousand different kinds of rot. I could smell the stench of the entire company.

•

Ad Hoc Meetings, Further Abnegating Process

Soon after the encounter with the Mord, my Manager began to visit me for reasons other than to ask her perpetual question. She would burst in near the end of the day and begin to rant, spittle flying from her mouth. Sometimes the language would be foreign to me. Sometimes I could understand the words but the context was incomprehensible. Other times, there would be no words, just shouts and shrieks and grunts.

My Manager's body would contort during these meetings, like a wet rag being wrung dry. She had become impossibly thin so that her eyes were cavernous in her face. The smell of wet burning plastic clung to her. Her hair had fallen out and she always wore a different wig, some of them living and some of them dead.

"I don't know how to help you," I would tell her, genuinely concerned about her. In the context of my current situation, I thought she was, if not a friend, then at least not an enemy.

Those of my spy beetles that had survived the change of purpose had recorded a variety of images in the myriad halls and passageways of the third floor. One of the most arresting involved my Manager. I had seen her, pensive and quietly weeping, walking across a cracked marble floor, only to stop and give out a cry of surprise. For hunching toward her with wet abandon was the fish with her face, and in that moment as the beast drew near, I saw an image that haunted me: of my Manager's shock registering simultaneously on two identical faces. I am sure this is the first time she knew of the discontinuation of the fish project.

As for the ad hoc meetings, she would invariably storm out of my office and my unease would become chronic, for I knew that I had been unable to give her any kind of solace.

Perhaps the only solace would have been for Slumber to be sucked back up into the distance of the perpetual clouds ringing the behemoth company grub, never to return.

•

Taking Further Steps

My beetles continued to bring me information in a halting fashion, but most of it just depressed me more. One report I watched while home at my apartment showed Scarskirt hunting down the fish project and stabbing it to death. Her knife sliced down, up, down, up, down as the fish tried to get away from her ever more slowly, spurting a thick green blood. The look on Scarskirt's face was as beatific and composed as during one of our status meetings. When the fish lay still, great ridges of exposed flesh quivering, Scarskirt reached forward and hacked off the copy of the Manager's face. Then she hunched down and showed it to my beetle, so I would get a good look at it, dripping, pale, and rubbery. She was smiling, of course.

After seeing this, my stress level went up exponentially. I grew so afraid I took to carrying weapons. I jury-rigged giant rhinoceros beetles into simple projectile weapons that fired either the remnants of less-fortunate beetles or old-fashioned shrapnel I'd found in the cathedral ruins. I made dung beetles into moldy grenades, using a liquid wrung out of my message bats as the fuel. I put up zones of foul-smelling molds outside my office, to discourage flesh-and-blood visitors. I devised subtle camouflage for myself, coating myself in the same fireflies that lined my walls, so that it was not always clear if I was in the office or not.

"Remember when" became how I started every conversation with my fellow employees during status meetings, although they did not like it. Scarskirt became openly contemptuous and Leer followed her lead. Scarskirt goaded Leer to send beetles to lazily, almost toyingly, attack my office defenses so that I would be forced to expend resources repelling them.

"Everything will be fine," Scarskirt would reassure me in the breakroom in the morning as I kept my distance.

In the afternoon, she would walk by me in the hall as I flinched away, and say loudly, "Why are your messages so abusive?" even though I had not communicated with her.

Leer by contrast would be professional when I bumped into her on my way to the bathroom, but with the kind of professionalism that one despises in a supposed friend. She was changing her appearance three or four times a morning by then. Sometimes she would give me a sickly half-smile, as if she had been caught in a monstrous lie.

•

One day I could have sworn I heard a sighing sound coming from the darkness that was the high ceiling of my office. The ceiling almost seemed alive. I told myself I was paranoid, but that afternoon I felt a vast wind and a huge black manta ray detached itself and flew out of my door and into the shadows. Such a creature was beyond Scarskirt's skill level, or even Leer's. It had to be reporting back to the Mord.

I now saw the Mord's almost unrecognizable features on the flounder's back at least twice a day. Those huge eyes stared out at me with some unrecognizable passion emblazoned on them. Sometimes the Mord would speak and say in a gravelly voice, "You never loved your manager" or "You should leave Scarskirt alone." Other times I intuited a pleading, pained look on his face as he murmured things like "Help me. Help me, Savante."

But I no longer trusted him.

How could I?

•

Additional Alterations Used to Isolate Me

At Slumber's urging, perhaps aided by a suggestion from Scarskirt, everyone on the creative team except me had themselves altered so that they shared certain uniform attributes. These attributes included green exoskeletons through which the familiar faces peered as if through a graveyard of excavated crustaceans. A lingering scent of brine became common to their type. The network of worms became mobile so that they remained connected wherever they went. Slumber took them personally to the company's recreational rooms, eschewing Human Resources and slugs alike to show his trust in them. They even began to talk the same. They all began to talk like Scarskirt.

I did not know how I felt about being left out of this phase of entitlements. I did not know how my Manager felt about being left out, either.

In my nightmares I was floating in a sea of cracked-open crab and lobster parts, miles from shore, under a fiery red moon. Beside me the corpse of the fish project floated, its face bobbing beside it, still screaming in death.

•

My Personnel File: More Attempts at Being Proactive

Despite all of the pressures I have detailed, I did complete several legitimate beetle projects, garnering a grudging praise from Slumber, who otherwise I saw not at all. In this way – through the quality of my work – I hoped to preserve my job.

I also decided to visit my personnel file in the basement. This was one of the perks of working for the company, especially as I did not require the Mord or another member of Human Resources to accompany me. I hoped my file might divulge some clue, some nuance, that would give me a way out of my increasingly perilous situation.

The elevator down was sleek and fast and had not been used for any company experiments, which was a relief. When I got to the records department, an attendant wearing a surgical mask led me to the right room. My large box was stacked amongst thousands of other such boxes, all studded with tiny breathing holes. Yelping and snorting noises came from some of the boxes, bird trills from others.

Although the attendant was at least six feet tall and made of muscle and steel, he grunted with the effort of pulling the box down and putting it on the table in front of me.

It had been eight months since I had visited my personnel file. At that time, I had taken it for a walk on the little hill and fed it some carefully hoarded treats. I had opened up to it and told it things about my father, my mother, and my arduous trek to the city that I had never told anyone. I remembered that moment as a lightening of a burden, a cathartic experience.

I opened up the box.

Inside lay the unrecognizable corpse of my personnel file. Anyone unfamiliar with it would have seen only some kind of large mammal. Rotting.

White maggots curling through the masses of intestines, organs, sinew, and soft tissue with the mindless motions of a baby's fingers. My flesh went cold and I think I stopped breathing for a time.

There were many, many knife wounds. I had seen those kinds of marks before.

Even beyond the fear, a feeling of intense sadness came over me. The killing seemed so vindictive, and so unnecessary.

"Do you still want to take it out – or, perhaps, look through it?" the attendant asked, offering me a pair of gloves.

"No," I said. "There's no need."

Everything was very clear.

●

The Beginning of the End

Trapped. I could not go to the Mord, Leer, Slumber, or my Manager. Should I throw myself on the mercy of Scarskirt, I felt certain I would end up like Winterlong. I dreamed of quitting, but could not see a future beyond the company. For a while, I tried desperately to act normal, but it was difficult under the circumstances.

After my visit to my personnel file, the black manta ray covered my ceiling all the time. All I could see on the flounder's back was the Mord's thick block of a face, its huge eyes staring at me, inscrutable. The image never spoke to me, but I studied that face for long minutes, trying to decipher some further message there. All I could really see is how the eyes still retained some essence of the old Mord – how, if I looked long enough, I could believe I was still looking at a picture of my old friend in a bear suit. The Mord who was always quick with a joke and liked nothing better than to spend lunch in a stairwell with a thermos of coffee and a pair of binoculars.

I kept making beetles at a ferocious rate, both to protect myself and prove I was still working at the company.

I no longer had messages from other employees.

I no longer could get Leer or Scarskirt or even Slumber to acknowledge my presence.

I began to live in memory. I would see my father's long, white fingers as

JEFF VANDERMEER

he sat at the piano in the old house that I remembered only from the few surviving photographs. Or I would see my mother playing chess with him, hunched over the board with intense concentration. Or conversations with Leer from years back that had made me laugh. Or the look on Mord's face when he saw a glimpse of a sparrow, which widened his features and made him seem almost childlike.

If I just concentrated hard enough on these images, I believe I thought I could survive all of it.

●

Another Meeting with My Manager

One night, after the manta ray had flown off, my Manager entered my office and sat down. She looked so tired and so thin that for the first time I thought she might be dying. Her eyes were so far back in their sockets that I almost couldn't see them except for the slight reflection, the glint from the whites. She smelled like limes, so I knew she had just visited with the rest of the team.

"I am giving you a raise," my Manager said, but she didn't seem happy about it.

She took an object from her pocket and placed it on my desk. It was an amorphous ball of clear flesh with a small brown frog inside of it.

"This will make everything like it was before. Slumber and I made it together. For you. Just eat it tomorrow morning and you will feel much better."

"Thank you," I said.

My Manager leaned forward, although it was more like a swaying motion from fatigue, and with her elbows on my desk, she whispered, "Do you love me?"

It was the first time, in that moment, looking at my Manager so frail and on the edge of some unknowable catastrophe, that I realized she had once been flesh-and-blood. That she might have had a history from before the company. That she might be as much a victim of circumstances as me.

Because she said it there, in my office, at that moment, and because I was tired and alone and no longer cared, I said, "It's possible," instead of "No."

My Manager's smile destroyed the worry lines radiating from the corners of her eyes. The smile was so unexpected that I smiled back.

Then she stumbled to her feet and was gone, leaving my raise on my desk.

•

The Nature of My Raise

The next morning, I came to work in a good mood. I had had uninterrupted sleep for the first time in months. I did not notice anything amiss, although Leer and Scarskirt had changed the color of their exoskeletons to black. For Scarskirt this meant that her pale perfect face shone like death from her mask, her red lips a feast of blood. For Leer, it made it seem as if only the exoskeleton held her up. Neither of them would look at me, but I took this in stride since things had been bad for some time. I knew it would take many months to restore normalcy.

I ate my raise right away – it tasted like moist chocolate cake – and started working on my beetles with newfound vigor.

Not twenty minutes later, a member of Human Resources cradling a slug in her arms summoned me to my Manager's office. By then, my stomach was feeling queasy.

As we neared the elevators, my last thought before the slug kicked in was: *Why are all of the offices empty?*

•

I woke in a chair in the Human Resources office on the seventh floor. The HR representative who had brought me stood to my left, holding the slug. My Manager sat behind Mord's desk. To her left stood Slumber, looking solemn. To her right stood the Mord, large and terrible, holding the rotting remains of my personnel file, from which he scooped entrails into his mouth with a kind of absent-minded hunger.

My heart began to beat so fast I could feel it thudding. My throat closed a little. My arms became shaky and my legs didn't seem to work. I'm sure they could hear my breathing, shallow and quick.

Looking very solemn, my Manager leaned forward and said, "We have decided to terminate your employment with this company due to a pattern of unprofessional communication. Do you have anything to say in your defense?"

Shocked, anguished, I opened my mouth to speak, and realized I had been poisoned by my raise. For nothing eloquent or even faintly coherent came from between my lips. Instead, frog eggs poured out, falling heavy to the floor, and coating my chin and shirt in green slime. Nothing could be further from the definition of professional.

My Manager gave me a look of sorrow while the Mord growled in his corner and a thin smile animated Slumber's solemn face. I believe that somewhere in the building Scarskirt smiled at that exact moment as well.

But as they led me away, attaching the slug as I struggled, I regained my voice long enough to shout at my Manager as the doors began to close on me, "I love you. I've always loved you."

A sharp intake of breath. The sound of the paper encasing her bursting into flame once more.

•

The Results

Images of Leer, of Mord, of Scarskirt filled my head as Human Resources threw me out of the front door, the place on my spine where they had just ripped off the slug still stinging. It was a bitterly cold day and no one was walking on the plaza in front of the building. I'm sure people had been told to avoid it until I was gone.

The doors shut on the pragmatic faces of my tormentors. I staggered backwards, looking up at the place that had been my home for so many years – that had, in this incomprehensible world of ours, been all that was left to me of family. Now, I realized, I would have to find my way alone.

But there was one last surprise.

As I stared up at the window of Mord's office, so far away, it opened and there my Manager stood: on fire from head to toe, and no extinguishing it this time. She looked down at me, and although I could not read the expression on her face I would like to think she was happy, for a moment.

Then the Mord rose behind her, roaring as he rose and rose and rose, as if he might never stop growing, to fill the entire window. A slap of a paw and my Manager jerked back out of sight.

The fire spread from window to window, room to room, while the Mord raged, thrashing and fighting. Once, he stopped to stare down at me, paws against the glass. Once, he looked out into the gray sky as if searching for something.

A shadow, tiny and on fire, began to drift down from the burning windows.

Was it a leaf? Who could tell? By the time it reached the ground, it would have fallen away into nothing.

This, then, was the situation at the time I left the company.

PREDECESSOR

❋

The great man's home lay within thick woods, beyond a churning river crossed only by a bridge that looked like it had been falling apart for many years. The woods were dark and loamy and took the sound of our transport like a wolf taking a rabbit. The leaves passed above us in patterns of deep green shot through with glints of old light. There was the smell of something rich yet suspect in the chilled air.

The house rose out of the forest like a cathedral out of a city: unmistakable. It had an antique feel. Two levels, although the second story was gutted and unusable to us, the off-white color stained with the amber-and-green dustings of pollen and pine needles. A steeple of a roof that contained nothing but rotted timbers, descending to a screened-in porch, beyond which lay the horseshoe construction of the interior passageways. The house might have been a hundred years old. It might have been two hundred years old. It might have always been there.

Our tread on the gravel driveway startled me; it was the first true sound I'd heard for many miles.

The screen door was broken – someone had slashed through it, and the two pieces had curled back. We walked onto the porch and found, beside two large wicker chairs like decaying thrones, the mummified remains of two animals the size of dogs but with skulls more like apes. They looked as if they'd fallen asleep attempting to embrace. They looked, in the way their paws had crossed, as if they had been attempting to cross the divide between animal and human.

My partner looked at them with revulsion.

"Corruption," she said.

"Peace," I said.

In answer she took out her keys and moved toward the door that led into the house.

The door had been hacked at with some kind of axe or other crude weapon. The gouges and cuts had turned black against the weathered white. The knob dangled from the door as if it belonged somewhere else.

"Nothing did that," I said. "Nothing that lives here now. Remember that."

"I'll remember," she said, and turned the key in the lock. It made a sound like metal scraping, but also of something released.

She glanced at me before she opened the door. "We don't know what he left."

The iron-gray of her eyes wanted something from me, but all I had was: "The power's gone from it. He hasn't slept for a long time."

I had no weapon. She had no weapon.

●

Beyond the door, a long, straight corridor waited for us, badly lit by glimmering lamps set into walls that seemed to both jut outward and recede into shadow. It was like the throat of a beast, except at the far end we could see where it curved to enter into the second half of the "U." Where did it come out? There had been no other door on the porch.

From where we stood, the corridor clearly changed as it progressed. What was near to us had a weathered opulence – rosewood panels and graying chandeliers long since gone dark. The burgundy carpet lay flat under our feet, and something had been dragged so violently down its length that the fibers had been flattened in a swerving pattern. But farther down we could see plants or little trees, and there came from the far end a suggestion of an underlying funk, the smell of unnatural decay. There came also a throaty murmur, as of a fading congregation or something ursine.

"Vestiges," I said.

"Of what?"

"Of the man himself."

I walked forward. Her boots scuffed the carpet behind me as if compelled to follow against her will.

Nothing happened for several minutes. We did not investigate the rooms we passed, which lay behind closed doors. We did not stop to look at the paintings. Side tables, lamps, and the like did not interest us. Instead, it was as if we followed the swerving pattern in the carpet to see where it led. I began to think of it now less as the imprint of a body being pulled as the trail of something that had no legs, like a giant slug. There was a suggestion, at the edges of the swerve, of a curious mixture of a deeper red and an amber resin.

We had no specific brief. She knew this, and still she asked, "What are we looking for?"

"Everything," I said, and it was true. Nothing angered him more than the wrong focus. But she was nervous. I could tell.

The corridor seemed to collapse into forest, even though I knew this could not be true. It was simply the overgrowth of potted plants and trees run amok, aided by the bulge of a domed skylight mottled dark green with debris. The trees were almost bony, but tall, and their leaves spread out like emerald daggers. What once were regimented bushes had become feral explosions of branches. Between them lichen and vine had taken hold in cracks in the floor where the carpet had been cut away. The trail of the thing without legs led over the underbrush. Recent.

"What's that? In there – beneath?" she asked. I felt rather than heard a tremor in her voice.

"Something dead," I said. It did not seem important to say more.

"Spectacularly dead," she said, and I thought perhaps I had not felt a tremor after all.

We moved on, farther into the great man's house. Now there were glass cages set into the inner wall and no doors at all, but the cages held only mold and things that had expired a long time ago. Some of them lay close to the glass as if trying to burrow through it. Others had died with their forearms banging against it. We did not examine them closely.

●

Then we began to encounter the living. The inner wall pulled into itself and left room for more than just glass cages. A muttering rose from the displays that had been left there, behind a torn, bloodied, sometimes shredded cross-hatching wire. What lay behind was squirming flesh mottled with fur, an eye or two glancing out from the mess with an odd acknowledgment of fate. A spasming claw. A quivering snout. There was no great seriousness, nor order, to this exhibit. These creatures, neglected and left without food or water, had half-devoured each other, and by their nervous natures had consigned themselves to an ever-contracting existence. They would not leave the ledge on which they'd lived their lives to that point. Now they were deranged, and lay on the border between life and death without knowing the difference.

"Survivors," she said.

"No," I said. "Not yet."

We walked further. By now, we were almost two-thirds of the way to the curve of the "U." The stain trail on the carpet had resumed, seemed again to lead us.

Now came the parrotlike birds that had the mange and stumbled across the floor, too weak to fly. Now came cats and dogs that had been combined in peculiar ways and left to stagger, something wrong with their brains that made them lose their balance. Now came the fish tanks full of slop and mewling and naked, shivering tissue. Now came things living inside of other things, gone so completely wild that they were innocent of us.

The vines had crawled up the sides of the walls.

The vines were hiding other things, which peered out at us. Or had they become part of the vines?

She was looking around as if for a weapon, but we had decided against weapons.

"It will be over soon," I said. For some, it was already over.

She nodded. I knew she trusted me. We were not without weapons now that we had abandoned them.

What had looked like ornamentation ahead, at the join of the "U," was actually a row of faces jutting out of the wall, set slightly above what appeared to be a long love seat with thin crimson cushions. These faces – twenty or thirty of them – ranged from that of a boar to that of a kind of thick lizard to a thing very much like a woman. They were all undergoing a slow transmutation of expressions, as if sedated. None looked peaceful. None could speak, and where you could see their throats it was clear some surgery had been required of them. This was to be expected. But what were they supposed to be looking at?

My partner knelt and stared into the face of the woman-thing. There was not so much distance between them. Not really.

"These cushions were once white," she said, staring into the open, gray eyes of the woman-thing. Its lank hair fell straight. It gave off a smell of corruption.

"There has been spillage," I said. "And slippage."

"Can we free them?"

She, like me, had understood that these were not just faces. The bodies behind them must descend in living coffins behind the love seat. Did their feet touch the edge of some surface? Or did they hang, torsos held in harnesses? And if so, what lay beneath them?

I couldn't put my hand on her shoulder. When you let some things in you never get them out.

"Don't you see that they are already free?" I asked.

It was in the eyes. While the muscles in their cheeks, their jowls, their snouts, their muzzles, winced and pulled back in soundless rage or sadness, those eyes stared straight ahead, as dead as anything dead we'd yet seen.

"This is the work of a great man," she said, but I could hear the question.

"We should continue," I said.

For the row of faces led to a doorway, and the doorway led to the second corridor – the one that should lead back even though there had only been one entrance on the porch.

She rose, and on a whim peered back down the corridor we had just traveled through. "The lights are out," she said. "The lights are going out."

And they were. One by one, each lamp, each dim-glowing chandelier, was blinking out, leaving more and more shadow. More and more darkness. Into that space shapes moved where no shapes had been.

Was the shiver I felt one of anticipation? I don't know. Soon there would be an ending.

"We should continue," I repeated. Perhaps there was a tremor in my voice this time. I do not know.

•

Beyond the doorway lay the second corridor. Gone the rosewood. Gone the carpet. Gone the paintings on the wall. The walls were as off-white as the outside of the house. The stench of blood came from everywhere, and the lights here were bare bulbs and flickering fluorescent strips. The floor was linoleum and the stain of whatever had come through formed a long snarl of red disappearing into the distance. Now, though, it trailed up the walls, onto the ceiling, not just the floor. Spun crazily. Did not take a straight line.

We could not see the end of the corridor. We could see no trees or bushes. Now the lights went out one by one as we passed, and when I looked back there appeared to be a long shadow with one arm against the doorway staring at us. Then it was gone.

"Is he here?" she said.

"Yes," I said.

She took a step, then another, and I followed for a time and let her lead.

We came to a place where the wall gave way to a huge glass cage that held a wet, flickering, shifting mass of blackish-brown broken only by shimmers of red.

"What is it?" This time I asked.

She was quiet for a moment. "Starlings. So many starlings, so close together that they cannot move, held up by each other's bodies."

Now I could see the wings and beaks and feathered heads. The eyes bright, feverish, anguished.

"What purpose could this serve to him?" I asked.

She only laughed harshly, took my arm, tried to pull me away. I would not go.

"What purpose could this serve to him?" I asked again, and still she had no answer.

There was a way into the cage. A small chamber at the bottom that would allow a man to crawl in, shut the door, and then open another, translucent door into the space with the birds. The red trail led inside and then back out again.

She saw me looking at it. "What purpose would it serve to go in?" she asked.

"Then I would know *why*," I said.

"You might know why, or you might not. But you would come out mad."

"Am I not already mad?"

I couldn't find an individual starling within that glass cage. They had become something else.

"Trap," I said, wrenching my gaze away.

She nodded, led me forward. We had no weapons.

I had said no weapons.

Was I right?

•

The lights, they went out behind us. Now the few windows showed us not forest but darkness. Night had come, and kept encroaching while we walked down the corridor. I kept thinking about the starlings. I kept thinking about the soundless scream that must be rising within them.

We came to a massive enclave hollowed out from the inner wall. I did not think that there could be such a space within the house, until I remembered the second floor and the way the steepled roof had looked like a chapel.

Within this enclave lay a giant human body composed of many other bodies. And within its belly, which had been ripped open, there lay the bodies of animals too various to describe. And these bodies too had been torn apart and remade to create still stranger creatures. And those creatures had their own as well. The scene seemed to recede from us as we watched it, as if my mind wanted to put as much distance there as possible. The face of the giant human body was various – a patchwork of so many different possibilities that culminated in a gashed, bearlike muzzle. *Flesh is only flesh, skin only skin, muscle only muscle. It can all change and be changed.* There was a desperation to it, as of someone frustrated, thwarted, looking for a solution that never came.

The stain across the walls, across the ceiling, across the floor, had smashed through the glass divide between us and that tableau. The stain ended here even if the corridor did not. Somehow this change in logic unnerved me more than the box of starlings – more even than the body within bodies laid out before us.

"What is the meaning of us?" she whispered.

I know she meant "What is the meaning of this?" but that is not what she said.

"Keep moving," I said. "We are almost at the end now."

"What kind of end can that be?"

"The great man is nearby, I can tell."

"But we have no weapons."

"That is our weapon."

"I expected…"

"Stop."

•

At first, the corridor seemed to end in a blank wall – as disconcerting as following an arm with one's gaze only to have it end in a nub. But no: it curved once again, and beyond the curve was the office of the great man. A sparse desk. A windowless existence. Parts of things all over the floor, red and various. No chair. It was not needed.

In the light from the lamp on the desk, we could see that a giant raven stood there. It had a beak huge and ominous, which had the sheen of steel but the riddled-through consistency of driftwood, riven with wormholes and fissures. A clacking black tongue within the beak. A head like a battering ram. A body the size of a mastiff. Instead of legs and claws it had thick human forearms and hands. The fingernails were long, curved, and yellowing.

The raven inclined its head and turned one giant, bottomless eye toward us – an almond of pure black with just a hint of light reflecting from it.

"It didn't take them long," the raven said, in a deep, refined voice. "It didn't take them long at all."

At the sound of that voice, my partner began to cry: a soft weeping that I echoed from somewhere deep inside.

But I had a mission. *We* had a mission. Now, when it didn't matter, I took her limp, cold hand in mine and held it tight.

"We have a message to deliver," I said.

"Oh?" the raven said, considering me coldly. I saw now that dried blood had flaked all across his razor beak. "And what message is that? I'm busy here."

"You are to stop. You are to *stop*," I said.

"Stop what?" Bemusement beneath the dark feathers.

"*Out there*, they want you dead."

A soft, chuffing laugh that a bird should not be able to make. "There is no *out there*. Anymore."

"No," I admitted. "We didn't find much. But every time you change something, it changes there."

"Some day it may be enough," he said.

My partner made a sound, as if to speak.

"Don't you recognize her?" I asked.

"Her?" he said. "Her?" Peering.

"Don't you recognize me?" she said. "I recognize you."

The raven with the human hands turned back to his desk. Beyond that desk was a formless darkness. "That was a long time ago. That wasn't here. That wasn't this."

"It could be," she said, and took a hesitant step forward. And then another. I saw the courage that took, although I don't believe in courage.

The raven's head whipped around, and it said, almost with a snarl, "Stay back."

She stopped.

I heard a lurching sound now, coming from down the corridor. Every light behind us was dark. We existed only in the round glow of the lights in the office. I was trying to remember a life before this that might have been nothing but smoke: a cottage by a stream and a cool night with friendly stars and the weight of a woman's head against my chest as we looked up from the wet grass.

"We are here to make you stop," I said.

"I know," he said.

"Don't you remember?" she said, as the dead talk to the dead. But she was staring into the darkness beyond.

I was close enough now. I lunged across at him, in the motion I had practiced a thousand times under his watchful eye.

My arm around the surprisingly delicate neck. A quick, wrenching twist. The raven's eyes rolled up. It dropped to the floor. Dead.

I stood there, staring. Was it to be that easy?

It was not.

The darkness moved, came out into the light. It was him. Again. Much larger, but the same. The eye regarding me from above was not without love.

"I couldn't let you after all," he said. "The work is too important."

"Don't you remember?" she said, again. My partner now seemed caught in a loop. I could not help her.

The lurching came nearer.

"Your predecessor is almost here," the raven said. "I cannot stop, and you cannot stop me."

"Some day you will be convinced," I said. "And you will let me."

"Some day I will finally sleep," came the rumbling voice.

There was a wetness behind me, and a soft guttural sound as of a throat that has been cut and yet the flesh lives.

"Don't you remember?"

A sadness entered the eyes of the great man. "I remember enough to let you decide."

It was useless, but I tried. I lunged up at him, but my predecessor had caught up to me. A hand that was not a hand on my arm. A kind of intensity of motion that sucked its way into my skin, all of my skin. Tore it off. Tore it all off. All of it.

Brought me struggling to the box of starlings. Shoved me in. Left me there. Waiting for the moments when the great man and his new-old queen walk by. Waiting to sense them from the way the wings ripple differently across my face, the way the beaks and heads and claws suppurate and wriggle and try to escape, and keep trying to escape. Breathing in the spaces between.

One day, he will let me go, with or without her. He will release the starlings up through the ruined second story, through the chimney, to explode out into the sky, over the old woods. They will no longer know they are birds, as I no longer remember what I was before. But we will be flying and falling, falling and flying, and against that beating of atrophied wings, against that sharp blue, I will see the gravel path and the bridge beneath us. Returning. Remembering.

While my predecessor feeds upon me.

FIXING HANOVER

✳

When Shyver can't lift it from the sand, he brings me down from the village. It lies there on the beach, entangled in the seaweed, dull metal scoured by the sea, limpets and barnacles stuck to its torso. It's been lost a long time, just like me. It smells like rust and oil still, but only a tantalizing hint.

"It's good salvage, at least," Shyver says. "Maybe more."

"Or maybe less," I reply. Salvage is the life's blood of the village in the off-season, when the sea's too rough for fishing. But I know from past experience, there's no telling what the salvagers will want and what they will discard. They come from deep in the hill country abutting the sea cliffs, their needs only a glimmer in their savage eyes.

To Shyver, maybe the thing he'd found looks like a long box with a smaller box on top. To me, in the burnishing rasp of the afternoon sun, the last of the winter winds lashing against my face, it resembles a man whose limbs have been torn off. A man made of metal. It has lamps for eyes, although I have to squint hard to imagine there ever being an ember, a spark, of understanding. No expression defiles the broad pitted expanse of metal.

As soon as I see it, I call it "Hanover," after a character in an old movie back when the projector still worked.

"Hanover?" Shyver says with a trace of contempt.

"Hanover never gave away what he thought," I reply, as we drag it up the gravel track toward the village. Sandhaven, they call it, simply, and it's carved into the side of cliffs that are sliding into the sea. I've lived there for almost six years, taking on odd jobs, assisting with salvage. They still know next to nothing about me, not really. They like me not for what I say or who I am, but for what I do: anything mechanical I can fix, or build something new from poor parts. Someone reliable in an isolated place where a faulty

105

water pump can be devastating. That means something real. That means you don't have to explain much.

"Hanover, whoever or whatever it is, has given up on more than thoughts," Shyver says, showing surprising intuition. It means he's already put a face on Hanover, too. "I think it's from the Old Empire. I think it washed up from the Sunken City at the bottom of the sea."

Everyone knows what Shyver thinks, about everything. Brown-haired, green-eyed, gawky, he's lived in Sandhaven his whole life. He's good with a boat, could navigate a cockleshell through a typhoon. He'll never leave the village, but why should he? As far as he knows, everything he needs is here.

Beyond doubt, the remains of Hanover are heavy. I have difficulty keeping my grip on him, despite the rust. By the time we've made it to the courtyard at the center of Sandhaven, Shyver and I are breathing as hard as old men. We drop our burden with a combination of relief and self-conscious theatrics. By now, a crowd has gathered, and not just stray dogs and bored children.

First law of salvage: what is found must be brought before the community. Is it scrap? Should it be discarded? Can it be restored?

John Blake, council leader, all unkempt black beard, wide shoulders, and watery turquoise eyes, stands there. So does Sarah, who leads the weavers, and the blacksmith Growder, and the ethereal captain of the fishing fleet: Lady Salt as she is called – she of the impossibly pale, soft skin, the blonde hair in a land that only sees the sun five months out of the year. Her eyes, ever-shifting, never settling – one is light blue and one is fierce green, as if to balance the sea between calm and roiling. She has tiny wrinkles in the corners of those eyes, and a wry smile beneath. If I remember little else, fault the eyes. We've been lovers the past three years, and if I ever fully understand her, I wonder if my love for her will vanish like the mist over the water at dawn.

With the fishing boats not launching for another week, a host of broad-faced fisher folk, joined by lesser lights and gossips, has gathered behind us. Even as the light fades: shadows of albatross and gull cutting across the horizon and the roofs of the low houses, huddled and glowing a deep gold-and-orange around the edges, framed by the graying sky.

Blake says, "Where?" He's a man who measures words as if he had only a few given to him by Fate; too generous a syllable from his lips, and he might fall over dead.

"The beach, the cove," Shyver says. Blake always reduces me to a similar terseness.

"What is it?"

This time, Blake looks at me, with a glare. I'm the fixer who solved their well problems the season before, who gets the most value for the village from what's sold to the hill scavengers. But I'm also Lady Salt's lover, who used to be his, and depending on the vagaries of his mood, I suffer more or less for it.

I see no harm in telling the truth as I know it, when I can. So much remains unsaid that extra lies exhaust me.

"It is part of a metal man," I say.

A gasp from the more ignorant among the crowd. My Lady Salt just stares right through me. I know what she's thinking: in scant days she'll be on the open sea. Her vessel is as sleek and quick and buoyant as the water, and she likes to call it *Seeker*, or sometimes *Mist*, or even just *Cleave*. Salvage holds little interest for her.

But I can see the gears turning in Blake's head. He thinks awhile before he says more. Even the blacksmith and the weaver, more for ceremony and obligation than their insight, seem to contemplate the rusted bucket before them.

A refurbished water pump keeps delivering from the aquifers; parts bartered to the hill people mean only milk and smoked meat for half a season. Still, Blake knows that the fishing has been less dependable the past few years, and that if we do not give the hill people something, they won't keep coming back.

"Fix it," he says.

It's not a question, although I try to treat it like one.

•

Later that night, I am with the Lady Salt, whose whispered name in these moments is Rebecca. "Not a name men would follow," she said to me once. "A land-ish name."

In bed, she's as shifting as the tides, beside me, on top, and beneath. Her mouth is soft but firm, her tongue curling like a question mark across my body. She makes little cries that are so different from the orders she barks out ship-board that she might as well be a different person. We're all different people, depending.

Rebecca can read. She has a few books from the hill people, taught herself with the help of an old man who remembered how. A couple of the books are even from the Empire – the New Empire, not the old. Sometimes I want to think she is not the Lady Salt, but the Lady Flight. That she wants to leave the village. That she seeks so much more. But I look into those eyes in the dimness of half-dawn, so close, so far, and realize she would never tell me, no matter how long I live here. Even in bed, there is a bit of Lady Salt in Rebecca.

When we are finished, lying in each other's arms under the thick covers, her hair against my cheek, Rebecca asks me, "Is that thing from your world? Do you know what it is?"

I have told her a little about my past, where I came from – mostly bed-time stories when she cannot sleep, little fantasies of golden spires and a million thronging people, fables of something so utterly different from the village that it must exist only in dream. *Once upon a time there was a foolish man. Once upon a time there was an Empire.* She tells me she doesn't believe me, and there's freedom in that. It's a strange pillow talk that can be so grim.

I tell her the truth about Hanover: "It's nothing like what I remember." If it came from Empire, it came late, after I was already gone.

"Can you really fix it?" she asks.

I smile. "I can fix anything," and I really believe it. If I want to, I can fix anything. I'm just not sure yet I want Hanover fixed, because I don't know what he is.

But my hands can't lie – they tremble to *have at it,* to explore, impatient for the task even then and there, in bed with Blake's lost love.

●

I came from the same sea the Lady Salt loves. I came as salvage, and was fixed. Despite careful preparation, my vessel had been damaged first by a storm, and then a reef. Forced to the surface, I managed to escape into a raft just before my creation drowned. It was never meant for life above the waves, just as I was never meant for life below them. I washed up near the village, was found, and eventually accepted into their community; they did not sell me to the hill people.

I never meant to stay. I didn't think I'd fled far enough. Even as I'd put distance between me and Empire, I'd set traps, put up decoys, sent out false rumors. I'd done all I could to escape that former life, and yet some nights, sleepless, restless, it feels as if I am just waiting to be found.

Even failure can be a kind of success, my father always said. But I still don't know if I believe that.

•

Three days pass, and I'm still fixing Hanover, sometimes with help from Shyver, sometimes not. Shyver doesn't have much else to do until the fishing fleet goes out, but that doesn't mean he has to stay cooped up in a cluttered workshop with me. Not when, conveniently, the blacksmithy is next door, and with it the lovely daughter of Growder, whom he adores.

Blake says he comes in to check my progress, but I think he comes to check on me. After the Lady Salt left him, he married another – a weaver – but she died in childbirth a year ago, and took the baby with her. Now Blake sees before him a different past: a life that might have been, with the Lady Salt at his side.

I can still remember the generous Blake, the humorous Blake who would stand on a table with a mug of beer made by the hill people and tell an amusing story about being lost at sea, poking fun at himself. But now, because he still loves her, there is only me to hate. Now there is just the brambly fence of his beard to hide him, and the pressure of his eyes, the pursed, thin lips. *If I were a different man. If I loved the Lady Salt less. If she wanted him.*

But instead it is him and me in the work room, Hanover on the table, surrounded by an autopsy of gears and coils and congealed bits of metal long past their purpose. Hanover up close, over time, smells of sea grasses and brine along with the oil. I still do not *know* him. Or what he does. Or why he is here. I think I recognize some of it as the work of Empire, but I can't be sure. Shyver still thinks Hanover is merely a sculpture from beneath the ocean. But no one makes a sculpture with so many moving parts.

"Make it work," Blake says. "You're the expert. Fix it."

Expert? I'm the only one with any knowledge in this area. For hundreds, maybe thousands, of miles.

"I'm trying," I say. "But then what? We don't know what it does."

This is the central question, perhaps of my life. It is why I go slow with

Hanover. My hands already know where most of the parts go. They know most of what is broken, and why.

"Fix it," Blake says, "or at the next council meeting, I will ask that you be sent to live with the hill people for a time."

There's no disguising the self-hatred in his gaze. There's no disguising that he's serious.

"For a time? And what will that prove? Except to show I can live in caves with shepherds?" I almost want an answer.

Blake spits on the wooden floor. "No use to us, why should we feed you? House you…"

Even if I leave, she won't go back to you.

"What if I fix it and all it does is blink? Or all it does is shed light, like a whale lamp? Or talk in nonsense rhymes? Or I fix it and it kills us all."

"Don't care," Blake says. "Fix it."

•

The cliffs around the village are low, like the shoulders of a slouching giant, and caulked with bird shit and white rock, veined through with dark green bramble. Tough, thick lizards scuttle through the branches. Tiny birds take shelter there, their dark eyes staring out from shadow. A smell almost like mint struggles through. Below is the cove where Shyver found Hanover.

Rebecca and I walk there, far enough beyond the village that we cannot be seen, and we talk. We find the old trails and follow them, sometimes silly, sometimes serious. We don't need to be who we are in Sandhaven.

"Blake's getting worse," I tell her. "More paranoid. He's jealous. He says he'll exile me from the village if I don't fix Hanover."

"Then fix Hanover," Rebecca says.

We are holding hands. Her palm is warm and sweaty in mine, but I don't care. Every moment I'm with her feels like something I didn't earn, wasn't looking for, but don't want to lose. Still, something in me rebels. It's tiring to keep proving myself.

"I can do it," I say. "I know I can. But…"

"Blake can't exile you without the support of the council," Lady Salt says. I know it's her, not Rebecca, because of the tone, and the way her blue eye flashes when she looks at me. "But he can make life difficult if you give him cause." A pause, a tightening of her grip. "He's in mourning. You know it makes him not himself. But we need him. We need him back."

A twinge as I wonder how she means that. But it's true: Blake has led Sandhaven through good times and bad, made tough decisions, and cared about the village.

Sometimes, though, leadership is not enough. What if what you really need is the instinct to be fearful? And the thought as we make our way back to the village: *What if Blake is right about me?*

•

So I begin to work on Hanover in earnest. There's a complex balance to him that I admire. People think engineering is about practical application of science, and that might be right, if you're building something. But if you're fixing something, something you don't fully understand – say, you're fixing a Hanover – you have no access to a schematic, to a helpful context. Your work instead becomes a kind of detection. You become a kind of detective. You track down clues – cylinders that fit into holes in sheets of steel, that slide into place in grooves, that lead to wires, that lead to understanding.

To do this, I have to stop my ad hoc explorations. Instead, with Shyver's reluctant help, I take Hanover apart systematically. I document where I find each part, and if I think it truly belongs there, or has become dislodged during the trauma that resulted in his "death." I note gaps. I label each part by what I believe it contributed to his overall function. In all things, I remember that Hanover has been made to look like a man, and therefore his innards roughly resemble those of a man in form or function, his makers consciously or subconsciously unable to ignore the implications of that form, that function.

Shyver looks at the parts lying glistening on the table, and says, "They're so different out of him." So different cleaned up, greased with fresh fish oil. Through the window, the sun's light sets them ablaze. Hanover's burnished surface, whorled with a patina of greens, blues, and rust red. The world become radiant.

When we remove the carapace of Hanover's head to reveal a thousand wires, clockwork gears, and strange fluids, even Shyver cannot not think of him as a statue anymore.

JEFF VANDERMEER

"What does a machine like this *do?*" Shyver said, who has only rarely seen anything more complex as a hammer or a watch.

I laugh. "It does whatever it wants to do, I imagine."

By the time I am done with Hanover, I have made several leaps of logic. I have made decisions that cannot be explained as rational, but in their rightness set my head afire with the absolute certainty of Creation. The feeling energizes me and horrifies me all at once.

•

It was long after my country became an Empire that I decided to escape. And still I might have stayed, even knowing what I had done. That is the tragedy of everyday life: when you are in it, you can never see your *self* clearly.

Even seven years in, Sandhaven having made the Past the past, I still had nightmares of gleaming rows of airships. I would wake, screaming, from what had once been a blissful dream, and the Lady Salt and Rebecca both would be there to comfort me.

Did I deserve that comfort?

•

Shyver is there when Hanover comes alive. I've spent a week speculating on ways to bypass what looked like missing parts, missing wires. I've experimented with a hundred different connections. I've even identified Hanover's independent power source and recharged it using a hand-cranked generator.

Lady Salt has gone out with the fishing fleet for the first time and the village is deserted. Even Blake has gone with her, after a quick threat in my direction once again. If the fishing doesn't go well, the evening will not go any better for me.

Shyver says, "Is that a spark?"

A spark?

"Where?"

I have just put Hanover back together again for possibly the twentieth time and planned to take a break, to just sit back and smoke a hand-rolled cigarette, compliments of the enigmatic hill people.

"In Hanover's...eyes."

Shyver goes white, backs away from Hanover, as if something monstrous has occurred, even though this is what we wanted.

It brings memories flooding back – of the long-ago day steam had come rushing out of the huge iron bubble and the canvas had swelled, and held, and everything I could have wished for in my old life had been attained. That feeling had become addiction – I wanted to experience it again and again – but now it's bittersweet, something to cling to and cast away.

My assistant then had responded much as Shyver is now: both on some instinctual level knowing that something unnatural has happened.

"Don't be afraid," I say to Shyver, to my assistant.

"I'm not afraid," Shyver says, lying.

"You should be afraid," I say.

Hanover's eyes gain more and more of a glow. A clicking sound comes from him. Click, click, click. A hum. A slightly rumbling cough from deep inside, a hum again. We prop him up so he is no longer on his side. He's warm to the touch.

The head rotates from side to side, more graceful than in my imagination. A sharp intake of breath from Shyver. "It's alive!"

I laugh then. I laugh and say, "In a way. It's got no arms or legs. It's harmless."

It's harmless.

Neither can it speak – just the click, click, click. But no words.

Assuming it is trying to speak.

●

John Blake and the Lady Salt come back with the fishing fleet. The voyage seems to have done Blake good. The windswept hair, the salt-stung face – he looks relaxed as they enter my workshop.

As they stare at Hanover, at the light in its eyes, I'm almost jealous. Standing side by side, they almost resemble a King and his Queen, and suddenly I'm acutely aware they were lovers, grew up in the village together. Rebecca's gaze is distant; thinking of Blake or of me or of the sea? They smell of mingled brine and fish and salt, and somehow the scent is like a knife in my heart.

"What does it do?" Blake asks.

Always, the same kinds of questions. Why should everything have to have a function?

"I don't know," I say. "But the hill folk should find it pretty and perplexing, at least."

Shyver, though, gives me away, makes me seem less and less from this place: "He thinks it can talk. We just need to fix it *more*. It might do all kinds of things for us."

"It's fixed," I snap, looking at Shyver as if I don't know him at all. We've drunk together, talked many hours. I've given him advice about the blacksmith's daughter. But now that doesn't matter. He's from here and I'm from *there*. "We should trade it to the hill folk and be done with it."

Click, click, click. Hanover won't stop. And I just want it over with, so I don't slide into the past.

Blake's calm has disappeared. I can tell he thinks I lied to him. "Fix it," he barks. "I mean really fix it. Make it talk."

He turns on his heel and leaves the workshop, Shyver behind him.

Lady Salt approaches, expression unreadable. "Do as he says. Please. The fishing…there's little enough out there. We need every advantage now."

Her hand on the side of my face, warm and calloused, before she leaves.

Maybe there's no harm in it. If I just do what they ask, this one last time – the last of many times – it will be over. Life will return to normal. I can stay here. I can still find a kind of peace.

●

Once, there was a foolish man who saw a child's balloon rising into the sky and thought it could become a kind of airship. No one in his world had ever created such a thing, but he already had ample evidence of his own genius in the things he had built before. Nothing had come close to challenging his engineering skills. No one had ever told him he might have limits. His father, a biology teacher, had taught him to focus on problems and solutions. His mother, a caterer, had shown him the value of attention to detail and hard work.

He took his plans, his ideas, to the government. They listened enough to give him some money, a place to work, and an assistant. All of this despite his youth, because of his brilliance, and in his turn he ignored how they talked about their enemies, the need to thwart external threats.

When this engineer was successful, when the third prototype actually worked, following three years of flaming disaster, he knew he had created something that had never before existed, and his heart nearly burst with pride. His wife had left him because she never saw him except when he needed sleep, the house was a junk yard, and yet he didn't care. He'd done it.

He couldn't know that it wouldn't end there. As far as he was concerned, they could take it apart and let him start on something else, and his life would have been good because he knew when he was happiest.

But the government's military advisors wanted him to perfect the airship. They asked him to solve problems that he hadn't thought about before. How to add weight to the carriage without it serving as undue ballast, so things could be dropped from the airship. How to add "defensive" weapons. How to make them work without igniting the fuel that drove the airship. A series of challenges that appealed to his pride, and maybe, too, he had grown used to the rich life he had now. Caught up in it all, he just kept going, never said no, and focused on the gears, the wires, the air ducts, the myriad tiny details that made him ignore everything else.

This foolish man used his assistants as friends to go drinking with, to sleep with, to be his whole life, creating a kind of cult there in his workshop that had become a gigantic hangar, surrounded by soldiers and barbed-wire fence. He'd become a national hero.

But I still remembered how my heart had felt when the prototype had risen into the air, how the tears trickled down my face as around me men and women literally danced with joy. How I was struck by the image of my own success, almost as if I were flying.

The prototype wallowed and snorted in the air like a great golden whale in a harness, wanting to be free: a blazing jewel against the bright blue sky, the dream made real.

I don't know what the Lady Salt would have thought of it. Maybe nothing at all.

●

One day, Hanover finally speaks. I push a button, clean a gear, move a circular bit into place. It is just me and him. Shyver wanted no part of it.

He says, "Command water the sea was bright with the leavings of the fish that there were now going to be."

Clicks twice, thrice, and continues clicking as he takes the measure of me with his golden gaze and says, "Engineer Daniker."

The little hairs on my neck rise. I almost lose my balance, all the blood rushing to my head.

"How do you know my name?"

"You are my objective. You are why I was sent."

"Across the ocean? Not likely."

"I had a ship once, arms and legs once, before your traps destroyed me."

I had forgotten the traps I'd set. I'd almost forgotten my true name.

"You will return with me. You will resume your duties."

I laugh bitterly. "They've found no one to replace me?"

Hanover has no answer – just the clicking – but I know the answer. Child prodigy. Unnatural skills. An unswerving ability to focus in on a problem and solve it. Like…building airships. I'm still an asset they cannot afford to lose.

"You've no way to take me back. You have no authority here," I say.

Hanover's bright eyes dim, then flare. The clicking intensifies. I wonder now if it is the sound of a weapons system malfunctioning.

"Did you know I was here, in this village?" I ask.

A silence. Then: "Dozens were sent for you – scattered across the world."

"So no one knows."

"I have already sent a signal. They are coming for you."

Horror. Shock. And then anger – indescribable rage, like nothing I've ever experienced.

•

When they find me with Hanover later, there isn't much left of him. I've smashed his head in and then his body, and tried to grind that down with a pestle. I didn't know where the beacon might be hidden, or if it even mattered, but I had to try.

They think I'm mad – the soft-spoken blacksmith, a livid Blake, even Rebecca. I keep telling them the Empire is coming, that I am the Empire's chief engineer. That I've been in hiding. That they need to leave now – into the hills, into the sea. *Anywhere but here…*

But Blake can't see it – he sees only me – and whatever the Lady Salt thinks, she hides it behind a sad smile.

"I said to fix it," Blake roars before he storms out. "Now it's no good for anything!"

Roughly I am taken to the little room that functions as the village jail, with the bars on the window looking out on the sea. As they leave me, I am shouting, "I created their airships! They're coming for me!"

The Lady Salt backs away from the window, heads off to find Blake, without listening.

After dark, Shyver comes by the window, but not to hear me out – just to ask why I did it.

"We could at least have sold it to the hill people," he whispers. He sees only the village, the sea, the blacksmith's daughter. "We put so much work into it."

I have no answer except for a story that he will not believe is true.

•

Once, there was a country that became an Empire. Its armies flew out from the center and conquered the margins, the barbarians. Everywhere it inflicted itself on the world, people died or came under its control, always under the watchful, floating gaze of the airships. No one had ever seen anything like them before. No one had any defense for them. People wrote poems about them and cursed them and begged for mercy from their attentions.

The chief engineer of this atrocity, the man who had solved the problems, sweated the details, was finally called up by the Emperor of the newly minted Empire fifteen years after he'd seen a golden shape float against a startling blue sky. The Emperor was on the far frontier, some remote place fringed by desert where the people built their homes into the sides of hills and used tubes to spit fire up into the sky.

They took me to His Excellency by airship, of course. For the first time, except for excursions to the capital, I left my little enclave, the country I'd created for myself. From on high, I saw what I had helped create. In the conquered lands, the people looked up at us in fear and hid when and where they could. Some, beyond caring, threw stones up at us: an old woman screaming words I could not hear from that distance, a young man with a bow, the arrows arching below the carriage until the airship commander opened fire, left a red smudge on a dirt road as we glided by from on high.

This vision I had not known existed unfurled like a slow, terrible dream, for we were like languid Gods in our progress, the landscape revealing itself to us with a strange finality.

On the fringes, war still was waged, and before we reached the Emperor I saw my creations clustered above hostile armies, raining down *my* bombs onto stick figures who bled, screamed, died, were mutilated, blown apart... all as if in a silent film, the explosions deafening us, the rest reduced to distant pantomime narrated by the black humored cheer of our airship's officers.

A child's head resting upon a rock, the body a red shadow. A city reduced to rubble. A man whose limbs had been torn from him. All the same.

By the time I reached the Emperor, received his blessing and his sword, I had nothing to say; he found me more mute than any captive, his instrument once more. And when I returned, when I could barely stand myself anymore, I found a way to escape my cage.

Only to wash up on a beach half a world away.

Out of the surf, out of the sand, dripping and half-dead, I stumble and the Lady Salt and Blake stand there, above me. I look up at them in the half-light of morning, arm raised against the sun, and wonder whether they will welcome me or kill me or just cast me aside.

The Lady Salt looks doubtful and grim, but Blake's broad face breaks into a smile. "Welcome stranger," he says, and extends his hand.

I take it, relieved. In that moment, there's no Hanover, no pain, no sorrow, nothing but the firm grip, the arm pulling me up toward them.

●

They come at dawn, much faster than I had thought possible: ten airships, golden in the light, the humming thrum of their propellers audible over the crash of the sea. From behind my bars, I watch their deadly, beautiful approach across the slate-gray sky, the deep-blue waves, and it is as if my children are returning to me. If there is no mercy in them, it is because I never thought of mercy when I created the bolt and canvas of them, the fuel and gears of them.

●

Hours later, I sit in the main cabin of the airship *Forever Triumph*. It has mahogany tables and chairs, crimson cushions. A platter of fruit upon a dais. A telescope on a tripod. A globe of the world. The scent of snuff. All the debris of the real world. We sit on the window seat, the Lady Salt and I. Beyond, the rectangular windows rise and fall just slightly, showing cliffs and hills and sky; I do not look down.

Captain Evans, aping civilized speech, has been talking to us for several minutes. He is fifty and rake-thin and has hooded eyes that make him mournful forever. I don't really know what he's saying; I can't concentrate. I just feel numb, as if I'm not really there.

Blake insisted on fighting what could not be fought. So did most of the others. I watched from behind my bars as first the bombs came and then the troops. I heard Blake die, although I didn't see it. He was cursing and screaming at them; he didn't go easy. Shyver was shot in the leg, dragged himself off moaning. I don't know if he made it.

I forced myself to listen – to all of it.

They had orders to take me alive, and they did. They found the Lady Salt with a gutting knife, but took her too when I told the Captain I'd cooperate if they let her live.

Her presence at my side is something unexpected and horrifying. What can she be feeling? Does she think I could have saved Blake but chose not to? Her eyes are dry and she stares straight ahead, at nothing, at no one, while the Captain continues with his explanations, his threats, his flattery.

"Rebecca," I say. "Rebecca," I say.

The whispered words of the Lady Salt are everything, all the Chief Engineer could have expected: *"Someday I will kill you and escape to the sea."*

I nod wearily and turn my attention back to the Captain, try to understand what he is saying.

Below me, the village burns as all villages burn, everywhere, in time.

Shark God Versus Octopus God
(Based on a Fijian Myth)

*

1. The Shark God Cometh

A long time ago, when Dakuwaqa the Shark God was young and not so wise, he made all who lived in or near the sea fear him. They feared him for his knives that posed as teeth. They feared him for his relentlessness. They feared him for his speed. They feared him because the bloodlust was buried so deep in him that he loved to fight for no good reason.

Dakuwaqa could take many shapes, but he enjoyed the shape of shark the best in those early days. It fit him. It fit his appetite.

When Dakuwaqa swallowed up a fish, he would give a big, bloody, toothy smile, and say, "One more. I'm still hungry! I'm the fucking Shark God. Give me more!"

No matter how full Dakuwaqa was, he still wanted at least one more fish. This made Dakuwaqa dangerous. It also made him take risks.

Sometimes, when Dakuwaqa was bored, he would take human form. In that form, he was a handsome, tall, dark-eyed youth with gleaming white teeth. Then, he would visit an island and lure a young woman down to the edge of sand and tide. Returning to his shark form, he would devour her, the water runneling red against the white of the surf.

Such pastimes reflected the most animal part of his shark nature. But the game he liked best of all was defeating other gods throughout the ocean. It seemed to be his calling.

"It's what I'm fucking good at," he liked to say, with a bloodstained leer, to his remora advisor, Selqu, as they loitered in some underwater cavern.

•

II. Selqu, the Remora Advisor

Selqu had perfected the art of the simpering suck-ass. His bloated gray-black body shuddered with a wild pleasure whenever he was called upon to approve of Dakuwaqa's tyranny. His mad gaze, performing endless circles of his surroundings no matter how motionless he floated, reflected the strain of his abandonment of self.

Selqu longed to become the Lord of the Remoras. He longed to be brought tribute from the least and the mightiest among his species – the flakes and flecks, the cartilage and the bone they had gleaned from whatever species of shark they had attached themselves to.

Smelling of blood seemed to be no great thing to Selqu. Not if he could remain the Shark God's Remora.

So he fed Dakuwaqa the tale of his invincibility in a thousand words as golden as the light that slides through the reef at dawn, making of that heartless, cut-throat community of eaters an illumined castle of enchantment.

"Just one more," Selqu often murmured to himself at night, as he lay attached to the sleeping Shark God's body, the light of deep ocean a blue-black flecked with the tiny pulses of miniature jellyfish. "Just one more."

Soon, they would rule over all.

•

III. The Shark God's Invincible Army

Dakuwaqa had an army of ten thousand steel-gray sharks at his command: hammerheads, great whites, tigers, and more. Their eyes were cold black coral dots, their hunger as ceaseless as his, their fins sharp as their teeth. With them came their battle-hardened remoras, eager for morsels of stray flesh, starved for foreign parasites. Behind them came battalions of skates, rays, and lion fish, all ready to gobble up whatever remains the sharks and remoras left for them.

This army did not know the value of mercy. When they swam into battle, the water turned the color of storm from their passage. Hundreds of miles away, fish would pause in their travels because they could hear the swish-swish of ten thousand dorsal fins, because they could hear the muttered underwater echo, washing across their hearing in waves, that was the shark army's mantra: *justonemore, justonemore, justonemore, justonemore...*

The sea in their wake turned red with the memories of living flesh.

•

IV. The Relationship Between the Shark God and His Army

Dakuwaqa led this shark army, of course, and he had an excellent record against the other gods. He had to. Because of the rules by which the gods are bound, Dakuwaqa's shark army could not move in until Dakuwaqa had first vanquished the god being attacked. If the attacked god defeated him, or he showed any other sign of weakness, Dakuwaqa would find his shark army attacking him. Nothing would please the remoras, the lion fish, the skates, more than to feast upon rich god-flesh. For Dakuwaqa may have been a god, but he was not invincible; he could be sorely wounded by mortal teeth.

At the thought of this possibility, Dakuwaqa always laughed and told Selqu, "Those bastards can't take me. I'm Dakuwaqa, the Shark God – the most ruthless killer in all the ocean."

"Yes," Selqu would say. "Yes, you are."

Dakuwaqa was very young. He loved the thrill of dominion so much that he had never acquired any fear of defeat, of limitation. He had come fully formed from the Sacred Egg Sac and never known his father or his mother. This had made him think of himself as deathless and ageless. Dakuwaqa did not know that immortality could contain a kind of death within its endless span.

Every morning, he would swim out from his sumptuous coral palace to inspect his shark army, secure in the knowledge that they would always be loyal because he would never be vulnerable.

•

v. The Shark God's Excellent Record Against the Other Gods –
And Why This Was a Bad Thing

In a matter of just a few years, Dakuwaqa and his army had beaten the God
of the Dolphins, the God of the Whales, the God of the Moray Eels, the
God of the Lobsters, the God of the Lesser Fish, and the God of the Greater
Fish. Not only had he defeated these gods, he had eaten most of them, ran-
sacked their seas, and taken from them the islands under their protection.

Dakuwaqa became more powerful with each victory. His gleaming gray
legions grew in size as he grew in size. His name evoked fear from Easter
Island to Viti Levu, from Papua New Guinea to Tonga.

The people of the defeated islands could no longer fish in the seas for fear
of Dakuwaqa and his army of sharks. The animals in the sea cowered in
their homes, hoping that Dakuwaqa or his remora messengers would not
knock on their doors and say, "We need one more, just one more."

The women of the islands no longer smiled at dark-eyed muscular young men.
They looked away. They boarded up their huts and homes when they heard, carried by the breeze, from the sea, the breathy thick whisper of "Come down to
the water, my beautiful ones. Come down here." Often now followed by, as the
women grew more wary, the words "Come *the fuck down here!* Now!"

"Why won't they come out of their homes? Why won't they come down to
the sea?" Dakuwaqa would moan to Selqu. "Why do they disobey me so?"

"They are not like the creatures of the sea," Selqu would respond. "They,
my God-Emperor, do not understand your glory."

"Well, you might be right about that," Dakuwaqa would say. "It is not an
easy weight to bear, my glory. But the hell with it – I'll manage somehow."
And so saying, he would have another tuna fish brought to him for dinner.

For a long time, it looked as if the God-Emperor Dakuwaqa would defeat
all of the other gods and become God of the Sea.

•

vi. The Previous God of the Sea

Now, it should be revealed that no god had been powerful enough to become the God of the Sea for centuries. The last God of the Sea had been the

God of the Turtles, many centuries before. The God of the Turtles was the size of a large island. In fact, he *was* an island – a slow-floating island carried by the current, atop which birds had, over the years, dropped seeds and soil. Until now, from his back, there grew a great jungle of plants and trees. Animals roamed the surface of his covered shell like fleas upon an uncaring dog.

The God of the Turtles could have beaten Dakuwaqa with his size and his implacable calm, garnered from thousands of years of slow, deep thought. But he was very old and, for his own unknowable reasons, had abdicated his place as God of the Sea in favor of finding the deepest, most remote oceans. And there he floated, lost in deep turtle thought, surrounded by the most ancient of waves, while creatures lived and died upon his shell.

Some said he dreamed – that he had dreamed for centuries now, and that the God of the World had recruited him to dream the World through its next few thousand years of existence so that the God of the World could take a brief vacation from that duty.

As the God of the Manta Rays, whom Dakuwaqa had always considered inedible, said from his prison deep beneath the sea, "The God of the Turtles dreams the dream of this world, and woe to him who goes against that dream."

"That's bullshit," Dakuwaqa had responded, wondering how they'd even gotten on the subject. "Dreaming is bullshit." He had always hated the way that the God of the Manta Rays spoke.

Dreaming the world. What a load of whale crap. *Why,* Dakuwaqa thought to himself as he swam through the coral outcroppings of his crab-built palace, *I never dream. I never have time to dream – I just swim endlessly forward, and that is enough for me.*

Still, in building his empire, Dakuwaqa had been very careful to avoid the Turtle.

•

VII. Kadavu Island and the Octopus God

Soon Dakuwaqa ruled all of the ocean except for the Turtle and one island: Kadavu Island, on the western fringes of his empire.

Kadavu Island was large and bountiful. Its clear streams provided water for animals and people alike. Its forests provided shelter and food. Its hills and small mountains provided relief from heat in the hottest part of the year. Banana and breadfruit grew there. A barrier reef encircled most of the island, and within its embrace lay many lagoons in which to fish. Not a single shark patrolled those lagoons. The god that protected the lagoon would not permit it.

Kadavu Island's guardian was the Octopus God. He had large, deep eyes that seemed to contain a vortex of shooting stars. He had eight tentacles that could act as hands or feet or tools – or rip a whale in half. If he wanted the day to end early, he would shoot his ink into the sky and the sun and sky would disappear into new-born night. (It was said that were he to release all of his ink, the world would be black for a thousand years.) The Octopus God could not change shape, but he could change size – from the size of the smallest of fiddler crabs to the largest whale, or so large that four of his tentacles could reach around one side of the island while the other four reached around the other, to meet in a menacing embrace.

The Octopus God had lived for thousands of years, and was said to be slightly mad. Sometimes, the ocean would strobe with emerald-ruby-gold-blue-green phosphorescence late at night and even Kadavu's many nocturnal fishers, from people to eels to crabs to herons, would retire for the evening. They were certain the Octopus God was having an episode. (Others thought he was merely perfecting the details of what he called the Octopus God Triumphant, an underwater light show reenacting his greatest victories; he had been working on it for centuries.)

No one living at that time had ever spoken to the Octopus God, but they knew the Octopus God had been friends with the God of Turtles for many centuries. They knew that the Octopus God had consulted with the God of Turtles on many matters. Some believed that the Octopus God knew the secret of the Turtle's dreaming, that he was as smart as the God of Turtles.

"But not as smart as me," Dakuwaqa said, as he relaxed in his seaweed bath, being cleaned by a pair of exotic remoras.

"No, not as smart as you," said Selqu, lost in a daydream where even the two remoras cleaning Dakuwaqa brought him tribute and let him mate with them.

"I am close now to what I've wanted since I popped out of that stupid egg sac," Dakuwaqa said. "The Turtle doesn't matter. All that matters is the

Octopus. Remove the Octopus and I can be the God of the Sea. And then what soft plump girl will be able to say no to me then? What defeated god will dare fuck with me, then?"

"No one," Selqu said softly. "No one. It is time. Just one more." His gills rippled with excitement.

Behind him, Dakuwaqa reflexively ate one of the remoras that was cleaning him and let out of a mighty God-burp. Selqu did not notice.

•

VIII. Dakuwaqa Reviews His Troops

The next morning, Dakuwaqa, Selqu at his side, consulted with his shark army underlings. They were lined up in the green-blue water outside of his palace while he floated in the entrance hole. Behind them the army of sharks they commanded formed a circle that went round and round without end.

"What do you think?" roared Dakuwaqa at his army. "Do you think I will be the God of the Sea? Or do you think the Octopus God will kick my tail? Tell me the truth, or I'll need one more, just one more, *right fucking now!*"

Dakuwaqa sometimes ate one or two of his lieutenants, just to make sure that the others didn't get any ideas about disobeying him. Nothing inspired fear in his army like seeing him shit out a fellow soldier and piss the unfortunate's blood through his skin.

With one voice, the shark army shouted, "You will be the God of the Sea. You will be the God of the Sea! No one can defeat you! The Octopus God will become one more! One More! One More! One More!"

"That's what I thought," Dakuwaqa said, cleaning the space between his teeth with a piece of seaweed before, to his ever-lasting humiliation, Selqu could do it for him. "I thought you might say that." He admired his toothy smile in a shiny piece of sailfish scale Selqu held up to him. "I can't say I disagree. No, not at all."

"This will be a glorious day, God-Emperor," Selqu said. "You will become God of the Sea and, lo! the tales of centuries will revolve around your God-Head."

Dakuwaqa frowned. He hated it when Selqu sounded like the God of the Manta Rays. And not just because it sounded false, but because then he was reminded of what the manta ray had said about the God of the Turtles.

•

IX. The Battle for Kadavu Island

So brash, bloodthirsty Dakuwaqa swam out to do battle with the old, crafty, insane Octopus God. Once he had defeated the Octopus God, his army of sharks would swim in and take over, leaving just enough tentacle bits for the skates, rays, and lion fish to be happy.

As always, Selqu came with Dakuwaqa, and, as always, Selqu had drawn up the battle plan. The battle plan was always the same: attack, attack, attack, ceaselessly.

Dakuwaqa swam through a gap in the reef and entered the peaceful lagoons of Kadavu, the first shark to do so for thousands of years. The fish swam away screaming watery screams. The people – the ones Dakuwaqa did not surprise and eat – headed for shore, and once there retreated to the interior of the island.

Dakuwaqa searched the reef and lagoons for the Octopus God. He swam and swam, bellowing, "Come out, Octopus God. Come out right now, so I can eat you! Let's just get it over with. Be a shark about it!"

In response, from deep inside the darkest fissures and rifts in the reef, Dakuwaqa and Selqu heard a deep, chuckling laughter. The sound echoed through the coral and the seaweed. The laughter seemed to come from everywhere and nowhere, changing direction and speed with great and confusing swiftness.

"Maybe if you shout louder, God-Emperor," Selqu suggested from the place right above Dakuwaqa's forehead where he grasped the Shark God's skin with his suckers.

"Good idea," Dakuwaqa snarled. *"Come out!"* he roared again, so loud that the birds of the island rose in flocks, unsettled. "Come out and die!"

He could smell the Octopus God, but the scent was everywhere.

•

Several hundred feet beyond the reef his army circled restlessly – a gleam of gray silver, a suggestion of white teeth on a white foam surf.

Finally, as he began to tire, he heard the Octopus God say, "I'm right over here" – and saw the tip of a tentacle over the top of some coral.

Teeth gnashing – octopus flesh within his grasp – he swam at the tentacle at top speed, only for it to disappear into a crack in the coral.

Dakuwaqa was furious.

"Stop hiding!" he shouted in a bubbly shout. "Coward! Stop hiding! You are making it very difficult for me to get one more."

By now, he was really out of breath. It had been a long time since his prey had successfully hidden from him. He found himself gasping, his fins moving slower.

Again, he saw a tip of tentacle. Again, he raced toward it. Again, it disappeared.

"God dammit," snarled Dakuwaqa, and started swimming back and forth across the top of the reef again, fuming. This couldn't be looking too good to his countless minions.

Again, the tentacle. Again, it disappeared into a hole.

Dakuwaqa screamed his displeasure. Fish for hundreds of miles swam for cover.

Selqu dared say nothing.

"King Octopus!" Dakuwaqa roared. "I'm going to eat you slowly when I find you. I am going to savor each tentacle and each little suction cup on each tentacle. There won't be any of you left, you coward!"

Dakuwaqa was winded now. All of the eating he had done over the years had left him a little out of shape. If he was honest with himself, he would have realized that in human form he had become a somewhat flabby island youth over the last year or two.

"Coward?" he heard a sly voice say in his right ear just as eight tentacles lashed into his sides and held him motionless. "How about some other words, shark? How about some other words?" The tentacles continued to hold him tight.

"I don't need any other words, asshole," Dakuwaqa said. "I'm going to make you an eight-time amputee, and then I'm going to crush your head between my teeth and grind your beak down to dust."

The Octopus God laughed. "Let me welcome you to Kadavu Island with a hug. I don't think you'll soon be free of me."

And he was right.

JEFF VANDERMEER

The battle raged all day and into the night, but the Octopus God was right.

Dakuwaqa thrashed about. He spun, rolled, squirmed, pulled, pushed, opened his jaws, and slammed them shut. But no matter what he did, he could not get free of the Octopus God's tentacles. In fact, he began to get a bit dizzy. Selqu had gotten dizzy a long time before, and was in danger of losing his grip on the God-Emperor's skin. Even worse, the Octopus God had sometimes loosened just one tentacle long enough to grab a snack of crab from the nearby reef, but even then Dakuwaqa had not been able to get free. Worst of all, the Octopus God would not stop talking about the underwater light show he was working on...

"Just...one...more..." he said slowly. He was beginning to feel as if he were going to be sick.

"You can't get free of me," the Octopus God said in his sly, mad voice. "I can hold you here until you drown if you like."

"Fuck you," Dakuwaqa said, but the Octopus God was, again, right. Like most sharks, he couldn't stand still for long – he had to keep moving forward to bring water through his gills. If he didn't he would drown. He wouldn't die, but he would drown, and keep drowning, and all during the process of drowning, there would be no way he could get free of the Octopus God, and it would hurt more than anything he had ever known.

Dakuwaqa thrashed again, shouting out to Selqu, "Do something! Do something, Selqu!"

At which point, the Octopus God ended Selqu's ambitions by pulling him off of Dakuwaqa and grinding him up with his beak. (Selqu's last thought had nothing to do with ambition, and everything to do with surprise.)

Dakuwaqa thrashed and changed into a flabby youth holding his breath, but the Octopus God held on. He changed into a ray. He changed into a giant lobster. He changed into a slippery eel. He changed into a whale. But still the Octopus God held on. Not only that, the Octopus God was squeezing the life out of him.

The Octopus God squeezed harder. "Do you give up?"

Dakuwaqa began to see black spots in front of his eyes. He was painfully aware of his waiting shark army. He knew, even without looking, that some of them would be trying to take a bite out of him later, even if he won.

Around them, the water was now darker and colder, the sky above the water pressing down and blue-black. All around, the phosphorescent glow of the coral illuminated them – and the flitting stars of glowing fish too stupid to have hidden already. The Octopus God strobed red and green, blue and orange, content to battle Dakuwaqa to the end of time.

"I can do this forever," he whispered in Dakuwaqa's ear. "I can do this forever and a day. I can continue to recite lines to you from my underwater light show. I can sing, if you like. I do not mind. It is interesting. It is something to do."

Something gave inside of Dakuwaqa. Something broke. He stopped struggling and went back to his shark shape. All the ferocity had left his eyes. He could have been a young sharklet just out of his unknown mother's egg sac again. He remembered how helpless he had felt, coming out of the sac, squirming past its rough edges, for an instant held motionless by it.

"I give up!" Dakuwaqa wheezed. "I give up." He hated saying it. He had never said "I give up" before in his life. He had always said, "Just one more."

"Why should I let you go?"

Dakuwaqa snarled, then fell silent.

"Well," the Octopus God said. "I'm waiting."

"What do you want?"

"If I let you go, this is what I want – you will release all of the gods you have not already devoured. You will leave this island alone and protect all creatures that live on land and in the waters here from your sharks. You will never conspire to be the God of the Sea again."

Dakuwaqa groaned. He could feel water entering his body through his mouth. It did not feel good.

"Yes, yes, yes. Just let me go."

"You promise on your life?"

"On my life."

The Octopus God laughed. "I'm not sure I believe you, but let me tell you this: I've been talking to the God of the Turtles, and he says that if you cause me any more trouble, he will come back and be the God of the Sea again."

"I promise," Dakuwaqa said. He was turning blue now, and not a nice seablue, either. More of a my-gills-need-water blue.

"Remember what I have said, Dakuwaqa," the Octopus said, and released Dakuwaqa.

Dakuwaqa circled the Octopus God four or five times, forcing water back through his gills. He sputtered and coughed. Then he said, "It may not even matter, my promise. Because, when I go back to them, my shark army will try to tear me apart."

"Yes," the Octopus God said, "but you are the God of the Sharks. I am sure you will have no problem dealing with them. And if you do, I will just defeat the next Shark God."

Dakuwaqa was tired and hungry, and suddenly he knew that one day he would die. He did not feel young anymore.

"Goodbye," he said. "I hope I never see you again."

The God of the Octopi just laughed a watery laugh.

●

x. What Happened After...

Dakuwaqa did not die that day, although he received many scars. He did as he said he would, and released the other gods. Since that day, no god has ever again challenged the God of Kadavu Island. The people who live on the island can go out to fish and never worry. The Octopus God still lives in the reef beyond the island, guarding his people, and working on his light show.

Dakuwaqa no longer eats young women. For one thing, even in human form he is scarred, even on his face, and no longer handsome. For another, he has lost the taste for them. Some days, he does not eat at all, but simply rejoices at the feel of water pushing around his body. As he grows older and wanders through his kingdom, he finds that sometimes he is content with what he has. Sometimes, he does take human shape, now, but only to sit by a fire and to talk, or to listen.

Dakuwaqa will never rule Kadavu Island, but now that he is wiser, it does not matter much to him. An odd mood grips him now; his expression becomes serious. Someday, he thinks, walking along the beach at sunset, I will visit the God of the Turtles and learn what dream he dreams.

Errata

✳

When I received Jeff VanderMeer's "story," reproduced below, my first impulse was to forward it to the writer's family, to whom it might be more relevant than to the readers of Argosy. *(The two photographs that accompanied the story – one of a kitchen freezer and the other of a waterlogged lobby – were more than a little disturbing to both myself and my wife, and I have declined to reproduce them within these pages.)*

Unfortunately, my brother James had been quite explicit when he called to check on the progress of the issue two weeks before Mr. VanderMeer's story arrived. He insisted that I include the story in the magazine "no matter how unorthodox it may appear to be." At James' request, I had already slapped – rather bemusedly – some images of farm equipment and seals into the allotted space in the main volume ready to be replaced with the tardy story whenever it came in. According to James, whom I have not heard from since, VanderMeer's story "must be published both in the magazine and in a separate chapbook entitled simply Errata." *James pays the bills, so despite any instincts to the contrary, I have no choice but to publish this "story" as he desires – although that doesn't mean I have to do so without comment or fair warning to the reader.*

— Jeremy Owen

●

Lake Baikal, Siberia – North of Yolontsk, Near Olkhon Island

Dear Jeremy:

I am writing this sitting in the waterlogged lobby of a rotting, half-finished condominium complex. I am surrounded by cavorting freshwater seals and have two pearl-handled revolvers in my lap, a bottle of vodka in my right

133

hand, a human body in the freezer in the kitchens behind me, and a rather large displaced rockhopper penguin staring me in the face. Upstairs, on the second floor, is the room I've made my headquarters. It has a bidet but no bath. The toilet seat refuses to stay up. The wallpaper has succumbed in places to a grainy black fungus, despite the moderate climate. I smell mold everywhere. (Would you believe fish have appeared in the lobby on occasion?) Sometimes the electricity works, but mostly I hope it doesn't because I'm convinced that with all the water everywhere I'm likely to be electrocuted, perhaps even while I sleep.

I don't know the name of the condominium complex because the dilapidated sign out front is in Cyrillic, but it almost certainly includes the words "Lake Baikal" in the title. Lake Baikal Prison Camp Suites, perhaps. Or, Lake Baikal Indoor Swimming Pool & Seal Habitat. Or, Lake Baikal Zoo Suites.

Still, it has a magnificent view. The front wall of the lobby has eroded to the point that the windows have fallen out, so there's nothing between me and the lake but a bit of mortar and marble. Sunsets are particularly magnificent, even if the atmosphere is marred by the seals snuffling in to sleep on the soggy carpeting, on the couches, and sometimes even on the tables. As for the penguin, her name is Juliette.

Did James tell you that the local shaman has inscribed my contact lenses with tiny mystical symbols? The shaman goes by the name of "Ed" because his real name is so convoluted that he long ago gave up making anyone learn it. The symbols supposedly bring me luck and ward off the Devil. I'm not sure it's working. I'm also not sure how he managed the inscription.

I also admit to being more than a little confused as to how I wound up here. (And, for a while, I was confused as to how Juliette got here. Trade winds? Hitchhiking?) But, then, anyone would share this feeling, if put in my position. That I blame your brother is understandable, I think. That the vodka permeating this part of the world like a particularly harsh cliché dulls most of my anger is also understandable.

My splendid isolation – although how can one truly feel isolated surrounded by a convocation of such magnificently oratory mammals? – has been interrupted by several calls from your brother. Right here in the lobby. On this weathered battle tank of a telephone next to me, a black phone that looks like a prop from *Dr. Strangelove*. The last call came just a few days ago. Did James tell you about it? I imagine not.

"Jeff," came his voice crackling through the bad connection, with what sounded like traditional Russian folk Muzak bleeding into the background.

"James," I said. "What the fuck am I still doing here? Tell me *exactly* what you want me to do."

Your brother's money had just about run out, rubles drifting through my hands, and I was thinking about asking Juliette to go hunt me up some fish.

"It's time," James replied with a kind of quivering anticipation in his voice. "It's time."

"No shit, it's time. It's past time," I said.

"You must write now."

"I must write now. Great. *What* do you want me to write about?" He'd told me while I was still in Florida that I would be writing a short story, but since I'd gotten to Lake Baikal, it had quickly become clear that I wasn't just writing a "story."

"All of it," James said. "Even this."

I paused for a second to think about that statement. "Even this?"

"Yes, even this."

"And how about...*this?*"

"Yes, yes – all of it! It's all important. Phone conversations. The shaman. Gradus. Your life. Hell, even the penguin. Just start at the beginning – whatever you think is the beginning. And don't forget the Errata part. That's important for the Change."

"Jesus Christ."

"It's so important, Jeff," James said, and I could tell he was pleading now. He thought he had to convince me. He'd forgotten I had been talking to Ed a lot. He'd forgotten what I'd left behind. He'd even forgotten what I'd had painstakingly etched into the edges of my contacts.

James' voice broke with some unidentifiable emotion as he said, "Jeff, it'll all be worth it. You'll see."

"I hope so," I said. "Because my room doesn't even have a bath. And that lake is fucking *freezing.*"

That's when I hung up. Juliette, standing patiently by the chair, looked up at me with a stare that said, "Maybe you shouldn't have done that. Maybe he had more to say."

Well, if he did, it couldn't have been important, because he hasn't called back.

•

So let me throw both you and James a bone: Here's your first correction. Ed helped me with it by consulting his Book (more about that later). Hell, in a way even Juliette helped me with it. Finding it. Picking this bit over any other. Weighing the "exact pressure of each word as it impacts the world," as James had once said. I can almost feel that pressure in the way the ice hanging on branches in the early morning seems brittle, ready to fall.

And when it does? What will happen then?

Erratum #1: "Box of Oxen," Alan Dean Foster, forthcoming in issue four

The son of Russian immigrants, one of the observers peering through powerful binoculars immediately recognized the Cyrillic letters stamped on the side of the cylinder. His hasty translation provoked consternation and not a little alarm among his co-workers. Frantic, coded messages were sent to various parts of the country.

should read:

The son of Russian immigrants from the Lake Baikal region of Siberia, one of the observers, named Sergi, peered through powerful binoculars and immediately recognized the Cyrillic letters and shamanistic symbols stamped on the side of the cylinder. There were also some mutterings in Russian. His hasty translation of the Cyrillic provoked consternation among his co-workers. Frantic coded messages were sent to various parts of the country. As for the symbols, Sergi failed to mention them to his co-workers, for they promised both the destruction and redemption of humankind. They brought back to Sergi memories of vacations with his family, of walking through a forest of silent fir trees only to emerge at the banks of Lake Baikal near Shaman Rock, which rose from that limitless blue like a shrine. His father had told him that the strongest of the heavenly gods lived there, and negative or bad thoughts

could disturb the god's slumber. He had always been careful, therefore, to never complain while on their vacation, and to live always
in the moment, absorbing the mysteries of that clear water and the
stillness that wavered forever between peaceful and watchful.

Deathless prose it ain't, but according to Ed and the Book, that is the
appropriate correction. We are now Closer than we were to the Change, as
James would say.

But James also said to start at the beginning, and that's a good deal more
difficult. How do you determine that? Beginnings are continually beginning. Time is just a joke played by watchmakers to turn a profit, don't you
think, Jeremy? Well, maybe not. That could just be the vodka talking.

Maybe it starts with meeting James for the first time at the World Fantasy
Convention in 2003, where he was debuting *Argosy*. But I talked to him for
about four minutes, tops, so that's probably not it.

Perhaps it starts with the writers' convention in Blackpool, England,
where a dozen or so of us writer-types – Liz Williams, Jay Caselberg, Neil
Williamson, Jeffrey Ford, and others – wound up trapped in a small wood-
paneled room at the butt-end of a couple of spiral staircases and a maze of
corridors. We were there for a reading, but found no audience, so Gwyneth
Jones told us the uplifting story about how she walked downstairs one night
to the sounds of a frog screaming as a cat disemboweled it.

That was the first time I felt my world *shift* in a way that signaled potential
cataclysm. I mean, there were less personal harbingers, like 9/11, the war in
Iraq, and any number of other calamities. But for some reason, sitting there
next to Jeffrey Ford in that town that seemed like a combination of hell and
a carnival, where the next event slated for the convention hall was a double
bill of Engelbert Humperdinck and David Cassidy – somehow *that* moment
signaled a downward spiral. I remember thinking, *Is this what being successful is going to be like? Trapped in a closet with a bunch of other successful people?*
Somehow, even though the rest is murky, I can see the connection between
that moment and this one – sitting here, drinking vodka and talking to a
penguin.

I've tried giving vodka to the penguin, by the way. She doesn't like the
taste. The seals, on the other hand, seem designed to imbibe the stuff. Clearly,
they are Russian, while the penguin is not. Ed explained Juliette to me the

first time he came over. An escapee from a passing circus. In love with an Antipodes or Falklands that she (he? sexing penguins is one skill level beyond me) will probably never see. Far from home, just like me and the man in the freezer.

"When you get to your room at Lake Baikal, you'll find a box on the bed in your room. There will be a pair of pearl-handled revolvers in the box," James told me after he'd sent me the plane ticket.

"Guns?"

"That's what I said."

"What the fuck will I need guns for?"

There was a pause. Then: "Nothing to worry about, Jeff. If you need to hunt game or anything."

"Hunt game? With pearl-handled revolvers?" I asked, incredulous. "Isn't that a bit…I dunno…*fancy?* Do I just run out into the forest with my pearl-handled revolvers, or do I invite some deer to a cocktail party and then gun them down?"

But it wasn't until I actually reached Lake Baikal and brought up the subject again over the phone that James told me the truth. "Actually, I should be honest. There are people who would like to see us fail."

For the first time, my bullshit detector went off. I realize now it should have gone off much sooner. "Fail at what? Writing a short story?"

A pause. Then, "It's more complicated than that. You'll have to read everything I left you in your room to understand."

"So there's someone after me?"

"Yes."

"Who is it?"

"I don't know. It could be one of several people. Let's just call him 'Gradus' for now."

"That's fucking hilarious," I said. "Should I start calling myself Shade? Perhaps I can call you Kinbote?"

"Call me whatever you like," James said. "I know you're bitter. You're self-hating – and you have every right to be. But don't worry – when you truly take in what Lake Baikal has to offer, all of that will change. Now, go up to your room on the second floor. Everything you need is there."

And he hung up.

Leaving me to worry about a faceless shadow named Gradus that might one day, one night, appear in the seal-choked lobby and force me to use those pearl-handled revolvers. From that moment forward, I could not rid my dreams of him: a silhouette, a too-white glint of eye, a swift and certain death.

●

When you truly take in what Lake Baikal has to offer, all of that will change.
Mark Sergeev, an Irkutsk poet, once wrote:

If you are stopped suddenly by a penetrating blue and your heart pauses, as it sometimes happens only in childhood, from astonishment and delight... if all petty worries, all the vanities of the world, fall away like autumn leaves, and the soul takes wing and is filled with light and silence. If, suddenly, the real world holds back, and you feel that nature has its own language and that it is now clearly understood. If a simple earthly wonder has entered your life and you have felt ennobled by this encounter – it means, this is Baikal.

And that's how it was for me from my first glimpses of Lake Baikal, in the back seat of the world's most ancient and rusty cab, to the truly stunning view available at my condominium digs. (And such interesting facts! Did you know, Jeremy, that twenty percent of the world's fresh water can be found in Lake Baikal? Or that it would take all the rivers of the world one year to fill its basin? I was still absorbing these facts as we pulled up.)

Of course, Jeremy, you have to understand: such a feeling, such a state of grace, can be destroyed by the wrong context, the wrong events. Like being surrounded by seals and a displaced penguin. Like having to put a dead body in a freezer. That kind of thing can kill your ability for wonder, no matter how much you wish to retain the feeling that the world as we know it is fundamentally *sound*.

I ask Juliette for advice sometimes. "Juliette," I say. "Is Ed for real? Is the Book for real? Is James for real? Is this really going to work? Or is it a form of madness?"

"I dunno," Juliette says. "I'm just a penguin. But I can bring you some fish, if you'd like."

"That would be nice," I say, "because this Russian beef jerky tastes like it's made from a mixture of bear and rubber."

Lake Baikal is nearly a mile deep. If Juliette could dive deep enough, she could bring me fish that had never felt the light upon them. She could bring me treasures rarely seen by humans. Mysteries long unsolved, brought into the sun.

●

Correction alert. I'll feed you these slowly, so you don't get stuffed.

Erratum #2: "The Telephone," Zoran Živković, issue three

I put the receiver to my ear and said sharply, "Hello!"

"Good evening!" said someone at the other end of the line. I'd been certain it would be a younger person, most likely under the influence of a substance that had put them in a very happy mood. Instead, I heard the deep, serious voice of a middle-aged man, so my hackles came down a little. I'd been ready to deliver a tirade on bad manners to the unknown young caller, but now I just replied, "Good evening," although still in a surly tone.

"This is the Devil," said the man evenly, just like one of my friends who was calling.

I sat there speechless for several moments and then hung up the telephone.

should read:

I put the receiver to my ear and said sharply, "Da?"

"Guten evening," said the person on the other end of the line. The connection crackled and popped as if I were hearing grease dance on a stovetop.

I'd thought it would be a young person, most likely under the influence of vodka. Instead, I heard the deep, gravelly voice of an old man. The voice had an undertone I can't describe except to say it sounded like the spring loam of deep forest, the glimpse of sky through thick branches. Which doesn't make sense, but there it is.

The man's voice made my hackles come down a little. I'd been ready to deliver a tirade on bad manners to the unknown caller, but now I just replied, "Good evening," although still in a surly tone.

"This is the shaman," said the man unevenly, the inconsistency of his tone oddly calming. "Have you ever envisioned a better world? A world where silence is a blessing and snow is like peace?"

For a moment I was held by a terrible fascination, and a glimpse of a half-formed image of immense power, but with a shiver I managed to deny it and hang up the phone.

And so on, Jeremy, substituting "shaman" for "the Devil," with frequent allusions to snow, ice, the frozen north, etc. I don't have the patience or attention span to set it out right now. If that ruins everything, so be it. But I rather think at this point that any decision I make is the right decision.

•

The old shaman in Zoran's story certainly was right. It gets bitterly cold up here in the winter. The locals tell me that waves freeze in mid-crash against the shore, that you can see every individual ripple and striation in the resulting ice sculptures – and they have the photographs to prove it.

At what passes for the local bar (the only business within miles: a tin shack a mile down the road), the owner sells these photographs to the rare tourist, along with a local myth that "in the extremest cold words themselves freeze and fall to earth. In spring they stir again and start to speak, and suddenly the air fills with out-of-date gossip, unheard jokes, cries of forgotten pain, words of long-disowned love." That's not how the bartender put it; that's a quote from Colin Thubron's *In Siberia*, which was left on my bed along with the pearl-handled revolvers. The quote makes me sad and hopeful at the same time. It speaks to my mission, such as it is.

But, then, everything has been speaking to me in that way, lately. The day I left Tallahassee, Florida to come here, my stepdaughter Erin gave me a kind of anarchist's handbook called *Days of War, Nights of Love: Crimethink for Beginners*.

"I don't need it anymore," she said, "but I thought you might."

At that point, she had no reason to give me anything other than a black eye, so I was touched. "I'll read it," I said. But the truth is, I read one page and just haven't gotten around to the rest.

That first page (page 126) was titled "The Concert at Baku" and related the events of November 7, 1922, when the Russian experimental composer Arseny Mikhailovich Avraamov ascended to the roof of a tall building and directed a concert of factory sirens, steam whistles, artillery, and everything else in the city of Baku capable of making loud noise; for the climax of the piece, the entire fleet of the Caspian Sea joined in with their foghorns.

Of course, the book tried to make it logical, part of the people's struggle: "a moving demonstration of what is possible when art and cooperation are considered integral to social life, rather than quarantined to our private lives and leisure time."

But even then, before I truly knew what James meant to do, what *Argosy* meant to him, I saw Mikhailovich Avraamov's act differently. I thought about all of the people who participated in his experiment. Surely some of them sought more from it than just *music*. Surely some of them saw it as *transformative*, as a kind of *liberation*. I saw it as his attempt at change – to find the right sounds and symbols to alter the world at its core, to split it open and reform it. To, in an odd way, heal it.

After all, Jeremy, do you really think James sent me all the way to fucking Lake Baikal to write a short story? I don't think so. I don't think so at all. Not now.

I should probably tell you what I found when I got here. After paying the Mongolian cab driver his rubles, I walked into the water-soaked lobby of this place, noting the seals with a small sound of surprise, but ignoring them long enough to call James and let him know I had arrived. Then I walked up to my room on the second floor, just as James had directed me to do.

In addition to a desk with a manual typewriter on it (which I have disdained to use, preferring my pretentious customized Moleskine notebooks with gold leaf inlay, and utilitarian ballpoint pens), I found a box with two pearl-handled revolvers on the bed, along with a scrawled note that said to look under the bed.

I put my suitcase down and looked. What did I find? Nothing as dramatic or as fancy as the revolvers. Just the following:

- Copies of *Argosy* #1-#3
- Printouts of parts of *Argosy* #4
- *The Lake Baikal Guidebook* by Arthur D. Pedersen and Susan E. Oliver

- an envelope containing a badly typed letter (on annoying onion-skin paper) that must have been dictated to someone local over the phone
- an envelope inside that envelope, containing a second letter
- contact information for Ed the Shaman
- reminders of how to reach James by phone
- the address to which I should send my finished story

The first letter read as follows (errors corrected):

Dear Jeff:

Now that you have reached your destination, you no doubt have questions about the scope of your mission, and why it required you to travel so far across the world.

The answer is not that easy to provide, although at its simplest level your mission does require you to write a story, while also correcting "mistakes" made in *Argosy* since its inception.

The truth is, I can give you hints as to how to carry out your mission. I can give you the tools you need to complete it. I can even give you an explanation (see the second letter, should you need it). But even after all of that, you will change the context of the assignment by your very involvement in it. There are variables I cannot and do not wish to control. Mutations and permutations will mean the result is not exactly as I have intended, but it will also ensure that the result is truly unpredictable and thus worthy of our work. To some extent, I have factored all of this into my calculations.

The errata part of your assignment is perhaps the most straightforward. In short, I need you to read through each issue of *Argosy* and issue corrections for certain stories. I cannot tell you which stories, but I believe you will, as you become attuned to the power of Lake Baikal and your own natural instincts, recognize the right ones when you see them. Ed the Shaman will then help you by consulting his Book for you, a holy tome that has been passed down from generation to generation. I believe this step is essential, and so does Ed. I can personally vouch for him, as I have met with him

143

several times while traveling through the area. (On my father's side, I am descended from ancient Siberian tribes, and I know that the shaman's wisdom runs very deep indeed.)

After you have performed this step and learned everything you need from the guidebook, I believe that your assignment will become much clearer. You will know what to write and how to write it, in the exact way necessary.

You can always open the second letter if you find yourself needing a "why." I leave it up to you as to when you open it. I will say only that the timing of this action is important.

Your colleague,
James Owen

Did it feel like starting over, after everything I had been through? The hell it did. It felt like a bad dream. Isn't that right, Juliette? *Yes, that's right, Jeff.*

I didn't open the second letter for a long time. Normally, I would have opened something like that immediately, but somehow, at that moment, I couldn't handle any of James' whys. I could hardly handle the seals in the lobby. Comical. Sinister. Surreal. I don't know how to describe my first impressions.

A new life. Guns. A composer who used a whole town for his orchestra. A place where words freeze in the winter and thaw in the spring. And over it all, the shadow of Gradus waiting to envelop me. Slowly progressing, feeling his way toward James' plan.

Aren't you scared? I was scared. I'd have pissed my pants if it would have helped relieve the fear.

Only Juliette wasn't scared. Over the centuries, I'm sure her kind had seen much worse – doomed Antarctica expeditions, men eating the frozen bodies of their comrades, sled dogs reduced to whimpering piles of bones, ships frozen in the ice, strife and conflict: a whole history of failure witnessed by her forebears. And throughout it all, a question on the cellular level rising slowly in the communal, generational penguin mind: *Why?*

Why does it have to be this way?

•

Erratum #3: "The Gate House," Marly Youmans, forthcoming in issue four

In October, the cold and snow would begin, sealing the stream in ice, sagging the limbs outside the kitchen window. The land would look stainless and white, as if the world knew nothing of blood and dirty deeds. She would build a snow maiden in the courtyard and feed the birds who had the courage to stay and not fly south. Consolation might sift from the sky, like soft crystal. It could be a new life, now dimly seen, like the humpbacked shape of a camel in a dispersing cloud.

should read:

In October, the snow and ice would come, sealing the lake in silence, weighing down the trees outside her kitchen window. The land and lake would look seamless and white, as if it knew nothing of blood or pain. She would build a snow maiden on the edge of the lake and feed the birds that had no choice but to stay in that frozen place. And through that act, consolation might settle over her as gently as the snow. The world seemed to tell her that she could have a new life, now dimly seen, like a shadowy figure walking slowly across the ice-laden lake to the near shore.

•

I wonder if Gradus was stalking me long before I came to Lake Baikal. I wonder if he has been there since the Beginning. (Whichever beginning you prefer, Jeremy.)

As I may have mentioned, I have a fine view of the lake from here, given that the water comes right up to and beyond my doorstep. Sometimes, oddly enough, this lobby feels like a landing pad on the Death Star, with seals lunging in and lurching out every few minutes, their heads bobbing, their large eyes alive with hidden meaning. Mostly, they seem to be mocking me.

Because, honestly, would I be sitting here in a rotting condominium complex halfway around the world if I hadn't, at some point, hit rock bottom?

Your brother may be persistent and good at persuading people to do things, but no one's *that* good.

•

I shared my story with Ed a couple of weeks ago, when he came around in his battered pickup to take me to Shaman Rock and his Book. After I had finished my account, Ed turned to me and said, "You are a fortunate man. You are still alive and you have a purpose."

Possibly. Possibly not.

The truth is, Jeremy, by April of this year, my life had begun to fall apart. The coming schism, the disintegration that I'd sensed in Blackpool, had reached fruition. Constant book tours, fan e-mails, re-imagining my lump of a body into something more approximating fitness, and my complete inability to relax into all of this new success had warped my mind. The vodka helps me see this. (Juliette reminds me of it with her innocent, non-judgmental stare.)

I became ever more vain and superficial. I bought fifteen pairs of shoes, for fuck's sake. I got contacts. I spent more time primping than a supermodel. Worse, I took my wife Ann for granted. I took Tallahassee for granted. I had a restlessness in me that led to driving around late at night dressed to the nines with the music turned up loud, as a poor substitute for...what?

Sometimes everything seems hopeless on the macro level – global warming, war, murderously corrupt politicians, terrorism. Sometimes it is much more personal and internalized.

I began to drink too much. I began to indulge in self-pity. I began to see myself as some kind of victim in all of this, and that led to worse things still. I had an affair with a co-worker at my day job. Ann left me as a result. I turned for comfort to my new lover, only for her to reveal that she was a born-again Christian. "Accept Jesus and we can be together," she said. When I refused, she lodged a harassment complaint with Human Resources. My supervisor told me it would be best if I quit. I told her what she could do with that suggestion, and by mid-June, I had lost my marriage, my day job, and most of my self-esteem and had been reduced to living in a tiny cockroach-infested apartment with only the slim thread of intermittent royalties keeping me off the streets.

I was in shock by then, I think. I was beyond feeling guilt or anything else. I'd gotten what I wanted only to find out it wasn't what I wanted at all.

I hung out at a bar called Gill's, dulling myself into a stupor with cheap beer and whiskey by night and trying to think up ideas for blockbuster commercial novels to pitch to my agent by day. I tried to make out to all but my closest friends that everything was fine. I limped along with some freelance work for *Publishers Weekly* and the local newspapers, but I knew that would dry up eventually, because I was always missing deadlines.

By July, I had stopped doing even that and just drank all day and night. I even stopped bathing and shaving. Sometimes, during my erratic sleep, I'd dream of my former life and it would seem exactly that: a dream of something that had never been. When I woke, I'd call Ann, no matter what the time, even though I knew there was no hope she'd take me back, just to reassure myself that once upon a time I'd had that life.

I try to convince myself now that it would have gotten better without outside intervention, but I think I'm wrong. If James hadn't called one night while I was at Gill's, trying to convince Katie, the owner, to give me a beer on credit, I don't know what would have happened.

The phone at the bar rang and Katie answered it, then handed the receiver to me with a puzzled look on her face. "It's for you. Says he's an old friend. Keep it brief, okay?"

"Hello," I said.

"Jeff? Jeff VanderMeer?"

"Yeah. Who the fuck is this?"

A thin laugh. "James Owen. Remember me?"

For a second, I didn't. James Owen might as well have been from another planet.

"World Fantasy 2003? *Argosy*?"

Then I did remember, which confused me even more. "How'd you get this number?"

"It doesn't matter. Let's just say a couple of concerned friends gave it to me."

"Why would they do that?"

"Because I have an opportunity for you."

"What kind of opportunity?"

There was a pause. I think he knew this was a hard sell. "I need you to go to Lake Baikal in Siberia and write a story."

"You want me to write a story about Lake Baikal?"

"No. I need you to *go* to Lake Baikal and write me a story. For *Argosy*."

"You're full of shit."

"I don't blame you for thinking so, but I'm not. You'll be paid. Your expenses will be taken care of…. Don't you think a change of scenery might be a good idea?"

"Lake Baikal?" I was trying to get my wits about me. "That's the place with the freshwater seals?" As I would soon know all too well.

"Among other things. A property there has recently come into my possession and it would be perfect for you. You can get some peace and quiet there and write."

James chose not to reveal at that point that he thought a man would one day come walking along the lakeshore with the express purpose of killing me.

•

That first time James called me at Gill's, I hung up on him and went back to drinking. And the next night. And the night after that. It was not until the night after I got into a fight in the parking lot over something so stupid I can't remember what it was and had my nose broken that I realized that I needed to say "yes" or I was going to find my way to rock bottom.

"Great," James said. "I knew you'd come around."

He gave me the flight information, assured me of money coming in the mail, and told me his instructions would be waiting for me at Lake Baikal.

"That all sounds fine to me, James," I said, as if I was talking to a crazy person.

I drank my way through the countless hours of flights, the bus and train and car rides, until I finally wound up here.

•

Gradus remained in my thoughts. I could not get him out. He was the great Unknown in a world that had become as simple as the ice and snow, but no less mysterious.

"When can I expect this mystery man to arrive, James?"

"I don't know. It could be any time."

"Any time, huh?"

"Yes. You should carry the revolvers with you wherever you go."

"Even down to the grocery store?"

"There is no grocery story near you."

"Exactly my point! Neither I nor Juliette is thrilled about that. No movie theater, either."

"Appreciate the natural beauty."

"I'm trying. I'm also reading the guidebook for the fiftieth time. I'm on the verge of switching to the crimethink book and becoming an anarchist."

"Stay calm. It'll all be over soon."

"I just wish this 'Gradus' would get here soon so I can show him these fancy revolvers and scare him on his way."

"Jeff, this kind of person doesn't get scared. You will probably have to kill him."

I didn't believe him, at the time.

•

A week after my arrival, I met Ed the Shaman for the first time. I hadn't been putting it off so much as acclimating to my surroundings – getting used to having conversations with Juliette; taking hikes along the lakeshore, through the stunning, bird-filled forests; familiarizing myself with the tin shack bar and its twelve different brands of vodka. James hadn't indicated any constraint for my "Literary Work of Great Import and Inestimable Redeeming Value" other than "I'll let you know when you have to start it," so I'd decided to take my time.

But, finally, I called Ed. He arranged to pick me up early on a Monday morning. I had with me an Erratum segment – or, at least, what I thought might serve as one – taken from John Grant's "The Dragons of Manhattan." It contained long tracts of rant that I thought might be James applying the nudge of his own beliefs.

Ed pulled up in a battered pickup truck that needed a coat of paint and new shocks. The back was filled with fishing tackle, old tires, and wooden boxes that appeared to be stuffed with hay.

He got out, said hello in decent English, and shook my hand. He didn't look like a shaman, even allowing for the fact that I'd only ever seen them in photos in books and read about one in Angela Carter's *Nights at the Circus*.

"You're the shaman?" I asked.

"Yes – I'm Ed. James wrote to me a while back, so I was expecting your call."

"Ed" wore a baseball cap of indefinite origin, a denim jacket over a worn T-shirt, and a pair of faded blue jeans. He had a gold earring shaped like an otter in his left ear and a silver earring shaped like a seal in his right ear. His broad, wrinkled face had the half-Caucasian, half-Asian look shared by many in the area. He had eyes so blue and piercing it was hard to hold his gaze.

I felt like asking, "Is this your traditional dress? Because it's not very convincing." But I resisted. Instead, I asked, "Where are we going?"

Ed smiled. "We're going to consult the Book. It's near Shaman Rock."

I had heard of Shaman Rock from the travel guide. It was the holiest of holy sites in the old religions. Even going near it was hazardous according to some. But what the hell – this was what I was here to do. So I hopped into the passenger seat, held the door shut with a piece of electrical cord, and off we went, Ed using a series of dirt roads to get to our destination. (There wasn't anything paved within twenty miles of the condominiums. Not anymore. No need for it.)

"You know you need to pay me to see the Book?" Ed asked along the way.

I didn't, but luckily James had provided enough money.

●

Warning: Here comes another correction.

Erratum #4: "The Dragons of Manhattan," John Grant, issue three

> Any internally coherent set of explanations of the phenomena we observe around us starts off as the cutting-edge science of its day. Assuming it is widely accepted, it becomes a fixed dogma: To disagree with it is a stupid and indeed evil revolt against supposedly absolute knowledge. Even though humanity's retaliations against the rebels can be vicious in the extreme, eventually there are enough revolutionaries, and they are persistent enough, that the existing Grand Universal Theory is forced to adapt or give way to a new, improved version.

should be:

Any internally coherent set of explanations of the phenomena we observe around us becomes the cutting-edge science of its day. Assuming it is widely accepted, it devolves into dogma: To disagree with it is a stupid, evil revolt against supposedly absolute knowledge. But even though humanity's retaliations against the rebels can be vicious, eventually the revolutionaries are persistent enough that the existing Grand Universal Theory is forced to adapt or give way to a new, improved version.

I can't tell you where the Book is housed in relation to Shaman Rock. I can't tell you much of anything about it, because I promised Ed I wouldn't. And, besides, it's irrelevant to this story. What *is* relevant to this story is the Book itself.

It lay in its hiding place like something made from the earth – more than a thousand years old, according to Ed, and containing all the wisdom of his shaman forebears. It was fashioned from broad leaves and red bark. Dead beetles and the pelts of animals had been woven into its spine. Large and bulky, it smelled light, of mint and sea salt. The languages in which it had been set down were various and incomprehensible to me. Its cover, wood shot through with silver and bronze, had a worn, smooth feel that was pleasant to the touch. But the cover is all I got to touch, and all I saw of the pages was a quick five-minute glimpse before Ed motioned for me to move back, away from the Book.

In short, Jeremy, it was the most extraordinary object I have ever seen, and it is mostly my glimpse of the Book that allows me to maintain faith in this whole mad project. Certainly it wasn't James' reassurances or the all-too-ordinary appearance of Ed himself.

That first day, all I did was read the erratum excerpt to Ed, who then consulted the Book, burned some incense, and told me after about an hour, "You've got the right manuscript. But that's the wrong part. And the change is small in this one. A slight change is all you need. Bring another part tomorrow and we'll start over."

Then he took me fishing in his cockleshell of a boat. We caught some white graylings, which we cooked over an open fire in the lobby back at the condo. It drove the seals away temporarily, but fascinated Juliette, who even seemed to like the taste of cooked fish. That's the kind of barbarism a circus will drive you to.

●

I repeated this process for weeks as I strove to find the right parts for the Errata. James called every once in a while to check up on me. For the most part, I didn't appreciate these calls.

Once he said, apropos of nothing, "I am a direct descendent of Cotton Mather and Increase Mather. Make of that what you will."

I haven't made much of it, let me tell you.

"Dave Eggers might read this issue," he said during his next-to-last call.

Of all the things he said, this made me angriest. "So the fuck what? After everything else you've told me, who gives a flying fuck about that? Fuck Dave Eggers. I'm freezing my ass off here, trying to believe in some shamanism thing that's probably bullshit, and you're thinking about Eggers?"

"Well," James said, "by my calculations, he's one of those who has to read it for us to be successful."

During another call, I was telling him about an unstable artist friend of mine, and he said, "At the age of eleven, I was a long-term patient in a hospital in Phoenix. On a single day, I was visited by the Pope, with whom I discussed superhero comics, and Mickey Mouse, with whom I discussed being visited by the Pope. An hour later, President Reagan was shot. These events helped to cement my thoughts about synchronicity."

"What the hell was that?" I said. I'd been telling him about the seals when he went off into his soliloquy. "Did you read that off a note card or something?"

"I did," he said.

"*Why?*"

"Fuel for your story. It needs to be in there. As does a mention of farm equipment."

●

Most of the time, we both tried to avoid the subject of Gradus, even though I would go to sleep thinking of him and wake up in the morning with a start, certain he was standing over me, and reach like a drowning man for my pearl-handled revolvers.

James' reasons for putting me in this position still remained cloudy, but I had decided not to open the second letter until after I finished the mind-numbing task of perfecting the Errata. And, after a while, I stopped asking James, because he refused to tell me over the phone. Which meant that only the letter could answer my remaining questions. Still, I resisted its pull.

Juliette helped me. I kept asking her if I should open the letter, and she refused to answer – for which silent advice I would reward her with some grayling.

•

Correction!

Erratum #5: "My General," Carol Emshwiller, issue two

> They'd given up on getting any information out of him. They said he was mine to do with as I wished. We always take them along with us and get them back in shape for our farms. "Don't be treating him too nice," they said. "He's dangerous." They say that every time. Nothing has happened so far and it's unlikely considering the shape they're always in.

should read:

> They'd given up on getting any information out of him. They said he was mine to do with as I wished. We always take them along with us and get them back in shape for our farms. "He's dangerous," they said. "He killed a man. He'll kill you if you give him half a chance." They say that every time. Nothing has happened so far and it's unlikely considering the shape they're always in. Most of them are so shocked that their vision of the world has proven false

that they fall into a stupor, as if their minds cannot adjust to their new situation. Their new world.

•

By now, I've grown used to the seals, and grown fond of Juliette. (In a reversal of our established roles, I've taken to buying fish for Juliette from Ed.) I've grown used to the rhythms of the lake and the sounds that begin at dusk – the sounds of owls, of bats, of the occasional night fisherman working without lights: rasping pieces of words in a foreign tongue, distorted by the water. I don't even mind bathing in the lake anymore. I jog and I do push-ups and have forgotten weight machines even exist. Even better, my readers can't get to me here, and neither can my editors. Really, all things considered, it should be peaceful. Except for the man in the freezer.

That happened the day before yesterday. Yesterday, I had visitors, strangely enough. The author and explorer Liz Williams had heard a rumor that I was in the area and stopped by with a couple of her friends on their way south, into China. You don't think of there being "explorers" today, but there are in this part of the world, and Liz is one of them.

They didn't stay as long as I might have liked, although I still was glad of the company. Juliette is not what one might call a sparkling conversationalist. And Ed either talks in riddles or asks for money.

While Liz's companions explored my surreal abode and were in turn investigated by the local seal community, Liz and I sat and talked, reliving Blackpool and various other adventures. After all that had happened in the twenty-four hours before that, I was relieved to experience a veneer of normalcy. Even if I was babbling. Even if my heart was pounding in my chest.

As I may have mentioned, one thing they have in abundance around here is vodka. We drank a lot of it. For a long time.

Eventually, she noticed the pearl-handled revolvers on the table next to us.

"Oh, those are nice," she said. "I used to have a pair like that back in Brighton. Used them for magic shows."

"I killed a man with them yesterday," I blurted out.

Liz laughed, said, "These things happen. Just can't be avoided."

"No, I mean it. I killed a man. He's in the freezer in the kitchen. I mean, the freezer isn't working, but it seals the smell in. I mean, it keeps the seals out."

Liz laughed even harder at that – was it forced? – but when I invited her and her companions to stay the night, they told me they had to be farther south by dusk if they wanted to cross into China on schedule.

I asked Juliette her opinion. She thought it was a convenient excuse.

Then I read her another correction.

Erratum #6: "The Mystery of the Texas Twister," Michael Moorcock, issue one

From Zodiac's quarters, there now issued the unworldly strains of a violin. Even Begg was astonished. Then he smiled broadly, remembering his old opponent's only apparent passion – his passion for music. The strains were assured and subtle, from an instrument of extraordinary age and maturity. At first Begg tried to identify the piece. Clearly, he thought, some modern master. But then he realised that the composer was Zodiac himself. Gradually it moved from classical to romantic to contemporary structure, a perfectly integrated piece, that led the listener slowly into the nuances of the music. Moreover it was somehow in perfect resonance with the landscape itself.

should read:

From Zodiac's quarters, there now issued the unworldly strains of a violin, in a Russian mode. Even Begg was astonished. Then he smiled broadly, remembering his old opponent's only apparent passion – his passion for the types of music that he had always claimed would change the world. The strains were assured and subtle, from an instrument of extraordinary age and maturity. They conjured up a landscape of deep water and thick forests. At first Begg tried to identify the piece. Clearly, he thought, some modern master. But then he realized that the composer was Zodiac himself. Gradually it moved from gypsy-classical to romantic to contemporary structure, a perfectly integrated piece, that led the listener slowly into the nuances of the music. Moreover, it was somehow in perfect resonance with the landscape itself, as if it had brought the pristine world of the north to the south. Underlying this resonance: a subtle strain of menace, for transformation is not without peril.

•

The day before Liz arrived at my doorstep – two days after I had finished the last session with Ed and four days after James called me for the last time – I was sitting in my favorite chair in the lobby, staring out at the lake, when I realized a figure was standing twenty feet to my left, having apparently just entered the lobby through one of the holes that led to the lakeside. His boots were wet. He was dressed all in black. He wore a ski mask, also black. He was tall, over six feet. I could see the white of his eyes through the holes in the mask. He was looking at me intently and pulling out something ominous from beneath his overcoat. I raised my pearl-handled revolvers and shot him before he could complete the motion. It happened as if preordained. It happened as if we were both part of some stage production. There was a tiny puff of smoke, a burning sensation in my hands, and two small holes opened up in the man's chest. He made a huffing sound, almost of surprise. His hands dropped to his sides and he crumpled against the wall. The sound of the guns had been so inconsequential that it hadn't startled the seals or Juliette.

For a long time, I continued to sit in my chair, holding the revolvers. That the man was dead seemed certain. That it had been Gradus seemed self-evident. That it had all occurred in a vastly different way than I'd expected bothered me. In my imagination, Gradus always approached from afar, visible from a distance, and I had time to think about what I was going to do. In reality, it had been quick, decisive, and without thought.

As I looked at the body, I began to cry. I began to weep, hunched over in my chair. But I wasn't grieving for Gradus. As if the bullets that had entered Gradus had instead taken the breath out of me, had expelled something from me, I was crying for my past life. I was weeping for everything I had thrown away to get to that point. In that moment, it had finally hit me how irrevocable my decisions had become, and how few decisions I had left before me. I would never again be Jeff VanderMeer. Not in any meaningful way.

Then, after a while, I dragged the body over to the freezer in the kitchen. I didn't remove the mask. I didn't want to see his face.

•

Erratum #7: "The Carving," Steve Rasnic Tem, issue three

Then following the flight of chips, white and red and trailing, over the railing's edge and down onto the rocks, she saw the fallen form, the exquisite work so carelessly tossed aside, the delicate shape spread and broken, their son.

She turned to the master carver, her mouth working at an uncontrolled sentence. And saw him with the hammer, the bloody chisel, the glistening hand slowly freed, dropping away from the ragged wrist.

This man, her husband, looked up, eyes dark knots in the rough bole of face. "I could not hold him," he gasped. "Wind or his own imagination. Once loose, I could not keep him here."

And then he looked away, back straining into the work of removing the tool that had failed him.

should read:

Then following the flight of chips, white and red and trailing, over the railing's edge and down onto the snow-strewn rocks of Burkhan Cape, she saw the fallen form, the exquisite work so carelessly tossed aside, the delicate shape that had sacrificed itself spread and broken.

She turned to the man, her mouth working at an uncontrolled sentence, words that must, in their order, be perfect or remain unreleased. And saw him with the hammer, the bloody chisel, the glistening hand slowly freed, dropping away from the ragged wrist.

The man looked up, eyes dark knots in a rough bark face. "I could not hold him," he gasped. "I could not keep him here. He wanted to be somewhere else. He needed to be somewhere else."

And then he looked away, back straining into the work of removing the tool that had freed him.

●

After I had disposed of the body, and made sure Gradus hadn't left a vehicle out front (he hadn't), I poured myself a glass of vodka and went up to my room on the second floor, leaving Juliette at the bottom of the stairs looking forlorn. I wanted to read James' other letter. I wanted to know why Gradus had come all this way to kill me. I wanted to have had a good reason not to let him kill me.

The second letter was also on that annoying onionskin paper, but it had no errors and appeared to have been typed by James himself.

Dear Jeff:

If you haven't yet seen Ed's Book, you will soon, and once you do, I know that any doubts will leave you. For that reason, this letter may be irrelevant. But I still had to write it, if for no other reason than to clarify where I stand in my own mind.

Let's be clear: You are coming in late to this whole scenario. From the very beginning, I planned *Argosy* to represent a major shift in the world, a way to change it irrevocably. Every page, every story, every interview, even every typo has been calculated to produce one certain result: transformation. And that transformation will become apparent upon the publication of your story "Errata." Your work is the final missing piece that will effectuate the Change.

I know you, like me, believe the world is in a terrible state right now, from the environment to political systems to hypocrisy to "sleepwalking on the tracks," as Thoreau put it. This has troubled me deeply since I was very young, and the feeling has only gotten worse as I have gotten older. I built a time machine when I was a kid just so I could try to go back in time and fix things from the moment they began to break. Of course, that didn't work. How could it? There would be so many things to fix. No one could do it all. Even if the machine worked.

But now, as an adult, and having talked to Ed and having experienced the Book, my life is committed to this change. For I believe that words *can* Change the world. I believe that after "Errata" is published, and as the right people in the right combinations read it, you will see a transformation of the world. Like in the old myth I left on your bed: A thaw will come and words will be spoken and heard that have been frozen for years, if not centuries. Like some sort of virus, the world will become a better place. Everything will begin to make sense. There will be some kind of balance again.

For this, I needed you. I needed a final refocus and correction to what had already been done. I needed someone outside of the system, someone who had given up hope, to undertake the final part of the project. For this, I also needed someone so torn out of their normal balance, their normal world, that they could kill if need be. Because I don't know when you will read this letter. Because *Argosy* may need a final sacrifice, like those made by the shamans of old. Perhaps my life is needed to bring this all to fruition. Maybe that's what it will take. And maybe not.

If it has, and you read this letter after, know that I forgive you, and that you are almost done. All you must do is finish the story and send it to my brother.

I'm telling you: There will be an epiphany. There will be a shift. You will feel it. You just have to wait for it and be patient. And, depending on your timing, either I will be there to experience it too, or I won't. I am at peace with either future.

Thank you for your time and your efforts.

Your friend,
James Owen

Ever since reading his letter, Jeremy, I've been sitting in a chair in the lobby, drinking steadily, becoming more and more numb. Because I'll be damned if I go to that freezer and remove the mask of the man I've killed. But mostly because, regardless of anything else he was, your brother was a nutcase. He was completely and utterly cracked in the head. And I was stupid enough to follow all of his insane directions and thus make it to this point, which once seemed like a plateau on the way up, but now feels like a slide into the deeper depths.

James Owen. Publisher. Author. Entrepreneur. It strikes me that I never really knew him – didn't know nearly enough about his childhood, his parents, his upbringing, his education, to trust him the way I did, to let him manipulate me this way.

But now that it's almost time, I must tell you that the most extraordinary calm has come over me. Why? Because I have only one hope left, even though it's a fool's hope. Tomorrow, I will hand this entire account over to the toothless Japanese man who – fleeing from horrible crimes of his own devising, no doubt – plays the role of postal worker in these parts. Whether he is competent enough to be trusted, I don't know. (Although he was reliable enough in handing over the money orders James sent me until about a week ago.)

Hopefully, you will receive and publish this Errata and thus fulfill James' vision. Hopefully, enough people will read it in the right combinations. And then, hopefully, the world will Change as he, in his twisted and yet idealistic way, believed it would.

In the meantime, I'll wait in this lobby, talking to Juliette. "James promised me," I will say to her. "James told me the world would Change if I wrote a short story."

"Who is James?" Juliette will reply. "Do I know him?"

"You may have even met him," I'll say.

Here's your story, James Owen. Now where's my epiphany?

God help me, some part of me still believes it could happen.

And if it doesn't, well, then, I'll just have to put these pearl-handled revolvers to good use, won't I?

THE GOAT VARIATIONS

*

It would have been hot, humid in September in that city, and the Secret Service would have gone in first, before him, to scan for hostile minds, even though it was just a middle school in a county he'd won in the elections, far away from the fighting. He would have emerged from the third black armored vehicle, blinking and looking bewildered as he got his bearings in the sudden sunlight. His aide and the personal bodyguards who had grown up protecting him would have surrounded him by his first step onto the asphalt of the driveway. They would have entered the school through the front, stopping under the sign for photos and a few words with the principal, the television cameras recording it all from a safe distance.

He would already be thinking past the event, to the next, and how to prop up sagging public approval ratings, due both to the conflict and what the press called his recent "indecision," which he knew was more analogous to "sickness." He would be thinking about, or around, the secret cavern beneath the Pentagon and the pale, almost grub-like face of the adept in his tank. He would already be thinking about the machine.

By the end of the photo op, the sweat itches on his forehead, burns sour in his mouth, but he has to ignore it for the cameras. He's turning a new word over and over in his mind, learned from a Czech diplomat. *Ossuary.* A word that sounds free and soaring, but just means a pile of skulls. The latest satellite photos from the battlefield states of Kansas, Nebraska, and Idaho make him think of the word. The evangelicals have been eschewing god-missiles for more personal methods of vengeance, even as they tie down federal armies in an endless guerilla war. Sometimes he feels like he's presiding over a pile of skulls.

The smile on his face has frozen into a rictus as he realizes there's something wrong with the sun; there's a red dot in its center, and it's eating away

JEFF VANDERMEER

at the yellow, bringing a hint of green with it. He can tell he's the only one who can see it, can sense the pulsing, nervous worry on the face of his aide.

He almost says "ossuary" aloud, but then, sunspots wandering across his eyes, they are bringing him down a corridor to the classroom where he will meet with the students and tell them a story. They walk past the open doors to the cafeteria – row on row of sagging wooden tables propped up by rusted metal legs. He experiences a flare of anger. Why *this* school, with the infrastructure crumbling away? The overpowering stale smell of macaroni-and-cheese and meatloaf makes him nauseous.

All the while, he engages in small talk with the entourage of teachers trailing in his wake, almost all overweight middle-aged women with circles under their eyes and sagging skin on their arms. Many of them are black. He smiles into their shiny, receptive faces and remembers the hired help in the mansion growing up. Some of his best friends were black until he took up politics.

For a second, as he looks down, marveling at their snouts and beaks and muzzles, their smiles melt away and he's surrounded by a pack of animals.

His aide mutters to him through clenched teeth, and two seconds later he realizes the words were "Stop staring at them so much." There have always been times when meeting too many people at once has made him feel as if he's somewhere strange, all the mannerisms and gesticulations and varying tones of voice shimmering into babble. But it's only lately that the features of people's faces have changed into a menagerie if he looks at them too long.

•

They'd briefed him on the secret rooms and the possibility of the machine even before they'd given him the latest intel on China's occupation of Japan and Taiwan. Only three hours into his presidency, an armored car had taken him to the Pentagon, away from his wife and the beginnings of the inauguration party. Once there, they'd entered a green-lit steel elevator that went down for so long he thought for a moment it was broken. It was just him, his aide, a black-ops commander who didn't give his name, and a small, haggard man who wore an old gray suit over a faded white dress shirt, with no tie. He'd told his vice president to meet the press while he was gone, even though he was now convinced the old man had dementia.

The elevators had opened to a rush of stale cool air, like being under a mountain, and, beneath the dark green glow of overhead lamps, he could see rows and rows of transparent, bathtub-shaped deprivation vats. In each floated one dreaming adept, skin wrinkled and robbed of color by the exposure to the chemicals that preserved and pacified them. Every shaven head was attached to wires and electrodes, every mouth attached to a breathing tube. Catheters took care of waste. The stale air soon faded as they walked silent down the rows, replaced by a smell like turpentine mixed with honeysuckle. Sometimes the hands of the adepts twitched, like cats hunting in their sleep.

A vast, slow, repeating sound registered in his awareness. Only after several minutes did he realize it was the sound of the adepts as they slowly moved in their vats, creating a slow ripple of water repeated in thousands of other vats. The room seemed to go on forever, into the far distance of a horizon tinged at its extremity by a darkening that hinted of blood.

His sense of disgust, revulsion grew as the little man ran out ahead of them, navigated a path to a control center, a hundred yards in and to the left, made from a luminous blue glass, set a story up and jutting out over the vats like some infernal crane. And still he did not know what to say. The atmosphere combined morgue, cathedral, and torture chamber. He felt a compulsion, if he spoke, to whisper.

The briefing papers he'd read on the ride over had told him just about everything. For years, adepts had been screened out at birth and, depending on the secret orders peculiar to each administration, either euthanized or imprisoned in remote overseas detention camps. Those that managed to escape detection until adulthood had no rights if caught, not even the rights given to illegal immigrants. The founding fathers had been very clear on that in the constitution.

He had always assumed that adults when caught were eliminated or sent to the camps. Radicals might call it the last reflexive act of a Puritanical brutality that reached across centuries, but most citizens despised the invasion of privacy an adept represented or were more worried about how the separatist evangelicals had turned the homeland into a nation of West and East Coasts, with no middle.

But now he knew where his predecessor had been storing the bodies. He just didn't yet know *why*.

In the control center, they showed him the images being mined from the depths of the adepts' REM sleep. They ranged from montages as incomprehensible as the experimental films he'd seen in college to single shots of dead people to grassy hills littered with wildflowers. Ecstasy, grief, madness, peace. Anything imaginable came through in the adepts' endless sleep.

"Only ten people in the world know every aspect of this project, and three of them are dead, Mr. President," the black-ops commander told him.

Down below, he could see the little man, blue-tinted, going from vat to vat, checking readings.

"We experimented until we found the right combination of drugs to augment their sight. One particular formula, culled from South American mushrooms mostly, worked best. Suddenly, we began to get more coherent and varied images. Very different from before."

He felt numb. He had no sympathy for the men and women curled up in the vats below him – an adept's grenade had killed his father in mid-campaign a decade before, launching his own reluctant career in politics – but, still, he felt numb.

"Are any of them dangerous?" he asked the black-ops commander.

"They're all dangerous, Mr. President. Every last one."

"When did this start?"

"With a secret order from your predecessor, Mr. President. Before, we just disappeared them or sent them to work camps in the Alaskas."

"Why did he do it?"

Even then, he would realize later, a strange music was growing in his head, a distant sound fast approaching.

"He did it, Mr. President, or said he did it, as a way of getting intel on the Heartland separatists."

Understandable, if idiosyncratic. The separatists and the fact that the federal armies had become bogged down in the Heartland fighting them were the main reasons his predecessor's party no longer controlled the executive, judicial, or legislative branches. And no one had ever succeeded in placing a mole within evangelical ranks.

The scenes continued to cascade over the monitors in a rapid-fire nonsense-rhythm.

"What do you do with the images?"

"They're sent to a full team of experts for interpretation, Mr. President. These experts are not told where the images come from."

"What do these adepts see that is so important?'

The black-ops commander grimaced at the tone of rebuke. "The future, Mr. President. Its early days, but we believe they see the future."

"And have you gained much in the way of intel?"

The black-ops commander looked at his feet. "No, not yet, we haven't. And we don't know why. The images are jumbled. Some might even be from our past or present. But we have managed to figure out one thing, which is why you've been brought here so quickly: something will happen later this year, in September."

"Something?"

Down below, the little man had stopped his purposeful wandering. He gazed, as if mesmerized, into one of the vats.

"Something cataclysmic, Mr. President. Across the channels. Across all of the adepts, it's quite clear. Every adept has a different version of what that something is. And we don't know *exactly* when, but in September."

He had a thousand more questions, but at that moment one of the military's top scientific researchers entered the control room to show them the schematics for the machine – the machine they'd found in the mind of one particular adept.

The time machine.

●

The teachers are telling him about the weather, and he's pretending to care as he tries to ignore the florescent lighting as yellow as the skin that forms on old butter, the cracks in the dull beige walls, the faded construction paper of old projects taped to those walls, drooping down toward a tired, washed-out green carpet that's paper-thin under foot.

It's the kind of event that he's never really understood the point of, even as he understands the reason for it. To prove that he's still fit for office. To prove that the country, some of it, is free of war and division. To prove he cares about kids, even though this particular school seems to be falling apart. Why this class, why today, is what he really doesn't understand, with so many world crises – China's imperialism, the Siberian separatist movement, Iraq as the only bulwark against Russian influence in the Middle East. Or a vice president he now knows may be too old and delusional to be anything other than an embarrassment, and a cabinet he let his family's political cronies bully him into appointing, and a secret cavern that has infected his thoughts, infected his mind.

And that would lead to memories of his father, and the awful silence into which they told him, as he sat coked up and hung-over that morning on the pastel couch in some sleazy apartment, how it had happened while his father worked a town hall meeting in Atlanta.

All of this has made him realize that there's only one way to succeed in this thing called the presidency: just let go of the reality of the world in favor of whatever reality he wants or needs, no matter how selfish.

The teachers are turning into animals again, and he can't seem to stop it from happening.

●

The time machine had appeared as an image on their monitors from an adept named "Peter" in vat 1023, and because they couldn't figure out the context – weapon? camera? something new? – they had to wake Peter up and have a conversation with him.

A time machine, he told them.

A time machine?

A time machine that travels through time, he'd clarified.

And they'd believed him, or if not believed him, dared to hope he was right. That what Peter had seen while deprived of anything but his own brain, like some deep-sea fish, like something constantly turning inwards and then turning inwards again, had been a time machine.

If they didn't build it and it turned out later that it might have worked and could have helped them avert or change what was fated to happen in September…

That day, three hours after being sworn in, he had had to give the order to build a time machine, and quickly.

"Something bad will happen in late summer. Something bad. Across the channels. Something awful."

"What?" he kept asking, and the answer was always the same: *We don't know.*

They kept telling him that the adepts didn't seem to convey literal information so much as impressions. and visions of the future, filtered through dreamscapes. As if the drugs they'd perfected, which had changed the way the adepts dreamed, both improved and destroyed focus, in different ways.

In the end, he had decided to build the machine – and defend against almost everything they could think of or divine from the images: any attack against the still-surviving New York financial district or the monument to the Queen Mother in the New York harbor; the random god-missiles of the Christian jihadists of the Heartland, who hadn't yet managed to unlock the nuclear codes in the occupied states; and even the lingering cesspool that was Los Angeles after the viruses and riots.

But they still did not really know.

●

He's good now at talking to people when it's not a prepared speech, good at letting his mind be elsewhere while he talks to a series of masks from behind his own mask. The prepared speeches are different because he's expected to *inhabit* them, and he's never fully inhabited anything, any role, in his life.

They round the corner and enter the classroom: thirty children in plastic one-piece desk-chairs, looking solemn, and the teacher standing in front of a beat-up battlewagon of a desk, overflowing with papers.

Behind her, posters they'd made for him, or someone had made to look like the children made them, most showing him with the crown on his head. But also a blackboard, which amazes him. So anachronistic, and he's always hated the sound of chalk on a blackboard. Hates the smell of glue and the sour food-sweat of unwashed kids. It's all so squalid and tired and oddly close to the atmosphere in the underground cavern, the smell the adepts give off as they thrash in slow-motion in their vats, silently screaming out images of catastrophe and oblivion.

The children look up at him when he enters the room like they're watching something far away and half-wondrous, half-monstrous.

He stands there and talks to them for a while first, trying to ignore the window in the back of the classroom that wants to show him a scene that shouldn't have been there. He says the kinds of things he's said to kids for years while on the campaign trail, running for ever-greater office. Has said these things for so many years that it's become a sawdust litany meant to convince them of his charm, his wit, his competence. Later, he won't remember what he said, or what they said back. It's not important.

But he's thought about the implications of that in bed at night, lying there while his wife reads, her pale, freckled shoulder like a wall above him. He could stand in a classroom and say nothing, and still they would be fascinated with him, like a talisman, like a golden statue. No one had ever told him that sometimes you don't have to inhabit the presidency; sometimes, it inhabits you.

He'd wondered at the time of coronation if he'd feel different. He'd wondered how the parliament members would receive him, given the split between the popular vote and the legislative vote. But nothing had happened. The parliament members had clapped, some longer than others, and he'd been sworn in, duly noting the absence of the rogue Scottish delegation. The Crown of the Americas had briefly touched his head, like an "iron kiss from the mouth of God," as his predecessor had put it, and then it was gone again, under glass, and he was back to being the secular president, not some sort of divine king.

Then they'd taken him to the Pentagon, hurtled him half a mile underground, and he'd felt like a man who wins a prize only to find out it's worthless. *Ossuary.* He'd expected clandestine spy programs, secret weapons, special powers. But he hadn't expected the faces in the vats or the machine.

●

Before they built the time machine, he had insisted on meeting "Peter" in an interrogation room near the vats. He felt strongly about this, about looking into the eyes of the man he had almost decided to trust.

"Are you sure this will work?" he asked Peter, even as he found the question irrelevant, ridiculous. No matter what Peter said, no matter how impossible his scientists said it was, how it subverted known science, he was going to do it. The curiosity was too strong.

Peter's eyes were bright with a kind of fever. His face was the palest white possible, and he stank of the chemicals. They'd put him in a blue jumper suit to cover his nakedness.

"It'll work. I pulled it out of another place. It was a true-sight. A true-seeing. I don't know how it works, but it works. It'll work, it'll work, and then," he turned toward the black one-way glass at the far end of the room, hands in restraints behind his back, "I'll be free?"

There was a thing in Peter's eyes he refused to acknowledge. A sense of something being held back, of something not quite right. Later, he would never know why he didn't trust that instinct, that perception, and the only reason he could come up with was the strength of his curiosity and the weight of his predecessor's effort to get to that point.

"What, exactly, is the machine for? Exactly. Not just...time travel. Tell me something more specific."

The scientist accompanying them smiled. He had a withered, narrow face, a firm chin, and wore a jumpsuit that matched Peter's, with a black belt at the waist that held the holster for an even blacker semi-automatic pistol. He smelled strongly of a sickly sweet cologne, as if hiding some essential putrefaction.

"Mr. President," he said, "Peter is not a scientist. And we cannot peer into his mind. We can only see the images his mind projects. Until we build it, we will not know exactly how it works."

And then, when the machine was built, and they took him to it, he didn't know what to make of it. He didn't think they did, either – they were gathered around it in their protective suits like apes trying to figure out an internal combustion engine.

"Don't look directly into it," the scientist beside him advised. "Those who have experience a kind of...disorientation."

Unlike the apes examining it, the two of them stood behind three feet of protective, blast-proof glass, and yet both of them had moved to the back of the viewing room – as far away from the artifact as possible.

The machine consisted of a square housing made of irregular-looking gray metal, caulked on the interior with what looked like rotted beef, and in the center of this assemblage: an eye of green light. In the middle of the eye, a piercing red dot. The machine was about the size of a microwave oven.

When he saw the eye, he shuddered, could not tell at first if it was organic or a metallic lens. The effect of the machine on his mind was of a thousand maggots inching their way across the top of a television set turned on but not receiving a station.

He couldn't stop looking, as if the scientist's warning had made it impossible not to stare. A crawling sensation spread across his scalp, his arms, his hands, his legs.

"How does it work?" he asked the scientist.

"We still don't know."

"Does the adept know?"

"Not really. He just told us not to look into it directly."

"Is it from the future?"

"That is the most logical guess."

To him, it didn't look real. It looked either like something from another planet or something a psychotic child would put together before turning to more violent pursuits.

"Where else could it be from?"

The scientist didn't reply, and anger began to override his fear. He continued to look directly into the eye, even as it made him feel sick.

"Well, what do you know?"

"That it shouldn't work. As we put the pieces together…we all thought… we all thought it was more like witchcraft than science. Forgive me, Mr. President."

He gave the scientist a look that the scientist couldn't meet. Had he meant the gravity of the insult? Had he meant to imply their efforts were as blasphemous as the adept's second sight?

"And now? What do you think now?"

"It's awake, alive. But we don't see how it's…"

"It's what?"

"Breathing, Mr. President. A machine shouldn't breathe."

"How does it take anyone into the future, do you think?'

The temperature in the room seemed to have gone up. He was sweating. The eye of the thing, impossibly alien, bored into him. Was it changing color?

"We think it doesn't physically send anyone into the future. That's the problem. We think it might somehow…create a localized phenomenon."

He sighed. "Just say what you mean."

The pulsing red dot. The shifting green. Looking at him. Looking into him.

"We think it might not allow physical travel, just mental travel."

In that instant, he saw adept Peter's pale face again and he felt a weakness in his stomach, and even though there was so much protection between him and the machine, he turned to the scientist and said, "Get me out of here."

Only, it was too late.

The sickness, the shifting, had started the next day, and he couldn't tell anyone about it, not even his wife, or they would have removed him from office. The constitution was quite clear about what do with "witches and warlocks."

•

At this point, his aide would hand him the book. They'd have gone through a dozen books before choosing that one. It is the only one with nothing in it anyone could object to; nothing in it of substance, nothing, his people thought, that the still-free press could use to damage him. There was just a goat in the book, a goat having adventures. It was written by a Constitutionalist, an outspoken supporter of coronation and expansion.

As he takes the book, he realizes, mildly surprised, that he has already become used to the smell of sweating children (he has none of his own) and the classroom grunge. (*Ossuary*. It sounded like a combination of "osprey" and "sanctuary.") The students who attend the school all experience it differently from him, their minds editing out the sensory perceptions he's still receiving. The mess. The depressed quality of the infrastructure. But what if you couldn't edit it out? And what if the stakes were much, much higher?

So then they would sit him down at a ridiculously small chair, almost as small as the ones used by the students, but somehow he would feel smaller in it despite that, as if he was back in college, surrounded by people both smarter and more dedicated than he was, as if he is posing and being told he's not as good: an imposter.

But it's still just a children's book, after all, and at least there's air conditioning kicking in, and the kids really seem to want him to read the book, as if they haven't heard it a thousand times before, and he feeds off the look in their eyes – *the President of North America and the Britains is telling us a story* – and so he begins to read.

He enjoys the storytelling. Nothing he does with the book can hurt him. Nothing about it has weight. Still, he has to keep the pale face of the adept out of his voice, and the Russian problem, and the Chinese problem, and the full extent of military operations in the Heartland. (There are cameras, after all.)

It's September 2001, and something terrible is going to happen, but for a moment he forgets that fact.

And that's when his aide interrupts his reading, comes up to him with a fake smile and serious eyes, and whispers in his ear.

Whispers in his ear and the sound is like a buzzing, and the buzzing is numinous and all-encompassing. The breath on his ear is a tiny curse, an infernal itch. There's a sudden rush of blood to his brain as he hears the words and his aide withdraws. He can hardly move, is seeing light where there shouldn't be light. The words drop heavy into his ear as if they have weight.

And he receives them and keeps receiving them, and he knows what they mean, eventually; he knows what they mean throughout his body.

The aide says, his voice flecked with relief, "Mr. President, our scientists have solved it. It's not time travel or far-sight. It's alternate universes. The adepts have been staring into alternate universes. What happens there in September may not happen here. That's why they've had such trouble with the intel. The machine isn't a time machine."

Except, as soon as the aide opens his mouth, the words become a trigger, a catalyst, and it's too late for him. A door is opening wider than ever before. The machine has already infected him.

There are variations. A long row of them, detonating in his mind, trying to destroy him. A strange, sad song is creeping up inside of him, and he can't stop that, either.

●

>>> He's sitting in the chair, wearing a black military uniform with medals on it. He's much fitter, the clothes tight to emphasize his muscle tone. But his face is contorted around the hole of a festering localized virus, charcoal and green and viscous. He doesn't wear an eye patch because he wants his people to see how he fights the disease. His left arm is made of metal. His tongue is not his own, colonized the way his nation has been colonized, waging a war against bio-research gone wrong, and the rebels who welcome it, who want to tear down anything remotely human, themselves no longer recognizable as human.

His aide comes up and whispers that the rebels have detonated a bio-mass bomb in New York City, which is now stewing in a broth of fungus and mutation: the nearly instantaneous transformation of an entire metropolis into something living but alien, the rate of change has become strange and accelerated in a world where this was always true, the age of industrialization slowing it, if only for a moment.

"There are no people left in New York City," his aide says. "What are your orders?"

He hadn't expected this, not so soon, and it takes him seven minutes to recover from the news of the death of millions. Seven minutes to turn to his aide and say, "Call in a nuclear strike."

•

>>> ...and his aide comes up to him and whispers in his ear, "It's time to go now. They've moved up another meeting. Wrap it up." Health insurance is on the agenda today, along with social security. Something will get done about that and the environment this year or he'll die trying...

•

>>> He's sitting in the chair reading the book and he's gaunt, eyes feverish, military personnel surrounding him. There's one camera with them, army TV, and the students are all in camouflage. The electricity flickers on and off. The school room has reinforced metal and concrete all around it. The event is propaganda being packaged and pumped out to those still watching in places where the enemy hasn't jammed the satellites. He's fighting a war against an escaped, human-created, rapidly reproducing intelligent species prototype that looks a little bit like a chimpanzee crossed with a Doberman. The scattered remnants of the hated adept underclass have made common cause with the animals, disrupting communications.

His aide whispers in his ear that Atlanta has fallen, with over sixty-thousand troops and civilians massacred in pitched battles all over the city. There's no safe air corridor back to the capital. In fact, the capital seems to be under attack as well.

"What should we do?"

He returns to reading the book. Nothing he can do in the next seven minutes will make any difference to the outcome. He knows what they have to do, but he's too tired to contemplate it just yet. They will have to head to the Heartland and make peace with the Ecstatics and their god-missiles. It's either that or render entire stretches of North America uninhabitable from nukes, and he's not that desperate yet.

He begins to review the ten commandments of the Ecstatics in his mind, one by one, like rosary beads.

•

>>> He's in mid-sentence when the aide hurries over and begins to whisper in his ear – just as the first of the god-missiles strikes and the fire washes over and through him, not even time to scream, and he's nothing anymore, not even a pile of ashes.

•

>>> He's in a chair, in a suit with a sweat-stained white shirt, and he's tired, his voice as he reads thin and raspy. Five days and nights of negotiations between the rival factions of the New Southern Confederacy following a month of genocide between blacks and whites from Arkansas to Georgia: too few resources, too many natural disasters, and no jobs, the whole system breaking down, although Los Angeles is still trying to pretend the world isn't coming to an end, even as jets are falling out the sky. Except, that's why he's in the classroom: *pretending*. Pretending neighbor hasn't set upon neighbor for thirty days, like in Rwanda except not with machetes, with guns. Teenagers shooting people in the stomach, and laughing. Extremist talk radio urging them on. Closing in on a million people dead.

His aide comes up and whispers in his ear: "The truce has fallen apart. They're killing each other again. And not just in the South. In the North, along political lines."

He sits there because he's run out of answers. He thinks: *In another time, another place, I would have made a great president.*

•

>>> He's sitting in the classroom, in the small chair, in comfortable clothes, reading the goat story. No god-missiles here, no viruses, no invasions. The Chinese and Russians are just on the cusp of being a threat, but not there yet. Adepts here have no real far-sight, or are not believed, and roam free. Los Angeles is a thriving money pit, not a husked-out shadow.

No, the real threat here, besides pollution, is that he's mentally ill, although no one around him seems to know it. A head full of worms, insecurity, and pure, naked *need*. He rules a country called the "United States" that waivers between the First and the Third World. Resources failing, infrastructure crumbling, political system fueled by greed and corruption.

When the aide comes up and whispers in his ear to tell him that terrorists have flown two planes into buildings in New York City, there's blood behind his eyes, as well as a deafening silence, and a sudden leap from people falling from the burning buildings to endless war in the Middle East, bodies broken by bullets and bombs. The future torques into secret trials, torture, rape, and hundreds of thousands of civilians dead, or displaced, a country bankrupted and defenseless, ruled ultimately by martial law and generals. Cities burn, the screams of the living are as loud as the screams of the dying.

He sits there for seven minutes because he really has no idea what to do.

•

...and *his* fate is to exist in a reality where towers do not explode in September, where Islamic fundamentalists are the least of his worries.

There is only one present, only one future now, and he's back in it, driving it. Seven minutes have elapsed, and there's a graveyard in his head. Seven minutes, and he's gradually aware that in that span he's read the goat story twice and then sat there for thirty seconds, silent.

Now he smiles, says a few reassuring words, just as his aide has decided to come up and rescue him from the yawning chasm. He's living in a place now where they'll never find him, those children, where there's a torrent of blood in his mind, and a sky dark with planes and helicopters, and men blown to bits by the roadside.

At that point, he would rise from his chair and his aide would clap, encouraging the students to clap, and they will, bewildered by this man about whom reporters will say later, "Doesn't seem quite all there."

An endless line of presidents rises from the chair with him, the weight almost too much. He can see each clearly in his head. He can see what they're doing, and who they're doing it to.

Saying his goodbyes is like learning how to walk again, while a nightmare plays out in the background. He knows as they lead him down the corridor that he'll have to learn to live with it, like and unlike a man learning to live with missing limbs – phantom limbs that do not belong, that he cannot control, but are always there, and he'll never be able to explain it to anyone. He'll be as alone and yet as crowded as a person can be. The wall between him and his wife will be more unbearable than ever.

He remembers Peter's pale, wrinkled, yearning face, and he thinks about making them release the man, put him on a plane somewhere beyond his country's influence. Thinks about destroying the machine and ending the adept project.

Then he's back in the wretched, glorious sunlight of a real, an ordinary day, and so are all of his reflections and shadows. Mimicking him, forever.

Three Days in a Border Town

*

You remember the way he moved across the bedroom in the mornings, with a slow, stumbling stride. His black hair ruffled and matted and sexy. The sharp line down the middle of his back, the muscles arching out from it. The taut curve of his ass. The musky smell of him that kissed the sheets. The stutter-step as he put on his pants, the look back at you to see if you'd noticed his clumsiness. The way he stared at you sometimes before he left for work.

•

Day One

When you come out of the desert into the border town, you feel like a wisp of smoke rising up into the cloudless sky. You're two eyes and a dry tongue. But you can't burn up; you've already passed through flame on your way to ash. Not all the blue in the sky could moisten you.

The border town, as many of them did, manifested itself to you at the end of a second week in the desert. It began as a trickle of silver light off imagined metal, a suggestion of a curved sheen. *A mirage has more substance.* You could have ignored it as false. You could have taken it for another of the desert's many tricks.

But *The Book of the City* corrected you, with an entry under "Other Towns":

> Often, you will find that these border towns, in unconscious echo
> of the City, are centered around a metal dome. This dome may be
> visible long before the rest of the town. These domes often prove to
> be the tops of ancient buildings long since buried beneath the sand.

Drifting closer, the blur of dome comes into focus. It is wide and high and damaged. It reflects the old building style, conforming to the realities of a lost religion, the metal of its workmanship predating the arrival of the desert.

Around the dome hunch the sand-and-rock-built houses and other structures of the typical border town. The buildings are nondescript, yellow-brown, rarely higher than three stories. Here and there, a solitary gaunt horse, some chickens, a rooting creature that resembles a pig. Above: the sea gulls that have no sea to return to.

Every border town has given you something: information, a wound, a talisman, a trinket. At one, you bought the blank book you now call *The Book of the City*. At another, you discovered much of what was written in that book. The third had taken a gout of flesh from your left thigh. The fourth had put a pulsing stone inside of your head. When the City is near, the stone throbs and you feel the ache of a pain too distant to be of use.

It has been a long time since you felt the pain. You're beginning to think your quest is hopeless.

About the City, your book tells you this:

> There is but one City in all the world. Ever it travels across the face of the Earth, both as promise and as curse. None of us shall but glimpse It from the corner of one eye during our lifetimes. None of us shall ever fully see the divine, in this life.
>
> It is said that border towns are ghosts of the City. If so, they are faint and tawdry ghosts, for those who have seen the City know that It has no Equal.

A preacher for a faith foreign to you quoted that from his own holy text, but you can't worship anything that has taken so much away from you.

•

He had green eyes and soft lips. He had calloused hands, a fiery red when he returned from work. His temper could be harsh and quick, but it never lasted. The moodiness in him he tried to keep from you. Most of the time he hid it well. The good humor, when he had it, he shared with you. It was a good life.

•

At the edge of town, you encounter the sentinel. He sits in his chair atop a tall tower, impassive and sand-worn, sun-soaked. An old man, wrinkled and white-bearded. You stand there and look up at him for a long time. Perhaps you recognize some part of yourself in him. Perhaps you trust him because of it.

The sentinel stares down at you, but you cannot tell if he recognizes you. There is about him an immutable quality, as if beneath the coursing red thirst of his flesh, the decaying arteries and veins, the heart that fights against its own inevitable stoppage, there is nothing but fissured stone. This quality comes out most vividly in the color of his eyes, which are like gray slate broken by flashes of the blue sky.

"Are you a ghost?" the sentinel asks you. A half smile.

You laugh, shading your eyes against the sun. "A ghost?" There'd be more moisture in a ghost, and more hope. "I'm a traveler. Just passing through. I'm looking for the City."

You catch a hint of *slippage* in the sentinel's impassive features, a hint of disappointment at such an ordinary quest. Half the people of the world seek the City.

"You may enter," the sentinel says, and suddenly his gaze has shifted back to the horizon, and narrowed and deepened, no doubt due to some ancient binocular technology affixed to his eyes.

The town lies open to you. What will you make of it?

•

Your father didn't like him, and your mother didn't care. "He's shallow," your father said to you. "He's not good enough for you." You knew this was not true. He kept his own counsel. He got nervous in large groups. He didn't like small talk. These were all things that made him seem unapproachable at first. But, over time, they both grew to love him almost as much as you loved him.

Everyone eventually wanted to like him, even when he was unlikeable. There was something about him – a presence that had nothing to do with words or mannerisms or the body. It followed him everywhere. Sometimes now, you think it must have been the presence of the City, the distant breath and heat of it.

•

Are you a ghost? The sentinel's question circles in your mind. As you reach the outskirts of the border town, the sand somehow finer and looser, you stop for a second, hands on your hips, like a runner who has reached the end of a race. Your solitude of two weeks has been broken. It is as if you have breached an invisible bubble. It's as if you had lunged through a portal into a different place. The desert is done with.

If not a ghost, then perhaps a pariah? As you walk farther into the town, no one acknowledges you. These are short, dark-skinned people who wear brown or gray robes, some with a bracelet or necklace that reveals a sudden splash of color, some without. Their eyes are large and either brown or black. Small noses and thin lips or wide noses and thick lips. Some of them have skin so black it almost looks blue. They speak to each other in the border town patois that has become the norm, but you catch a hint of other languages as well. A smell of spice encircles them. It prickles your nostrils, but not in the same way as a hint of lime. Lime would indicate the presence of the City.

For a moment, you think that perhaps your solitude has entered the town with you. That somehow you really have become a wisp of smoke. You are invisible and impervious, as unnoticeable as a speck of dust. You walk the streets watching others ignore you.

Soon, a procession dawdles down the street, slower then faster, to the beat of metal drums. You stand to one side as it approaches. Twenty men and women, some with drums, some shouting, and in the middle four men holding a box that can only be a coffin. The coffin is as plain as the buildings in this place. The procession travels past you. Passersby do not acknowledge it. They keep walking. You cannot help feeling the oddness of this place. To ignore a stranger is one thing. To ignore twenty men and women banging on drums while shouting is another. Even the sea gulls rise at its approach, the chickens scattering to the side.

When the procession is thirty feet past you, an odd thing happens. The

coffin opens and a man jumps out. He's naked, penis dangling like a shriv-
eled pendulum, face painted white. He has a gray beard and wrinkled skin.
He shouts once, then runs down the street, soon out of sight.

As he does so, the passersby stop and clap. Then they continue walking.
The members of the procession recede into the side alleys. The empty coffin
remains in the middle of the street.

What does it mean? Is it something you need to write down in your book?
You ponder that for a moment, but then decide this is not about the City.
There is nothing about what you saw that involves the City.

Then dogs begin to gather at the coffin. This startles you. When they bark,
you are alarmed. In *The Book of the City* it is written:

> Dogs will not be fooled. They will not live silent in the presence of
> the City – they will bark, they will whine, they will be ill-at-ease.
> And the closer the City approaches, the more these symptoms will
> manifest themselves.

Was a piece of the City nearby? An inkling of it? Your heart beats faster.
Not the source, but a tributary. Otherwise, your head would be aching,
trying to break apart.

But no: as they nose the coffin lid open, you see the red moistness of
meat. There is raw meat inside the coffin for some reason. The dogs feast.
You move on.

Above you, the silver dome seems even more enigmatic than before.

•

His name was Delorn. You were married in the summer, under the heat of
the scorching sun, in front of your friends and family. You lived in a town
centered around an oasis. For this, your people needed a small army, to
protect it against those marauders who might want to take it for themselves.
You served in that army, while Delorn worked as a farmer, helping pick dates,
plant vegetable seeds, and maintain the irrigation ditches.

You were in surveillance and sharp-shooting. You could handle a gun as
well as anyone in the town. After a time, they put you in charge of a small
band of other sharp shooters. No one ever came to steal the land because

the town was too well-prepared. Near the waterhole, your people had long ago found a stockpile of old weapons. Most of them worked. These weapons served as a deterrent.

Delorn and you had your own small home – three rooms that were part of his parents' compound, at the edge of town. From your window, you could see the watchfires at night, from the perimeter. Some nights, you watched your house from that perimeter. On those nights, the air seemed especially cold as the desert receded further from the heat of the day.

When you came home, you would crawl into bed next to Delorn and bring yourself close to his body heat. He always ran hot; you could always use him as a hedge against the cold.

•

So you float like a ghost again. You let your footfalls be the barometer of your progress, and release the idea of solitude or no solitude.

As night approaches, you become convinced for a moment that the town is a mirage, and all the people in it. If so, you still have water in your backpack. You can make it another few days without a border town. But can you make it without company? The thirst for contact. The desiccation of only hearing your own voice.

Someone catches your eye – a messenger or courier, perhaps – weaving his way among the others like a sinuous snake, clearly with a destination in mind. The movement is unique for a place so calm, so measured.

You stand in front of him, force him to stop or run into you. He stops. You regard each other for a moment.

He is all tufts of black hair and dark skin and startling blue eyes. A pretty chin. A firm mouth. He could be thirty or forty-five. It's hard to tell. What did he think of you?

"You come out of the desert," he says in his patois, which you can just understand. "The sentinel told us. But he also said he thought you might be a ghost. You're not a ghost."

How had the sentinel told them already? But it doesn't matter…

"Could a ghost do this?" you say, and pinch his cheek. You smile to reassure him.

People are staring.

He rubs his cheek. His hands are much paler than his face.

"Maybe," he says. "Ghosts from the desert can do many things."

You laugh. "Maybe you're right. Maybe I'm a ghost. But I'm a ghost who needs a room for the night. Where can I find one?"

He stares at you, appraises you. It's been a long time since anyone looked at you so intensely. You fight the urge to turn away.

Finally, he points down the street. "Walk that way two blocks. Turn left across from the bakery. Walk two more blocks. The tavern on the right has a room."

"Thank you," you say, and you touch his arm. You can't say why you do it, or why you ask him, "What do you know of the City?"

"The City?" he echoes. A wry, haunted smile. "The ghost of it passes by us sometimes, in the night." His eyes become wider, but you don't think the thought frightens him. "Its ghost is so large it blocks the sky. It makes a sound. A sound no one can describe. Like…like sudden rain. Like…" As he searches for words, he is looking at the sky, as if imagining the City floating there, in front of him. "Like distant drum beats. Like weeping."

You're still holding his arm. Your grip is very tight, but he doesn't notice.

"Thank you," you say, and release him.

As soon as you release him, it's as if the border town becomes real to you. The sounds of shoes on the street or pavement. The trickling tease of whispered conversations, loud and broad. It is a kind of illusion, of course: the border town comes alive at dusk, after the heat has left the air and before the cold creeps in.

What did *The Book* say about border towns?

> Every border town is the same; in observing unspoken fealty to the
> City, it dare not replicate the City too closely. By necessity, every
> border town replicates its brothers and sisters. In speech. In habits.
> If every border town is most alive at dusk, then we may surmise that
> the City is most alive at dawn.

You find the tavern, pay for a room from the surly owner, climb to the second floor, open the rickety wooden door, hurl your pack into a corner, and collapse on the bed with a sense of real relief. A bed, after so long in the desert, seems a ridiculous luxury, but also necessity.

You lie there with your arms outstretched and stare at the ceiling.

What more do you know now? That the dogs in this place are uneasy. That a messenger-courier believes the ghost of the City haunts this border town. You have heard such rumors elsewhere, but never delivered with such conviction, hinting at such frequency. What does it mean?

What do you want it to mean?

●

Despite the bed, you don't sleep well that night. You never do in enclosed spaces now, even though the desert harshness has expended your patience with open spaces, too. You keep seeing a ghost city superimposed over the border town. You see yourself flying through like a ghost, approaching ever closer to the phantom City, but becoming more and more corporeal, until by the time you reach its walls, you move right through them.

In your book, you have written down a joke that is not really a joke. A man in a bar told it to you right before he tried to grope you. It's the last thing you remember as you finally drift away.

> Two men are fighting in the dust, in the sand, in the shadow of a mountain. One says the City exists. The other denies this truth. Neither has ever been there. They fight until they both die of exhaustion and thirst. Their bodies decay. Their bones reveal themselves. These bones fall in on each other. One day, the City rises over them like a new sun. But it is too late.

You loved Delorn. You loved his sly wit in the taverns, playing darts, joking with his friends. You loved the rough grace of his body. You loved the line of his jaw. You loved his hands on your breasts, between your legs. You loved the way he rubbed your back when you were sore from sentinel duty. You loved that he fought his impatience and his anger when he was with you, tried to turn them into something else. You loved him.

●

Day Two

On your second day in the border town, you wake from dreams of a name-less man to the sound of trumpets. Trumpets and...accordions? You sit up in bed. Your mouth feels sour. Your back is sore again. You're ravenous. Trumpets! The thought of any musical instrument in this place more opti-mistic than a drum astounds you.

You quickly get dressed and walk out to the main street in time to watch yet another funeral procession for a man not yet dead.

The sides of the streets are crowded and noisy – where have all these people come from? – and they are no longer drab and dull. Now they wear clothing in bright greens, reds, and blues. Some of them clap. Some of them whistle. Others stomp their feet. From the edge of the crowd it is hard to see, so you push through to the front. A man claps you on the back, another nudges you. A woman actually hugs you. Are you, then, suddenly accepted?

When you reach the curbside, you encounter yet another odd funeral pro-cession. Six men dressed in black robes carry the coffin slowly down the street. In front and back come jugglers and a few horses, decorated with thin colored paper – streamers of pale purple, green, yellow. There is a scent like oranges.

To the sides stand children with boxy holographic devices in their hands. They are using these toys to generate the images of clowns, fire eaters, danc-ing bears, bearded ladies, and the like. Because the devices are very old, the holograms are patchy, ethereal, practically worn away at the edges. The old-est holograms, of an m'kat and a fleshdog, are the most grainy and yet still send a shiver up your spine. Harbingers from the past. Ghosts with the very real ability to inflict harm.

But the most remarkable thing is that the man in the coffin is, again, not dead! He has been tied into the coffin this time, but is thrashing around. He looks foreign, with a cast to his skin that's neither dark nor light.

"Put it back in my brain!" he screams, over and over again. "Put it back in my brain! Please. I'm begging you. Put it back!" His eyes are wide and moist, his scalp covered in a film of blood that looks like red sweat.

You stand there, stunned, and watch as the procession lurches by. Some-times someone in the crowd will run out to the coffin, leap up, and hit the man in the head, after which he falls silent for a minute or two before resum-ing his agonized plea.

You watch the dogs. They growl at the man in the coffin. When the coffin is past you, you stare at the back of the man's neck as he tries to rise once again from "death." The large red circle you see there makes you forget to breathe for a moment.

You turn to the person on your left, a middle-aged man as thin as almost everyone else in town.

"What will happen to him?" you ask, hoping he will understand you.

The man leers at you. "Ghost, they will kill him and bury him out in the desert where he won't be found."

"What did he do?" you ask.

The man just stares at you for a moment, as if speaking to a child or an idiot, and then says, "He came from the outside – with a *familiar*."

Your body turns cold. A familiar. The taste of lime. The sudden chance. Perhaps this town does have something to add to the book. You have never seen a familiar, but an old woman gave you something her father had once written about familiars. You added it to the book:

> The tube of flesh is quite prophetic. The tube of flesh, the umbilical, is inserted at the base of the neck, although sometimes inserted by mistake toward the top of the head, which can result in unexpected visions. The umbilical feeds into the central nervous system. The nerves of the familiar's umbilical wind around the nerves in the person's neck. Above the recipient, the manta ray, the familiar, rises and grows full with the knowledge of the host. It makes itself larger. It elongates. The subject goes into shock, convulses, and becomes limp. Motor control passes over to the familiar, creating a moving yet utilitarian symbiosis. The neck becomes numb. A tingling forms on the tongue, and taste of lime. There is no release from this. There should be no release from this. Broken out from their slumber, hundreds are initiated at a time, the tubes glistening and churling in the elision of the steam, the continual need. Thus fitted, all go forth in their splendid ranks. The eye of the City opens and continues to open, wider and wider, until the eye is the world.

So it says in *The Book of the City*, the elusive City, the City that is forever moving across the desert, powered by...what? The sun? The moon? The stars? The sand? What? Sometimes you despair at how thoroughly the City has eluded you.

•

You stand in the crowd for a long time. You let the crowd hide you, although what are you hiding from? A hurt and a longing rise in your throat. Why should that be? It's not connected to the man who will be dead soon. No, not him – another man altogether. For a long, suffocating moment you seem so far away from your goal, from what you seek, that you want to scream as the man screamed: *Give me back the familiar!*

In this filthy, run-down backwater border town with its flaking enigmatic dome, where people believe in the ghost of the City and kill men for having familiars – aren't you as far from the City as you have ever been? And still, as you turn and survey your fate, does it matter? Would it have been any different walking through the desert for another week? Would you have been happier out in the Nothing, in the Nowhere, without human voices to remind you of what human voices sound like?

Once, maybe six months before, you can't remember, a man said to you: "In the desert there are many other people. You walk by them all the time. Most all of them are dead, their flesh flapping off of them like little flags." A bitterness creeps into the back of your throat.

You look up at the blue sky – that mockery of a sky that, cloudless, could never give anyone what they really needed.

•

"We should harvest the sky," Delorn said to you once. You remember because the day was so cool for once. Even the sand and the dull buildings of your town looked beautiful in the light that danced its way from the sun. "We should harvest the sky," he said again, as you sat together outside of your house, drinking date wine. It was near the end of another long day. You'd had guard duty since dawn and Delorn had been picking the last of the summer squash. "We should take the blue right out of the sky and turn it into water. I'm sure they had ways to do that in the old days."

You laughed. "You need more than blue for that. You need water."

"Water's overrated. Just give me the blue. Bring the blue down here, and put the sand up there. At least it would be a change."

He was smiling as he said it. It was nonsense, but a comforting kind of nonsense.

He had half-turned from you as he said this, looking out at something across the desert. His face was in half-shadow. You could see only the outline of his features.

"What are you looking at?" you asked him.

"Sometimes," he said, "sometimes I think I can see something, just on the edge, just at the lip of the horizon. A gleam. A hint of movement. A kind of...presence."

Delorn turned to you then, laughed. "It's probably just my eyes. My eyes are betraying me. They're used to summer squash and date trees and you."

"Ha!" you said, and punched him lightly on the shoulder. The warmth you felt then was not from the sun.

•

The rest of the day you spend searching for the familiar. It might already be dead, but even dead, it could tell you things. It could speak to you. Besides, you have never seen one. To see something is to begin to understand it. To read about something is not the same.

You try the tavern owner first, but he, with a fine grasp of how information can be dangerous, refuses to speak to you. As you leave, he mutters, "Smile. Smile sometimes."

You go back to the street where you found the courier. He isn't there. You leave. You come back. You have nothing else to do, nowhere else to go. You still have enough money left from looting desert corpses to buy supplies, to stay at the tavern for a while if you need to. But there's nothing like rifling through the pockets of dead bodies to appreciate the value of money.

Besides, what is there to squander money on these days? Even the Great Sea rumored to exist so far to the west that it is east is little more than a lake, the rivulets that tiredly trickle down into it long since bereft of fish. It's all old, exhausted, with only the City as a rumor of better.

You come back to the same street again and again. Eventually, near dusk, you see the courier. You plant yourself in front of him again. You show him your money. He has no choice but to stop.

"There is something you did not tell me yesterday," you say.

The courier grins. He is older than you thought – now you can see the wrinkles on his face, at the sides of his eyes.

"There are many things I will not tell a ghost," he says. "And because you did not ask."

"What if I were to ask you about a familiar?"

The grin slips. He probably would have run away by now if you hadn't shown him your money.

"It's dangerous."

"I'm sure. But for me, not for you."

"For me, too."

"It's dangerous for you to be seen talking to me at all, considering," you say. "It's too late now – shouldn't you at least get paid for the risk?"

Some border towns worship the City because they fear it. Some border towns fear the City but do not worship it. You cannot read this border town. Perhaps it will be your turn for the coffin ride tomorrow.

The courier says, "Come back here tomorrow morning. I might have something for you."

"Do you want money now?"

"No. I don't want to be seen taking money from you."

"Then I'll leave it in my room, 2E, at the tavern, and leave the door unlocked when I come to meet you."

He nods.

You pull aside your robe so he can see the gun in your holster.

"It doesn't use bullets," you say. "It uses something much worse."

The man blanches, melts into the crowd.

●

He wanted a child. You didn't. You didn't want a child because of your job and your duty.

"You just want a child because you're so used to growing things," you said, teasing him. "You just want to grow something inside of me."

He laughed, but he wasn't happy.

•

That night, you still can't sleep. Your head aches. It's such a faint ache that you can't tell if it's from the stone in your head. This time the sense of claustrophobia and danger is so great that you get dressed and walk through the empty streets until you have reached the desert. Standing there, between the town and the open spaces, it reminds you of your home.

There's a certain relief, the sweat drying on your skin although there is no wind. You welcome the chill. And the smell of sand, almost like a spice. Your headache is worse, but your surroundings are better.

You walk for a fair distance – this is what you've become most used to: walking – and then turn and look back toward the town. There is a half-moon in the sky, and so many stars you can't count them. Looking at the lights in the sky, the sporadic dotting of light from the town, you think, with a hint of sadness, that the old stories, even those told by a holographic ghost, must be wrong. *If humans had made it to the stars we would not have come to this. If we had gone there, our collapse could not have been so complete.*

You fell asleep, then, or so you believe. Perhaps your headache made you pass out. When you wake, it is still night, but your head pounds, and the stars are *moving*. At least, that is your first thought: *The stars are moving.* Then you realize there are too many lights. Then, with a sharp intake of breath, you know that you are looking at the ghost of the City.

For you have seen the City before, if only once and not for long, and you know it like you know your home. This sudden apparition that slides between you and the stars, that seems to envelop the border town, looks both like and unlike the City.

There were underground caverns near where you grew up. These caves led to an underground aquifer. In those caves, you and your friends would sometimes find phosphorescent jellyfish in the saltish water. By their light you would find and catch fish. They were like miniature lighted domes, their bodies translucent, so that you could see every detail of their organs, the lines of their boneless bodies.

This "City" you now see is much like that. You can see *into* and *through* it. You can examine every detail. Like a phantom. Like a wraith. Familiars and people transparent, gardens and walls, in so much detail it overwhelms you. The City-ghost rises over the border town ponderously but makes no sound. The edges of this vision, the edges of the City crackle and spark, discharging energy. You can smell the overpowering scent of lime. You can taste it on your mouth, and your skull is filled with a hundred hammers as your headache spins out of control. You think you are screaming. You think you are throwing up.

The City sways back and forth, covering the same ground.

You start to run. You are running back toward the border town, toward this Apparition. And then, just as suddenly as it appeared, the City puts on speed – a great rush and flex of speed – and it either disappears into the distance or it disintegrates or…you cannot imagine what it might or might not have done.

●

Sometimes you argued because he was sick of being a farmer, because he was restless, because you were both human.

"I could do what you do," he said once. "I could join your team."

"No, you couldn't," you said. "You don't have the right kind of discipline."

He looked hurt.

"Just like I don't have the skills to do what you do," you said.

They seemed like little arguments at the time. They seemed like nothing.

●

When you reach the outskirts of the border town, you find no great commotion in the streets. The streets are still empty. You spy a stray cat skulking around a corner. A nighthawk worshipping a lamp post.

You approach the sentinel's chair. He peers down at you from the raised platform. It's the same sentinel from the other day.

"Did you see it?" you ask him.

"See what?" he replies.

"The City! The phantom City."

"Yes. As usual. Every two weeks, at the same time."

"What do you see? From inside the town."

He frowns. "See? A hologram, invading the streets. Just an old ghost. A molted skin – like the snakes out in the desert."

Your curiosity is aroused. You hardly know this man, but something about his dismissal of such a marvelous sight bothers you.

"Why aren't you excited?" you ask him.

A sad smile. "Should I be? It means nothing." He stands on his platform, looking down. "It doesn't bring me any closer to the City."

In his gaze, you see a hurt and a yearning that you recognize. You mistook his look when you first met him. He wasn't disappointed in you, but in himself. Maybe all reasons are the same when examined closely.

•

You walk home through a border town so empty it might as well be a mirage itself. No one to document the coming of the wraith-City. How had it manifested? Had, for an instant, the dome of the border town and the dome of the City been superimposed as one?

When people begin to ignore a miracle, does that mean it is no longer miraculous?

•

A man stands in your room. You draw your gun. It's the courier. He has a sad look on his face. Startled, you draw back, but he puts out a hand in a gesture of reassurance, and you're so tired you choose to believe it.

"It is not what you think," he says. "It's not what you think."

"What is it then?"

"I need a place. I need a place."

In his look you see a hundred reasons and explanations. But you don't need any of them. This is a man you will never know, that you will never come to know. It doesn't matter what his reasons are. Lonely, tired, lost. It's all the same.

"What's your name?" you ask.

"Benkaad," he tells you.

He sleeps on the bed with you, facing away from you. His skin is so dark, glinting black in the dim light from the street. His breathing is rapid and short. After a time, you put your arm around his chest. Sometime during the night, you reverse positions and he is curled at your back, his arm around your stomach.

"There is a scar on the back of your head."

"Yes. That's where the doctor put the stone inside of me."

"The stone?"

"The stone that pines for the City."

"I see."

He begins to rub your head.

It is innocent. It is different. It's not like before.

●

Once, you had to shoot someone – a scavenger, a rogue, a man who would have killed someone in your community. He'd gone bad in the head. It was clear from his ranting. He had a gun. He came out of the desert like a curse or a blight. Had he been crazy before he went into the desert? You'll never know. But he came toward the guard post, aiming his gun at you, and you had to shoot him. Because you let him get too close before you shot him – you shouting at him to drop his weapon – you had to shoot to kill.

The man lay there, covered in sand and blood, arms crumpled underneath him. You stood there for several minutes as your team ran up to you. You stood there and looked out at the desert, wondering what else might come out of it.

They told Delorn, and he came to take you home, you dazed, staring but not seeing. Once inside, Delorn took off all of your clothes. He placed you in the bathtub. He used precious water to calm you, massaging your skin. He rubbed your head. He cleaned the salt and sweat from your body. He toweled you dry. And then he laid you down on the bed and he made love to you.

You had been far away, watching the dead man in the sand. But Delorn's tongue on your skin brought you back to yourself. When you came, it was in a rush, like the water in the bath, as you reconnected with your body.

You remember looking at him as if he were unreal. He was selfless in that moment. He was a part of you.

●

Day Three

In the morning, Benkaad is gone, leaving just the imprint of his body on your bed. The money you'd promised him has been taken from what you'd left in your bag. You try to remember why you let him sleep next to you, but the thought behind the impulse has fled.

Out into the sun, past the tavern keeper, cursing at someone. The day is hot, almost oppressive. You can walk the desert for two weeks without faltering, but after two days of a bed, you've already lost some of your toughness. The sun finds you. It makes you uncomfortable.

Benkaad waits for you on the street. As soon as he sees you, he drops a piece of paper and walks away. His gaze lingers on you before he's lost around a corner, as if to remember you, for a time at least.

You pick up the paper. Unfold it. It has a map on it, showing you where to find the familiar. A contact name and a password. Is it a trap? Perhaps, but you don't care. You have no choice.

That morning, you had woken refreshed, for the first time in over a year, and somehow that makes you feel guilty as you follow the map's instructions – through a warren of streets you wouldn't have believed could exist in so small a town. You forget each one as soon as you leave it.

As you walk, a sense of calm settles over you. You're calm because everything you face is inevitable. *You have no choice.* This is the missing piece of *The Book.* This replaces *The Book.* You're afraid, yes, but also past caring. Sometimes there's only one chance.

●

Finally, a half hour later, you're there. You knock on a metal door in a run-down section of town. The directions had been needlessly complex, unless Benkaad meant to delay you.

You've got one hand on your gun as the door opens. An old woman stands there. You give her the password. She opens the door a little wider and you slip inside.

"Do you have the money?" she asks.

"Money? I paid the one who led me here."

"You need more money to see it and connect to it."

Suddenly, the surge of adrenalin. It *is* here. A familiar.

Two men appear behind the woman. Both are armed with bullet-fed guns. Ancient. They've the look of hired guns, their tans deep, leathery.

You walk past them to the room that holds the familiar.

"Only half an hour," the one man says. "It's dying. Any more and it'll be too much for you, and for it."

You stare past him. Someone is just finishing up with the familiar. He has detached from its umbilical, but there is still a look of stupefied wonder on his face.

The umbilical is capped by an odd cylindrical device.

"What's that?" you ask the old woman.

"The filter. You don't want that thing all the way into your mind. You'd never get free."

"Strip," one of the men says.

"Strip? Why?"

"Just strip. We need to search you," the man says, and raises his gun. The old woman looks away. The other man has a hunger in his eyes you've seen too many times before.

There's no other way out. You shoot the two men, the old woman, and the customer. None of them seem to expect it. They fall with the same startled look of surprise.

You don't know if they'll wake up. You don't care. It surprises you that you don't care.

Your head is throbbing.

You enter the room.

●

There, in front of you, lies the familiar, its wings fluttering on the bed. It seems to both press down into the bed and try to float above it. Its wings are ragged. Instead of being black, it is dead white. It looks as if it were drifting, wherever the air might take it.

You take the umbilical and bring it around to the back of your head. The umbilical slides through the filter. You feel a weak pressure, a probing presence, then a firm, more assured grasp, a prickling – then a wet piercing. The taste of lime enters your mouth. A scratchiness at the back of your throat. You gasp, take two deep breaths, and then you hear a voice inside your head.

You are different.

"Maybe," you say. "Maybe I'm the same."

I don't think you are the same. I think you are different. I think that you know why.

"Because I've actually seen the City."

No. Because of why you want to find it.

"Can you take me there?"

Do you know what you are asking?

"I attached myself to you."

True. But there is a filter weakening our connection.

"True. But that might change."

You don't know how I came to be here, do you?

"No."

I was cast out. I was defective. You see my color. You see my wings. I was created this way. I was meant to die in the desert. I let a man I found attach himself so that would not happen. Eventually, it killed him.

"I'm stronger than that."

Maybe. Maybe not.

"Do you know your way back to the City?"

In a way. I can feel the City. I can feel it sometimes, out there, moving...

"I have a piece of the City in my head."

I know. I can sense it. But it may not help. And how do you plan to leave this place? Do you know that even with the filter, in a short time, it will be too late to unhook yourself from me. Is that what you want? Do you want true symbiosis?

Is it what you want? You don't know. It seems a form of madness, to want this, to reach for it, but there is a passage in *The Book of the City* that reads:

> Take whatever the City gives you. If it gives you a cane, take it and use it. If it gives you dust, take the dust and make a house of it. If it gives you wisdom, take wisdom. The City does not give gifts lightly. It is not that kind of City.

You're crying now. You've been strong for so long you've forgotten the relief of being weak. What if it's the wrong choice? What if you never get him back even after all of this?

Are you sure? the familiar says inside your mind. It is different than connecting for a short while. It is a surrender of self.

You wipe the tears from your face. You remember the smell of Delorn, the feel of his body, his laugh. The smell of lime is crushing.

"Yes," *I'm sure,* you say, and you find that it is true, even as you disconnect the filter, even as you begin to feel the tendrils of unfamiliar thoughts intertwining with your own thoughts.

You have chosen.

•

The most secret part of *The Book of the City*, which you have never reread, is hidden on the back pages. It reads:

> I lived in a town called Haart, where I served as a border guard and my husband Delorn worked as a farmer at the oasis that sustained our people. We loved each other. I still love him. One night, he was taken from me, and that is why I keep this book. One night, I woke and he was not beside me. At first, I thought he had gotten up for a glass of water or to use the bathroom. But I soon discovered he was not in the house. I searched every room. Then I saw the light, through the kitchen window, saw the light, flooding the darkness, and heard the quiet breath of the City. I ran outside. There it lay, in all its glory, just to the west. And there were the imprints of my husband's boots, illumined by the City – heading toward it. The City was spinning and hovering and gliding back and forth across the desert. Then it was gone.
>
> In the morning, we followed my husband's tracks out into the desert. At a certain point, they stopped. The boot prints were gone. Delorn was gone. The City was gone. It was just me, screaming and shrieking, and the last set of tracks, and the friends who had come out with me.
>
> And every day since I have had a question buried in my head: *Did he choose the City over me? Did he go because he wanted to, or because it called to him and he had no choice?*

•

At dusk, you escape, the familiar wrapped around your body, under the robes you've stolen from a dead man. Your collar is high to disguise the place where it entered you and you entered it. Out into the desert, where, when the border town is far distant, you can release him from beneath your robes and he, unfurling, can rise above you, your familiar, crippled wings beating, and together you can seek out the City.

It is a cool night, and a long night, and you will be miles away by dawn.

The Secret Life of Shane Hamill

✳

Here is everything that I know about the strange events that happened in and around the area of our bookstore, starting eighteen months ago. This is also everything I know about Shane Hamill. We never liked him. I want that on the record, first and foremost. We never liked him, and I'm fairly sure he never liked us. There may have been some good reasons for this situation, and some bad reasons, too, but I doubt any of it is important now.

Shane once made out with a girl in a graveyard. I don't know if he met the girl there or if they came there together. I mention it because Shane told us about it so often, or referred to it. For my part, I found this fact kind of creepy, not cool. Others, more attuned to the Goth scene, I believe made Shane into a sort of hero over it, behind his back. Although, as I've stated, we didn't like him. He was a good worker, and some even said he was a good supervisor, I'll admit that – but no better than the rest of us. We're all good workers.

Sometimes, even early on in his employment with our bookstore, Shane had a far-off stare, which was strictly against bookstore policy. I cannot stress that enough: Shane often said or did things that were against corporate policy. Not explicitly against policy – not the formal policies – but still things no one else said or did.

For example, once, during a slow day, we were both standing around the cash register, Shane staring out the window, when he said to me, "I'll bet it's not snowing in Sarajevo." Now, the weirdest thing about what he said is that it wasn't snowing here. So I don't know *why* he would say that. It didn't make sense. Besides, who's to say it *wasn't* snowing in Sarajevo at that moment? It might very well have been snowing in Sarajevo. There might have been a blizzard for all Shane knew. That bothered me for a long time, to tell the truth.

Another time, Shane actually paid for a book for a customer, and it wasn't even because he liked her, if you know what I mean. He felt sorry for her!

Which also doesn't make sense. When someone can't afford groceries, that's a tragedy. When they can't afford a book, that's just a shame. Maybe she told him it wasn't snowing in Sarajevo. I have no idea.

But all of this happened before the boat, and it was manageable, these little things he did that made him unlike the rest of us. (Although I think it's all relevant. Even the kiss in the graveyard, which I may get back to later in this report; I was given no directions to follow in making this report, so I think it's best if I just get it all down and let you guys in HQ worry about what should be in it and what shouldn't be in it.)

The boat was just like…like a physical manifestation of his strangeness. He'd been borrowing books about boats secretly for a while before he asked our manager if he could build one on a lot not far from our bookstore.

I still remember hearing our manager snort when Shane asked him. I was kneeling in the History section, facing copies of William Vollman's latest, and they were in Politics, just one shelf over. He snorted and said something like, "What would you want to do that for?"

And Shane replied, "I'm going to build the boat and then I'm going to leave for the ocean."

Our manager snorted again and said, "No, really. Is it some kind of hobby?"

Slowly, Shane said, "I guess you could call it that."

And our manager was so amused – and bored, too, probably – that he told Shane that he could build a boat if he wanted to.

●

That was eighteen months ago. Now that the boat is built and Shane is gone, it doesn't seem funny anymore, even to those of us who are still bored. At first, it didn't seem like he was serious. A boat? Near the bookstore? How could one man build a boat, anyway? It turned out he could, but very slowly. He started out by buying lumber for scaffolding. Then he bought lumber for the hull. One weekend, his friends must have come out and helped him, because when I got there on Monday (I don't work weekends; that's what seniority and an assistant manager badge can get you), about two months after he'd started, the scaffolding was all in place, along with ten long curved beams for the hull. I remember looking at it and thinking it was some abstract sculpture, like the stuff in the more boring books in our Art section.

It didn't look like a boat back then. It looked like a mess. A few of us stood out back at lunchtime and we laughed as we watched Shane work on it. He'd get no more done than bolting something in place to something else in an hour – I can't pretend to know enough about boat-building to give you the technical terms. To us it was clear: Shane had gone mad. Something in his head had gotten loose and inside he was thinking "I'll bet it's not snowing in Sarajevo" over and over again. Or maybe he was thinking about the girl in the graveyard.

I should tell you that I looked through his knapsack once, while he was working on the boat. I couldn't help myself. I didn't like Shane, but it fascinated me that he was doing something so insane. I wanted to know why. I wanted to have some clue. I found a little notebook inside and quickly took it to the photocopier, but could only run off a couple of pages before another employee came by, so I put the notebook back. But I've still got those two pages. I'll transcribe them here for you, in case it's useful:

Once, I made out with a girl in a graveyard. I didn't realize it was a portent of the future. It was the kind of thing thousands of people have done before me, and if it had personal significance, if it symbolized a certain individual daring, a frisson of experience outside of the every day, well, then, I seem to have psychoanalyzed all the mystery out of it by now, haven't I? The fact is, the world is generally indifferent to such acts. They do not reverberate or echo. No quiver or ripple comes unbidden to others because of it. But I still think of this event, if not often, then often enough; the softness of her lips, the intensity of her tongue, the feel of her against me, and, also, I can remember feeling the tombstones all around us, almost a dulling comfort against the burning. What am I to make of it? As much as "I'll bet it isn't snowing in Sarajevo." Later, we sat there, gazing at the dead. Perhaps it was then that I decided I'd rather leave than stay.

There's more, but it's not particularly useful to relate it. Some things are too personal, and I do not feel I deserve the comments anyway.

So it wasn't until month five or six that we really began to see the shape of the thing, and to realize the extent of Shane's Folly, as some of us began to call it. It took the form of a Roman galley, or so Shane said. It had five slots on each side for oars and one main mast in the middle. Typical for him, when I asked him where he'd gotten the blueprints for it, he just smiled and flipped me a coin. I'm going to take a rubbing of it with a pencil and show it to you here, right in this report, so you can see just how disrespectful Shane was to those around him.

A coin with a tiny, rough image of a boat on it. My first thought was outrage – that he had wasted the time of my fellow employees on building something that wouldn't even work. Later, I realized that this thought meant Shane had gotten to me in a way. I thought about the ramifications of this while in my apartment enjoying a glass of cheap brandy and some jazz music and looking over the heirlooms my father had left me (if any of you are ever in the market for antiques for around the house, you might consider checking with me first). For a time, I even thought about going to the manager and handing in my resignation. Shane had compromised my integrity as a corporate employee. He had tried to substitute his vision for the corporate vision in my mind. He had almost succeeded.

At the time he tossed me the coin, I didn't let him know the extent of his almost-victory. I flipped the coin right back to him and said, "If you're not going to be serious, why should I listen to you?" He replied, "Because if you don't, you'll be left out." I didn't realize at the time what he was talking about. Left out of what? His talk of graveyards and kisses? His grotesque utterances about Sarajevo? His frequent lunches with some of the other employees, to which I was never invited? It didn't faze me.

You must understand – I was never angry at Shane. Never. I merely understood better than anyone that we had a job to perform in the bookstore and Shane was making it more difficult to do that job.

●

After nine months, the entire outline of the galley lay before anyone who cared to step around the back of our bookstore. For this reason, Shane had bought a huge tarp and thrown it across the frame. Somehow he managed to get the help of most of the other employees in pulling the tarp off when he wanted to work on the ship and then again in pulling it back on afterwards. It was probably easier to help than have to listen to Shane's messages disguised as small talk. However, I must report that the manager of our bookstore cannot be forgiven for his actions. Time and time again, even during busy periods, he would allow Shane to take breaks to work on the galley. At night, when Shane worked by flashlight and the headlights of his beat-up old car, it was even worse. Shane would be gone for fifteen to twenty minutes at a time, with our manager pretending not to notice. Shane would give any number of excuses to engage in his lazy and demoralizing behavior; our manager never saw them as excuses, though, even when I pointed it out to him. This, then, I cannot forgive, since we looked to our manager for guidance and for the strength to follow the corporate rules. Even more importantly, to keep track of the corporate rules, which were so many. (I can, in some sense, forgive Shane simply because I came to believe that it was in Shane's nature to be lazy; however, my observations of the manager had previously yielded the notion that he cared about his duties.)

A year had passed when Shane announced at an employee function at the local tavern that the initial phase of work had ended on his precious galley. "Thank you for your help," he said. "Thank you for your good wishes. Thank you for not firing me," he said, and gave a nod to the manager, who grinned ear-to-ear, looking for all the world like something hideous from the cover of a book in our Nature section.

To which Shane Statements (as I'd taken to calling them behind his back), to their credit, his fellow employees gave only a tepid smattering of applause, even, might I say, to the trained ear, a mocking amount of applause. This did not depress him. It did not affect him at all. He acted as if they loved him, and loved his "sacred task," as he had taken to calling it whenever I was around. Nothing, I can see now, would have stopped him, short of death. For whatever reason, the boat was locked into his thoughts in a way that I would never understand. I am not by nature obsessive.

When I saw that Shane's Folly would not soon end, I began to accept the world he had created for us – but accept it only so I could shatter it and return us to the state in which we had existed Before Shane (or B.S., as I called it when talking to my fellow employees). I began to think of the bookstore as a ship and all of us as its sailors, guiding it from safe port to safe port. In that light, it was clear that Shane had called for a mutiny, a term I was familiar with from my work shelving books in the History and Sports sections. Not only had Shane called for a mutiny, but our manager had joined the mutiny! I began to sort my employees by those who appeared to be listening to the teachings of the Shane and those on whom his siren song seemed to have no effect. It was a difficult process I had undertaken, and one that I eventually hoped would be documented in a company report. Unfortunately, one of those Leaning Shane crumpled up my notes on a particularly difficult evening in the bookstore, some 17 months into the period of Shane's Folly, and tossed them in a waste basket. I have only my memories, as a result, although I am happy, at some future time, to reconstruct whom I suspected of mutiny, even though it may no longer matter.

The only effect of my change in worldview, I see now, was to distance myself from the loyal employees who still remained, and for this I bear full responsibility. Most of them took my interrogations and probings in the gracious spirit with which I offered them. However, some did not see my work for what it was. If I had to do it over again, I might have stayed more within the powers of my assistant managership, for twice the manager of the store reprimanded me for what he said was "intrusive and inappropriate behavior."

I couldn't take him seriously, of course. How could I? He had gone in with Shane and the rest of them. Now it was not just Shane saying things about Sarajevo, it was other employees, although, as is the way with statements handed down, they became changed by the time I heard them from the other employees. One employee, a girl I rather liked until that moment, said, as we stood at the cash register, "I wonder if it's snowing where Sara is." "Sara?" I said. "Who is Sara?" "No one," she said, gazing with a strange, strange look on her face out the window. It wasn't until later that I caught the odd similarity.

By this point, 17 months and 2 weeks into Shane's Folly, the galley was finished. He had painted it, added caulking, furnished the galley, and even – of all the audacious things! – let some of the employees "ride" in the boat and practice pulling on the oars. They all, including the manager, seemed in awe of this oddity Shane had created; Shane himself seemed awed by it. Now all Shane was doing, it seemed, was waiting. As was I. I had by then decided all I could do was watch and wait and record, so that if a report was required by corporate HQ, I could provide one, as I am now doing. I am not violent by nature, nor persuasive; I am a simple assistant manager, devoted to the company, and to the idea of our bookstore. What else could I do? I could not stop Shane, although I was fairly sure Shane would stop himself.

So Shane waited. One day, 17 months, 3 weeks, and 2 days since he had started, I overcame my mental objections long enough to stand in front of the galley with Shane. It glistened in the morning sun and the sail whipped in the wind. The sail had a huge "S" in red on it. What it stood for was not immediately clear to me. It could have stood for Shane, or it could have been a mocking "Sarajevo," intended to get to me. The whole thing looked like a hideous monster made of wood, and no doubt un-seaworthy to boot. We were, after all, in the middle of Iowa. What could any of us possibly know about building boats like this one? Especially using an old coin to design it?

"What are you waiting for?" I asked Shane.

Shane stood there with his hands in his pockets, smiling up at his folly.

Then he stared at me, with what I can only call ill intent, and he said, "I'm waiting for the girl I kissed in the graveyard. Once she gets here, I'm gone. Because you know" – and as he said it I could hear the laughter in his voice, and the echo, as if he had been waiting for this moment for a long time – "Because you know, I'll bet it isn't snowing in Sarajevo now."

I'm afraid I broke down. I'm afraid almost 18 months of this nonsense had gotten to me. I turned red. I stood there, trying to control myself, but could not.

"You bastard!" I said. "You complete and utter bastard! What the hell are you talking about?! What can you possibly mean?! Why did you build this ridiculous ship? Why does the manager like you so much? You bastard! Bastard!"

After a while, I could not stop saying bastard, although after a time I could not look Shane in the eyes anymore, and my "bastard" became a groan and then a mumble and then a whisper. By the time I had stopped, Shane had gone inside, no doubt to spread more mutiny and to tell the employees who reported to me about my little episode.

I admit, it was a clear violation of corporate policy for assistant managers – but it was in direct response to Shane's own violation of hundreds and hundreds of corporate policies, repeatedly flaunted day after day, minute after minute, for months and months and months. What else could I do? My own mouth knew it had to mutiny against this mutiny.

But when I went back inside, no one would talk to me, not even the manager, not even to reprimand me. And that is when I knew beyond any doubt how far things had gone.

●

Exactly 18 months after Shane started his little project, his folly, his insanity, he disappeared along with the Roman galley built using an image on a coin as his guide. It is believed that he took all of our bookstore employees with him, including the manager. When I got into work that dreary Monday morning, I had to open the bookstore myself. At first, I thought there must have been some emergency, someone from the bookstore in the hospital. But no: when I unlocked the back door to prepare for the daily delivery of books via truck, I saw the truth. The ship was gone. They must have gone with it. The first thought that went through my head was actually a series of images: of a girl, of a graveyard, of Shane, of Sarajevo, a place I'd never been. The second thought was an actual *thought*, a treacherous one: a sudden pang in my heart, a sudden pain there – that I had been forgotten, that they all had abandoned me here, in Iowa, in our bookstore, while they'd left…for where? As you know, it is still unclear, which is why you have asked for this report. To stop it from happening again? To explain what happened at our store? To track down Shane wherever he might be? This is unclear to me, too.

But I know my thought, my pain, was just the last poison Shane brought to us making its way to the surface – my body, my brain, betraying me to Shane's mutiny, just for a second. Just for that second when part of me wanted to join them. I know that now, and I have consulted the corporate policy book many times for guidance on how to stop it from ever happening again to me. I know it is not behavior appropriate in an assistant manager, even if it constitutes a betrayal by thought not deed.

I suppose what bothers me the most, though, is the simple mystery behind what Shane said and the way in which Shane's encounter in a graveyard will not leave me, and the way in which I still, now, six months after the disappearance, see that huge sail in my dreams, flapping in a sudden breeze. I wish I could stop thinking about it.

That's all I know. If you have any further questions, please do not hesitate to ask. I am happy to try to answer them – as much for my own benefit as for yours.

The Surgeon's Tale

(with Cat Rambo)

✻

I.

Down by the docks, you can smell the tide going out – surging from rotted fish, filth, and the briny sargassum that turns the pilings a mixture of purple and green. I don't mind the smell; it reminds me of my youth. From the bungalow on the bay's edge, I emerge most days to go beachcombing in the sands beneath the rotted piers. Soft crab skeletons, ghostly sausage wrappers, and a coin or two are the usual discoveries.

Sometimes I see an old man when I'm hunting, a gangly fellow whose clothes hang loose. As though his limbs were sticks of chalk, wired together with ulnar ligaments of seaweed, pillowing bursae formed from the sacs of decaying anemones that clutter the underside of the pier's planking.

I worry that the sticks will snap if he steps too far too fast, and he will become past repair, past preservation, right in front of me. I draw diagrams in the sand flats to show him how he can safeguard himself with casings over his fragile limbs, the glyphs he should draw on his cuffs to strengthen his wrists. A thousand things I've learned here and at sea. But I don't talk to him – he will have to figure it out from my scrawls when he comes upon them. If the sea doesn't touch them first.

He seems haunted, like a mirror or a window that shows some landscape it's never known. I'm as old as he is. I wonder if I look like him. If he too has trouble sleeping at night. And why he chose this patch of sand to pace and wander.

I will not talk to him. That would be like talking to myself: the surest path to madness.

•

I grew up right here, in my parents' cottage near the sea. Back then, only a few big ships docked at the piers and everything was quieter, less intense. My parents were Preservationists, and salt brine the key to their art. It was even how they met, they liked to tell people. They had entered the same competition – to keep a pig preserved for as long as possible using only essences from the sea and a single spice.

"It was in the combinations," my dad would say. "It was in knowing that the sea is not the same place here, here, or here."

My mother and father preserved their pigs the longest, and after a tie was declared, they began to see and to learn from each other. They married and had me, and we lived together in the cottage by the sea, preserving things for people.

I remember that when I went away to medical school, the only thing I missed was the smell of home. In the student quarters we breathed in drugs and sweat and sometimes piss. The operating theaters, the halls, the cadaver rooms all smelled of bitter chemicals. Babies in bottles. Dolphin fetuses. All had the milky-white look of the exsanguinated – not dreaming or asleep but truly dead.

At home, the smells were different. My father went out daily in the little boat his father had given him as a young man and brought back a hundred wonderful smells. I remember the sargassum the most, thick and green and almost smothering, from which dozens of substances could be extracted to aid in preservations. Then, of course, sea urchins, sea cucumbers, tiny crabs and shrimp, but mostly different types of water. I don't know how he did it – or how my mother distilled the essence – but the buckets he brought back did have different textures and scents. The deep water from out in the bay was somehow smoother and its smell was solid and strong, like the rind of some exotic fruit. Areas near the shore had different pedigrees. The sea grasses lent the water there, under the salt, the faint scent of lemons. Near the wrecks of iron-bound ships from bygone eras, where the octopi made their lairs, the water tasted of weak red wine.

"Taste this," my mother would say, standing in the kitchen in one of my father's shirts over rolled up pants and suspenders. Acid blotches spotted her hands.

I could never tell if there was mischief in her eye or just delight. Because some of it, even after I became used to the salt, tasted horrible.

I would grimace and my father would laugh and say, "Sourpuss! Learn to take the bitter with the sweet."

My parents sold the essence of what the sea gave them: powders and granules and mixtures of spices. In the front room, display cases stood filled with little pewter bowls glittering in so many colors that at times the walls seemed to glow with the residue of some mad sunrise.

This was the craft of magic in our age: pinches and flakes. Magic had given way to Science because Science was more reliable, but you could still find Magic in nooks and crannies, hidden away. For what my parents did, I realized later, could not have derived from the natural world alone.

People came from everywhere to buy these preservations. Some you rubbed on your skin for health. Some preserved fruit, others meat. And sometimes, yes, the medical school sent a person to our cottage, usually when they needed something special that their own ghastly concoctions could not preserve or illuminate.

●

My dad called the man they sent "Stinker" behind his back. His hands were stained brown from handling chemicals and the reek of formaldehyde was even in his breath. My mother hated him.

I suppose that is one reason I went to medical school – because my parents did not like Stinker. Does youth need a better excuse?

As a teenager, I became contemptuous of the kind, decent folk who had raised me. I contracted a kind of headstrong cabin fever, too, for we were on the outskirts of the city. I hated the enclosing walls of the cottage. I hated my father's boat. I even hated their happiness with each other, for it seemed designed to keep me out. When I came back from my studies at the tiny school created for the children of fishermen and sailors, the smell of preservatives became the smell of something small and unambitious. Even though poor, the parents of my schoolmates often went on long journeys into the world, had adventures beyond my ken. A few even worked for the old men who ran the medical school and the faltering mages' college. I found that their stories made me more and more restless.

When the time came, I applied to the medical school. They accepted me, much to the delight of my parents, who still did not understand my motivation. I would have to work for my tuition, my books, but that seemed a small price.

•

I remember a sense of relief at having escaped a trap. It is a feeling I do not understand now, as if my younger self and my adult self were two entirely different people. But back then I could think only of the fact that I would be in the city's center, in the center of civilization. I would matter to more than just some farmers, cooks, fisherfolk, and the like. I would be saving lives from death, not just preserving dead things from decay.

The day I left, my father took me aside and said, "Don't become something separate from the work you do." The advice irritated me. It made no sense. But the truth is I didn't know what he meant at the time.

His parting hug and her kiss, though, were what sustained me during my first year of medical school, even if I would never have admitted it at the time.

•

The brittle-boned old man stands at the water's edge and stares out to sea. I wonder what he's looking at, so distant. The sargassum's right in front of him, just yards from the shore.

That's where I stare, where I search.

•

As a medical student, I lost myself in the work and its culture, which mainly meant sitting in the taverns boasting. I had picked up not just a roommate but a friend in Lucius, the son of a wealthy city official. We roamed the taverns for booze and women, accompanied by his friends. I didn't have much money, but I had a quick tongue and was good at cards.

Many long nights those first two years we spent daydreaming about the cures we would find, the diseases we would bring to ground and eradicate, the herbs and mixes that would restore vitality or potency. We would speak knowingly about matters of demonic anatomy and supposed resurrection, even though as far as anyone knew, none of it was true. Anymore.

Lucius: They had golems in the old days, didn't they? Surgeons must have made them. Sorcerers wouldn't know a gall bladder from a spoiled wineskin.

Me: Progress has been made. It should be possible to make a person from some twine, an apple, a bottle of wine, and some cat gut.

Peter (Lucius' friend): A drunk person, maybe.

Lucius: You are a drunk person. Are you a golem?

Me: He's no golem, he's just resurrected. Do you remember when he began showing up? Right after we left the cadaver room.

Lucius: Why, I think you're right. Peter, are you a dead man?

Peter: Not to my knowledge. Unless you expect me to pay for all this.

Lucius: Why can't you be a resurrected woman? I have enough dead male friends.

●

During the days – oh marvel of youth! – we conquered our hangovers with supernatural ease and spent equal time in the cadaver room cutting up corpses and in classes learning about anatomy and the perilous weakness of the human body. Our myriad and ancient and invariably male instructors pontificated and sputtered and pointed their fingers and sometimes even donned the garb and grabbed the knife, but nothing impressed as much as naked flesh unfolding to show its contents.

And then there was the library. The medical school had been built around the library, which had been there for almost a thousand years before the school, originally as part of the mages' college. It was common knowledge, which is to say unsubstantiated rumor, that when the library had been built thaumaturgy had been more than just little pulses and glimpses of the fabric underlying the world. There had been true magic, wielded by a chosen few, and no one had need of a surgeon. But none of us really knew. Civilization had collapsed and rebuilt itself thrice in that span. All we had were scraps of history and old leather-bound books housed in cold, nearly airless rooms to guide us.

Lucius: If we were real surgeons, we could resurrect someone. With just a little bit of magic. Medical know-how. Magic. Magic fingers.

Me: And preservations.

Richard (another of Lucius' friends): Preservations?
Lucius: He comes from a little cottage on the –
Me: It's nothing. A joke. A thing to keep fetuses from spoiling until we've had a look at them.
Peter: What would we do with a resurrected person?
Lucius: Why, we'd put him up for the city council. A dead person ought to have more wisdom than a living one.
Me: We could maybe skip a year or two of school if we brought a dead person back.
Richard: Do you think they'd like it? Being alive again?
Lucius: They wouldn't really have a choice, would they?

●

Do you know what arrogance is? Arrogance is thinking you can improve on a thousand years of history. Arrogance is trying to do it to get the best of the parents who always loved you.

Me: There're books in the library, you know.
Lucius: Quick! Give the man another drink. He's fading. Books in a library. Never heard of such a thing.
Me: No, I mean –
Lucius: Next you'll be telling us there are corpses in the cadaver room and –
Richard: Let him speak, Lucius. He looks serious.
Me: I mean books on resurrection.
Lucius: Do tell…

●

For a project on prolonged exposure to quicksilver and aether, I had been allowed access to the oldest parts of the library – places where you did not know whether the footprints in the dust revealed by the light of your shaking lantern were a year or five hundred years old. Here, knowledge hid in the dark, and you were lucky to find a little bit of it. I was breathing air breathed hundreds, possibly thousands, of years before by people much wiser than me.

In a grimy alcove half-choked with old spider webs, I found books on the ultimate in preservation: reanimation of dead matter. Arcane signs and symbols, hastily written down in my notebook.

No one had been to this alcove for centuries, but they *had* been there. As I found my halting way out, I noticed the faint outline of boot prints beneath the dust layers. Someone had paced before that shelf, deliberating, and I would never know their name or what they were doing there, or why they stayed so long.

Lucius: You don't have the balls.

Me: The balls? I can steal the balls from the cadaver room.

Richard: He can have as many balls as he wants!

Peter: We all can!

Lucius: Quietly, quietly, gents. This is serious business. We're planning on a grandiose level. We're asking to be placed on the pedestal with the greats.

Me: It's not that glorious. It's been done before, according to the book.

Lucius: Yes, but not for hundreds of years.

Peter: Seriously, you wonder why not.

Richard: I wonder why my beer mug's empty.

Peter: Barbarian.

Richard: Cretin.

Me: It seems easy enough. It seems as if it is possible.

•

One night, Lucius and I so very very drunk, trying too hard to impress, I boasted that with my secret knowledge of reanimation, my Preservationist background, and my two years of medical school, I could resurrect the dead, create a golem from flesh and blood. Human, with a human being's natural life span.

"And I will assist him," Lucius announced, finger pointed at the ceiling. "Onward!"

We stumbled out of the tavern's soft light, accompanied by the applause of friends who no doubt thought I was taking a piss – into the darkness of the street, and carried by drunkenness and the animating spirit of our youth, stopping only to vomit into the gutter once or maybe twice, we lurched our debauched way up the hill to the medical school, and in the shadows stole past the snoring old guard, into the cadaver room.

I remember the spark to the night, cold as it was. I remember the extravagant stars strewn across the sky. I remember the euphoria, being not just on a quest, but on a drunken quest, and together, best of friends in that moment.

If only we had stayed in that moment.

•

"Preservation is a neutral thing," my mother told me once. "It prolongs a state that already exists. It honors the essence of something."

She stood in the back room surrounded by buckets of pungent water when she said this to me. I think I was twelve or thirteen. She had a ladle and was stirring some buckets, sipping from others. Glints and sparkles came from one. Others were dark and heavy and dull. The floor, once white tile, had become discolored from decades of water storage. The bloody rust circles of the buckets. The hemorrhaging green-blue stains.

"But the essence of preservation," my mother said, "is that it doesn't last. You can only preserve something for so long, and then it is gone. And that's all right."

My father had entered the room just before she said this. The look of love and sadness she gave the two of us, me sitting, my father standing behind me, was so stark, so revelatory, that I could not meet her gaze.

Looking back at that moment, I've often wondered if she already knew our futures.

•

In the cadaver room, we picked a newly dead woman who had drowned in the sea. Probably the daughter of a fisherman. She lay exposed on the slab, all strong shoulders and solid breasts and sturdy thighs. Her ankles were delicate, though, as were the features of her face. She had frozen blue eyes and pale skin and an odd smile that made me frown and hesitate for a moment.

It will come as no surprise we chose her in part because her body excited me. Although Lucius' presence had helped me in this regard, women, for all our boasting, are not drawn to impoverished medical students. Even on those rare occasions, it had been in the dark and I had only had glimpses of a woman's naked form. The dissections of the classroom did not count;

they would drive most men to celibacy if not for the resilience of the human mind.

"This one?" Lucius asked.

I don't know if he still thought this was a lark, or if he knew how serious I was.

"I think so," I said. "I think this is the one."

And, although I didn't know it, I did mean the words.

We stood there and stared at her. The woman reminded me of someone the more I stared. It was uncanny, and yet I could not think of who she looked like. So taken was I by her that I pushed her hair from her face.

Lucius nudged my shoulder, whispered, "Stop gawking. That guard might wake up or his replacement come by at any minute."

Together, we bundled her in canvas like a rug, stole past the guard, and, by means of a wagon Lucius had arranged – from a friend used to Lucius' pranks – we took her, after a brief stop at my apartment to pick up some supplies, to a secluded cove well away from the city. I meant to preserve her tethered in the water, in the sargassum near the rockline. It was a variation on an old preservation trick my mother had once shown a client.

The physical exertion was intense. I remember being exhausted by the time we hauled her out of the cart. Her body would not cooperate; there was no way for her not to flop and become unwound from the canvas at times. It added to the unreality of it all, and several times we collapsed into giggles. Perhaps we would have sobered up sooner if not for that.

Luckily the moon was out and Lucius had brought a lantern. By then, my disorganized thoughts had settled, and although I was still drunk I had begun to have doubts. But this is the problem with having an accomplice. If Lucius hadn't been there, I would like to think I'd have put a stop to it all. But I couldn't, not with Lucius there, not with the bond between us now. As for what kept Lucius beside me, I believe he would have abandoned me long before if not for a kind of jaded hedonism – the curiosity of the perpetually bored.

●

It was hard. I had to think of the woman as a receptacle, a vehicle, for resurrection, not the end result. We laid her out atop the canvas and I drew symbols on her skin with ink I'd daubed onto my fingers. Holding her right hand, I said the words I had found in the books, knowing neither their meaning nor their correct pronunciation. I rubbed preservatives into her skin that would not just protect her flesh while she lay amongst the sargassum but actually bring it back to health. I had to do some cutting, some surgery, near the end. An odd autopsy, looking for signs of the "mechanical defect" as one of my instructors used to say, that would preclude her reanimation. I cleared the last fluid from her lungs with a syringe.

By this time I could not tell you exactly what I was doing. I felt imbued with preternatural, instinctual knowledge and power, although I had neither. What I had were delusions of grandeur spurred on by alcohol and the words of my friends, tempered perhaps by memories of my parents' art.

Lucius held the lantern and kept muttering, "Oh my God" under his breath. But his tone was not so much one of horror as, again, morbid fascination. I have seen the phenomenon since. It is as if a mental list is being checked off on a list of unique experiences.

By the time I had finished, I knew the dead woman as intimately as any lover. We took her down to the sargassum bed and we laid her there, floating, tethered by one foot using some rope. I knew that cove. I'd swum in it since I was a child. People hardly ever came there. The sargassum was trapped; the tide only went out in the spring, when the path of the currents changed. The combination of the salt water, the preservatives I'd applied to her, and the natural properties of the sargassum would sustain her as she made her slow way back to life.

Except for the sutures, she looked as if she were asleep, still with that slight smile, floating on the thick sargassum, glowing from the emerald tincture that would keep the small crabs and other scavengers from her. She looked otherworldly and beautiful.

Lucius gave a nervous laugh. He had begun to sober up.

"Any suggestions on what we do next?" he said, disbelief in his voice.

"We wait."

"Wait? For how long? We've got classes in the morning. I mean, it's already morning."

"We wait for a day."

"Here? For a whole day?"

"We come back. At night. She'll still be here."

218

●

There's nothing in the nature of a confession that makes it any more or less believable. I know this, and my shadow on the beach knows it, or he would have talked to me by now. Or I would have talked to him, despite my misgivings.

I haven't seen Lucius in forty years. My shadow could be Lucius. It could be, but I doubt it.

●

II.

In the morning, for a time, neither Lucius nor I knew whether the night's events had been real or a dream. But the cart outside of our rooms, the deep fatigue in our muscles, and the blood and skin under our fingernails – this evidence convinced us. We looked at each other as if engaged in some uneasy truce, unwilling to speak of it, still thinking, I believe, that it would turn out to have been a hallucination.

We went to classes like normal. Our friends teased us about the bet, and I shrugged, gave a sheepish grin while Lucius immediately talked about something else. The world seemed to have changed not at all because of our actions and yet I felt completely different. I kept seeing the woman's face. I kept thinking about her eyes

Did the medical school miss the corpse? If so, they ignored it for fear of scandal. How many times a year did it happen, I've always wondered, and for what variety of reasons?

That night we returned to the cove, and for three nights more. She remained preserved but she was still dead. Nothing had happened. It appeared I could not bring her back to life, not even for a moment. The softly hushing water that rocked her sargassum bed had more life to it than she. Each time I entered a more depressed and numbed state.

"What's her name, do you think?" Lucius asked me on the third night.

He was sitting on the rocks, staring at her. The moonlight made her pale skin luminous against the dark green.

"She's dead," I said. "She doesn't have a name."

"But she had a name. And parents. And maybe a husband. And now she's here. Floating."

He laughed. It was a raw laugh. I didn't like what it contained.

On the afternoon of the first day, Lucius had been good-natured and joking. By the second, he had become silent. Now he seemed to have lost something vital, some sense of perspective. He sat on the rocks drawn in on himself, huddled for warmth. I hated his questions. I hated his attitude.

Even though it was I who pined for the woman, who so desperately wanted her to come to gasping life, to rise from the sargassum, reborn.

Everywhere I went, I saw those frozen blue eyes.

•

Once, before I left home, in that time when I was arguing with my parents almost every day, restless with their world and my place in it, there was a pause because each of us regretted something we had said.

Into this silence, my mother said, "You've got to know who you are, and even when you think you've been treated unfairly still *be* that person."

I said something sarcastic and stormed out of the cottage – to feel the salt air on my face, to look across the water toward distant, unseen shores.

I didn't know that I would one day find so much more so close to home.

•

The fourth night Lucius refused to go with me.

"It's pointless," he said. "Not only that, it's dangerous. We shouldn't have done it in the first place. It's still a crime, to steal a body. Let it go. She'll be taken out to sea or rotting soon enough. Or put her out to sea yourself. Just don't mention it to me again."

In his face I saw fear, yes, but mostly awareness of a need for self-preservation. This scared me. The dead woman might have enthralled me, but Lucius had become my anchor at medical school.

"You're right," I told him. "I'll go one last time and put her out to sea."

Lucius smiled, but there was something wrong. I could feel it.

"We'll chalk it up to youthful foolishness," he said, putting his arm over my shoulders. "A tale to tell the grandchildren in thirty years."

She was still there, perfectly preserved, on that fourth night. But this time, rising from the sargassum, I saw what I thought was a pale serpent, swaying. In the next second, breath frozen in my throat, I realized I was staring at her right arm – and that it was moving.

I dashed into the water and to her side, hoping for what? I still don't know. Those frozen blue eyes. That skin, imperfect yet perfect. Her smile.

She wasn't moving. Her body still had the staunch solidity, the draining heaviness, of the dead. What I had taken to be a general awakening was just the water's gentle motion. Only the arm moved with any purpose – and it moved toward me. It sought me out, reaching. It touched my cheek as I stood in the water there beside her, and I felt that touch everywhere.

I spent almost an hour trying to wake her. I thought that perhaps she was close to full recovery, that I just needed to push things a little bit. But nothing worked. There was just the twining arm, the hand against my cheek, my shoulder, seeking out my own hand as if wanting comfort.

Finally, exhausted, breathing heavily, I gave up. I refreshed the preservation powders, made sure she was in no danger of sinking, and left her there, the arm still twisting and searching and alive.

I was crying as I walked away. I had been working so hard that it wasn't until that moment that I realized what had happened.

I had begun to bring her back to life.

Now if only I could bring her the rest of the way.

As I walked back up into the city, into the noise and color and sounds of people talking – back into my existence before her – I was already daydreaming about our life together.

•

The quality of the silence here can be extraordinary. It's the wind that does it. The wind hisses its way through the bungalow's timbers and blocks out any other sound.

The beach could be, as it sometimes is, crowded with day visitors and yet from my window it forms a silent tableau. I can watch mothers with their children, building sandcastles, or beachcombers, or young couples, and I can create the dialogue for their lives. How many of them will make decisions that become the Decision? Who really recognizes when they've tipped the balance, when they've entered into a place from which there is no escape?

The old man knows, I'm sure. He has perspective. But the rest of them, they have no idea what awaits them.

•

For another week I went to her nightly, and each time the hand reached toward me like some luminous, five-petaled flower, grasping toward the moon. There was no other progress. Slowly, my hopes and daydreams turned to sleeplessness and despair. My studies suffered and I stammered upon questioning like a first-year who couldn't remember the difference between a ligament and a radial artery. My friends stared at me and muttered that I worked too hard, that my brain had gone soft from overstudy. But I saw nothing but the woman's eyes, even when Lucius, without warning, while I was visiting her, moved out of our quarters. Leaving me alone.

I understood this, to some extent. I had become a bad roommate and, worse, a liability. But when Lucius began avoiding me in the halls, then I knew he had intuited I had gone farther, gone against his advice.

Finally, at the end of an anatomy class, I cornered him. He looked at me as if I were a stranger.

"I need you to come down to the water with me," I said.

"Why?" he said. "What's the point?"

"You need to see."

"What have you done?"

From Lucius' tone you would have thought I'd murdered someone.

"You just need to see. Please? For a friend?"

He gave me a contemptuous look, but said, "I'll meet you tonight. But I won't go down there with you. We meet there and leave separately."

"Thank you Lucius. Thank you so much."

I was so desperately grateful. I had been living with this secret in my head for almost a week. I hadn't been bathing. I hadn't been eating. When I did sleep, I dreamt of snow-white hands reaching for me from the sea. Hundreds of them, melting into the water.

•

I no longer think of my parents' bungalow as a trap. It's more of a solace – all of their things surround me. I can almost conjure them up from the smells alone. There is so much history here, of so many good things.

From the window, I can see the old man now. He seems restless, searching. Once or twice, he looked like he might come to the door, but he retreated and walked back onto the beach.

If I did talk to him, I don't know where I'd begin my story. I don't know if I'd wait for him to tell his or if mine would come out all in a mad rush, and there he'd be, still on the welcome mat, looking at this crazy old man, knowing he'd made a mistake.

●

Lucius at the water's edge that night. Lucius bent over in a crouch, staring at the miracle, the atrocity my lantern's light had brought to both of us. Lucius making a sound like a crow's harsh caw.

"It's like the movement of a starfish arm after you cut it off," he said. "It's no different from any corpse that flinches under the knife. Muscle memory."

"She's coming back to life," I said.

Lucius stood, walked over to me, and slapped me hard across the face. I reeled back, fell to one knee by the water's edge. It hurt worse than anything but the look in the woman's eyes.

Lucius leaned down to hiss in my ear: "This is an abomination. A mistake. You must let it go – into the sea. Or burn it. Or both. You must get rid of this, do you understand? For both of our sakes. And if you don't, I will come back down here and do it for you. Another thing: we're no longer friends. That can no longer be. I do not know you anymore." And, more softly: "You must understand. You must. This cannot be."

I nodded but I could not look at him. In that one whisper, my whole world had collapsed and been reformed. Lucius had been my best friend, but I hadn't been his. He was leaving me to my fate.

As I stood, I felt utterly alone. All I had left was the woman.

I looked out at her, so unbelievably beautiful floating atop the sargassum. "I don't even know your name," I said to her. "Not even that."

Lucius was staring at me, but I ignored him and after a time he went away.

The woman's smile remained, as enigmatic as ever. Even now, I can see that smile, the line of her mouth reflected in everything around me – in the lip of a sea shell, or transferred to a child walking along the shore, or leaping into the sky in the form of a gull's silhouette.

•

Maybe things would have been different had I been close to any instructors, but outside of class, I never talked to them. I could not imagine going up to one of those dusty fossils, half-embalmed, and blurting out the details of my desperate and angst-ridden situation. How could they possibly relate? Nor did I feel as if I could go to my parents for help; that had not been an option in my mind for years.

Worst of all, I had never realized until Lucius began to avoid me that he had been my link to my few other friends. Now that Lucius had cast me adrift, no one wanted to talk to me. And, in truth, I was not good company. I don't know if I can convey the estrangement surrounding those days after I took Lucius to see her. I wandered through my classes like an amnesiac, speaking only when spoken to, staring out into nothing and nowhere. Unable to truly comprehend what was happening to me.

And every night: down to the sea, each time the ache in my heart telling me that what I believed, what I hoped, must have happened and she would be truly alive.

In that absence, in that solitary place I now occupied, I realized, slowly and with a mixture of fear and an odd satisfaction, that my interest in the woman's resurrection no longer came from hubris or scientific fascination. Instead it came from love. I was in love with a dead woman, and that alone began to break me down. For now I grieved for that which I had never had, to speculate on a life never lived, so that every time I saw that she had been taken from me, a part of my imagined life seemed to recede into the horizon.

•

"The arm grew stronger even as she did not," I would tell my fellow castaway, both our beards gray and encrusted with barnacles and dangling crabs. I'm sure I would have practically had to kidnap him to get him into the bungalow, but once there I'd convince him to stay.

Over a cup of tea in the living room I'd say this as he looked at me, incredulous.

"Something in the magic I'd used," I'd say. "There was a dim glow to the arm. It even seemed to shimmer, an icy green. So I had succeeded, don't you see? I'd succeeded as well as I was ever going to. Magic might be almost utterly gone from the world now, but it still had a toehold when we were both young. Surely you remember, Lucius?"

In the clear morning light, the old man would say, "My name isn't Lucius and I think you've gone mad."

And he might be right.

•

Ultimately, my love led to my decision, not any fear of discovery. I couldn't bear the ache anymore. If she no longer existed, that ache would be gone. Foolish boys know no better. Everything is physical to them. But that ache is still here in my heart.

It was a clear night. I stole a boat from the docks and rowed my way to the hidden cove. She was there, of course, unchanged. I had with me jars of oil.

I had a hard time getting her from the bed of sargassum into the boat. I remember being surprised at her weight as I held her in my arms in the water for a time and cried into her hair, her hand caressing the back of my head.

After she was in the boat, I took it out to where the currents would bring it to deep water. I poured the oil all over her body. I lit the match. I stared into those amazing eyes one last time, then tossed the match onto the oil as I jumped into the sea. Behind me, I heard the whoosh of air and felt a rush of heat as flames engulfed the rowboat. I swam to shore without looking back. If I had looked back, I would have turned around, swum out to the burning boat, and let myself be immolated beside her.

As I staggered out of the water, I felt relief mixed with the sadness. It was over with. I felt I had saved myself from something I did not quite understand.

•

"What happened then," old man Lucius would say, intent on my story, forgetting the thread of his own.

"For three days, everything returned to a kind of normal," I'd tell him. "Or as normal as it could be. I slept. I went out with a couple of the first-years who didn't know you had abandoned me. I felt calm as a waveless sea."

"Calm? After all of that?"

"Perhaps I was in shock. I don't know."

"What happened after the third day?"

My guest would have to ask this, if I didn't tell him right away.

"What happened after the third day? Nothing much. The animated right arm of a dead woman climbed up the side of my building and crawled in through the window."

And with that, Lucius would be frozen in time, cup cantilevered toward his mouth, shock suffusing his face like honey crystals melting in tea.

•

I woke up with the arm beside me in bed. I tried to scream, but the hand closed gently over my mouth. The skin was smooth but smelled of brine. With an effort of will, I got up, pulled the arm away, and threw it back onto the bed. It lay there, twitching. There was sand under its fingernails.

I began to laugh. It was after midnight. I was alone in my room with a reanimated, disembodied arm.

Her arm. Her hand.

It had come to me from the depths of the sea, crawling across the sea floor like some odd creature in an old book.

What would you have done? I remembered Lucius' comment that the arm displayed the same mindless motion as a wounded starfish.

I took the arm downstairs and buried it in the backyard, weighed down with bricks and string like an unwanted kitten. Then I went back to bed, unable to sleep, living with a constant sense of terror the next day.

The next night, the arm was in my room again, last remnant of my lost love.

I buried it three more nights. It came back. I tossed it into the sea. It came back. I became more creative. I mixed the arm in with the offal behind a butcher's shop, holding my nose against the stench. It came back, smeared with blood and grease. I slipped it into an artist's bag at a coffee shop. It came back, mottled with vermillion and umber paint. I tried to cut it to pieces with a bone saw. It reconstituted itself. I tried to burn it, but, of course, it would not burn.

Eventually, I came to see it meant me no harm. Not really. Whatever magic bound it, it did not seek revenge. I hadn't killed the woman. I just hadn't brought her fully back to life. In return she hadn't come fully back to me.

●

"So then you kept it locked in a box in your room, you say?"

"Yes," I would tell my shadow. "There was no real danger of discovery – no one came to visit me anymore. And I rarely went to classes. I was searching for answers, for a way out. You have to understand, I was in an altered state by then."

"Of course."

A sip of tea and no inclination to divulge his own secrets.

The sea beyond the window is the source of the biggest changes for me now. It goes from calm to stormy in minutes. The color of it, the tone of the waves, varies by the hour. Over the months, it brings me different things: the debris of a sunken ship, a flotilla of jellyfish, and, of course, strands of sargassum washed up from the bay.

"I was insane," I tell him.

"Of course you were. With grief."

Youth is a kind of insanity. It robs you of experience, of perspective, of history. Without those, you are adrift.

●

Back to the libraries I went, and back again and again. But it was as if the floors had been swept and I could not trace my own footprints. In those echoing halls, I found every book but the one that would have helped me. Had my long-ago counterpart, standing there deliberating, thought about stealing the book? No matter now, but I found myself reliving the moment when I had slid the tome back into the stacks rather than hiding it in my satchel with at first horror and then resignation.

I even visited the remnants of the mage's college, following the ancient right wing of the library until it dissolved into the even more crumbling walls of that venerable institution. All I found there was a ruined amphitheater erupting in sedgeweeds, with a couple dozen students at the bottom, dressed in black robes. They were being lectured at by a man so old he seemed part of the eroded stones on which he sat. If magic still remained in the world, it did not exist in this place.

All I had left were the more modern texts and the memory of a phrase among the signs and symbols I had used to animate the arm: "Make what you bring back your own."

Each time I took the arm out of the box, it came garlanded with thoughts I did not want but could not make go away. Each time, I unraveled a little more. Dream and reality blended like one of my parents' more potent concoctions. Day became night and night became day with startling rapidity. I had hallucinations in which giant flowers became giant hands. I had visions of arms reaching from a turbulent, bloody sea. I had nightmares of wrists coated with downy hair and mold.

I stopped bathing entirely. I wore the same clothes for weeks. Her skin's briny taste filled my mouth no matter what cup I drank from. Her eyes stared from every corner.

●

"What did you do then?" my guest would prod once again. He'd have finished his tea by now and he would be wanting to leave, but ask despite himself.

"Don't you know, Lucius?" I'd reply. "Don't you remember?"

"Tell me anyway," he'd say, to humor the other crazy old man.

"One night, sick with weariness, with heartache, I took the arm to the medical school's operating theater and performed surgery on myself."

A rapid intake of breath. "You did?"

"No, of course not. You can't perform that kind of surgery on yourself. Impossible. Besides, the operating theater has students and doctors in it day and night. You can't sneak into an operating theater the way you sneak into a cadaver room. Too many living people to see you."

"Oh," he'd say, and lapse into silence.

Maybe that's all I'd be willing to tell my Lucius surrogate. Maybe that's the end of the story for him.

•

One night, sick with weariness, with heartache, I took the arm to the medical school's operating theater and performed surgery on myself.

It wasn't the operating theater and I wasn't alone. No, my friend was with me the whole time.

Me, tossing the proverbial pebbles from some romantic play at the window of Lucius' new apartment one desperate, sleepless night. Hissing as loud as I could: "Lucius! I know you're in there!"

More pebbles, more hissing, and then he, finally, reluctantly, opening the window. In the light pouring out, I could see a woman behind him, blonde and young, clutching a bedsheet.

Lucius stared down at me as if I were an anonymous beggar.

"Come down, Lucius," I said. "Just for a moment."

It was a rich neighborhood, not where one typically finds starving medical students. Not the kind of street where any resident wants a scene.

"What do you want?" he hissed down at me.

"Just come down. I won't leave until you do."

Again, that measured stare. Suddenly I was afraid.

He scowled and closed the window, but a minute later he stood in the shadow of the doorway with me, his hair disheveled, his eyes slits. He reeked of beer.

"You look half-dead," he said. "Do you need money? Will that make you go away?"

Even a few days earlier that would have hurt me.

"I need you to come down to the medical school."

"Not in a million years. We're done. We're through."

I took the arm out of my satchel and unwrapped it from the gauze in which it writhed.

Lucius backed away, against the door, as I proffered it to him. He put out his hand to push it away, thought better of that.

"She came back to me. I burned the body, but the arm came back."

"My god, what were you *thinking?* Put it away. Now."

I carefully rewrapped it, put it back in the satchel. The point had been made.

"So you'll help me?"

229

"No. Take that abomination and leave now."

He turned to open the door.

I said: "I need your help. If you don't help, I'll go to the medical school board, show them the arm, and tell them your role in this." There was a wound in me because of Lucius. Part of me wanted to hurt him. Badly.

Lucius stopped with his hand on the doorknob, his back to me. I knew he was searching furiously for an escape.

"You can help me or you can kill me, Lucius," I said, "but I'm not going away."

Finally, his shoulders slumped and he stared out into the night.

"I'll help, all right? I'll help. But if you ever come here again after this, I'll…"

He didn't need to say it. I knew exactly what he was capable of.

•

My parents had a hard life. I didn't see this usually, but at times I would catch hints of it. Preservation was a taxing combination of intuition, experimentation, and magic. It wasn't just the physical cost – my mother's wrists aching from hundreds of hours of grinding the pestle in the mortar, my father's back throbbing from hauling buckets out of the boat nearly every day. The late hours, the dead-end ideas that resulted in nothing they could sell. The stress of going out in a cockleshell of a boat in seas that could grow sullen and rough in minutes.

No, preservation came with a greater cost than that. My parents aged faster than normal – well-preserved, of course, even healthy, perhaps, but the wrinkles gathered more quickly on their faces, as did the age spots I thought were acid blotches and that they tried to disguise or hide. None of this was normal, although I could not know it at the time. I had no other parents to compare them to or examine as closely.

Once, I remember hearing their voices in the kitchen. Something in their tone made me walk close enough to listen, but not close enough to be seen.

"You must slow down," she said to him.

"I can't. So many want so much."

"Then let them *want*. Let them go *without*."

"Maybe it's an addiction. Giving them what they want."

"I want you with me, my dear, not down in the basement of the Preservation Guild waiting for a resurrection that will never come."

"I'll try…I'll be better…"

"…Look at my hands…"

"…I love your hands…"

"…so dry, so old…"

"They're the hands of someone who works for a living."

"Works too hard."

"I'll try. I'll try."

●

III.

I'll try. I'll try. To tell the rest of the story. To make it to the end. Some moments are more difficult than others, and you never know which are which until it's too late.

When Lucius discovered what I planned to do, he called me crazy. He called me reckless and insane. I just stood there and let him pace and curse at me. It hardly mattered. I was resolute in my decision.

"Lucius," I said. "You can make this hard or you can make this easy. You can make it last longer or you can make it short."

"I wish I'd never known you," he said to me. "I wish I'd never introduced you to my friends."

In the end, my calm won him over. Knowing what I had to do, the nervousness had left me. I had reached a state so beyond that of normal human existence, so beyond what even Lucius could imagine, that I had achieved perfect clarity. I can't explain it any other way. The doubt, in that moment, had fallen from me.

"So you'll do it?" I asked again.

"Let's get on with it," Lucius growled, through gritted teeth, "But not at the operating theater. That's madness. There's a place outside the city. A house my father owns. You'll wait for me there. I'll get the tools and supplies I need from the school."

●

Desperation, lack of sleep, and a handful of pills Lucius had been able to steal served as my only anesthetics. I had no idea, even with Lucius' help, even with my knowledge of preservation powders, if it would work. In effect, it might have been the equivalent of an assisted suicide attempt. I lay spread out on a tarp covering the long dining room table of that house while Lucius prepared his instruments, knowing that these minutes, these seconds, might be my last among the living.

The pain was unbelievable. I jolted in and out of consciousness to hear Lucius panting like a dog. Lucius sawing. Lucius cursing. Lucius cutting and suturing and weeping, blood everywhere, me delirious and singing an old nursery rhyme my mother had taught me, Lucius bellowing his distress in counterpoint.

"I never want to see you again," he gasped in my ear as he finished up. "Never."

I smiled up at him and reached out with my good arm to touch his blood-stained face, to say thank you, though no words came out. The pain burned through my skull like a wildfire. The pain was telling me I was alive.

•

When Lucius was done, he slumped against the side of the table, wiping at his hands, mumbling something I couldn't understand. It wasn't important. All I knew was that my own right arm had been consigned to the morgue and the woman's arm had replaced my own.

Lucius saw to it that I got back to my apartment, although all I have are vague flashbacks to the inside of a cart and a painful rolling sensation. Afterward I spent two feverish weeks in bed, the landlady knocking on the door every day, asking for the rent. I think Lucius visited me to clean and check the wound, but I can't be sure.

My memory of that time comes and goes in phases like the tide.

•

In the end, the same sorcery that animated the woman's arm saved me. Over time, I healed. Over time, my new arm learned to live with me. I worried at first about gangrene in the place where the arm met my flesh, but I managed to prevent that. In the mornings, I woke with it as though it was a stranger I had brought home from a tavern. Eventually, it would wake me, stroking my forehead and touching my lips so delicately that I would groan my passion out into its palm.

It was the beginning of my life, in a way. A life in exile, but a life nonetheless, with a new partner. Lucius had helped me see to that.

So it was that when I went back to my parents' bungalow, I had a purpose and a plan.

They met me at the door and hugged me tight, for they hadn't heard from me in months and I was gaunt, pale.

I did not have to tell them everything. Or anything. I tried to hide the new arm from them, but it reached out for my mother as though gathering in a confidante. What did it say to her, woman to woman? What secrets did it spell into her hands? I had to look away, as though intruding on their conversation.

"What will you do?" my father asked.

As my mother held my new arm, he had run a fingertip across it, come away with a preserving dust.

I wanted to say that I had come to ask his advice, but the truth was I had only returned after I had settled my fate. In the days, the hours, before everything had become irrevocable, I hadn't sought their counsel. And he knew that, knew it in a way that filled his eyes with bewilderment, like a solution of cobalt chloride heated to its purest color.

"What will I do?" I knew, but I didn't know if I could tell them.

My father had his hand on my shoulder, as if needing support. My mother released the arm and it returned to me and tucked its hand into my pocket, taking refuge. She had not yet said a word to me.

I told them: "I've signed on as a ship's doctor. I've enough experience for that. My ship leaves for the southern islands in three days." The arm stirred, but only barely, like an eavesdropper that has overheard its own name.

Lucius' father owned the ship. It had been Lucius' last favor to me, freely and eagerly given. "As far from the city as possible," he said to me. "As far and for as long as possible."

My father looked crushed. My mother only smiled bravely and said, "Three days is not enough, but it will have to do. And you will write. And you will come back."

JEFF VANDERMEER

Yes, I would come back, but those three days – during which I would tell them everything, sometimes defiant, sometimes defeated and weeping – were my last three days with them.

•

Even in the shallow water near the bungalow, you learn to find shapes in shadow, if you look long enough. Staring into deep water as it speeds past and sprays white against the prow of a large ship, the wind lacerating your face, you see even more.

But I never saw *her*. I never saw her. I don't know why I expected to, and yet on all of the hundreds of voyages I took as a ship's doctor, I always looked. The sailors say mermaids live down there, with scaly hair and soft fingertips and cold, clammy kisses. I cared for none of that. I yearned to see her face by some strange necromancy, her blue eyes staring up at me through the ocean's darker blue.

Worse yet, whether on deck or in my cabin, whether during ferocious, stomach-churning storms or trying to save a man with a piece of broken-off deck board forced through his sternum, I wanted a dead woman to tell the story of her life. I wanted to know if she had been a sister, a niece, a grand-daughter. I wanted to know if she'd liked cats or tormented them. Did she drink tea or coffee? Did she have an easy sense of humor? Was her laugh thin or full? How did she walk? What did she like to wear? So many questions came to me.

Because I had no idea of her personality, I imagined her, probably wrongly, as my double: embarrassed by her parents' eccentricities, a little amazed to find herself touched by life and led as though by the nose to this point of existence, this moment when I searched a hundred flavors of water for her smile.

It wasn't an academic point, and yet I experienced the sweet agony of living with a part of her every day. At first, I had little control over the arm, and it either flopped loosely at my side, uncooperative, or caused much trouble for me by behaving eccentrically. But, over time, we reached an accord. It was more skillful than I at stitching a wound or lancing a boil. The arm seemed to so enjoy the task that I wondered if the woman had been a thwarted healer or something similar – an artist of the domestic, who could sew or cook, or perform any arcane household task.

234

Sometimes, at night, it would crawl outside the counterpane, to the limits of its span, and lie in the cold air until the shivers woke me and forced me to reclaim it. Then I would besiege it with the warmth of my own flesh until it succumbed and became part of me again.

•

"Did you enjoy being a ship's doctor?" my guest would ask, if only to change the topic, and I would be grateful.

"It was boring and exhausting," I would say. "Sailors can injure themselves in a thousand different ways. There's only so much medicine you can carry on a ship."

"But did you enjoy it?"

"When it was busy, I would get pleasure from doing good and necessary work."

Keeping busy is important. My parents taught me that the utility of work was its own reward, but it also fills up your mind, gives you less time to think.

"Sounds like it wasn't half-bad," he'd say, like someone who didn't know what I was talking about.

Would I tell him the rest? Would I tell him about the times on the docks or at sea that I saw the pale white of drowning victims laid out in rows and immediately be back in the cadaver room? That some part of me yearned for that white dead flesh? That when I slept with women now it must be in the dark so that the soft yet muscular feel of them would not interfere with the image in my head of a certain smile, a certain woman. That I tried to fall in love with so many women, but could not, would not, not with her arm by my side.

•

In time, I gained notoriety for my skills. When docked, sailors from other ships would come to me for bandaging or physicking, giving themselves over to my mismatched hands. My masculinity had never seemed brutish to me, but laid against her delicate fingers, I could not help but find myself unsubtle. Or, at least, could not help but believe she would find them so.

And, indeed, her hand never sought out the other hand, as if to avoid the very thought of its counterpart.

I settled into the life easily enough – every couple of years on a new ship with a new crew, headed somewhere ever more exotic. Soon, any thought of returning to the city of my birth grew distant and faintly absurd. Soon, I gained more knowledge of the capriciousness of sea than any but the most experienced seaman. I came to love the roll of the decks and the wind's severity. I loved nothing better than to reach some new place and discover new peoples, new animals, new cures to old ailments. I survived squalls, strict captains, incompetent crews, and boardings by pirates. I wrote long letters about my adventures to my parents, and sometimes their replies even caught up to me, giving me much pleasure. I also wrote to Lucius once or twice, but I never heard back from him and didn't expect to; nor could I know for sure my letters had made it into his hands, the vagaries of letters-by-ship being what they are.

In this way many years passed and I passed with them, growing weather-beaten and bearded and no different from any other sailor. Except, of course, for her arm.

At a distant river port, in a land where the birds spoke like women and the men wore outlandishly bright tunics and skirts, a letter from my mother caught up with me. In it, she told me that my father had died after a long illness, an illness she had never mentioned in any of her other letters. The letter was a year old.

I felt an intense confusion. I could not understand how a man who in my memory I had said goodbye to just a few years before could now be dead. It took a while to understand I had been at sea for three decades. That somewhere in the back of my mind I had assumed my parents would live forever. I couldn't accept it. I couldn't even cry.

Six months later, slowly making my way back to my mother, another letter, this time from a friend of the family. My mother had died and been laid next to my father in the basement of the Preservation Guild.

It felt as if the second trauma had made me fully experience the first. All I could think of was my father, and the two of them working together in their bungalow.

I remember I stood on the end of a rickety quay in a backwater port reading the letter. Behind me the dismal wooden shanty town and above explosions of green-and-blue parrots. The sun was huge and red on the horizon, as if we were close to the edge of the world.

Her hand discarded the letter and reached over to caress my hand. I wept silently.

•

Five years later, I tired of life at sea – it was no place for the aging – and I returned home. The city was bigger and more crowded. The medical school carried on as it had for centuries. The mages' college had disappeared, the site razed and replaced with modern, classroom-filled buildings.

I stored my many trunks of possessions – full of rare tinctures and substances and oddities – at a room in a cheap inn and walked down to my parents' bungalow. It had been abandoned and boarded up. After two days, I found the current owner. He turned out to be a man who resembled the Stinker of my youth in the fatuousness of his smile, the foulness of his breath. This new Stinker didn't want to sell, but in the end I took the brass key, spotted with green age, from him and the bungalow was mine.

Inside, beneath the dust and storm damage, I found the echoes of my parents' preservations – familiar fond splotches across the kitchen tiles – and read their recipes in the residue.

From these remnants, what they taught me of their craft, and the knowledge I brought back from my travels, I now make my modest living. These are not quite the preservations of my youth, for there is even less magic in the world now. No, I must use science and magic in equal quantities in my tinctures and potions, and each comes with a short tale or saying. I conjure these up from my own experience or things my parents told me. With them, I try to conjure up what is so easily lost: the innocence and passion of first love, the energy and optimism of the young, the strange sense of mystery that fills midnight walks along the beach. But I preserve more prosaic things as well – like the value of hard work done well, or the warmth of good friends. The memories that sustain these concoctions spring out of me and through my words and mixtures into my clients. I find this winnowing, this release, a curse at times, but mostly it takes away what I do not want or can no longer use.

Mine is a clandestine business, spread by word-of-mouth. It depends as much on my clients' belief in me as my craft. Bankers and politicians, merchants and landlords hear tales of this strange man living by himself in a preservationists' bungalow, and how he can bring them surcease from loneliness or despair or the injustice of the world.

Sometimes I wonder if one day Lucius will become one of my clients and we will talk about what happened. He still lives in this city, as a member of the city council, having dropped out of medical school, I'm told, not long after he performed the surgery on me. I've even seen him speak, although I could never bring myself to walk up to him. It would be too much like talking to a ghost.

Still, necessity might drive me to him as it did in the past. I have to fill in with other work to survive. I dispense medical advice to the fisherfolk, many driven out of work by the big ships, or to the ragged urchins begging by the dock. I do not charge, but sometimes they will leave a loaf of bread or fish or eggs on my doorstep, or just stop to talk.

Over time, I think I have forgiven myself. My thoughts just as often turn to the future as the past. I ask myself questions like *When I die, what will she do?* Will the arm detach itself, worrying at the scar line with sharpened fingernails, leaving only the memory of my flesh as the fingers pull it like an awkward crab away from my death bed? Is there an emerald core that will be revealed by that severance, a glow that leaves her in the world long after my passing? Will this be loss or completion?

For her arm has never aged. It is as perfect and smooth and strong as when it came to me. It could still perform surgery if the rest of me had not betrayed it and become so old and weak.

Sometimes I want to ask my mirror, the other old man, what lies beyond, and if it is so very bad to be dead. Would I finally know her then? Is it too much of a sentimental, half-senile fantasy, to think that I might see her, talk to her? And: have I done enough since that ecstatic, drunken night, running with my best friend up to the cadaver room, to have deserved that mercy?

One thing I have learned in my travels, one thing I know is true. The world is a mysterious place and no one knows the full truth of it even if they spend their whole life searching. For example, I am writing this account on the beach, each day's work washed away in time for the next, lost unless my counterpart has been reading it.

I am using my beloved's hand, her arm as attached to me as if we were one being. I know every freckle. I know how the bone aches in the cold and damp.

I can feel the muscles tensing when I clench the purple stick and see the veins bunched at the wrist like a blue delta. A pale red birthmark on the heel of her palm looks like a snail crossing the tidal pool at my feet. We never really knew each other, not even each other's names, but sometimes that's not important.

APPOGGIATURA

(Fragments from the legendary city of Smaragdine's Green Tablet)

Autocthonous

At the university today, I cracked an egg yolk into my co-worker Farid's coffee while he was off photocopying something. The yolk looked like the sun disappearing into a deep well. The smell made me think of the chickens on my parents' farm and then it wasn't long before I was thinking about my father and his temper. It made me almost regret doing it. But when Farid came back he didn't even notice the taste. He was too busy researching the architecture of some American city for one of the professors. My yolk and his research were a good fit as far as I was concerned, especially since that was supposed to be my project. But he was always pushing and he was an artist, whereas I was just getting a history and religion degree. I wouldn't have anything to show for that until much later.

After he left and the building was empty, I set a fire in the wastebasket on the fourth floor, being careful to use a bit of string as a fuse so it wouldn't start to blaze until after I'd gotten on the bus down the street.

On the way home to my apartment, through the usual road blocks and searches, I embedded a personal command into the minds of the other people on the bus using the image of the saintly Hermes Trismegistus. He said to them, "Tomorrow, you will do something extraordinary for the Green of Smaragdine."

When I got to the complex, I stopped at each landing and used a piece of chalk to draw a random symbol. If there was a newspaper in front of someone's door, I would write on it or rip it or whatever came to mind.

I walked into my box of an apartment, gray walls, gray rooms, and took off my clothes. I painted myself green and leapt at the walls until the green mixed with the red of my blood and the gray was gone. Exhausted, I stopped, and pissed once again on my long-suffering copy of the blasphemous book Farid liked so much. Then I turned on the family TV that my mother had made me take when I came to the city and at the same moment I drove a paperweight through the screen. My fingers and arm vibrated from the shock.

But nothing else happened. There was no revelation. No sign.

I crumpled to the floor and began to cry.

When will the Green move through me? What will it take?

•

Cambist

At the Anadolubank in Istanbul, Hazine Tarosian has handled them all. Crinkled and smooth, crisp and softly old. To her, new bills smell like ink and presses moving at high speed. There's a hint of friction in the paper, of burning smoke, that gives motion to the images. A burst of sunflower, bee in orbit around pollen, for the Netherlands. Ireland's beefy headshot of James Joyce, with *Ulysses* on the other side. The sibilance of Egypt's Arabic letters against a backdrop of Caliph-era battlements, in the distance a verdigris dome, last link to fabled Smaragdine. The careful detail of Thai King Bhumibol calm upon his throne, sword across his lap, a flaming mandala at his back. Or even Portugal's massed galleons listing, sails taut against the whorled wind, sun a complex compass.

Hazine has begun to believe that the value of such wonders should be based on something more lasting than the rate of exchange. The verdigris dome in particular has so enthralled her that she even bought a book about Smaragdine called *The Myths of the Green Tablet*, and got her cousin to send her a few old coins she keeps in a display at her bank office.

For months now the image of the dome has come to her at night. She is floating over it and it is floating up toward her, until she's falling down through the dome and she can see, distant but ever closer: a green tablet, a ruined tower, an entire ancient city.

This dream is so vivid that Hazine always wakes gasping, the solution to some great mystery already receding into the darkness. Friends tell her the dream is about her job, and yet it informs her waking life in unexpected ways, imbues certain people and things with vibrant light and color. She keeps the Egyptian bill in her wallet. The suggestion, the hint, of Smaragdine, is so potent, as if a place must be hidden to become real.

Is this, then, the power of money? Hazine thinks, bringing tea and the newspaper back to bed with her in the mornings, her lover asleep and dreamless beside her.

●

Chiaroscuro

I was still searching for the missing daughter of a wealthy industrialist from Cyprus when the locals brought me in on another case. They'd heard I was staying at the Hilton – an American and a detective, in a city where neither passed through with any regularity. The police deputy, a weathered old man with a scar through his left eyesocket, made it clear that it would be best if I got into his beat-up Ford Fiesta with the lonely siren on top, and venture out into the sun-beaten city to help him.

It was a crap ride, through a welter of tan buildings with no hint anymore of the green that had made the place famous since antiquity. The river had become a stream. The lake that it fed into was entombed in salt. The cotton they turned to as a crop just made it all worse. They'd survived a dictator, too, who had starved and disappeared people while building a monstrous palace. Becoming modern is a bitch for some people.

The dead guy, a painter, the deputy told me, turned out to have lived on the seventh floor of what looked like a Soviet-era housing project made from those metal shelves you see at hardware stores. The smell of piss and smoke in the stairwell almost made me want to give up cigarettes again and find a bar. Most of the complex was deserted.

The painter's place had an unwashed, turpentine-and-glue smell. Several large canvases had been leaned against the wall, under cloth. Through a huge window the light entered with a ferocious velocity. Somewhere out in that glare lay the ruins of the old city center.

In the middle of the floor: a young man in the usual pool of blood. I could see a large, tissue-filled hole in his back. The piss smell had gotten worse. Behind him, one canvas remained uncovered on an easel.

Against a soft dark green background so intense it hit me like the taste of mouthwash, a girl sat on a stone bench in an explosion of light. A dark complexion or just a deep tan, I couldn't tell. A simple black dress. No shoes. No nail polish. A sash around her waist that almost hid a pack of cigs shoved in at the left side. Her head was tilted, chin out, as if looking up at someone. A thin smile that could have been caution or control. The way she sat I found strange, her torso almost curved inward so that it made her seem like a puzzle piece lacking its mate. She held something even greener than the background, but someone – the murderer I guessed – had scratched it out with a knife. It could have been a book; at least, she held it like a book, although there was something too fleshy about the hints of it still left on the canvas.

For a mistaken moment, I thought I'd found the missing girl. For a moment, I thought I'd found something even more important.

I looked around the apartment a bit, but my gaze kept coming back to the painting. It was signed in the corner: "Farid Sabouri."

I kept thinking, *Why did they defile the painting?*

After a while, the police deputy asked me in his imperfect English, "You know what happen? Who?"

Somewhere in this rat's warren of apartments there was probably a man whose wife or daughter the artist had been screwing. Or someone he owed a lot of money to. Or just a psychopath. You get used to the options after a while. They aren't complicated.

I breathed in the smoky air. They weren't ever going to find the guy who had done this. Not in this country. It was still reinventing itself. Deaths like these were part of the price you paid. The police deputy probably didn't expect it to be solved. He probably didn't really care, so long as he could say he'd tried.

"I have no fucking idea," I said. "But how much to let me take that painting?"

•

Dulcimer

From the *Book of Smaragdine*, 212th Edition:

> The dulcimer has many esoteric uses in the spiritual and medical worlds. Playing the dulcimer while attaching a wresting thread to a

person with a sprain will hasten the winding of the thread and the healing of the sprain. A man who plays the dulcimer over the grave of his dead wife will ensure that she stays dead and does not pay unexpected visits. A woman who plays the dulcimer holding it backwards will reverse her bad luck and bring home a wayward lover. A child who stands on one leg and attempts the dulcimer with chin and left hand while the right arm is tied behind the back will inevitably fall. If making a doppelganger using the priests' emerald powder, the dulcimer should be played during the mixing; otherwise, your monster may coalesce with a vestigial tale or tail. It is also known that playing the dulcimer after dinner increases the chance of pleasant conversation, if accompanied by wine and a nice dessert.

●

Eczema

Anyone who has seen Eczema's act for the Babilim Traveling Circus knows it is only enhanced by the equal and opposite reaction created by Psoriasis. Touring erratically throughout Central Asia and the Far East (where not banned), the circus has only rarely been captured on film or in still photographs.

Although myths about Eczema's act abound, most eyewitnesses agree on the basics: Eczema, so nicknamed by her late father, a doctor, for the predominant condition of her formative years, enters the ring accompanied by helpers who carry several small boxes under their arms. Eczema is heavily made up in white face and wears a man's costume more fitting for a sultan, including curved shoes. A fake mustache completes the illusion. In the background a local band plays something approximating circus music.

Eczema's assistants, dressed all in black, fan out around her. Some of them place shiny blue-and-gray models of buildings upon the floor while others arrange a variety of insects in amongst the buildings, including scarab beetles, praying mantises, and grasshoppers. Some are green or have been painted green, while others are red or have been painted red. A few flies, large moths, and butterflies weakly buzz or flutter above on long, glittering strands of hair plucked from the heads of Tibetan holy men, the leads held by specially trained insect handlers.

Eczema stands in the background as an announcer or ringmaster comes forward and says, "The King of Smaragdine now re-creates for you, using his minions, the Great Battle between the Smaragdineans of the Green Tablet and the Turks."

Reports differ on the battle's historical accuracy. Certainly, the Turks ruled the area around Smaragdine for some three hundred years, but records from the time are often incomplete.

As for the act itself, some describe it as "insects wandering around a badly made scale model of an ancient city, after which the crowd rioted to show their displeasure." Others describe "the incredible sight of beetles, ants, and other insects re-creating miniature set pieces of ancient battles amongst the spires and fortifications of a realistic and highly detailed cityscape. One of the most marvelous things ever seen."

During this spectacle, Eczema stands to the side, gesturing like an orchestra conductor and blowing on a whistle that makes no sound.

Most accounts agree that the act comes to an abrupt end when the insects that have not escaped are swept up by the helpers. A few eyewitnesses, however, tell tales of an ending in which "huge basslike mudskippers hop on their fins through the cityscape, gobbling up the insects."

Eczema then comes forward and says, in a grave tone, "What is below is like that which is above, and what is above is like that which is below for performing the miracle of one thing. And as all things were produced from one by the Meditation of one, so all things are produced from this one thing by adaptation."

After this short speech, the audience usually leaves in confusion.

Psoriasis does not join Eczema until the end of the act. That Eczema and Psoriasis are Siamese twins only becomes evident when they stand together and bow, and the declivity between them – that outline, that echo – tells the story of another act altogether.

•

Elegiacal

Brown dust across a gray sky, with mountains in the distance. A metallic smell and taste. A burning.

Abdul Ahad and his sister Parveen were searching for a coin she'd lost.

They stood by a wall of what was otherwise a rubble of stone and wood. A frayed length of red carpet wound its way through the debris.

"It has to be here somewhere," Parveen said. It had been a present from her uncle, a merchant who was the only one in their family to travel outside the country.

Her uncle had pressed it into her hand when she was eight and said, "This is an old coin from Smaragdine. There, everything is green." Her uncle made a living sometimes selling coins, but this one was special.

The coin was heavy. On the front was a man in a helmet and on the back letters in a strange language, like something from another world. For weeks, she had held it, smooth and cool, in her right hand – to school, during lunch, back at their house, during dinner. She loved the color of it; there was no green like that here. Everything was brown or gray or yellow or black, except for the rugs, which were red. But this green – she didn't even need a photograph. She could see Smaragdine in her mind just from the texture and color of the coin.

"I don't see it," Abdul Ahad said, his voice flat and strange.

"We should keep looking."

"I think we should stop." Abdul Ahad had a sharp gash across his forehead. Parveen's clothes had ash on them. Her elbows and the back of her arms were lacerated from where she had tried to protect herself from the bomb blasts.

"We should keep looking," Parveen said. She had to keep swallowing; her throat hurt badly. She heard her brother's words through a sighing roar.

The muddled sound of sirens.

A harsh wind roiled down the brown street, carrying sand and specks of dirt.

Abdul Ahad sat down heavily on the broken rock.

Now Parveen could hear the screams and wails of people farther away. Flickers of flame three houses down the block, red-orange through the shadows of stones.

Their father had been dead for a year. Now their mother lay under the rubble. They'd seen a leg, bloodied and twisted. Had pulled away rocks, revealing an unseeing gaze, a face coated with dust.

Her brother had checked her pulse.

Now they were searching for the coin. Or Parveen was. She knew why her brother didn't want to. Because he thought it wouldn't make a difference. But Parveen felt that, somehow, if she found it, if she held it again, everything would be normal again. She had only survived the air strike because she was holding the coin at the time, she was sure of it, and Abdul Ahad had only survived because he had been standing next to her.

"You don't have to look, Ahad," she said, giving him a hug. "You should sit there for a while, and I'll find it."

He nodded, gaze lost on the mountains in the distance.

Parveen walked away from him, kneeled in the dirt. She stuck her arm into a gap between jagged blocks of stone, grasping through dust and gravel, looking for something smooth and cool and far away. In a moment, she knew she'd have it.

●

Eudaemonic

From the *Book of Smaragdine,* 1st Edition:

> People from far off places ask why we worship the Green. They think of us as fools or outcasts. Yet even an ape can understand that human beings are born, live, and die. Even a beggar knows the alchemy in this basic transformation. To achieve true understanding, then, and thus true happiness, it is important to understand that transformation. Otherwise, our stay here is a ceaseless wandering, whether we roam or not.
>
> "Would you like to hear a riddle?
>
> *What power is strong with all power and will defeat every subtle thing and penetrate every solid thing?*
>
> "In giving yourself to the Green you will know what it means to search for answers to questions such as these. You will become secure in your happiness.
>
> "People say that we do not know what happened to the Tablet, that it has been hidden from us for a reason. But this matters not. If

we fail in the finding or the reaching, should ever our own city fall
and be forgotten, then still we shall be eudaemonic in the failure."

•

Euonym

*That first night on the train, we were so free there was nothing to do but yell
out the window at the darkness, into the cool breeze laced with honeysuckle and
coal smoke.*

Our father always thought he knew the value of a good and true name. He
named us Eczema and Psoriasis much as he would name a medical proce-
dure. It was an odd choice by a sometimes secretive man. Yes, my sister and
I had had disfiguring skin conditions as children, but this was so minor
compared to our other problems. We were conjoined twins. Before our first
birthdays, our father performed three surgeries to separate us. (In a sense, he
not only named us twice, he created us twice.) Psoriasis looked as if someone
had attached the male part of a puzzle piece to her side. I looked like a shark
had taken a bite out of me.

My real name was Kamilah and my sister's real name was Anbar, but our
father used Eczema and Psoriasis so much that around the house in Tashkent we learned to give up those names.

We had come to Tashkent because of our father's skill as a surgeon; despite
the repressive regime, the medical facilities there were "second to none," as
he liked to say. And it was at a dinner party our parents hosted for colleagues
from the medical school that someone called me "Kamilah" and, for the first
time, I did not respond. Who was "Kamilah"? I was Eczema. I did not realize then that I might have a third name, one I could choose myself. I was ten.

After everyone had left the house that night, our mother berated our
father for his cruelty. She was a beautiful, intelligent, tough woman who
loved us too much.

"How can you continue to call them that?" she asked him as he sat drinking scotch in the living room. "Haven't they been through enough?"

At the time, we were having terrible trouble in school. We didn't fit in.
We would never fit in.

Our father replied, "When I was growing up, I gave myself horrible nicknames. That way nothing the other boys said could be worse."

It was true that our father never treated anyone worse than he treated himself. A childhood disease had crippled his left arm: it was smaller and paler than his right arm. Because of it, our father was a kind of genius when he held the scalpel.

He never told us the names he'd given himself in school. Instead, he would tell us that he had used his skills and a green powder given to him by a Smaragdinean priest to reanimate a dead woman's arm, which he then used to replace his own, "the better to perform surgery." This tall tale wasn't funny the first time he told it, let alone the twentieth, but he didn't notice our reaction.

Another time – we must have been seventeen – we were sitting at the kitchen table, drinking coffee with our mother, when he walked out of his study in his bathrobe.

He smiled at us and said, "The real reason I call you what I do is that neither of you is comfortable. You never have been. Your brains are itchy – restless and curious – and there is no cure for that other than death. Never forget that."

Then he retreated into his study, padding along in the silly mouse slippers that he'd worn for as long as I could remember.

I would like to think that he already knew our plans and had forgiven us.

A month later, we ran away on the train, desperate to change the reality that had been imposed on us by the world.

A year later we found the Green in the form of the ringmaster who called himself Hermes Trismegistus and talked like a silk ribbon tied slowly around the wrist.

Two years and we came up with our first act for the Babilim Traveling Circus.

Four years and we began to have a sense of what our third, our self-chosen names might be, and how we might best serve the Green and thus ourselves.

Five years later our father died without either of us ever having had a chance to tell him any of this.

●

Insouciant

– boots smashing through brambles to the soft pine needle floor, left hand lacerated by branches from reaching out for support at the wrong moment, heart beat rapid, blood on the grip of his Glock, sharp pain in the shoulders as he whipped around long enough to get a few rounds off at an enemy that shattered in his vision because of the recoil, Lake Baikal behind him and more forest ahead and no hope in hell now of staking out the cabin where he suspected the girl was being held by the Russian toughs that had flushed him out, although he wondered as a bullet flecked a pine tree to his left and the bark exploded against his arm was the girl really there, how could he be sure and why the hell did his watch itch so badly against his sweating wrist and all the time trying not to fall, when he heard a bellowing behind him and the sound of his pursuers brought up short, followed by a cry of surprise, and he just kept running because he'd caught a hint of something green that reminded him of a painting he'd bought but didn't connect to his idea of reality, or anybody's idea of reality, and it wasn't until that moment that he realized all through the chase, until the sight of the smudge of green, that he'd been as carefree as he could ever hope to be in his line of work and how strange that was and yet so true, then tripped over something large and fleshy, fell on his side against some tree roots and, dazed, gasping for air, raised his head to find the smudge of green resolved into something so improbable that he lay there staring at it for far too long, knowing instinctively that this was part of some great mystery, a mystery he might pursue for years and never solve and yet must pursue anyway, and realizing too that because of it he would rarely know any kind of peace for the rest of his life –

•

Logorrhea

(Excerpted from "Yetis, Loch Ness, and Talking Fish?" in the English magazine *Strange Phenomenon*, April 1935)

> *"There is really no sight that stirs the blood more than witnessing a giant Logorrheic Coelacanth plowing its way across the floor of old-growth Siberian forest, bellowing for all it's worth." – Dr. G. Merrill Smith*

The freshwater walking fish called by some the "Logorrheic Coelacanth" has again been sighted in and around Siberia's Lake Baikal, as it has at regular intervals for hundreds of years. Most sightings occur miles from any water source, the fish reported to crawl awkwardly on its thick pectoral fins. Speculation leads this reporter to the conclusion that the Logorrheic Coelacanth must have a remarkable capacity to store water in pouches concealed by its gills. Third-hand accounts tell of hunters encountering the voice of this fish before ever sighting it. (This reporter believes that the force of cycling water through the gills creates the sibilant yet throaty noise.)

In August 1934, the Logorrheic Coelacanth's gill mutterings came under rigorous observation by Dr. G. Merrill Smith's zoological expedition to track and tag Lake Baikal's freshwater seals. Dr. Smith told this reporter that he saw "what looked like a squadron of raucous walking fish ugly as bulldogs at the edge of a clearing. Imagine my surprise when I realized they were speaking in an ancient shamanistic language associated with a lost race once close kin to the Smaragdineans." Independent analysis of the field recordings made by Dr. Smith confirms the resemblance to certain rare languages. Some scientists have postulated a kind of inadvertent mimicry to explain the phenomenon. (Dr. Smith has stated, "I think it might be as coincidental as a cat coughing up a hairball sounding like speech.") Others have proposed more outré theories, such as symbiosis between Neanderthals and the fish. Although no serious scientist accepts this theory, no one can explain the fish's wanderings, the long intervals between sightings, nor give any reason for the fish to have developed this "adaptation."

•

Lyceum

From the *Book of Smaragdine*, 543rd Edition:

> The Lyceum at Smaragdine began as a convalescence retreat for the children of the wealthy, often prescribed by court physicians. It also served as a center for teaching about medicine and philosophy, but during the Rule Without Kings, the Lyceum fell into disrepair. When finally refurbished by the insane Reformer King Jankamora,

the Lyceum took on ever more mystical undertones. King Jankamora had secret doors and tunnels added to the interior and made of the exterior a complex illusion. A facade created by skilled painters made it appear that it was always dusk inside. A certain organic quality began to permeate the architecture. Water features began to dominate the exterior gardens. Inside, King Jankamora had trees planted and knocked holes in the ceiling to accommodate them. Wherever possible, he lengthened the corridors and made them more difficult. Soon, it was nearly impossible to find the way from one room to another. The king also created what he called a "circus that is not a circus" and had it train and perform solely inside of the Lyceum, often to an audience of dead insects he had collected during his travels. Members of the court began to complain that the Lyceum had become "a hideaway for the uncanny and the unseemly." When King Jankamora disappeared, it was rumored that he had become trapped in the Lyceum. Sadly, when Smaragdine was taken during World War I by the British, the Lyceum was lost. Some claimed it had spontaneously sucked itself into the earth. Others, that King Jankamora reappeared and, with the help of his secret followers, disassembled the Lyceum and reassembled it far away, in the mountains. Claims that the Lyceum and all of its elements had been created by Jankamora to somehow assist in the search for the Green Tablet cannot be substantiated. Regardless, ever since that time there have been only hints of the Lyceum in the form of the brilliant green shards and wooden beams today found in the museums of other countries.

•

Macerate

To: The President of Emerald Delta River Cruises

Dear Sir or Madam:

I am writing to complain in no uncertain terms.

My wife and I are not rich people, nor extravagant. I, for example, work part-time at a grocery store since my retirement. But this past summer, we decided to treat ourselves to a river cruise. We chose your service because it had come highly recommended by one of our cousins and because the rates were reasonable. Five days on a river cruise! Nothing could have delighted us more, and my poor Macha, who works twelve-hour days in a factory, deserved it. Besides, the name of the boat seemed rather romantic: *The Light of the Moon*.

We departed in late August with the river calm and swallows skimming over the water. Our cabin seemed nice if cramped and the people on board were pleasant. It was a surprise to find that a number of pigs had been brought on board by another traveler, but they were kept below deck and made surprisingly little sound. We looked forward to a relaxing experience.

All was well until the second night, when, as you know, river pirates tried to board *The Light of the Moon*, under, well I must say it, the light of the moon. We were horrified, of course, but stayed in our cabin as the crew commanded. We heard all kinds of terrible noises and what sounded like shots fired, as well as a great uproar among the pigs. But this settled down and we were reassured by some new crew members in the morning that the pirates had been repelled and would no longer be a problem. Being a war veteran, I had remained calm and my poor Macha had been calm, too, although I made her take a sleeping tablet after.

Pirates simply made an adventure for us, this late in our lives. Nor did we mind the next day when two fellow travelers playing cards shot at one another before being subdued by members of the crew. Besides, Macha missed all of it, having overslept.

Shortly thereafter, however, the menu began to change and this is where I believe the nature of our complaint will become clear. It will also explain why we began to lose weight on this so-called "idyllic cruise downriver, ending at the site of ancient Smaragdine." Perhaps typing up a description from the menu will be enough to convince you of our claim:

Thrice-Shoved Frogs, Whole – Two whole emerald frogs, flayed alive and then lightly braised and macerated, after which the whole skin of one is pulled back over the other and vice versa. The frogs are then impaled, still fresh, on a two-headed skewer and cooked over an open flame. Both frogs are then put inside a hollowed-out river iguana, which is then stuffed into a large river fish and placed inside a box full of coals that is heated and tossed out behind the boat for further maceration. The resulting taste of the then-pan-fried Thrice-Shoved Frogs is indescribable.

For three days, your crew and the two women serving as cooks prepared a series of dishes that included macerating anything and everything, usually "shoving" or "stuffing" it inside of some other animal. I have never seen such senseless violence done to anything or anyone as to these creatures with their bulging eyes and gutted rears. When we complained, we were told by both women that we should be happy to receive such delicacies.

Many other strange things went on aboard that ship, sir or madam. Some of them I do not feel comfortable relating to you, even now, two months after our ordeal. The crew did not seem to sleep and once, when I peeked out from the door of our cabin after midnight, I saw two of them painted green from head to foot, stark naked, engaged in a dance involving scarab beetles. During the day, they would say odd things designed, I believe, to make us react in some specific way.

After a time, we did not know if perhaps the crew had gone mad or if they just practiced insolence as a cure for boredom.

When we arrived at our destination, the crew disappeared, leaving us there by the dock. We had to take a train back to our little apartment the very next day – a trip of some thirty hours, and very hard on my poor Macha.

We do not need or want apologies. We would like a refund of our money and vouchers for free meals from our favorite restaurant. It is only symbolic, of course, to have these vouchers separate from a general refund. But there is the principle involved, isn't there? We cannot get those "Thrice-Shoved Frogs" on *The Light of the Moon* out of our heads.

Thank you for your kind attention,

Saladin Davidos, Esq.

•

JEFF VANDERMEER

Pococurante

From the *Book of Smaragdine*, 212th Edition:

A careless person has no cure, unlike a careless thought or animal.
Calling a careless person a "pococurante" or other fancy name will
not, by the precision of the term, suddenly make the careless care-
ful. Once, a careless farmer living outside of Smaragdine lost his
own name and had to take the name of his ox, Baff, much to the
delight of the villagers (one of whom found the farmer's name and
used it as his own). A woman once lost her vagina and by the time
she found it she had twelve children. Losing one's shadow is perhaps the most common affliction of the careless, which explains
why, on a hot afternoon day, you will find so many little dribbles
of shadow in every lonesome crack and crevice. A lost shadow has
no wish to be found, because, inevitably, it will just be lost again.

"But the truly careless – the person who has descended into a
place that not many can understand – will lose much more than
that. These truly cursed people can lose even a love so strong that
it radiates like heat. The kind of love that creates laughter around
even the simplest act. When enough love is lost to this kind of in-
difference or carelessness, wars begin – sometimes in lands far distant from the occurrence, but always these wars come home. Such
effects are magnified depending on the status of the individual.
Thus, when statesmen, when queens, when caliphs, become careless, they lose whole armies and people die on vast scales in foreign lands. The innocent taste sand in their mouths, not the green
spring air of their native country. Their bones line the roads of
places so far away and exotic that not even the wind through their
skulls can say the names. A careless commoner often loses hate as
well, even though such hate will replace itself indefinitely and the
person therefore never realizes his own carelessness. But for this
reason, many careful kings and queens find the hate of others and
use it as if it were their own.

"Alas, a careless person has no cure, unlike a careless thought or
animal. It is just the way of the world."

256

•

Psoriasis

Anyone who has seen Psoriasis' act for the Babilim Traveling Circus knows it is only matched by the equal and opposite reaction created by Eczema.

Myths about Psoriasis' act abound, but this is what eyewitnesses report: Psoriasis, so nicknamed by her late doctor father for the predominant condition of her formative years, dressed as a man with a fake moustache, in clothes similar to whatever the locals favor, sits in the stands with the audience while below Eczema enters the ring in her sultan disguise accompanied by helpers who carry several small boxes. Eczema begins her act, which consists of an insect re-creation of a mythical Smaragdine battle.

At the same time, Psoriasis begins to complain about the act from the stands, in oddly modulated tones. The loudness and quality of this disturbance varies from city to city. Woven in with the complaints are phrases such as "The father of it is the sun," "The wind carried it in its belly," and "So the world was created," all delivered in a peculiar sing-song intonation. These phrases come from the fabled Emerald Tablet, attributed to the ancient alchemist Hermes Trismegistus.

After a time, the people listening to Psoriasis experience a heightened sense of happiness, followed by a profound drowsiness. One boy of thirteen recounts that "I know I must have fallen asleep, because my next memory is of feeling something smooth in my left hand and finding a strange green coin there."

That Psoriasis attempts to aid in the audience's enjoyment of her sister's insect battle seems apparent. Whether this is by simple hypnosis or some deeper technique is unknown. What, if anything, the audience does while under this possible hypnosis is also unknown. However, in the weeks and months after seeing the performance, many people report intense shifts of emotion, visions, and a desire for "all things that are green."

Psoriasis does not join Eczema until the end of the act. That Eczema and Psoriasis are Siamese twins only becomes evident when they stand together and bow, and the declivity between them – that outline, that echo – tells the story of another act altogether.

●

Semaphore

When Truewill Mashburn turned eighteen, he left the U.S. with forged documents and passed himself off as a thirty-something ESE teacher at a Costa Rican university. He'd always looked older than his age and at six-four with sandy-blond hair and a Viking's eyes and chin, people usually believed what he said. By the time he left Latin America at the age of twenty-two and headed for Europe, he'd hitchhiked through twelve countries, been a missionary, a doctor's aide, and a bank teller.

Now twenty-five, Mashburn found himself living in an abandoned semaphore tower on the banks of a Central Asian river that eventually wound its way down to the ruins of old Smaragdine and the tired modern city that surrounded it.

He'd read about the semaphore towers while hanging out in a Tashkent library. They'd once been vital in Smaragdine's epic battles against "the dreaded Turk." Now they were just free apartments ripe for the taking, in Mashburn's eyes.

Mashburn took the book – *The Myth of the Green Tablet* – and headed south. By the time he found the towers, he was ready to settle down awhile anyway, having been hassled at half a dozen borders. He could fish in the river, exchange some of his limited cash for food in the nearby village, read the book he'd stolen, or just hang out with the locals smoking dope. A few times a week, the village women walked past, giggling and talking about him. He couldn't understand them, but he knew what they were saying.

It should have been perfect, but an odd sense of responsibility began to grow inside him with each day he lived there. He felt it in his chest every time he walked up the three stories of crumbling stone steps to stare at the tower a half mile downriver that doubled his own.

The book was to blame, even though the author seemed contemptuous of the subject. On some level, the more Mashburn read about the fascinating history of Smaragdine, the more he couldn't help but feel an obligation to continue its ancient fight against the Turks. It didn't make sense, and yet it did.

Mashburn decided to become the true keeper of the tower. He removed the weeds inside and along the circular fringe. He did his best with his limited knowledge of drywall to repair the worst areas. He began to wear his tattered army-surplus jacket all the time. He bought a pair of old binoculars from a villager. He even assigned himself guard duty, more often at dusk than during the day.

At night, the tower looked less ruined and it was easier to imagine he was back in Time and that he might need to use the tower's windmill-like semaphore spokes to warn of some danger.

Then, too, Mashburn saw many strange things the longer he stood watch at night. Fish that bellowed at him from the water. Debris and bodies from some battle that had taken place many countries upriver. A man in a motorboat who looked vaguely American in a leather jacket and dark shades, a gun holster on his exposed ankle. Something was happening, Mashburn was certain. He just didn't know what.

One moonlit night just before dawn, he saw the most curious thing of all: a river cruise ship with several smaller boats pursuing it. When they caught up, what looked like a band of circus performers jumped on board: a couple of women dressed like caliphs, a snake charmer, a mime, and a fire-eater, among others. The battle raged as Mashburn looked on with mouth open.

By the time the conflict had subsided, far to the south of his position, he couldn't tell who had won, only that the boats remained empty and most of the river cruise crew were walking around on deck again.

Sometimes Mashburn felt prematurely old from all of his travels, but in that moment, he felt both dumbfounded and oddly blessed.

By mid-morning, he had the semaphore spokes turning for the first time in two centuries and he was sending his message out across the water. He didn't care if the next station was manned or not. That wasn't the point.

•

Smaragdine

In the vast city of Smaragdine on the edge of a dying sea-lake, from which come palm trees and a wasting disease, the color green is much prized. It matters not where it is found, nor the exact shade. The cloth-makers produce nothing but clothing in green, so that the people of the city are always swathed in it. The buildings are painted in emerald, in verdigris, edged in a bronze that quickly turns. Even the white domesticated parrots that the denizens have such affection for – these birds they dye green. Year by year the lake becomes smaller and the river that feeds into it more of a stream. Year by year, the palm trees become yellower and fewer. Yet the people hold vast and expensive festivals in celebration of the arcane and the uncanny. There is a constant state of celebration. Yet also it is a point of pride for buildings to fall into disrepair, if at the limits of their disillusion there creeps into the corners of rooms, across the ceilings, some hint of green. Someday, Smaragdine will be as a ruin and the lake will be gone and the river with it. But, in the end, it will not matter, for even when the last water is gone, this city will still be rich and fertile in color. This is all the inhabitants ask. It is all they can hope for. I know, for I lived in Smaragdine for a time. I knew the calm beauty of its streets, the dyed-green water of its many fountains, filled with green carp. I knew the slogans of the leaders in their green cloaks. I knew, too, the feel of the hot sun and was blinded by the mirage of sand eclipsed by the shimmer of the ever-more-distant lake. One day, I will return and know once again the richness of that place by its devotion to its color. One day I will walk through those empty streets and know the very definition of madness."

– Told to one of Marco Polo's men by a merchant selling green cloth in a Mumbai marketplace

•

Sycophant

The young man who sat down beside the writer Baryut Aquelus in a Tashkent coffeehouse wore a black blazer over a green T-shirt and blue jeans. He had sallow skin, an open, round face, and thick eyebrows. His mouth was fleshy, as if he'd suffered a split lip.

The writer thought he recognized the type. The first words confirmed it.

"Are you – ? Are you really – ?" The rasp of a mouth-breather, along with the stain and smell of betel nut.

"Yes."

He no longer bothered to smile or straighten his jacket when people came up to him. It had been a few years since he'd removed himself from the great, the smoldering, eye of fame, but he remembered its heat.

"I've read all of your work, sir. Especially *Myths of the Green Tablet*. A very brave book."

"You speak like a native Smaragdinean," the writer said.

The man looked away, actually blushed. The writer found this charming.

"Thank you. I came there as a child. I know English. And French, too. A little. I read you in French, at first."

How long ago? He'd been out of print in France for at least half a decade.

"That's very good, um…?"

"My name? Farid. You can call me Farid Sabouri."

"Nice to meet you, Farid."

The notebook in front of him now seemed inert, useless. The thoughts welling up behind the pen receded into some middle distance, waiting for him to call them forth again.

"Tell me, if I'm not bothering you," Farid said, "how you came to write *Myths of the Green Tablet*."

"You mean you don't know?" He'd meant it as self-deprecating but it came out vainglorious. "I guess I've told it so many times I expect anyone who wanted to know would know."

It had gotten him in trouble. Vague death threats from a bunch of doddering priests. A shorter stint at the university in Smaragdine than he would have liked. *The Green Tablet not the gospel, not even vaguely true?* He hadn't realized the effect it would have when he was writing it – he just wrote it.

"I know, but it's different reading it in the paper."

"Well, if you insist." *Do I really mind that much?* "I wrote it because I think that Smaragdine has suffered from its fetish for the color green. It keeps us looking at the past. I feel that, for the average Smaragdinean, the future is behind him. I mean, it's practically fantastical. Medieval. Alchemy? Airy-fairy about earth-air-water-fire? No offense," he added, noting the intent look on Farid's face.

Farid smiled, revealing yellowing teeth, and said, "I am fascinated by the bravery in the act. To become a…a lightning rod for many difficulties."

"Yes, well…"

Above them the fans swirled slowly and out on the street a steady procession of outdated vehicles used the worn street. The waiter came with two coffees.

"My gift for our meeting," Farid said. "Please, enjoy it."

"Thank you," the writer said. And he was, actually, surprised. Usually the people who came up to him wanted something but offered nothing, no matter how trivial, in return.

"So what brings you to Tashkent?" the writer asked.

Farid did not look away this time. "I came to see you. I studied your work at university. I've studied your life, too."

Oh no, the writer thought, *here it comes.* Sometimes he felt his personal life had become the size of a postage stamp.

"And did I measure up?"

"Oh, you are very brave," Farid said. "Although I don't know if you understand that."

"It's kind of you to say," the writer said, although Farid's syntax seemed odd.

Farid almost said something, stopped, bit his lip, leaned forward. "No, it's the truth. It makes me weep a little, thinking about it. If you don't mind me saying it. You've used your talent for things that don't always make sense to me."

The writer tried to shrug it off with a chuckle.

Is this where the conversation turns obsessional?

"And here I took you for a bit of a sycophant, Farid. A bit of a hanger-on, as the Brits here like to say."

"Not in the least – you believe too little but know too much," Farid said, and pulled out a gun and shot the writer in the stomach.

Baryut had the odd sensation of Farid walking over him and past while he lay there staring up at the ceiling fan and people were running away screaming. There was no pain. Nothing so fast could really be painful, could it?

Possessed of a sudden and terrible clarity, Baryut thought: *What can I write in the next few minutes?*

●

Transept

Why church broke? That question all ask when get Barakhad? Though no
many tourist now – just detective last week, bad circus week before. But I
tell you – even drunk sitting end of bar give answer if you want answer – he
say we run out money when no water. That man, head on table, see? He tell
you merchants. Merchants of Barakhad break church because priests too big,
too big. Or I, sir, I tell you Devil visit Barakhad when church of Smaragdineans building and break it.

Or it could be that the architect's plans were too complicated and they
planned not one but three transepts, with gold leaf that wouldn't flake off
for the archways and brushes made from the tongues of hummingbirds to
paint the column detail.

What? Oh, don't be mad. Just a little joke I like to play on tourists.
So many of you think that our command of English is crumbling along
with our infrastructure. But I went to university, even spent a summer at
the University of San Diego on an exchange program, a long time ago.
You're lucky you bumped into me, my friend. That drunk over there, for
example – he doesn't want to speak English anymore. His whole family
died last year.

But do you really want to know why the church isn't "finished"? Why
not get a drink and sit down. It won't take long, but you might need the
drink. Don't worry, I'll keep it simple. I know the names around here
confuse foreigners.

So: the real reason the church looks unfinished is that until recently we
had a civil war in this country. Hadn't heard of it? Well, we're not in an area
with anything of any value, really. Not anymore.

First one side held Barakhad. They starved us and killed some of us and
took some of us away. Then the other side took over. They starved us and
killed some of us and took some of us away. Then the peacekeepers came
to our country, although we never saw one in Barakhad, not once, and a
coalition of countries so far away that none of us here in Barakhad had ever
visited any of them began to use planes to bomb us. I believe your country
participated in that effort.

We already had little food, no electricity. Now when people walked down
to the market, they might become splintered bones and shredded flesh and a

stain of red on the roadside in a blink of the eye. We lost maybe half of the people in Barakhad during those months.

Now that the bombs have stopped, we are doing our best. The priests who might have helped are gone. There has been no time to rebuild the church, my friend. We haven't had time to rebuild many things, as you may have seen when you came in to town.

So at the moment the church is crumbling and overgrown with weeds. It's green enough to make even a Smaragdinean happy. The north side of the transept remains one wall and a promise of a roof. No one likes a church where the wind can catch you up like the breath of God. No one likes a church with the rain on the inside. Except me, since that's where I'm forced to live for now.

Am I talking to you? Are we speaking? Are you hearing me?

●

Vignette

Once, a very long time ago, an adventurer became a problem for the King of Smaragdine. Something to do with the king's daughter. Something to do with the king's daughter and wine and a dance hall. So the king decreed that this adventurer should be sent "on a long quest for the good of the Green." The quest? To find the lost Tablet and bring it back to Smaragdine. The Tablet was in Siberia or Palestine or somewhere in South America or even possibly on the Moon, depending on one's interpretation of the writings. Regardless, this fit the very definition of "a long quest." Unfortunately for the adventurer, he had earned the nickname of "Vignette" because his adventures, although intense and satisfying in the retelling, were always short and occurred in and around the city.

Vignette wasn't very happy about the king's decision, but a long quest was better than immediate death, so off he went. Through Samarkand and East Asia he traveled; up into Siberia and around Lake Baikal; down to Mongolia; across China to Japan; by sailing ship to India; a brief stop in North Africa; up into the Mediterranean; over to Greenland; doubling back to England; braving the trip to the New World for several storm-tossed months; finding nothing there and sailing briefly down to South America.

He talked to everyone he could find – Arabs, Jews, Christians, Bantus, Moslems. Holy men and beggars. Merchants and royalty. Over time, his body grew lean and weathered but strong. His eyes narrowed against the sun and yet he saw more clearly. Fighting brigands in the steppes. Running from tribesmen with blow darts in the Amazon.

If only they could see "Vignette" now, he thought as he pulled an arrow from his shoulder and prepared a charge with Sudanese warriors against the fortifications of some other tribe. Climbing a mountain in the Himalayas, eyelashes clotted with frost, an avalanche crushed over them in a blink and as he dug himself out, he thought, *I'll show you the good of the Green.*

After a time, though, it really didn't matter to him if he ever found the Tablet – in fact, he no longer believed in its existence. He was homesick for Smaragdine and his friends there. So one day he began to head back, slowly. Some months later, he was close enough that all he had to do was cross the river by ferry and the walls shimmering in the distance would be real once more.

But he wasn't a fool. He'd brought three miraculous things with him, in a chest banded with gold: an ancient book from Siberia made of broad, thick leaves, written in a secret language none alive knew; a healing tincture from the Yucatan that smelled like honeysuckle and chocolate; and a shiny green stone that tribesmen in the Amazon had told him was a god's eyeball that had fallen from the sky one night. At least he wasn't returning empty-handed. With any luck the king would reward his efforts, or at least forgive his trespasses.

Word must have spread about his return, for a royal pavilion awaited him on the far side of the river.

But it was not the king who greeted him there. Instead, it was a woman and her retinue. At first he did not recognize her. Then he realized it was the king's daughter, five years older. She had wrinkles at the corners of her eyes. She had let her hair grow long. It hung free to her shoulders, framing a face that seemed too wistful, too sad, for one still so young.

"Where is the king?" he asked.

"He died a year ago," she said, and he could feel her gaze upon him, lingering over every scar and bruise on his stubbled face. "I rule Smaragdine now."

"I didn't find the Tablet, but I brought back a chest of treasures," he said. It was somewhere behind him, but he couldn't stop looking at her.

"I don't give a damn about any of that," she said, and leaned up and kissed him on the lips.

•

Vivisepulture

And the Turk came down upon Smaragdine like a storm of plagues and breached the city gates and slew the defenders on the walls with arrows and their horsemen, led by their captain Baryut Aquelus, outstripped their infantry and so came unto the great Lyceum where the priests had hidden the Green Tablet, and Baryut took the heart of Smaragdine from that place, leaving the priests dead upon the steps as they rode out again.

And in the streets beyond they came upon the din of fierce battle, for the Smaragdineans had recovered from their surprise and now fought like demons for their city and men fell in great numbers on both sides as the city began to burn.

Raising his sword, Baryut led the way for the Turk, cutting down any who opposed them.

But when he rode under the shadow of the city gates and looked back, Baryut saw that the Smaragdinean prince Farid, upon a black charger, had come up behind and slain his riders and would soon overtake him.

Safety lay at the semaphore tower by the river, but Farid outstripped the Turk and forced him up into the hills and ravines and the coffeehouse beyond.

Farid was only a few paces behind him, driven by righteous conviction.

The Tablet became heavier and heavier in the Turk's hands and the prince shouted at him now, sword slicing the sky into jagged pieces.

"Bring it back or I'll feed you to my dogs!" Farid shouted. "You are very brave, although I don't know if you understand that!"

"And here I took you for a bit of a sycophant, Farid," Baryut shouted back. "A bit of a hanger-on."

"Not in the least. You believe too little and know too much."

Soon Baryut was trapped at the edge of a ravine. In a coffeehouse. A ravine. The prince would kill him now and the Tablet would go back to Smaragdine and he would never write another book. Or perhaps even another sentence.

Baryut wheeled around and drew his sword to make his stand at the edge of the ravine.

"Sacrilege!" Farid screamed, galloping forward. Their horses came together and they were now so close that he could smell the betel nut on Farid's breath, could see the design on the green T-shirt he wore under the blazer.

The force of their swords clashing shuddered up and down his arm and the ground beneath their horses' hooves caved away and they fell headlong into the ravine, still in their stirrups.

The horses were dead by the time they reached the bottom, necks snapped. The tablet had cracked into a hundred pieces.

Baryut and Farid were buried alive under the pebbles and rocks and boulders dislodged by their descent. Their mouths filled with dirt. Their bones broke.

Then, because Farid could not reach his sword, he shot Baryut in the stomach.

Baryut looked up at the ceiling fan and could hear a slow pounding that he knew was his blood abandoning his body.

As Baryut died, he had the satisfaction of knowing Farid would die, too, soon enough.

Within a month, the flesh decayed from the bodies of the two men, leaving only bones. In four months, the shifting of earth confused the collapsed skeletons of the horses and the men until there was no difference between the two.

That spring, the rains came and water trickled through the ravine, loosening the stones, picking through the bones and the pieces of the Green Tablet. Every year, the water dislodged more and more fragments until over time the Tablet became not a hundred pieces but two hundred and then a thousand, until no one piece was any larger than a Smaragdine coin.

Beyond the ravine, more wars were fought. Some the Turk won, some the Smaragdineans won. Men died searching for the Tablet. Smaragdine became a backwater held together by the weight of dead ritual and then, eventually, broken by a mad dictator who fancied himself an architect on a grand scale.

Pieces of the Tablet were carried away by the rainwater and entered the river. Fish ate them and became strange with the knowledge, uttering sentences in a language no one understood. Herons ate the fish and fishermen noticed how mournful and heavy their eyes became.

In a hundred ways, the Green Tablet re-entered the world, but like the men, it had been buried alive and its knowledge with it. Reborn, it became a hidden thing, seen in glimpses from the corner of the eye. Sometimes things happened because of the Tablet that no one could understand because no one knew what the Tablet said anymore. Perhaps they never had.

And still people searched for it, never realizing that they could search their whole lives, die because of it, and yet it was there all the time, in front of them, even in the pattern of green mold across a dirty floor in a Tashkent coffeehouse or somewhere in the blood leaking from my body or in the patient whir of the ceiling fan overhead or in anything in the world that received love or hate or some lingering attention or...*anything* always forever.

AFTERWORD
Jeff VanderMeer

❀

Sometimes you run out of words. Much of what I might have to say about these stories is inconsequential next to the evidence itself. This hasn't always been so. For my last major collection, *Secret Life*, I provided extensive story notes, using the opportunity to lay bare process, inspiration, frustrations, perceived triumphs, and other insight that I thought might be of use to other writers.

I'm reluctant to do the same here for a number of reasons, but in part because the stories in *The Third Bear* are so often about the search for, or encounter with, the inexplicable. What can I add that Seether or Savant or Sensio hasn't already said for me? These stories are also meant to reveal more and more of themselves, and the connections *between the stories,* over the course of multiple readings. They are, hopefully, the kinds of stories that *change* every time the reader experiences them. My thoughts on that process would just undermine the effect.

Perhaps, too, I'm not interested in my perception of the stories any more – I am interested in yours. My interpretation is on the page, encoded with the personal experience that makes almost every story, no matter how surreal, a secret diary entry. How you personalize them now is the most important thing.

In that context, let me end with one last story.

•

The Magician

There was a magician, of course. I say "of course" because we had no right to expect a magician, or anyone else. At first, he didn't seem that good. The

269

cards were still visible when the doves appeared from his hands. The sleeves of his shirt seemed loose, suspect. He smelled, inexplicably, of lime. His coattails were muddy. Only gradually did we realize that the magician was doing things we hadn't noticed. He turned Kotie's shirt from gray to a mélange of orange, red, and green. He gave Sewel a lisp and a moustache. The stupid sad tricks that dripped from his hands with a loose insolence, the limp shuffling of the cards, the way he flexed the singing saw before he cut his lackluster assistant (a sad-eyed terrier) in half – these were just the decoys to distract us as we began to tell him things we didn't want to, things we'd never told the guards, even when they were interrogating us. Details about our families, about our pasts, about our very blood. And so: our ID tags changed. Our opinions on a myriad of topics changed. We realized we were standing in the snow in our boots, chained together, with just a tent roof to protect us. The horizon was an engulfing yellow-black line and in front of it there was nothing but the camp and the dogs and the fence. None of that changed, but we changed. And kept changing. In the cold. Under the gray sky. During his entire routine, the magician did not speak, his arms and hands, in their deceptive motions, speaking for him. At the end of his performance, he stood there for a moment, waiting for the applause frozen in our minds. He nudged us with, "It's your turn now." But there was no turn for us. Why should there be? We had not asked for a magician. We wanted our tongues back. We wanted our words. Our lives. After awhile, the guards took him away, leaving us as we had been before, only a little more so. The doves lived for a day, but only because we waited until then to kill and eat them. The doves were all that remained of the magician, and our need to preserve that memory had been stronger than our hunger. For a time. And so we waited. Waited for the next. And the next.

– Jeff VanderMeer, March 3, 2010, Tallahassee, Florida

ACKNOWLEDGMENTS

✽

Thanks to my first readers: Kelly Barnhill, Laird Barron, Tessa Kum, Alistair Rennie, Jonathan K. Stephens, and Ann VanderMeer. Thanks to all of the editors who have championed my short fiction over the years. Finally, many thanks to Jacob McMurray for the design of this book, as well as Jill Roberts and Jacob Weisman from Tachyon, and Marty Halpern, for their many kindnesses.

About the Author

✳

Jeff VanderMeer grew up in the Fiji Islands and has had fiction published in over twenty countries. His books, including the bestselling *City of Saints & Madmen*, have made the year's best lists of *Publishers Weekly*, *LA Weekly*, *Amazon*, the *San Francisco Chronicle*, and many more. Considered one of the foremost fantasy writers of his generation, VanderMeer has won two World Fantasy Awards, an NEA-funded Florida Individual Writers' Fellowship and Travel Grant, and, most recently, the Le Cafard Cosmique Award in France and the Tähtifantasia Award in Finland. He has also been a finalist, as writer or editor, for the Hugo Award, Bram Stoker Award, IHG Award, Philip K. Dick Award, Shirley Jackson Award, and many others. The author of over three hundred stories, his short fiction has appeared recently in *Conjunctions*, *Black Clock*, Tor.com, and *Songs of the Dying Earth*, among several other original and year's best anthologies, and Library of America's *American Fantastic Tales*, edited by Peter Straub. Collections include *Secret Life* and *The Third Bear*.

He reviews books for, among others, the *New York Times Book Review*, the *Washington Post Book World*, and the *Barnes & Noble Review*, as well as being a regular columnist for the Omnivoracious book blog. Current projects include *Booklife: Strategies and Survival Tips for the 21st-Century Writer*, the noir fantasy novel *Finch*, and the forthcoming definitive *Steampunk Bible* from Abrams Books. He currently lives in Tallahassee, Florida, and serves as assistant director for Wofford College's Shared Worlds writing camp for teens (Spartanburg, South Carolina), in addition to conducting workshops and guest lecturing all over the world.